THE CITY OF CULL

CRIES OF MISERA: BOOK ONE

Z.J. BLIGHT

CONTENT WARNING

The City of Cull (Cries of Misera: Book One) is a fictional work of literature that takes place in an underground setting of a lost, forgotten city of scientific advancement. The protagonist soon discovers this new world and the terrifying reality that comes with it. Due to the circumstances of the atmosphere and contents contained in the story, it is essential to mention all the potentially explicit or otherwise questionable elements included in the narrative.

Reader discretion is strongly advised.

<u>The list of warnings goes as follows in alphabetical order:</u>

- Animal Hunting & Consumption
- Anxiety & Panic Attacks
- Assault
- Biohazards & Biological Horror
- Blades
- Blood
- Corpses & Cadavers
- Death
- Firearms
- Gore
- Hallucinations
- Medical Equipment & Themes
- Mental Health Issues & Trauma
- Misogyny
- Mutation & Transformation
- Murder
- Psychological Horror
- Religion
- Speciesism
- Strong Language
- Violence
- Vomiting

Readers who deem these topics as personal triggers should not read the story ahead or otherwise take note of caution before reading further about these themes. Mental health and triggers are serious matters to consider, and for your well-being, you have the right to know everything contained in this fiction. While this book is a dystopian adventure of the sci-fi horror subgenre, it is still important for an author to regard every possible reader interested in learning more about the narrative and the content it contains. Please be aware of the situations ahead.

For My Family, Friends, & Past Self

I've wanted to write a book for a long time, but never really took the leap. Well after twelve years of having this story in my mind, it's finally coming true, and I feel accomplished to fulfill this lifelong ambition. Thank you to my family and friends for encouraging me to develop this book into a legitimate work and supporting my efforts. As well as my past-self, who held onto this tale for all this time and not once let it go. This is only the beginning, and I hope to write more for *Cries of Misera*.

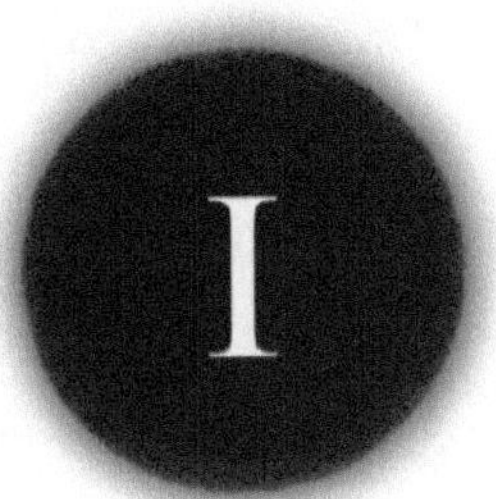

Nature numbered my days, but I cherished every one.

The sun graced me with warmth for another afternoon. Grateful to admire the sky's grandeur, I appreciated the billowing clouds lining the cerulean limits. In flowing harmony, they wisped for the horizon. Every day, I reached towards those delicate seraphs in the heavens, their wings so far from my grasp. I fantasized being one with them, soaring toward the horizon without care. To gaze across land's plains, the never-ending oceans, and behold how they mingled together. Behind me, as the clouds traveled further, the mountaintop reached for the sky and stretched towards the forest. Ahead of the wilderness was the beach where I stood. Ocean waves lapped my toes. My soles sank into the saturated sand, while the saltwater beckoned me to stay a little longer.

How could I deny that request?

The sea beyond, the sky above, the forest behind my back and the high mountain, they meant *everything* to me: my whole life.

The stratocumulus expanded, obstructing the sunlight above. Was the weather changing in a new, inexplicable way, or was it just a simple downpour? My contemplation drifted until a familiar voice called from the overhanging cliff behind my back. For a moment, the clouds parted, and the sunlight greeted the earth once more. A radiant beam shimmered upon the ethereal woman above. Adorned in nylon robes and a bag at her waist, a blessed messenger carried a portent of my future. Paving the path of my destiny, she spent every waking moment leading me towards happiness and fulfillment.

My motivation. My sister.

The only other human being I had ever known.

Narissa, the single leaf on my tree of heritage; the superior vein connected to my bloodline. Ever since I'd been born into the world, she was my light, and the angels were hers. She allowed me to be one with them, sharing their ways and teachings. They had divine rules to abide by, but there was one that could never be broken, lest you upset the heavens: never defy the orders you're given.

"Charissa! There you are!" Her voice rang like a bell in the calm. I tried to listen while lost in the ongoing collision between the waves and the shoreline. "Come on, it's your birthday! Let's make the most of it!"

It dawned on me; this day, I turned twenty-two. Birthdays never mattered much to me—at least, I never made *mine* a big deal. The older I grew, the more I understood concepts I'd never grasped during my youth—heart and mind, heaven and earth, life and death—and for every year I aged, the more I comprehended that I lived a constant repetition.

A routine.

As much as I loved the beach's beauty, the limitless sky, and the glorious sun, the same thing transpired every day. The unknown lingered out there, far from my grasp, inviting me to explore its mysteries and marvels. Even if I had everything I could ask for, was it wrong for me to go beyond this oceanic impasse to discover more? Would this monotony change, or did I have to continue the pattern without complaint?

Narissa called, "Oh, and I worked so hard on your surprise! I guess you won't mind if I just keep it for next year!" she laughed.

I jumped; My train of thought thrown me off track. My birthday came with a yearly surprise to always anticipate. Even if birthdays weren't my thing, gifts were, and Narissa made an earnest effort to make my birthdays special. I never demanded anything of her, but she always reminded me how much she cared, even when I already loved her as much as life itself.

"Yeah, yeah, I'm coming!" I hollered.

To return to the forest from the beach, we had two paths: take the long way along the steep hill ahead, or to climb the rocky, dangerous terrain. Perhaps because of my birthday, I dared to break the norm. I grabbed the stone chunks protruding forth and climbed upward, though Narissa wasn't the happiest with the more reckless choice. "What do you think you're doing? Climb down before you get yourself hurt!" She panicked, leaning over the edge.

But I couldn't give up what I had started. I couldn't let the distance to the ground below and my goal intimidate me. My palms ached with every jagged edge they encountered, but that didn't stop me from going for the top. I laughed, the excitement coursing through my nerves. Getting to the surprise faster was too good to pass up, and with a little more effort, I managed to dig my fingers into the edge of the finish line. A tiny achievement, yes, but a little victory I conquered myself.

The cliff crumbled. As the rocks broke apart and fell, so did I.

In a split second, destiny had decided what to do with me, until someone else intervened. "Hold on! I got you!" Narissa pulled me to the finish line with ease.

Once more, I'd given into the illusion of making my own choices, and she showed me that I was still incapable. Ever since I was a baby, she'd had to rescue me from the mud before I got too deep. That insecurity lingered, leaving me helpless no matter how simple the task. I always needed to depend on Narissa, and she had to take over whenever I fell. In this case, quite literally.

On my side, gasping for relief, Narissa cleared her throat. Her pale lips pinched together, and her slender eyebrows furrowed. "Honestly, Charissa, this is possibly one of the most ridiculous things you've tried to do…" She huffed. "But I can't stay mad at you." She extended her palm, and I gripped it with a grin. She couldn't help but do the same, pulling me on my feet and patting the dirt from my already messy clothes. "Just please be a little more careful, for your own sake, alright? If you do get hurt, it'd not only break my heart, but there'd be one less pair of hands to help with everything. Winter's coming, and we have to be at our best. I'm not getting any younger." At thirty-five, she was perhaps overstating her age.

"Sorry, Narissa. I promise that I won't try and do things like that again. No more rock-climbing from here on out."

Her soft face glowed, but as I studied her, I questioned our sisterhood. Our appearances and behaviors contrasted. Narissa, fairer and more elegant, had the palest ivory complexion from hair to toe. Unblemished in her likeness and personality, she strived for the best in everything—even for me, the flawed half of her.

Spending days in the sunlight, my skin was bronze and tarnished with freckles and moles. My auburn hair, straight and past my shoulders, always found a way to turn into a bird's nest by evening. As for my eyes, they were gray stones that dulled in comparison to my sister's white pearls. Everything about her was perfect, while I was the imperfections she left behind. A heaven-made diamond alongside a simple sand pebble.

"That's exactly right, *cherub*. No more rock climbing for birthday presents!" Narissa giggled, always dubbing me her innocent little lamb, her *darling angel.* I had grown to loathe the nickname long ago.

I wasn't a child.

"Speaking of which, I wanted to give you a little something that I have been working on for quite some time now. Are you ready for your surprise?" Her enthusiasm infectious, my sourness turned sweet.

"You know I am! What is it this time?"

I tried to guess—a homemade treat or another art project? Finally, she eased the butterflies in my stomach and fetched the gift from behind her: a carved maple bow, not a single mistake in its craftsmanship.

"Wow, you've really outdone yourself, sis!"

Longbow in my clutches, the surface smoother than my skin, the handle had the softest cottontail rabbit pelt. The bowstring tuned into each end of the recurve, and the threads for it had the same lightness as Narissa's hair. With finer animal hides and fibers being hard to come by in this wilderness, she gave me nothing but *her* best. A peculiar feature, but it added to the sentiment. Even more charming, a dried marigold tied on the nock.

My favorite flower.

"I knew you'd love it. It took me quite a while to gather all the right things, but I made it just in time. I even managed to make you a fresh set of these," she chirped, unstrapping a belt from her body, and pulling it off to reveal a quiver attached to the leather. Handing them to me, the weight of each arrow settled as I strapped the belt to my waist. I was astonished by the gifts bestowed upon me. She'd managed to make these without stirring any suspicion from me the whole time. I was just thankful I had a bow that could hold together for once.

Out with the old, in with the new.

"Would you like to do a test on the *real* game? See how it feels?" From the sounds of it, it would be more than shooting pinecones and stick figures off a log for weeks, if not years. When it came to meals, Narissa would capture the meat, while I scrounged for berries and speared fish. She had taught me plenty of things, and hunting proved the most crucial, but I wasn't allowed to do the dirty work. Not once did she allow me to prove myself—either because she thought I couldn't hit a moving target, or perhaps because she didn't want her baby sister growing up.

Either way, she now gave me a chance to try my new gift. Or rather, a chance to show her what I *could* do. "So, does this mean I can hunt on my own? Because you don't always need to hold my hand for everything,"

Her brows softened to my words.

"I don't mean to coddle you. I know you want to try and start doing things alone, but I just want to make sure you're ready for anything if I ever..." She sniffled. "Well, I'm not always going to be around forever, you know. My time here is fleeting."

There I went, making her upset. I had to fix this mishap. "Hey, hey, I know you're only watching out for me." I attempted to dam her tears. "Let's go get our meat for tonight's dinner, *together*. You can show me how to work this fancy new bow of mine, too."

The gloom on Narissa's face lifted, perking to my offer. "Then let's not waste time! Dinner can't come an evening too soon!"

She turned on her heels, and her iridescent hair flowed like a running river. I followed such "water," thankful I didn't make matters worse. There had been times I had to walk on eggshells to keep her from letting out her violet blues, and while I never liked having to comply with her every nuanced complaint, it was better than having her drown in her own tears. Such fragility came along with her vibrance. Not a day passed did she fail to make every waking moment one to be grateful for. Her brightest showered whenever we spent time together, especially when we were in the happiest place imaginable: our beloved home.

As we embarked on our hunt, we went through our *sanctuary*. The fecundity of the wilderness entranced me. The fresh waterfalls and breathtaking rivers sang, lush with animals and verdant growth. Crimson, umber, and sienna leaves decorated the tall trees, with ripe fruit nearly falling from their branches. A gentle breeze whispered past each thicket, bringing solace in my every step. Normally, it would inspire me to feel at one with life around me, but as I wandered among these same trees, the same grass, the same soil, I had never lived in an *actual home.*

Being isolated on a tranquil island, everything beyond the sea remained unclear to me. The only way I could interpret the rest of the world was through the wonder of books, old relics left by people of the past. Throughout my life, Narissa gave me these treasures comprised of paper and ink, and for every title, I left the last page a new person. Whether of fiction or of facts, each cover held invaluable knowledge. The more I learned, the more I needed to see it for myself. The ambition to escape this place remained persistent, and the works of literature made by those of my kind made the desire stronger. Ever since Narissa gave me my first book, I have craved the meaning to my life.

To know what it was like to be human.

Every time I reached deep into my past to recall such a memory of home, no semblance could be found other than the wild. Nature was all I had ever been familiar with. Even the faces of my mother and father never surfaced from the deepest crevices of my mind. Narissa not only took the role of the older sibling, but my guardian, too. The first thing I ever recalled was being in her arms in the dark. She was crying, the most I had ever seen. I must have been a baby, but our parents weren't there—just her and me. She brought purpose to my being, so I never questioned

Narissa about our existence before all this. Yet now, more than ever, there were answers that only she could possibly have.

As we kept alert, we treaded through the blackberry bushes, where most creatures sought food. For as long as I could've remembered, Narissa told me not to go where the blackberries grew. I never had permission to pick in this area without her watch, and for good reason. "Didn't you say that cave bears stick around here? Why are we going through these bushes?" I mentioned.

"I did, but the animals are getting ready to hibernate. The bears will be too busy stocking up, so if we're lucky, we might catch uncontested prey," she remarked.

I trusted her insight, until she stopped in her steps. Pulling me aside, still behind a tree trunk, she peeked and brought my attention to our mark. "Over there, do you see that?" she breathed, her voice so low that not a single soul could hear her except for me. A full-grown fox trotted about, its orange fur glowing through a blackberry bush.

"I see it. How should I do this?" I whispered.

"You already know what to do. Just take it slow and steady, like you practiced." Narissa held my shoulder, and with that, I drew an arrow from my side. Designed to take my mark with its tapering head, it was my time to make it shine. "Keep your mind clear and your breath still. No what-ifs, no hesitation. You know what you have to do now."

I had to prove myself capable.

"I…Okay. I'll—I'll try." I readied my arrow and pulled the bowstring until I held it straight, pointing toward the oblivious fox. Preparing my shot, the tips of my fingers trembled. Whenever it came to risks, I had only ever endangered myself; never anything else. Taking the life of another, even negligible, had never crossed my path before. The little creature had no idea what was about to come his way, but I tried hard not to let my heart get the better of me. I braced myself, steadied my breath, and clenched my teeth.

I let go.

The arrow whistled through the air, and my bittersweet prize squeaked. There it was: the dying fox, its blood soaking in the dry earth. To think he was alive only moments ago, but everything had changed when I came in. I wasn't sure how to process it.

Narissa bore a proud grin. "Excellent shot!" She wandered towards the fox and withdrew the arrow from the carcass. From her bag, she brought a cloth, stained from the countless captured prizes. Taking the dead fox, she wrapped it in a warm cotton embrace.

I followed behind her with an unpleasant ache in my chest. I could never be numbed to the burden like her.

"Good job. We'll be able to make a fine stew."

She praised, the unease in my stare lingered on the ground, toward the stain I made on the earth.

"What did I just do?"

Alert to my distress, she tried to soothe my heartbreak. "Charissa. I know you might feel bad, but there's no need. You should be proud of what you've done."

"What do you mean?"

"Hunting is vital. It's what we both have to do. If it means we can live, then it's important to do what is necessary to survive. We won't be hungry for another day, so you're doing what's right for both of us." Her words soaked into me, and I had to listen.

This was what had to be done, and what *I* had to do. Life required nourishment, sometimes at the cost of another, but it didn't mean that I had to find any satisfaction with it. The sinking tension that overwhelmed me dwindled away, but remaining here would've only made it return. "Can we go back home now?" I coughed.

"Of course, cherub. Maybe you could do something to make you feel better…ooh, I know. How about you pick some apples? Oh, and plenty of red ones!" she encouraged me as she took a route to our treehouse. I lingered behind to do what she asked.

Picking fruit had always been my usual business, and so on our way, I kept at her tracks while I plucked from the generous trees we passed. I cared for every apple in my arms, diligent not to let one stumble away. I even tempted myself by biting into the ripest one in my possession, but before I could delight myself with a chomp—something squirmed from its red skin.

"Agh!" I dropped the apple, and Narissa stopped.

"What's the matter?" she worried.

I gawked at the ruined fruit in the soil. "There's something wrong. I don't think we should eat these." I muttered, prompting her to pick up the apple. Seeing the white larvae wiggling from the tainted flesh, she grimaced as she tossed it back on the ground.

"That's odd. The air's been so cold, I didn't think any more bugs would be out here. Thankfully, it's only one bad apple, right? Just keep picking, and if we find more, I'll make some bait for tomorrow." She continued the path home, and with reluctance, I continued to pluck from the trees with shaky fingers.

I had eaten my fair share of bugs and insects, but that worm warranted unease. During my nervous harvest, I paused at the sight of a baby fox that waddled around one of the trees I picked at, black nose to the ground without noticing my presence. It sniffed at the discarded fruit on the soil and nipped at the squirming larvae.

The haunting guilt crept upon me once again.

While Narissa continued ahead, I detoured from the norm once more. Approaching the baby fox, I took a bite from an apple, afraid another worm might come out. To my luck, the flesh was clean, and I offered the cub a little nibble.

"Here, have some…" I mumbled.

Before I could get any closer, it scampered away. My regrets worsened, delving into my earlier interference. That because of me, the cub had been orphaned. Anxious that it would get lost, starve, or worse, I dropped my apples and chased after it. Following its tail through the bushes, I was about to get a hold of its body, until I found myself in an open, vast area.

One I had never discovered.

Wooden fences surrounded a large, perfect circle of hollowed earth ahead. The little fox darted towards the dark endlessness, about to dip beneath the borderline—about to plummet.

I needed to act fast.

I leaped and grabbed hold of the cub. My head barely over the edge, I peered down, nothing but obscurity culminated within.

Nothing but pitch-black.

The tiny kit cried in my hold. I pulled away from the void and slumped on my backside, keeping the creature close to my chest. It was so afraid of me, and it must have been left all alone; only substantiating my guilt further. "I'm so sorry, little guy."

Yipes came from the shrubbery, and a second fox rushed through. To my relief, I released the baby fox onto the ground, and it scurried to its mother. They cuddled one another, scuttling into the wilderness together. My heartstrings relaxed, but they pulled right back toward the pit right beside me.

I rose from the dirt and focused on the enormous cavern formed into the ground. This wasn't a predator's den or the steep drop of a waterfall. No, far more harrowing. The hole itself was humongous; you could pour an entire lake into it without sating its depths. A metal shell covered the void's walls, and its emptiness seemed to call louder the longer I stared, making the hairs on my neck stand.

This was the most fascinating thing I had ever found.

Such a malevolent oddity mustered my curiosity. Seeking a reason, I brought my fingertips to one of the fences. It was natural for a ground cavern to be in the wilderness, but the fact this one went so deep, only to be sectioned off with sticks and planks, was definitely unnatural. Whoever did this feared for the well-being of the creatures that could have met their demise with the pit, and there could have only been one person responsible for that: Narissa.

We knew this forest, from how many trees there were to which lake had the best water, so to find this unknown part of our home left me distraught.

But it only made sense.

There hadn't been a time where I could be on my own; she was always telling me where or where not to go every time, but that's because she cared about my wellness. I didn't interpret her intentions any other way. She would confide in me about everything, and if she did hide anything, it'd be for my livelihood—whether it'd be a dead animal, or dangers like the hollow mass before me. The longer I stared into the emptiness, the more I considered whether anything lived at the bottom.

Could anything have *survived* down there?

Not far ahead, an oddity peeked from the bushes. A strange shimmer shifted to the sunlight, and I investigated further. There appeared to be another metal construct, covered in shrubbery. Curious about what nature might have hidden from me, I pulled apart the bramble and snapped every twig in my way, only to find an extraordinary sight: a peculiar little shelter.

What made this?

A small door accompanied the rickety foundation. I grabbed its handle, pulling hard enough to unhinge it. I stumbled, with the door now on the ground. Brushing the rust off my palms, I went inside, careful not to break the little stairs. With leaves no longer obstructing the shelter, light peered through the open-view window, and the inner confines illuminated to reveal a chair. With wheels! A desk to match, with little etches made into the surface, but the rust left the scratch marks undiscernible.

Had I just discovered ancient history?

Or maybe…there was somebody else living in the wilderness I had never known about. The possibilities on the what-ifs piled on and on. After living with my sister for my entire life, seeing another human face would have been a breath of fresh air and good company. I had to find more clues and possibly figure out who might have last been here. I rummaged through the space, but didn't find anything worthwhile. Dirt and disappointment were the only things I could collect, until the flooring jostled to my weight. A flimsy square of metal dented in, loose for me to pry. Once I managed to get a grip and pull it, I found something: a book! Another for my collection.

I carefully replaced the square and relished the newfound gem. The leather cover peeled apart, as the pages inside suffered from prolonged water damage. I wiped the muck from its front, brushing the metallic words embellished on it.

Book of Immigration & Visitation—that word struck me.

My dictionary mentioned what *immigration* meant, "the process of coming to a foreign land with the intention of staying, or even living there." If the title were true, and the book remained here, it only gave me a further compulsion to learn more about the place I called home, and the people before me. I got comfortable in the chair, pondering such a peculiar title. I expected paragraphs, but the pages offered pictures, and names to pair with every different face. Catalogued entries of humanity: their ages, heights, weights, blood types, and other details. Flipping through the pages, I met more strangers, and the more I began to contemplate. Where were all these unfamiliar faces? There had to be a reason this book was hidden. If nobody came for it, these traces of human existence would have withered away. For preservation's sake, I stashed it in my bag to bring home.

I had to leave before Narissa found me.

I'd already wronged her by running off without her consent, but to have her to find out I'd been sticking my nose where it didn't belong would have been worse. Right as I was about to get up from the chair, another fascination caught the corner of my eye. I rolled the chair aside, where underneath the desk's frame, something red took my interest. A large button, square in shape and colored red with words embedded in the dull surface.

Ascend / Descend

Shifting between the button and the crater outside, I had to see what it did. I was about to uncover something amazing.

"Charissa! Get away from there now!"

My head slammed against the desk. Clenching my scalp, I stifled my whimpers once Narissa came in view of the window. I ran from the shelter and Narissa sprinted to me, still carrying the slain fox in her hold. She grabbed me by the wrist and pulled me away. "If a cave bear saw you, you would've been done for! What made you come over here?"

"I-I saw a baby fox and had to make sure it was—"

Yanking at me again, she stopped to face me directly. "I keep my eye off you for a—" Her grip eased on my jacket. "I'm not mad, I was just scared for you…I thought you might've—j-just promise me something from here on out."

"Yes, Narissa?"

She kept silent, only to bring her gaze to the void. "You will never set foot around here. Nowhere near the blackberries, nowhere past these trees. It's too dangerous to be here by yourself. Don't ever, ever leave me again. Please, Charissa, that's all I ask."

Having to save me twice in one day, on my birthday, no less? Narissa had the right to be furious. All I could mutter was— "Okay,"

She released me.

"Thank you. Stick close to me, please. Let's get home." She turned, slow in her walk, and I followed her path. We left behind the pit, and neither of us spoke afterward, but I continued to glance past my shoulder at the giant hole obscured beyond the red maple trees. Even through the rustling leaves, the abyss called for me.

After we had finished hunting earlier in the day, Narissa told me to do my daily reading while she tended to supper. I took the opportunity to catch up on my studies while I waited for her to call me to eat. Outside, the horizon went from the brightest blue to outspoken orange to vibrant violet as dusk crawled through the forest. But the calm of the night shaded different than usual. The stars didn't shimmer from the sky as the clouds shrouded the night in darkness, leaving the heavens above hollow. With a lit candle on the wall right next to the windowsill, I stared outside from the confines of my room. Laid across my mattress of twigs, leaves, and deer pelts, I basked in the crisp chill of the season. With summer long gone, I would admire the copper leaves dancing in the frigid wind from my bedroom. On cold days, I'd spend time here, reading books until my mind exhausted itself. Pages from my favorite stories lined the lumber walls, stuck to the bark with old honey. Narissa scolded me every time I took from the books too literally, but the pictures and words were too good not to hang up. If I ever stooped to my lowest, I would play out scenes in my head, pretending to be part of a bigger story, anticipating the next tale I'd embark in after.

I still remember from when I was younger how Narissa would wait until every December to get me a new book, or even two if my yearly behavior deserved it. How was it, though, was she able to do this? We couldn't cut down the trees here to make paper, and we certainly didn't have ink to make the words come true. No, she introduced me to the idea of "miracles."

Ever since Narissa taught me about the angels and their morals, she told me that for all the good things I did, I would be rewarded for my efforts. If I did well every day to contribute to our home, if I treated every creature here with kindness, and if I listened to every order she gave to me, I would be given anything I asked for. All she had to do was go to the angels with an earnest prayer, request the desire in her mind, and it would arrive a few days after.

Narissa offered to perform another miracle for me this year, and I had been thinking what new kind of title I'd devour: a fantasy, an adventure, or perhaps another collection of poems? The options seemed limitless, but they dulled in comparison to something else I wanted.

Something I had been yearning for in recent years.

The older I got, the more Narissa urged me to learn new vocabulary as well. One year, she had given me an old English dictionary, a paperback so tattered that the pages barely held to the spine. She told me that "We might be living out in the wild, but that doesn't mean we can't better enhance our capabilities to master the art of language." I couldn't imagine a scenario where I would use half of the advanced words, but I tried to retain some of them.

Many of the books might've given me glimpses of what lied beyond oceanic nowhere, though the more I gathered from this book, I learned about the world in its fullest. I went again, skimming through the seemingly endless list, and managed to find an interesting word. *Caelestis: derived from the Roman culture; heavenly, celestial, a dweller in heaven.*

But what did "Roman" pertain to? I flipped through the weathered pages to find *the relation to Rome.* That only answered my question halfway; was Rome a thing, or a place? *The capital city of Italy, a country located in Southern Europe.* As I kept learning through these connected words, it connected the dots to what my dreams amounted to.

The world beckoned me.

If I knew where every country, or even where I was, I could figure out how I could get to each distinct region. But without a boat to guide me, there was no possibility of reaching beyond the sea. Would I have to watch as the world passed me until my final day dawned? I envisioned myself living my existence behind the trees, seeing the same blades of grass, convincing myself that I could never go. By the time I had gray hair and wrinkles, I would still be in the woods. The wild might've been my home, yet I was a bird that would dwell in the same nest, from birth to passing. I couldn't let my dreams fade like my feathers, too old and frail to ever fly away. To make it change, I had to do something.

The book came to my mind: *Immigration and Visitation.*

From the moment I picked it up, the questions piled up so high. Was it true, that people of the past migrated here? Maybe a long time ago, there had been a civilization that shared the same grounds, but the shelter lacked any real trace: no food, no waste. Narissa and I had never seen another human, but the evidence brought new possibilities. With how displeased she was, she couldn't find out I had taken a souvenir from the place where she forbade me from trespassing.

But with her busy, now was the time.

I retrieved the leather book from its hiding place underneath my bed and slowly went through the pages again. The names of people I had never met flooded my memory once more. Each one had their distinct picture and personal information, but what got to me most were their origins. Every person came from a different background: France, Japan, Vietnam, Russia, Germany, Scotland, Canada…but where could they have gone? They made me envious of their lives. One thing was for sure: to seek others like me, I had to step away from my comfort zone. I had to ask Narissa if we could leave the wilderness behind and find a place we could call our *new home*, with people like us.

My days could no longer be idle.

"Charissa! I could use a hand!"

I stashed the book underneath my bedding. The best time to confront Narissa would be during our meal. I made my way through the claustrophobic confines of the hallway and into the main space. Given what we had to work with, we made the treehouse comfortable and secure. Wilted flowers decorated the log-stacked walls, their stems woven together. We kept our valuable keepsakes on shelves. Seashells, ores, or acorns—the little things we had made us further adore Mother Nature. The best thing we had was the *Everything Table:* a large wooden stump accompanied by two smaller, shorter ones for seats where Narissa and I did, well, *everything.* We used it to play games, practice writing, and eat our meals together whenever it snowed or rained. During our free time, Narissa and I would make our own tunes. While she sang, I used a *harmonica* that she had given to me for one of my birthdays.

We really did everything together.

My favorite part of the home, though, was the kitchen. We found ways to make it a whimsical place, preparing our fresh harvests and using the herbs we grew on the window whenever we needed to add zest to our delicious discoveries. We had the most fun making marinades or jams, storing them in makeshift clay jars to enjoy after long, laborious days. The best delicacy we concocted was a special recipe: a jam made with raspberries, grapes, cherries, and mint leaves. The cutting board and ceramic pot sat on the counter, mashed berries welling within the clay containers. With the jam finished, Narissa had to be tending to the brew outside, because a new scent filled the air. The savory smell of cooked fox meat flavored the gentle wind.

I went through the trapdoor and used the planked ladder attached to the tree trunk foundation of our home. At the bottom, Narissa tended to a stone crock nestled on burning logs. The broth, rich with diced potatoes, tomatoes, and freshly cut meat and spices, perpetuated my hunger. Narissa worked hard on the meal for my happiness, and her efforts always went above and beyond.

This was the most she had ever done for my birthday.

"The scent is wonderful, isn't it?" She gave me the ladle. "Keep stirring. I have to get the bowls and *another* little surprise for you." A devious chuckle followed as she hurried away.

As I mixed the broth, it made my belly grumble, but the anxiety of having to confront Narissa after supper made it twist. Perhaps I assumed the worst, but I hoped she would listen to me.

A couple more minutes breezed by, and Narissa returned with two bowls and spoons. She wore her satchel on her shoulder; the *surprise* had to be in there. Our dinner finished cooking, and she cooled the flames underneath the stone cauldron until there was only enough fire to keep us warm. She handed me my bowl and spoon, along with a bear pelt to keep snug, and picked up the lantern nearby, rekindling the chamber so we could have a cozy dinner between inseparable sisters.

"This is perfect! Let's dig in." Narissa allowed me to gather my first portion. I spooned in a few helpings and got extra fox meat, waiting until Narissa filled her bowl too. Once we got our first servings, we sat together to watch the clouds swimming through the dusky sky. Calmness filled the air, but the sharp cold it brought bristled on my nose and cheeks. The perfect birthday evening, and to enjoy a hot meal together as a family made it even better.

As Narissa got herself settled in, she raised her stew to me. "A toast to you, my little sister. May you have many more years to come in your happy, happy life. Cheers!" She beamed. Despite any sisterly differences we had, if any at all, I appreciated her ardent kindness.

I couldn't deny her gesture, and I raised my bowl and clinked the rim to hers. "Thank you so much for all of this. Cheers, Narissa."

We savored our supper, feasting with jubilant laughter until our dishes emptied. The tender meat and the rich vegetables offered a luscious sensation to my tongue: the honor of our best meal yet. Finishing our first helpings, we returned for seconds and indulged until we ached.

"Before I forget," Narissa interrupted, putting her bowl aside and digging in her bag, "let me give you your *second* present…Aha, there she is! Couldn't hide from me. Oh, I can't wait to see the look on your face!" She brought out a marvelous masterpiece.

A carved-pine tiger, my favorite animal. We'd never managed to find one here, but I read about them when I was a kid. The details were so accurate to the picture. My name, along with the year, was scratched in on the feline figure's stand.

Live Long, Charissa!

October 22nd, 2174

Handing me the figure, I took it with cautious palms to my chest and held it with the broadest smile I ever had.

The little tiger made me wish I could have seen a real one. From a distance, of course. Ever since I learned that they came from Northern China, it made me yearn to go there. To witness what those cats did in their natural habitat, and how their home compared to everything else in my life.

My grin wavered. "It's...It's awesome. Thanks a lot, Narissa."

Although I adored the gift, it further convinced me to talk to her about what had been worrying me earlier, and she could tell I had something to say.

"What's the matter? I thought you liked it."

"It doesn't have to do with this. I love it. I do. But there's something serious I wanted to talk to you about."

Narissa slid closer to me, leaning in and bringing my chin up. "You can tell me anything. You should never feel afraid to confront me about your troubles, and I'm here to listen."

Her words reassured me to speak out.

"Ever since you showed me what miracles were, it's made me wonder what life's really about."

To that question, she raised her brow. "It's not truly boiled down to what it's about, but the experience. To live it to the fullest." She pinched my cheek. "You probably think you're getting old, but trust me, there's still so much waiting for us."

She didn't understand.

"But these miracles...when you shared me my first book, it made me think of things I never thought of. People, the places they live in, *how* they live. Could a miracle give us what they have? Like a new house, or maybe...a boat?"

The soft color of her face paled. "Nothing *that* big."

"How come? The books, the dictionary tells me of all these amazing things."

"Well, sure, the books I gave you were so you didn't have to live life unaware, but that doesn't mean we can really have any of that. Not anymore, anyway."

"Couldn't a miracle just give us anything we'd ask for?"

"Did you already forget what I've told you?" She gave a gentle smile. "I only ask for miracles that give us what we need, not what we want. When I ask for seeds, it's because we have to survive. But ask for a house or a boat, those are things that we could live without… And the thing is, life isn't easy, and never will be. But with miracles, they allow us to get by, day to day. We can't be greedy by asking the angels for too much. They already carry many burdens."

"I know that. But wouldn't it be nice to have what everyone else does?"

Her body stiffened in the freezing air, as did her grin. "What're you trying to ask?"

The hesitation tried to pry me back from taking my leap, but I refused to be reduced to living here for the rest of my existence. This was my chance for a dream come true. "When will we…"

Our chance.

"When will we ever leave this place? To be with other human beings and make a new home where we could happily live forever?"

Narissa's expression hollowed, and her skin paled even lighter.

"Oh, cherub, this *is* our forever home!" she exclaimed. "There is no need to leave when we already have so much here, where *nobody* would ever find us. We're more than fine where we are now."

I had never perceived my own sister to be a liar, or someone who'd betray my trust, but I had to press on to understand her motive. "Sure, but why not? Shouldn't we be with other people like us?"

As I pressured, her ivory stare shifted. A forced smile plastered her face. "We don't need anybody else."

My faith dwindled. "But again, *why not?*"

Quiet enough to raise concern, she couldn't look me in the eye. "I mean, we have everything we could ever want here, all to ourselves. This whole place? We can't just *leave* it all behind!"

"Narissa, you can't keep trying to avoid—"

"Charissa, we've made a wonderful home here." Like that, her composure slipped. "I mean, I'm happy with how things are, aren't you? We've settled so well here that I didn't think we'd ever have to leave, unless I'm…wrong?" Her voice cracked.

"No. I've been feeling differently for a while."

From the way she trembled, I might have shattered her fragile heart into smithereens. "I…see," she mumbled.

"Narissa, we can't stay here forever. Eventually we need to be able to find people like us. Couldn't we make our own boat, or maybe—"

"We can't. There're too many *things* that're keeping us here. Things I don't think I'm ready to tell you of."

"…What have you been hiding from me?"

She did her best not to show her worst from coming out, lip quivering and brows strained. "It's not that I'm *trying* to hide anything from you," she retorted. As my confidence in her honesty faded, I began to see right through the deceptions. Since earlier in the afternoon, I'd speculated how many *years* she'd kept secrets from me.

"What about earlier, back over by the—"

"I've been doing this to protect you." Her words cut through mine as she stood. "There's nothing out there worth abandoning what good we have. You might not like it, but we're staying here…we have to."

I bowed my head, disappointed to be right. She was keeping something from me. I had nothing more to say, as she had cracked my trust. "So can we ever go?"

"We can't leave. I'm sorry. It's just not worth the risk, especially when…" She averted her eyes, refusing to look at me. "There's nothing left in this world."

My throat turned constricted. "What?"

Her stare lingered on the burning flames. "The books I gave you, they were only mementos of history, fragments of humankind. If any of those things you've read still existed, I'd give them all to you. But I can't…because it's all gone." She stared back at me, her lips thinning. "Even if we left this place, there'd be nothing for us. You and I may as well be the only ones left of this world."

No…None of this could be true. She had to be lying to me again.

"You're just saying that…"

Not once did she blink in her affirmation. "Charissa...Do you know what angels truly are?"

To that, I didn't want to answer. Instead, she did it for me.

"They used to be people that walked the same ground as we did, until they earned their wings. They watch over us here so that we can be able to learn from them and live on with the peace they've left. If we try to leave this place, we'd be leaving them. We'd have nobody to protect us out there."

Her deception got the better of me, and at that rate, the curious flames could no longer burn. I shut down, inevitably finding myself defeated. "Then why are we here? What's the point of all this?"

In my state of despair, she held my hand. "There's never a definite answer, but I know that *you're* the point of my life. So long as we have each other, I could never ask for more."

Bitter warmth crawled to my fingertips, and I yanked away. "Why would you keep all of this from me?"

"I..." Her frozen fingers trembled. "I'm trying to do what's best for you."

I had no control of my mouth, for the heat fired my lips. "No, all you're doing is lying to me! I see now...all you've ever done was lie to me, about everything!"

She reduced to the log beneath her. "P-Please, I'm sorry!"

In my seething rage, I shouted: "I don't even know you anymore!"

A soft gasp came from her, and her breath shook, tears trickling down her frosted cheeks. Clenching the tiger figure with resentment, I hurried into the treehouse. I got myself in my room to rest for the night, hoping to forget about what happened, but I couldn't shake off the frustration. *How dare I, for wanting a bit of freedom?*

She didn't have to coddle me the way she did, treating me like an infant. As a grown woman, I had the right to be my own person, and not somebody else's shadow. Yes, she might've tried to keep me safe, but I still couldn't imagine what she tried to keep me from. If there was nothing else to see, then what could she be so afraid of? Even with everything we had here, we couldn't live out pointlessly here. However, it was more than that. To live in the wilderness forever was folly. From everything I had read, written by *human beings,* we were designed to explore the unknown. To seek out possibilities not yet realized.

For me, I had to know what's truly come of the world.

My life was bigger than this bird's nest: or rather a cage, decorated to be pleasant. What was she really trying to protect me from?

***

Morning's golden sunshine shone through the treehouse's cracks, waking me with an ache in my chest. The whole night, I could barely sleep, not when I had so much to atone for. I crawled from bed, knowing Narissa had more than the right to be upset with me. To ostracize her like that, to delude myself to thinking she undermined me, and to make her turn to tears: what kind of sister did that make me? I had to make it up to her, but I didn't have the courage to do so.

Not right away, at least.

Before the falling out, Narissa told me that I had to go fishing while she went off to gather what little crops we had left. I hoped that if I caught us enough meat, she'd be able to forgive me.

A simple *sorry* wouldn't mend a broken heart.

Since the dawn brought a bitter cold, I donned a hefty coat and prayed that I didn't cross paths with Narissa. For each other's sake, it would have been best to put space between us.

As I was about to leave my room, Narissa leaned at the doorway, holding onto its edge. "Charissa, about last night."

Before she could say anything more, I had to settle things like an adult should. I had to know when to take fault. "You didn't do anything wrong, Narissa. I know I shouldn't have said what I said, and for that, I'm very s—"

"You deserve to know more. Or at the very least, see it," she interjected, and confusion overtook my remorse.

"I don't get it."

Narissa kept silent, withdrawing from the doorsill and giving me nothing but a firm stare and honest tone. "I'm not sure you're ready for it, but I've made my decision. I have something to show you." She rested her palms on my shoulders. "But promise me that you will not pursue anything further after I take you there. No more peeking, no more digging around. Okay?"

"Okay, but where are we going?"

"I'm taking you somewhere…different. It's some ways away, but we can make it by this afternoon. It'll be a brief visit, though."

My eyes lit up. "Really? Where?"

"The other side of the mountain. I found it only a few days ago during a hunt. But we do have a long hike ahead, so pack your things. We're leaving once the sun's fully risen."

Narissa left my bedroom, and I experienced something new: exhilaration. For the first time in forever, change would come.

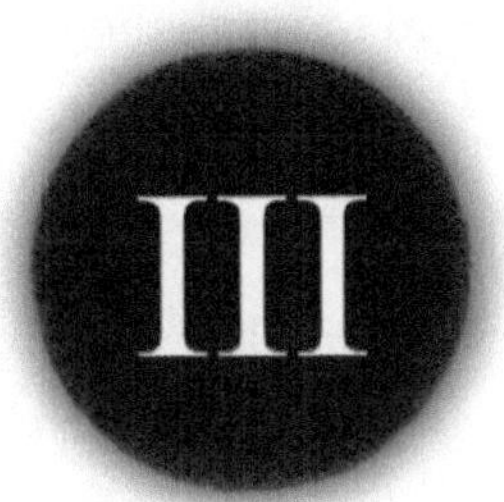

We embarked on our ultimate journey, the furthest I have traveled. Since we left home, Narissa kept us at a tense pace. Whenever I tried to talk to her during our trip, it was met with "have to keep moving." Despite the rush, the new, incomparable sights took my breath away: fields of wildflowers dancing in different shades of blue, and albatrosses soaring throughout the skies along the grand mountaintop. The valleys brought a different serenity the forest could not compare, and I never had been so alive. Though, as we stuck to the hillsides, my worries continued to linger for Narissa.

She kept forward gripping her magnum opus: her spear. Specially crafted with an obsidian shard, she used it for hunting the biggest beasts. The wild learned not to mess with the alpha: Narissa.

"You've brought *it* with you."

"This is necessary. We're going to unfamiliar territory."

"You don't know what we're going to find?"

"No need to be afraid, cherub. No matter what, we'll be alright. Just stick close to me and be ready for anything."

"Okay, but how much longer until we get there?"

"Very soon. We just need to get to the secret path."

"Secret path?"

A little further on, she brought me to a newfound marvel. From the side of the mountain, a cave was embedded, but the opening was rounded in a perfect arch, with the ground inside stretching into a smooth, black road. A speckle of light beckoned us at the end. "This'll lead us right where we need to go."

"For real? I really wanna know where we're heading. Tell me, please?" I begged.

"Like I told you, you need to see it to believe it,"

As we headed inside, the dark and wet path drew on, fissures crawling forth with dewed ivy. A howl of wind echoed through the passageway, and it only elevated my adrenaline more. Reaching the end of the tunnel, Narissa froze. I bore witness to a bewitching sight, and it was one for the books. A lost utopia lay beyond the other side, amassed with structures beyond natural rock and stone. They reached for the sky, clustered to create a paradise that had to be made by human hands. Wild growth crawled throughout the town, as if Mother Nature had reclaimed it for her own—nothing but flourishing viridian among the grays. Among the edifices, a signboard stood above with the canvas smothered in green grime, but through the vines did the oasis make its name.

Welcome to Commoneo, The Pride of Vinea!

Narissa and I remained speechless, fixated on the ruins of a place long neglected. As I stood there, I admitted that she had been right from the beginning. I had to see it to believe it. "Where are we?"

"When I came here the other day...it was a secret I was too nervous to tell, but I knew I had to show you since what happened at dinner." Narissa pointed to the array of houses and complexes at the hills not far from the main settlement. "Real houses too, just like you talked about."

"I thought you said there was nothing left in this world?"

"Maybe for our kind, but everything they've made still stands here." From ahead came a flock of birds, brisking above the lost land. Her eyes followed their movement. "This all must've been here for decades, a century perhaps."

"I wonder *who* built all this." My stupor overtook my reality. Squaring back to it, I took notice of the lack of human life. "But who in their right mind would also leave this all behind?"

The wind grew colder, making me shiver, and riddling Narissa in goosebumps. "Maybe it's not that their creators left them here, but perhaps their *creations* outlived them."

I glinted back at her. "What do you think happened to them?"

"I..." She shook her head. "I really don't know. But they're not here anymore. They're angels now, and they would never have wanted us to repeat their mistakes with...this."

"That can't be right." I focused back on the viridian, unable to contain the butterflies in my chest. "Someone, or even dozens built this place. They left it here for us for good reason, and it only took us this long to find it. We can't squander their gift…this miracle."

"…Maybe this was a mistake. I showed you what I wanted you to see, so I think we should turn back." Narissa was about to grab me. I sprinted along the downhill road and towards the ruins.

"Wait, hold on! Where are you going?"

"I wanna see what else is here!" I hollered.

She finally managed to get a grip on my wrist, preventing me from going any further into the lost town. "Stop, we don't know what we'd be getting ourselves into! Who knows what's there!"

I yanked away. "We didn't come this far for nothing. Let's see what's left here. Could bring back some worthwhile things."

After long consideration, Narissa didn't like the idea, but something made her bend. She might have still held guilt about what happened between us. "Alright, you have a point. Though we can't stay here for long. We'll look around, then go back home."

I couldn't help but laugh and made another run for it, doing a couple of spins, amazed by how high the buildings went and their numbers. There had to at least be a hundred constructs. There wasn't a single tree that could match their reach, although they still were so small compared to the mountain overshadowing them.

"Look at all of this! It's like they're touching the clouds!"

Natural life filled the area, but no trace of humanity. Not a living soul, except for the wild fauna prancing through. I kept exploring, in case anybody might have hidden away in the green. Narissa cautiously kept behind me the entire time, not bothering to speak as we traversed through the complex, but the warning signs only made her silent tensions rise. Massive claw marks streaked the pavement, and the bones of animals tangled with the overgrowth. Bears must have passed through for pickings, because nothing else would leave so many remains in their wake. It was only natural that the wilderness claimed Commoneo, but even so, this was a whole new world for me.

"You know what we should do?" I began framing the mental picture. "We should move here. Think of it, all of this to ourselves, so much—"

"No!" Narissa shouted.

She rarely raised her voice, and it unnerved me. "But why?"

Recognizing my pale face, she tendered her tone. "Just think about the hassle of gathering everything from home, bringing it here. This place wouldn't be good for us."

"But it's got shelter everywhere. We could fare well against the snow in something like this." My nails bristled to the corner foundation of a building, the inside and its contents in disarray. "Clean it up and fix up the surface damage, and it'd make for perfect hibernation."

"Look at all this, Charissa. It's all been run through, and any of these buildings could crumble." She pried my dawdling fingertips from the concrete wall. "Besides, where could we find food and water? Closest thing is the ocean now, and all this shade would ruin our crops."

"Well, how about…there!"

Brisking past the overgrown hotels and mossy restaurants, we came across a plaza lined with establishments. What struck me most was the grocery store that brandished a promising front. Shaded by red and white awning, the charming letters of *Melior Groceries* loomed right above. Empty bins and wilted posters with pictures of tempting produce lined the windows, covered in muck and cracks.

"Check this out, an actual supermarket! I've only read about these in books, but now one's right here! We should see if we can bring back any real food from here," I begged Narissa.

"I think we should leave. I doubt there's anything good left inside, or anywhere for that matter," she protested, but it was too late, for I had my hold on the rusted handles.

"I've read that they have all kinds of things to eat here. Please?"

"We have food at home."

I withdrew from the entrance, irritated by her unwilling attitude. "Okay. If you really don't want to be here, then I guess we can—hold on." Distracted by the next spectacle ahead, I passed Narissa.

The building wasn't shaped like its rectangular counterparts, but rather tapered like an apex towards the sky, angled in a wide pyramid. Only standing three stories high, glass panels lined the entire foundation, smothered in years of dried rainwater and gunge.

Commoneo Archives & Public Library.

"They even have a library here! But who's he?" My attention strayed away from the infrastructure to the bronze statue in front of the building. The concrete pedestal supported the figure of a bearded man in a lab coat, coated in an oxidized green and looking upward with dulled eyes, his hand reaching for the azure. I wiped the dirt from the plating, but the deteriorated alloy and scratches defaced his name.

"Amazing…" I muttered, turning to Narissa. Her stare was fixed on the bronze stranger's face.

"What's wrong?" I nudged her shoulder.

Once I broke her trance, she shuddered and blinked at me. "It's nothing. He just looks so lifelike."

I focused on the figure, then the building, driving me to discover what was inside its once-clear prominence. "Look, I know you really want to go home, but let's not leave empty-handed. I'd love to see if there's anything left in there at all." I gave my best effort to sway things my way, but Narissa was frozen in place once more.

After thinking about it, she walked for the front doors with slow, discontent steps. "Let's make this quick, then."

"Thanks!" I beamed and zipped past her, but the entrance offered an ominous welcome.

The shattered front led toward a dark hallway, where nothing could be seen until further inside. Alongside the walls, four more silhouettes accompanied the dark space. With a bed of matches from my pockets, I snapped a sprig, kindling the lantern attached to my backpack. The fire cleared away most of the obscurity, and with that, four figures showed themselves in their bronze shells, one accompanying each corner. They shared the same lab-coated appearance as the man outside, but they all had a unique likeness. Three more men, and one woman, with faces so realistic that their emotions emanated through the features.

"Who are these people?" I asked Narissa as she caught up to me, but when she shifted her gaze between all the figures, she bit her tongue.

"Wish I could say for certain."

Scrapes marred their names, leaving them impossible to read.

"Let's keep going then, we might be uncovering lost history," I told her as I moved forward. Pushing the transparent panes, we walked in on an inner sanctum, captivating me in its splendor. Past the front desk and beyond, the soft sunlight shined through the glass ceiling, illuminating the mossy environment and its treasure. Humid air accompanied the jungle of knowledge, as moths fluttered throughout the archives. A vast atrium centered the entire building, and surrounding it were balconied floors containing bookshelves entangled in green. In the center of the grand space was not just a simple artistic display, but a massive globe. From the way the shapes on the surface entwined with one another and how it rotated like our very planet, it became obvious what this was. Every country and every continent revealed itself, and my heart raced.

The entire *earth* greeted us with its glory.

My fingertips brushed along the cold cast. "This is so much bigger than I could have ever imagined. Think about the places we could still go to. It wouldn't be too late for us."

"We don't have too much daylight left," she reiterated, finding something peculiar nearby. Ducking under one of the tables, she retrieved an empty bag, one to be worn over the shoulder. Wiping the gunk on the nylon, she gave it to me. "How about you take this and find whatever you'd like, and I'll keep watch around here. Grab as many books as you want." The smile on her face quivered.

"Really? I can?" I snatched the bag.

"So long as we can make it out of here soon. Now, go on, and be sure to pick plenty of variety."

Without thinking where to go first, I ran to the closest shelves. "You're the best! Love you!"

She watched me in silence, not daring to take her eyes off me.

I grabbed whatever interested me the most. The more intact and dry it was, the better, although most of the books were so wet that the pages fell apart upon picking them up. Peering up from the first floor, the ambition of searching upward struck. My collection back home mainly consisted of make-believe, so a genuine article was the priority. *Science & Technology* caught my intrigue.

"I'm going to see what else I can find up there," I told her, spotting a spiral staircase. As I made my way, I glanced at Narissa, the smile on her face becoming more forced.

The steel bars and glass steps of the cyclone were tethered by vines, but with care, I made my way to the second floor. I passed the aisles, heading for my desired section. My hopes for finding more salvageable books grew thin, but once I made it to the Science & Technology catalog, each shelf had categories with titles aplenty. I strolled through Meteorology, Geology, and plenty more fields, until I happened upon a subject worth better understanding: Botany.

Although I spent my entire life surrounded by various plants, there could be some to my knowledge I didn't discover. Perhaps it was the hunger getting to me, but I sought to find edible greens in the pages. Brushing my fingers through the mossy book spines, I peeled away each one to see their names, only to find a worthy catch called *Flora and You*. I reached for its moist cover, delicate to pull it from the shelf.

Squawk!

I stumbled into the shelf behind me. Right above, a harpy eagle observed me from the top array of books, beady eyes blinking as its talons dug into the shelving. I was about to hightail myself, until it pecked at its own chest, where its blood shone on its feathers. Before I made any sudden movement, so as not to get torn apart, it shrieked again, soaring away for a broken gap in the ceiling. A gorgeous creature like that deserved to take roost in the tallest trees, not some library of a lost world. What could've compelled such a formidable predator to take shelter here? If anything, it drove me to be fast with my literary choice. I dared not to cause more disturbance to the wildlife here.

The botany book sat on the floor, but before I picked it up, something caught my eye from the empty space on the shelf. Between the books, a scrap of cloth peeked through. I reached into the case and pulled out a long black piece of fabric. Marigold flowers patterned its cotton, and it tied together to cover a square object. I undid the knot, unveiling the contents inside, which were protected by a kind of clear box. A little stack of photographs sat there, with a folded note on top. Facing down the aisle, checking to see if Narissa was there, the frantic butterflies in my chest fluttered as I undid the note.

I leave this as a warning to any who finds it.

Commoneo is nothing but a trap.

Vinea is not what it seems.

The ones in white have driven everyone below.

If you see the elevators, turn back while you can.

There's nothing here worth dying for.

Let the rest of the world know of this place and all its lies.

Tell them that Pietas holds no salvation.

The human race was never ready for this.

Anastasia G—

A streak of ink finished the rest.

The wings in my ribcage turned to ice. I flipped through the pictures. The first capture was an island from the viewpoint of the ocean, the grand mountain in frame. The second, the town, Commoneo. Rather than overgrowth, the constructs brimmed with people, everyone in the frame having prosperous faces. The following pictures were stills of flowers, distant captures of creatures, and some of the buildings I came across not long ago. Harmless at first, the last series of photos took a dark turn. Past the frames of nature came fire at the shore, boats at beaches engulfed in flame. In the next picture, people in panic, running from ghostly entities of white mist. The last one, a demon incarnate. Soulless, hollow pupils, unhinged chitinous jaws and rows of ravenous teeth, contained in an ivory veil. No more photos left.

"Charissa! Are you ready to head out?" Narissa called from the end of the shelves.

I stuffed away what I found into my coat, facing her. "N-Narissa! You scared me there. Didn't think you'd check on me, but yeah...I think we can go." Cold sweat beaded on my forehead.

She came down the aisle to spot the book on the floor, picking it up and handing it to me. "You were just taking a while, didn't mean to frighten you. Did you find all of books you can carry?"

I couldn't part with any words at that moment, but I showed her the contents inside the shoulder bag, and she dug through to gander at all my literary finds. "Looks like you'll have all winter to read through these. If we're all done here, let's make it back home before evening settles." She gave me another forced smile.

"Narissa, are you sure you don't know where everybody went?" I pried. "Surely they didn't just disappear..."

She shrugged, stare drifting to the glass ceiling. "They must've left."

"Well, something must've happened. You sure you don't know?"

"I—" she blurted.

"Narissa."

She spouted. "I can't tell you!"

Pacing out from the aisle, Narissa made a break for it. Stuffing the bandana and photos deeper in my coat, I gripped the bag of books and chased after her. Already pacing down the staircase, Narissa went for the front doors. I managed to catch up once she stepped foot outside.

"Please! Just talk to me!" I yelled, but she kept for the uphill road. "Come on, Narissa! You can't keep hiding things from me!"

She stopped in her haste, pale hair fluttering in the breeze.

"I—I don't think you should ever know," she stammered.

Before I could pry further truth from her, a slate-feathered bird wandered from the rubble—the same harpy eagle from inside. The gash on its chest had grown larger, and slimy white larvae squirmed from its flesh, gnawing on its body. Once the fearful bird spotted us, it took a wind toward the opposite direction of the forest. Afraid for its well-being, I ran after it. In my mind, it asked me to follow its flight so that I could somehow help. Narissa panicked and darted for me.

"Wait, Charissa! What're you doing!"

We ran past the plaza and found ourselves on new streets. I went further and further until the bleeding bird soared away into the distance. In the middle of my chase, I bumped into some rails, standing on a boardwalk overhanging from the edge of a wide, massive cliff. The azure in the sky reached afar, as a new beach lay ahead. The harpy faded away into the horizon, only to head over a series of docking bays. A swarm of husky clouds crawled through the sky, swamping the sun, and the light ceased to beam through. At the bay, the collapsed docks resided in the water, the wooden beams splintered into smithereens. Several massive boats strewed the beach ahead. Large debris covered the sand, the boats either lopsided amongst the shoreline or had sunken deep into the further waters, the last remains of their constructs barely floated above in blackened char.

The photos did not deceive me.

Narissa hurried alongside me, covering her mouth. She dropped her spear, the beam rattling to the stone. "Now you know why we never left..." she mumbled.

"Narissa, you know what happened here, don't you?"

"I thought I was ready to tell you, but perhaps I was wrong—no, I need to say it." She locked her eyes to mine. "Do you know why we stayed in the forest for all this time and for all our lives?"

"Because you said there was nothing else for us out here?"

"There's more to it than that. You might not remember it, but I think about it every night…you and me in that cavern."

My first memory.

Her lips quivered once she tried to speak again. "We were runaways. We had a part in all of this."

As she went to tell me more, I glanced at the ruins, to the bay, to her. After what I uncovered in the library, I had no reason to see her deception, though I had to double down. "What were we running from?" I asked, and her cold stare drew to the ground.

"The answer to that is beneath us." Her voice hollowed.

What did *we* do?

"W-What's down there?" I stuttered.

"...A new beginning for humanity."

There was no way *I* had to do anything with this.

"Okay, what's going on, Narissa? I don't know why you're acting this way. Why—"

All of it pieced together.

Why she never allowed me to explore, why she always told me to stay at her side. There was something she tried to make me avoid, and it began to make sense, the way she acted whenever I tried to pry. On my birthday, when I was on my own near that pit. Unjust conclusions came to mind. Did *she* have something to do with that?

"Are you talking about that massive hole in the ground? The one in the forest?" The cold silence stifled once more, and it had to break. "Narissa, you have to have to tell me what we did."

"...Do you remember what's down there?"

My memory had a blank space. Not a single trace of the past resonated here, nor whatever remained in that hole.

"Am I supposed to?" I replied.

She didn't speak. Enough was enough.

"Are you saying that there's something I should have known, but you don't want to tell me? Are you doing what's best for me, or are you just still keeping me in the dark?" I tried to comprehend her intentions and what scars tainted these ruins.

She drew a deep breath. "We were a part of something that never should have been humanly possible. There are things that happened here you couldn't even imagine. Things you should never know. But I knew I couldn't let you go and be a victim. That's why I had to take you away."

I continued to listen.

"We needed to escape, as far as we could. I took you into the forest where nobody could find us, and I couldn't handle the burden of losing you." Soft whimpers escaped her. Despite everything she'd told me thus far, and what she hid away, I had to be there for her.

I brought her close to me.

"Shhh…Narissa, please, it's alright," I comforted, and that was enough to let her recount her take.

"We stayed in that cave for weeks. I had no idea what to do. We had nowhere to go. I was scared that we would've never made it."

"But what…" It pained me to ask. "What about mom and dad?"

"I don't know…I don't know." She pulled away, her nails digging into her cheeks. "I don't even know who they truly were, but they never should've brought us here. To be born here."

"Narissa…" I mumbled.

"The only good thing that came from this place was you, and only you. You're the only thing that matters to me anymore…but we *can't* leave." Narissa gazed at the lifeless docks.

"We still can. We *have* to."

"But we're on an *island*…don't you get it?"

In that moment, I began to grasp just how isolated we truly were. We didn't know which ocean we resided in, and had no clue where the closest landmass would be, and no idea if there would be any other human being out there. The signs were everywhere, but I had been blissfully unaware and uncaring. I always found peace with Narissa, and only her. The reality made me feel smaller and smaller.

"There is nothing else out here but this. There's nowhere else to go…this is all we have. Do you understand now?" Narissa reiterated, despairing. She broke down. "We are in the middle of the ocean, the middle of nowhere. Nobody knows that we're here… nobody knows."

I couldn't stand to see her in such a state, and attempted to rationalize what she tried to voice. "Narissa, even if we are on an island, even if we didn't know where we were, that doesn't mean we couldn't try to leave. We don't know what's truly out there… And maybe, somebody could find this island. Help us. There's no chance everyone is all gone."

Her fingers fidgeted once more.

"Or…Are you saying nobody *should* find us?" I asked.

Her silence remained frigid until she broke the ice. "Yes, and that's why I kept you here."

I stepped away from her answer. Again with these lies. This was nothing like my sister. "Why would you do this?"

"If anybody were to find this island…if anybody were to know who we were? They'd do everything they could to make this place disappear…to make *us* disappear."

My legs tensed and my chest tightened. "Narissa, you're scaring me,"

"This was the only way we could survive. I had to keep you here, and I came to this town time and time again, to keep you alive."

Everything in my world fell apart.

"You've been here behind my back, and you never said a word?"

"I had to come here to get food, medicine, so many things to help us survive. I'd travel by night to get you everything you needed. Clothes to wear, books for you, too—" I had to stop her there.

"No, why wouldn't you tell me about any of this? The things we have. They all came from here? But the miracles…the books you had given me, the harmonica, the bow? They all came from—"

"I've been making everything up, Charissa!" she screamed, leaving me speechless. "I've been lying to you all this time. I've taken from that same library, and so much more…I even scratched away the names of those *scientists*, so nobody would ever know of their horrid, horrid contributions to this entire island." She couldn't contain herself, and she choked up. "There's no such thing as miracles…there's only so much I could do alone. I was only trying to give you a good life, and that meant hiding you away from the entire world."

What was even the truth anymore?

"Why did it take you this long to tell me any of this? To keep secrets from your own sister? Am…am I even your sister? Is my name even Charissa, or is that made up, too?"

She took my face in her hands.

"Don't even dare ask me any of that! Don't ever question who you are! You are my everything! You are my world!"

I turned my back, yet she still tried to get through to me, as if her words amounted to anything.

"I had to teach you *everything* and care for you for your whole life. You *are* my sister, and you've always meant more to me than life itself. You realize that don't you?"

She genuinely loved me, but she betrayed my trust. I didn't know what to say.

"To live in peace, I did what I had to do, making sure you never figured any of this out. Though the more you asked questions, the more you were bound to find out…I *had* to keep things a secret from you, but the guilt has eaten away at me every day."

I had to ask her one last thing.

"Can we ever be like other people?"

"…Nobody can ever know we exist."

My breath stopped.

"No matter what, there's no way we could ever live a normal life. We could never be normal people. Not when we have all *this* clinging to us." Her words trembled, her eyes turning glassy. "Many unspeakable things have happened here, and no matter where we go, we'd be bringing a part of that, and I just *can't* allow that."

I closed my eyes, clutching my scalp, as my entire universe turned to dust. If I couldn't even trust my sister, could I trust my own vision?

Could I have trusted anything at all?

"Charissa, you must understand that we don't need anybody when we already have each other." She attempted to convince me that there was no point in leaving this place, to find human beings, and to live like real people. "Isn't it better to live knowing there is nothing more out there but this? Knowing we weren't meant to see the rest of the world? That we don't *belong* anywhere else?"

But right then, I didn't know what I wanted anymore.

Her deluded words drowned in the sour tears streaking my face, and the wind made them brittle against my cheeks. I crumbled, pulling off the shoulder bag, clenching tighter on the handles, and threw it over the boardwalk. Narissa's hands covered her mouth. She had never seen me so angry. *I* do not think I have ever been so mad—so crushed. The books plummeted to the beach, but I didn't care anymore. I wanted to run away from everything. From these ruins. This island.

From her.

I didn't say anything else, and I walked back toward the wilderness far ahead. *Back home.* Narissa sobbed, dropping to her knees as she called out my name, reaching out for my forgiveness. "Charissa, come back! I did all this because I love you! Please, don't do this to me!"

There was no such thing as *miracles.*

I didn't pay attention to Narissa's stories or her delusions. No matter what, she still would have kept things hidden from me, trying to clog my mind with her *lies.* Everything she said could have been a fable of hers too, deceiving me still, to keep me trapped in this "paradise."

She said that we should never be found, and that we would be dead otherwise, but that all had to be a front to dissuade me from pursuing any form of civilization. Because if we were never found, what was the point? To live out until we died, never to be seen again?

If I were to defy my future of isolation, then I had to pursue the truth. What Narissa said earlier, about a *new beginning for humanity*, I needed to figure out what it all meant. If I were to ever find a chance of having a normal life, to be with other human beings, to be *human*, I had to go against her wishes. I had to unshackle the invisible chains that came from the depths, keeping me stranded here.

The answer was right below me, and I needed to be ready for it.

That dusk, heavy rain pelted the treehouse, the crackling thunder deafening me. The noise tried to take my mind off everything that happened after our trip to Commoneo, but it was impossible. The downpour grew stronger as the night continued, and not a single creature dared to make a peep during the approaching storm. I kept in bed, eyes closed as midnight came closer, waiting for the right time.

The moment to leave Narissa behind.

Deep down, I loved her so much, yet she'd spent a lifetime painting colorful lies. I could never have loved someone who deliberately kept me away from the rest of the world, and I certainly couldn't *live* with someone like that. Our entire life together had been an escape from reality, supposedly all for my own sake.

That wasn't her right.

A couple of weeks after Narissa took me to that paradise town, the distance I'd put between us was unconquerable. Any attempt she made to make amends; I offered her no peace of forgiveness. We lived our ignorant lives, exactly like she wanted, but with neither words nor absolution.

Instead of hunting together, she went for food and hides on her own, while I fished in the afternoons and chopped firewood for the biting dusks. Each time our duties concluded, my door went shut and I spent my evenings alone. Every night, Narissa tried to leave food in front of my room, but I didn't eat anything she made. Once a new morning came, I stepped around her meal and went about things my way. I didn't need her to survive, and I had to prove that to her.

On the one hand, I nearly dared to forget about everything that went down, just to try and make amends and pretend it was alright. But on the other hand, I had to unveil the shadows Narissa concealed over my life, including the darkest one of them all.

That pit.

There had to be something down there, but Narissa would never shed any light on the darkness that controlled our freedom. She couldn't be trusted, and I no longer fell for her schemes. After what happened at Commoneo, I gathered what I needed. Whenever I finished my duties before Narissa, I would return home to plan, packing my possessions in a spare bag and keeping everything hidden under my bed. I had to make the most of the supplies on this lone voyage. For my defense, I'd bring my longbow, along with arrows and a chiseled stone knife. To keep the cold at bay, I'd wear a deerskin coat, a couple of sweaters, and my spare clothes for next month. For food, I stashed some water, carrots, and turnips. Lastly, the most important possessions: the leatherbound book, and the lost photographs. If I were to find the owner of such artifacts, or her descendant, I'd need my research materials.

With my plan, I had second thoughts about traveling within the depths. If all else failed, my last solution would have been to go elsewhere. Somewhere far from the island, where I'd find a new home; free to be human, and to no longer be manipulated into a false bliss. A little more preparation and it would be my time to set out. During my rest, I waited until Narissa snuffed the lights, knowing she'd head for bed. However, things did not go according to plan.

The creaks of her footsteps came to my room instead. Skin becoming colder, I faked my sleep as her presence drew closer.

My breath slowed, but my heart raced.

"Charissa...I know you probably can't hear me, or want to, anyway." She sighed, sitting at the edge of my bed. "I'm sorry. Sorry about everything. I know how much you want to leave; I do...But I can't let you. Not yet. The world just isn't ready for us...at least here, we have each other. You're safe and sound, and *that* means the world to me." She tugged at my bed-pelt and drew in a deep, shaky breath. "But it hurts, knowing you don't want to talk to me...or even look at me. These have been the worst days of my life, and I wish we could go back to the way things used to be. I just want *you* back."

A lump dropped in my throat.

"I can't say when we can ever leave, but if this is your dream, I want to make your *miracle* come true one day. And I know this isn't much, but here's something sweet to enjoy in the morning. Maybe then, we can make things right, you and me. It's the only miracle I ever ask for anymore." She shuddered a sniffle. "Goodnight, cherub, I love you." She pecked my forehead, and a tear dripped onto my cheek. Clay clinked onto the nightstand beside me, and she exited my bedroom, heading to her quarters. I brought myself up to find a jar on the nightstand. Taking off the lid, a berried mash welled at the bottom.

It was my favorite jam, but the incentive didn't easily persuade me. The smell even sickened me, and the flavor could never compare to the taste of freedom I'd craved for so long. I reached for the side of my bed, pulling out the same bandana from the library. Ever since I first touched the marigolds on the black sea, I found my motivation. The woman who left behind her mementos could not be forgotten, nor could the people on those pages, and the same went for me. Her keepsakes warned me of the dangers that lay ahead, and to stray away from whatever remained below. But to fulfill the wishes she left behind, as well as my own, I had to find answers.

The only way to do that was to delve deeper.

***

For a couple more hours, the tempest outside worsened, and my time had come. In my mind, the same words repeated themselves.

Now, more than ever.

I stepped silently into the hall and into the living room; the continuous rain helped to nullify the creaks I made along the way. There was no sign of Narissa behind me, so I lit the lantern from my bag, bracing myself. As I opened the trapdoor, the rushing wind blasted inside, freezing my cheeks, but Mother Nature wouldn't stop me. I dropped into the mud and breathed in the biting air, prepared for what was to come. I had to go forward, and made the first steps on my long journey. The bushes and branches flailed in the violent storm, possibly the worst the forest had endured. The rain soaked the fur draped over my body, adding more weight and burdens to the challenge. The skin of my forehead flaked as my nose ran, chapping my lips, but I refused to falter. I pulled the collar, warming myself with my breath. I was only halfway through coming face-to-face with the pit once again.

I couldn't let it go.

Enduring for a little longer, pushing aside wavering twigs and tearing through naked shrubs, I finally approached the clearing, and ahead, the same immense pit drilled into the earth. The fences barricading the edges splintered from the ground, blown right into the massive maw by the midnight squall. Even as the rain poured, it wasn't remotely enough to fulfill the pit's insatiable thirst. My body froze as the gaping darkness howled in silent unison with the screeches of the storm. An intense ringing flooded my ears, and the abyssal voices all told me to jump in, even repeating my name. How did they know who I was? Separated from my mind, my toes drew closer and closer to the void. The invisible strings to my limbs guided me forward to the cacophony.

Come closer, Charissa...Come closer, Charissa...

I forced myself from going further. Plummeting to the bottom wasn't the method. There had to be another way into the depths.

It hit me: the shelter.

In the metal structure, the storm had blown off more of its leafy coverage, and the rain came through the open window. I ducked under the desk; the red button was my ticket downward. With my four fingers on the button, I pressed. Click. Nothing. Click. Still nothing. I pressed it in quick succession, my hopes dwindling as no result showed.

A vigorous quake rattled throughout the ground. The shaking grew more violent by the second, knocking me off my feet and down the steps of the shelter. I picked myself up through the weight of the rainwater and tremors, heading for the rattling abyss as the force within came upward. By miracle's grace, an immense metal platform arose from the depths. The howling winds brushed any wooden and skeletal remains from the alloy hoist, glistening. I imagined that the giant steel disc could have lifted a hundred people between the planet's surface and crust.

Finally, I would soon unfold the mystery beneath my feet. As the rain pattered an otherworldly melody on the metal, I stepped onto the platform. I tapped my boots against the metal, but…how was I supposed to make it go back down when the button was—

"Charissa! Get away from there, now!"

From the trees, dressed in only her robes, Narissa had darted ahead, drenched and shivering. She fidgeted with her spear, clenching it tight, her hair frozen into icicles. "Why are you doing this!" she screamed; her wails outmatched the storm's wrath.

I stood my ground. "Because you've done nothing but keep everything from me! I can't trust you anymore, Narissa!" I yelled, and she fumbled the weapon in her grip, struggling to stand.

"I only lied to protect us! I did all of this because—please, listen to me. I will explain everything to you. Give me another chance!" she pleaded, possibly deceiving me as she had time and time again.

"I can't. Not anymore. Not after what you did." The bottom of my heart relented, foolishly bending me to listen. "Tell me then. Why can't we start over? Why could we never be normal?"

Lightning flashed as Narissa took one of my hands. A wave of warmth came from her otherwise cold grasp. Glittering tears trickled from her pearlescent eyes, blending with the rain. "You mean too much to me. There are so many things in this world that could harm you, Charissa." She wept, refusing to let go. "And I should've never hurt you, the way I did. I never should have kept you in the dark...you deserve to know everything. I'll make this right. I promise you that."

I shuddered, not from the frozen storm, but from the way *she* made me falter. The claws of darkness tried to pull me into the void, but Narissa's grasp prevented me from falling. Her plea could not be tossed aside, for it only substantiated how much I mattered to her.

I was the only thing she had to live for.

"Please, come back home with me."

The truth could come later.

"I-I'm sorry...I'm so, so sorry, Narissa..."

"Don't be…" She wiped my tears. "I'm sorry, too. I wish I could have done it all differently, so you didn't have to run away from me…that you didn't have to feel like you could no longer love me."

I choked back more. Discovering what was down there meant little when my sister was the most important thing to me. We were both wrong, and we had to make this right. She deserved the chance to resolve her mistakes, as I could too. I loved her more than my lifelong dream. "I shouldn't have come out here to begin with. I should have listened, been a better sister. I lo–"

Two pale figures whispered from the forest.

Stare stuck to the entities, Narissa caught the horror on my face, and she turned. A nerve-wracked screech escaped her throat, but I was unable to make a sound. Materializing from their misty forms, they dragged their feet toward us. The twin glows appeared like wingless angels, yet their movements fidgeted, unlike any creature we recognized, and the closer they came, the more I wanted to unsee.

Under their hoods, their demonic guises hazed to view. Scarred and disfigured, horns protruded from their skulls, and their jaws hung at their joints. The raw skin on their chitinous bones peeled away in slivers, almost as if they melted alive. They chanted, repeating the same strange words, but I couldn't make them out.

Narissa shielded me with her body, leveling her spear at the figures. "Stay back!" she cried out. "Don't come any closer!"

They kept limping, their chants growing louder, more haunting. I reached around to get the longbow, my grip unsteady on the recurve. The fibers in my body became enslaved to their words, mesmerizing me in a frightful trance.

I couldn't do anything, but Narissa didn't hesitate to strike. She let out a blood-curdling cry as she lunged forward and pierced at one of the beasts, only to jerk the spearhead out from its chest in a gruesome pull. The figure froze, a massive gash in its chest staining its drenched white cloak. Foul, maggoty tendrils erupted from the wound, the nasty larvae squirming out and dropping into the mud one by one. The creature's claws clenched onto its chest, closing its injury with brutal snaps. The severed flesh mended itself together, and the beast glowered at Narissa. She was immobilized with the same terror I shared with her.

Its jagged claws split apart, only to take hold of her. Her spear fell as the creature locked Narissa back against its body, forcing her to watch the events unfold. "No! Stay away from her! Charissa, run!"

The second beast towered before me. My muscles tensed when my eyes met those empty sockets. In its husked pupils, there was no soul to be seen. A gurgling growl came from its throat, shrieking so loud that it siphoned my own screech of terror. Its head thrashed erratically until that chitinous maw pried itself farther apart. The humid stench of dead bellowed out. Its tongue lashed as its twin tusks and rows of teeth threatened to chew into my cerebrum, its throat clamoring to be sated.

To consume me.

Everything foretold my grisly demise, but I couldn't let death take hold. Not yet. After the moments from my life flashed, I pulled an arrow from my quiver and jammed it into the eye of the beast.

As it writhed and howled in pain, I kicked the abomination away and rushed off the metal platform. Narissa fended off her own demon, gripping it by the horns while it tried to sink its jaws into her flesh. Quickly, I picked up her spear, and amid the struggle, I skewered the head into the creature's spine, yanking it out. The ghastly monster convulsed in agony, collapsing into the mud, causing Narissa to fall as well. The constant downpour washed away the dark ichor that streamed from its fresh wound, and along with it came more white larvae wriggling out from within and burrowing themselves into the murky soil.

The sight made my stomach wrenched, but I had to know Narissa was safe. "Are you okay?" I pulled her close.

"Y-yes." she stuttered, clenching onto my shoulders. "Th-they're getting up!"

As the storm reached its full outburst, the howls toppled us to the mud. The closest monster crawled on its four limbs as the other beast yanked the arrow from its socket. They were both about to come for us once more, but Narissa grabbed her spear from the ground. Despite her fears, she swallowed them down and pulled me from the muck.

"Get to the platform."

"What did you say? No, we need to get out of here!" I shouted and clenched at her, but she pried off my grip, shoving me aside from harm's way as the creatures crept closer.

"Whatever you do, don't help me."

She sprinted, the twin horrors lunging at Narissa as she slipped away from their clutches. Darting for shelter, the robed demons chased her like hungry wolves. I couldn't let her do this!

I ran after her, getting back to the platform, but the harsh wind forced me to my knees. Hurriedly, I grabbed my longbow and drew an arrow from my quiver to provide Narissa cover. I fired my shot, but the wind brushed it past them, *thunking* into the ground. Dammit!

Once Narissa was inside the dwelling, she scrambled to find the controls. She collapsed onto the desk, finding the button, and tapping as fast as she could. She watched, hoping that I would descend to safety.

The platform didn't move.

The beasts broke into the shelter. In a state of panic, Narissa jammed the tip of her spear into the jaws of one of the beasts, subduing it, but the one with a lost eye continued to lash for her.

I needed to do something...*Do something!*

"Get to me! Hurry!" I yelled. "You can still make it!"

Narissa heard my voice and stuck her head outside. This was her only shot. She jumped out from the dwelling and slammed into the ground. Wailing in pain and trying to get herself up, the mud glued her down. She dug her hands into the soggy earth, desperate to crawl to me. The creature pounced from the window as it pursued her, and my instincts kicked in. I had to move. *I need to save her!*

The earth quaked again before I had the chance.

"No...no, no, no! Hold on! I'm coming!"

I dropped my longbow, about to run for her, but she lifted herself up, reaching out to me. She didn't reach out for help. No, she was telling me to *stop*. Her stare ensnared me, the light in her eyes fading. She had the most solemn smile on her face, but not of happiness. Instead, it was of acceptance. The beast had come to kill her, and she braced for it. Rain flooded her hollow eyes, yet there was still peace in her vision. What was the only thing she wanted in this world? It was for me to be *safe*.

"What are you doing!? No, no! Please, don't do this to me!" I pleaded to her with lung-clenching words. I fell to the metal beneath me, my nails digging into it as I reduced into miserable tears. *Get up, Narissa. Please, please, get up.* All I could do at that moment was watch as the abomination sheathed its crooked claws. I wailed to her one last time, "Don't...don't leave me alone!"

The platform shifted, and I descended.

I couldn't even witness my own sister's cruel fate as the darkness consumed me whole, and my cries echoed between the cold walls of the pit. Narissa's screeches pierced through the thunder above, and it left me with a burden far greater than any pain I ever bore.

There's...there's no way she's dead.

No...no! I couldn't believe it! I refused to!

Without the peace of telling her goodbye, the teeth of regret tore into me. Was that what the voices were? I lost consciousness as the regret numbed my senses, and all light dissipated from my core.

I became one with the void.

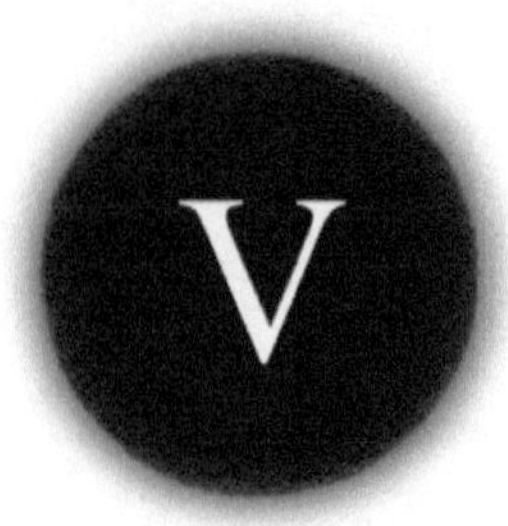

Nothing stripped me of my deepest fears more than loneliness.

Oh, Narissa, how I wish I could have told you...that I needed you.

That I loved you.

I had no idea if I was dead or alive, but for how long I drowned in black, the more the despair sank in. The shallow voices lingered the entire night, until they dissipated into nothingness. Once doomed to an empty eternity, the light within me renewed. Awoken to the everlasting dark, my flesh and bone strained to move. My body gained little spurs of strength, and a single breath was enough to bring a tinge of relief.

By divine intervention, I was alive. *Barely.*

The deerskin on my body flattened me to the cold, wet platform beneath. I tried to lift myself back up, but with every attempt, I slumped again and again. I was more of a corpse than a living soul.

Giving up wasn't acceptable, not when Narissa held onto the little light within. To waste my second chance would have been an insult, and I had to return to her.

No matter how hard it was, if I hadn't moved any sooner, I would have truly perished. With a long, drawn-out breath, the worst awaited me. Pulling the skin off, another gasp of air came through, and I brought myself to my knees. Frozen steel at my fingertips, I swept the moist remains of earth, trying to catch my bearings…the cloth of my sack.

Snatching up my belongings, I reached inside for the matches. Prayers weren't the only thing that could make them ignite. I swiped a stick across the striker. By grace, a spark flickered. With the lantern illuminated, a promising shine expelled the close darkness. The fire helped me as I dug through my pouch again, checking if the water container was intact and if the vegetables still fared well. Bruises and the onset of sourness fermented their skins. The hunger outweighed the concerns, and I crammed them into my mouth, washing it all down with whatever water was left. Days must have passed since I'd had anything if I treated this like my last meal. Rummaging through the rest of the supplies, I had to see how everything else held up.

The knife was in pieces, but the leatherbound book of faces remained safe, as did the photographs. The longbow and the arrows thankfully held together, despite them being damp.

With what little nourishment and supplies were available, I readied myself to seek a way out from these depths. The hollow environment offered nothing more than a stale, rank stench and a trail of muddied prints leading further into the bleakness. Something else came here, and I had to follow them. Burning glimmer of hope in hand, I creaked to walk again with blisters on my soles. Every step became heavier, and I had to get rid of the biggest burden on my shoulders. The damp sweaters slopped off, and instant ease washed over me. Bare skin to the air, a subtle humidity crept, as though the summer solstice made its way down below.

How far under the crust did I go?

The earthen walls echoed to my crunching boots, only to crinkle out into the emptiness. They turned silent once a twinkle shone in the distance. Even if it was so far away from reach, I had to go for it. The further down the tunnel I went, the more the glitter beckoned. Was this what it was like to find an escape from the lounge of purgatory, only to find heaven in the end? I finally reached it, and shielded my eyes until the soft glow dwindled, only to uncover them to a whole new realm.

Welcoming me was a trio of massive gates, connected in a triumphal arch of steel. The center entrance, the largest and most prominent, stood alongside its smaller counterparts—as tall as the most giant pine trees I had ever seen. Dim lights peered through each pathway, bound together in a massive barrier of metal. At the top of the proud entry, broken, golden bulbs flickered from large, slabbed letters, all on the verge of burning out into fading fireflies.

Metropolis Pietas
The start of a new world, a bright beginning for humanity.

What lay beyond the gates was beyond me, but my absolution was just on the other side. Those lost names could not be buried away, and soon, they and every secret within would be uncovered.

As for those abominations. *I would hunt down every single one.*

Peering through the gaps of the city entrance, a barricade blocked off the other side. Unknowing what lay beyond the bars, that same stale odor came through. I rattled the gate, but the hinges bolted tight to the arching steel. Stepping back to find another way, a subtle creak came to my right. At the smaller gate, hundreds of paper slips were left on the ground beside it. A glass window embedded into the metal wall nearby, where a heavy countertop extended forth. A slot was imbued into the alloy extension, and I picked up one of the paper pieces.

Emergency Ticket #2831

Above, a gilded sign lined the edge of the window. *Entry, Visitation, & Immigration* offered once-glittering letters, the glamor scuffed away. Everything must have been in place for a long time, but to say *how long* exactly: that was another mystery. Peering through the murky window as best as possible, I didn't see anything. Not far from the pane, a linear crack immersed into the wall. I dipped my fingers into the seam, only to pull aside a panel, sliding perfectly into the rest of the wall.

Found my way in.

In the musty, claustrophobic confines, particles of dust floated through the air. Posters were plastered on the walls, crumpling and peeling off. The floor had wads of paper and bits of debris all about, and at the far end of the ticket booth, another door awaited. I tried to shove it open, but something blocked it from the other side. Searching through the room for something that could help me, a booth desk was the first place to look. It had a four-wheeled chair, exactly like the one from the surface. Once I rolled it aside, I ducked under the desk to find another red button peeking from beneath. A perfect duplicate. I pressed it, hoping it would open the front gates.

Nothing happened, but something else was there.

A jacket with *Pietas Militia* stitched across the back laid on the floor. With a pinch and drag, an old axe, large enough to use both hands, became my ticket inside. I returned to the door, turning the axe until the flathead faced down, and with little space to work in, I smashed the knob. The rusted metal crumbled, and I slammed into the door, managing to crack it open. Even so, it still proved impassable. Force wasn't the only thing that would cut it. To my fortune, the hinges on the door were rusted too, on the brink of being pieces. I carefully tapped into each hinge until they broke off, and after chipping the three, the door broke loose. I put the axe aside, grabbing hold of the metal mass and pulling it out of its frame. The door popped out, slamming down. Heavy metal pinned my body, I stressfully pushed the door off, along with the mass on top before getting back on my feet. Some kind of bench had been blocking the way, but it now proved no obstacle.

Picking up the axe, I finessed further in.

The vast space proved refreshing compared to the booth, with rows of cushioned chairs and benches lining the vicinity. Bags, clothes, and personal belongings were tossed around the environment. So many things abandoned and in shambles. Broken light fixtures hung from the ceiling, going two levels high with a balcony centering the whole lobby. Large boards and banners lined the floor above, illustrating strange depictions with persuasive words to match.

Find your future at *Florence's University for the Gifted!*
Come see the Marvelous Mistress at *Fruor Falls!*
Have a Luxurious Stay at Pietas' *Sunset Resort!*

A loud creak groaned, only to be followed by breaking glass. The noise came from outside, and there wasn't a chance that this place was surrounded by only ghosts. Something else had to be with me. Shaking off the tension from my wet skin, I held the axe in my grip, stepped through the possessions on the floor, and tried to find a way out. Two front doors barely holding together caught my gaze, and I cautiously pulled them apart to step out into the unknown. Once immersed in the "outdoors," I witnessed the sight of the *new world* I fell upon. The woman said to turn away from the elevators, but never did I expect this—never could I fathom a place like this.

Fissures infested the concrete streets, the deep cracks crawling out for miles along a forsaken route toward the city's heart. Endless constructs filled the avenues, and I was insignificant among the colossi. While remnants of industrial waste obstructed the roads, strange railways stretched between the edifices above, disorienting me in its strange puzzle. Through the bleak shades of gray, not a single essence of life made itself known in the wake of the subterranean wasteland. No trees, no grass, nothing of nature was here, as there was above. No sun, no moon, no stars, no clouds.

The sky was empty.

Veins trembling, my heart palpitated up to my ears. I convinced myself that this was an afterlife, forged by every mistake I had ever made and fueled with every sin.

Behind, to my horror, carcasses piled at the gates. Not the kind that belonged to animals, but rather, people. Their remains had been there for a long time, to the point that the skeletons had meshed with one another, forming a blockade to prevent anyone from getting inside.

Or out.

The rancid fumes seeped into my chest, the sight and stink of decay made my gut churn and nearly expel. From how they clawed for the triumphal arch, their attempts at escape had been snuffed with a terrible twist of fate. There was nothing but dissolution down in the depths, and the exposure to such tragedy shook my mind. The anguish of the dead rattled my eardrums with their shrieks.

I fell to my knees, dropping my axe and clenching my head, my windpipe constricted as the municipality siphoned air from my lungs. The heap of lost souls overtook my senses, vocalizing their agony to me. From the start, they had beckoned me for my arrival. But being on the ground before them, I misconstrued their words all along. They weren't luring me in, but crying for salvation.

Can't escape. Can't get out.

Help. Help.

As my skull nearly ruptured, the howls of the dead fell to a hush. The trembles shook off, as did the strain in my temples. A gasp of air rushed through my throat, the blur clearing up.

I had to go back. *I had to go home.*

About to head the same way I came, my veins turned cold once more. Footsteps, breathing, and the sound of heavy metal dragging along the ground, came from behind. I scrambled to my feet and turned to face whatever lurked. From a nearby building, with a wide sign that had *Gift Shop* extending from it, the noises grew closer. From around the corner, a hand clung onto the edge, but it was so malformed that the fingers clumped into one appendage and ended with a rotted thumb.

"Somebody new?" a slushy voice bellowed, and the source lugged forward and showed itself. My heart sank to my stomach.

The face of a pig came into view, but it struggled to hold itself together, seemingly welded to its neck. It wore tattered and torn clothes, drenched in sweat and muck. It stood and limped on its two disfigured hooves; its body bloated, with boils on its greasy skin. In its other clunky, nubbed hand was a piece of steel that went several feet long—a rusty pipe. The moment it spotted me with its sunken, pus-filled eyes, its cross-bitten jaws stretched in a twisted smile, grinning from cheek to cheek with blackened gums foul with rotten teeth. A wheeze clamored from its drooling mouth. "You look a little lost. Let me take you someplace safe. You shouldn't be out in these streets. *"*

It—he—hobbled toward me, my back to the piles of deceased remains. This had to be make-believe, or the worst possible beast the devil made for me. "What's wrong? I'm trying to help you. I-I…" He started to weep, that vein-ridden gaze flooded with putrid tears. His snout, barely clinging to his grimy mug, dribbled with snot. But he stopped, his face scrunching, baring his teeth in a horrid grimace. "D-Don't back away from me! I'm not the bad guy here! Y-You hate me, don't you? No…no! I won't let you get away!" His wart-covered hooves stomped closer to me, bearing his towering bulk. In a fit of rage, he bulldozed for me, the concrete crinkled to his hobble. "Let me help you out!" he shouted.

I had to move! *Now!*

His blunt steel swung, but I rolled aside. The pipe slammed against the brittle corpses, old bones splintered into dust and bits. I got up and bolted. The pain in my body was unbearable, but I needed to keep it together. My mind raced, and I couldn't think of where to go.

Just away from here!

He cried out and slammed his pipe into the carcasses, over and over again, before redoubling momentum towards me again. "Don't run away! I was just a little upset, that's all!"

I tried to flee, but it was as though my legs were weighed down. Every breath became sharper; my ribcage nearly collapsed. His heaves rasped as he got closer, his wheezes reaching down my neck.

I needed to lose him!

I discovered a space between two of the ruined buildings. In between was a fence, patterned in a hexagonal wireframe, but it was an escape. I tossed the axe over and latched onto the steel, the tips of my boots prying into the gaps. I crawled over just as the pigman rammed himself into the fence. The wires rattled with his frame-denting impact, but he didn't break through. I scrambled to get my axe from the grimy ground and bolted again. The filthy brick walls were the only saving grace keeping me sound, but I didn't dare to stop.

The pigbeast swung his pipe into the fencing, failing to make it fall. He coughed from exhaustion, only to chuckle again and yell at me. "You're not gonna last long out here…I'm gonna find ya…and I'm gonna *eat* ya…" He hacked, his gurgles fading the further I paced.

I got out from the other end of the alley and into a new street, spattered with litter and remains. Soaked in sweat, my lungs strained to keep themselves intact, but despite it all, I was still alive. *For now.*

A newfound noise crinkled the dying air.

I couldn't pinpoint where it originated from, but I wandered toward the strange noise until it grew louder and scratchier. In the middle of the street was a small, chunky box. A prod stuck up from its rectangular shape, and there were numbers displayed in a little window.

Channel 1.901.

"—yran—re you—hear me—"

A voice came through.

Desperate, I found the compulsion to reach the voice on the other side. I didn't know how the contraption functioned, but I pressed the SPEAK button and cried out for help. "H-Hello? My name is Charissa—

I-I don't know who this is, and I don't know where I am, but something's coming after me—Save me, please!"

As I pleaded, the roots of my hair yanked. I screeched and dropped the device as my body lifted from the ground.

"—*who's there?—ello? —llo?*"

With my scalp on the verge of ripping off, I didn't even think, and I swung my axe from behind. A squeal broke the air again and I dropped back to the concrete. The pigman writhed as the curved red metal cleaved into his forehead, frantically trying to pull it out. "Ghhhhghr! You stuck it in me eye!"

I tried to escape, but he grabbed my arm, throwing my body, and as I soared, the air vanished from my throat. I crashed into the pavement, with the collision so strong that it staked a violent strain in my nerves.

My limbs couldn't move.

With an audible, gruesome pull, the pigbeast pried the axe head out of his skull, dark blood spurting out from the gash that scarred his mug. He threw the weapon aside, far more driven to kill me. "I sniffed you out good, and now...you're *mincemeat.*"

He approached me, his shadow covered my entire being. Leaning in, his disgusting mitts grabbed hold, nearly crushing my bones. One hand went on my shoulder, and the other on my skull, as he revealed my neck to himself. His drool dribbled onto my skin, and my eyes darted everywhere. "Mmm...I'm starving...*Don't. Mind. If. I. Do.*"

I turned into prey.

The maw of the nightmare dipped closer, rotted teeth coming to bear against my skin. All he had to do was sink in, and he would break through my flesh, helpless to his hunger. Absolutely helpless.

But he stopped.

A grunt of struggle squeaked out, his mass lifting from my numbed body. A white figure of menacing brawn held the pigman by the back of his neck, and my demon thrashed to escape. "Wh-what's going on!?"

The veiled individual threw him to the ground, and squeals of agony shattered the air as he collided with the concrete. The savior kicked him down, holding a weapon that extended from his shoulder, boasting a handle as the other hand gripped a handguard. The guardian angel aimed down the sight of a barrel, finger on the arch.

"N-No! Put that thing away! I-I wasn't gonna—"

A series of ear-shattering cracks followed.

Fire sparked in the air as jets of pellets soared for the pigbeast, each mark breaking through his malformed face and tumor-ridden chest until his features blurred into red. The monster wheezed, succumbing to his fatal wounds, and a wisp of smoke faded from the stranger's weapon. Metal bits and pieces rolled beside me; a burning hot warmth emanated from each one.

Amid the light show, it didn't occur to me until it was too late…the figure, my rescuer, wore the same white cloak that belonged to one of the monsters from the thunderstorm. The hooded entity peered at me, its eyes glowing gold from underneath its hood. My still body remained on the ground, where I prayed in silence to the true angels in heaven.

Save me.

"Someone else spoke through your transmitter, and then I heard the commotion. What happened?" A distant feminine voice called.

Another stranger appeared from the corner of my eye, one that was slender and a little shorter in comparison to the larger silhouette, but still tall and lanky. Masks obscured their faces underneath their hoods, and I couldn't tell what they were, but something else followed behind them both. I couldn't make it out initially, but it appeared to be a tail, covered in dark fur. My eyes shifted between her and the other stranger.

What were these things?

"Yeah, I know, I was coming back for it until I saw one of *them*, on top of this..." The broader figure paused in his words, his pitch deeper and gravellier than his counterpart. "She's...she's human."

He stood up from the corpse and walked to me, squatting. Without hesitation, he grabbed my face, and his claws grazed my skin, fossilizing me further in place.

"But that's impossible. Nobody from the outside has found this place in decades. Do you think—She's here to help us? An ambassador from above?" the mysterious woman speculated, peering behind him as he tapped his thumb against my cheek.

He hummed, examining my blank face. "If anyone were to be sent down here, it'd be a professional. Lady here nearly got killed. But either she's from the surface, or maybe..." He was close to tearing in. "She's a pawn of the *Ferecite*."

My jaw locked.

"No, if she were, she'd be able to handle her own…Look at her, she's terrified. I don't think she can even speak right now."

"Well, we can't leave her out here, that's for sure."

"I'm certainly not going to waste this opportunity. We need to bring her back to town and put her in recovery. When she's able, we can question her, see what brings her down here. After all, this is a monumental moment for us. I never dreamed I'd see a true human being."

What was going to happen to me?

"You're probably right. If anyone else found her, she'd wish she'd be dead. But still, I'm not sure if we should take our chances. What would *they* think? You really can't believe they wouldn't give us shit about this."

What were they going to do with me?

"I'm prepared for whatever *they* have to say. Pick her up carefully but be quick. For all we know, anything might've heard the gunfire."

Oh, angels above, where were they going to take me?

"On it. Just hope you're right."

"Not everyone out here is a monster, you know."

My body lifted from the ground, only to be hoisted over his shoulder. Utterly limp, I started to see black as he carried me away. All feeling dwindled from my fingertips and my toes, only for the numbness to run through my arms and legs. I struggled to keep myself conscious, until I went out entirely.

I want to go home.

The familiar darkness kept me company again. In my prayers that I would somehow find Narissa in the abyss, she was nowhere to be found. My body floated, becoming one with the null. Perhaps I'd finally arrived at my afterlife tribulation, and was waiting to see if the angels would bring me to heaven or if they'd leave me in the trenches of hell. I had to be dead this time. My trial was bound to come, and in the dark space of the *waiting room*, voices flooded around me.

"So, Virtue, how did you come across a true human?"

"She was in those streets on her own, a berserker nearly ate her alive. I don't know how this is all possible, but we couldn't just let her die."

I couldn't make out who the first voice belonged to, but the second came clear. The grit of his tone was familiar compared to the other's, grislier, deeper strew of words. In limbo, I listened with dread.

"You were a fool to bring her here. To have a genuine human being here? Do you have any idea of the catastrophe you have in the making? Let me get rid of her before *anybody else* knows she's here."

"Your Reverence, let's not be so rash. I'd like to know her deal before we just throw her back out, or take her in with open arms."

The fate of my future hung in the balance between the two disembodied entities. Regardless of the outcome, whether I succumb beyond my mortal vessel or live to see another day, I would perish in a nightmare fit to grapple with my sanity.

"If she proves to be a problem, you know what I'll do to you. You and Dr. Rhodes will risk banishment, or end up disposing of her yourself. After what you've been through, are you both willing to take the chances?"

"You're putting a lot on me, Reverence, but my sister has faith in this girl, so I might as well try and find some good in her too."

Silence followed afterward, and I didn't know what to expect next. Yet again, *death* gave me pitiful mercy.

My eyes fluttered to the dull yellow lights, with lustrous walls of iron closing me in. Despite the soreness of my body, the delicate sensation of cloth touched my skin. A pale blue gown silked over me, as did a pair of thin slippers. My body laid on something soft, and more comfortable than the leaf pile I had once grown so used to: A real bed. I turned over, where a plethora of gadgets surrounded me, humming low rhythms as they blinked and displayed strange, glowing windows. Numbers alternated within the glass, and a grid of rectangles centered the motion picture with a zigzagging line throughout the frame.

It synced to every palpitation.

As my senses cleared, a soft pain coursed through my arm. To my shock, a tube attached to me, connecting to a metal stand with a bag of liquid hanging from a hook. Past the pole, a bright hue glowed from a wide window that was covered in bolted grates. Ahead, a door resided on the other side of the room. Above the metal frame, there was another machine, displaying the date in red.

18:39 (17 | 11 | 2174)

Aside from the buzzing of the contraption, faint words came through the other side of the entryway. "Strange fluctuations. Checking her vitals, going to see why they're unstable." Afterward, the door opened, and a silhouette of white appeared in the frame. As it walked further into the room, the white clothes on its body blended seamlessly with its head…only to reveal the face of a mutt, covered in snow-like fur, carrying instruments of torture on a silvery tray. The Devil deceived me with another one of his abominations.

"Yes, I'll also check her I.V. and—" As the male talked to a strange device clipped to his chest, the dark gaze of the beast met mine. He dropped the equipment, the tools scattered on the floor. "She's awake! I repeat, she's awake!" he said, his barks echoing in the room.

He was going to kill me.

My veins pumped with adrenaline as I scrambled out of bed, knocking the metal stand beside it. Yanking the tube from my arm, where a dribble of blood beaded out from the wound, I struggled to get on my tingling feet. My legs were like jelly, my lungs wheezing for air as I made a bolt for the window.

"The patient's trying to escape! Get down here now, Virtue!" He called out to the device before he hurried to me. Clenching the metal grates, trying to pry them apart, the mutt's gloved paws grabbed my arms. I flailed them from his grip, only to fall to the cold floor. I attempted to crawl away from his clutches, but he held my ankles.

"Let me out of here!" I cried.

"I'm trying to help! Calm down!" he demanded, pulling at me. My nails dug into the iron below, and the little strength in my body resisted his efforts. I kicked him off, dragging myself to the door; my only way of getting out alive.

"You're not going to kill me too!" I screeched.

In a sick shift of fate, another stranger blocked the way. A pair of booted feet greeted me, and when my eyes dragged upward, his appearance left me petrified to the floor.

"What the hell's going on?"

A deep voice came from the figure of remarkable height, with his physique sporting strong muscles. Underneath his leather armor, fingerless gloves, and polished boots, dark fur with large rosettes covered every inch of him. His hair matched his deep pelt, woven into dreadlocks that reached the middle of his back. He shared the facial features of a panther, yet a body of human shape. His amber stare fixed on me in brief surprise, only to dart to the white figure.

A twist of a man and a black jaguar. "What happened here?"

"I don't know. None of us expected she'd wake up this soon, and when I came in, she went *berserk*. We should have restrained her the moment she arrived."

The pantherine man scoffed. "Don't be stupid. I told you she'd freak out but putting her in binds would've caused more issues. Get out of here; I'm going to see what she's all about. Oh, and inform Dr. Rhodes that her favorite patient is wide awake."

"Right. If this human tries anything else, you can handle it." The nervous dogman hurried past the other male. When it was only him and me, he leaned in with an open palm.

"Hello. You've been out for a few days—"

I crawled back, bumping against the bedframe behind me. "Stay away from me," I begged.

"Okay…" he kept his distance. The fangs in his maw inspired my worst fears, as if he might eat me like the pigbeast had tried to. "…do I really scare you?"

Unable to answer, I simply nodded.

I had nowhere to escape as he came closer, slow at his pace and still reaching out with that massive, clawed mitt. "There's nothing to be afraid of here. You can trust me." He tried to pacify me, but never in my life had I met face-to-face with a creature so humanlike in behavior, yet so monstrous in physicality.

"Wh-What are you?" I stammered.

Disheartened, he retracted his padded palm, brushing off the crest that punctured the leather on his left pectoral. The badge resembled a golden gladiolus. "The name's Kyran Rhodes, Virtue of Courage. How about you? Could you tell me your name?" His demeanor softened.

"I'm…" Before I darted to the crawlspace of the bed as a last resort, he huffed, leaning in. My breath stopped at his touch.

"Here, let's get you back up." He reached under my arms, and I almost fought back. However, when he lifted me from the frigid floor, he brought me to the bed, where he gently put me down. For a beast of his brawn, I hadn't expected his hold to be so considerate. "There you go, just relax a little. No reason to freak out," he assured, picking up the metal stand from the ground and collecting the wet, broken bag.

The way he moved and acted was so…*surreal.* After all the stories I'd read, where the characters interacted and developed between the pages, I always considered the way they connected. I struggled to put my knowledge to the test, considering how difficult it proved to find a way to communicate with a being so beastly, yet so human. Nothing prepared me to know how to best associate with someone half-man, or half-animal, but I resorted to playing on his safe side.

Do not deem myself as a threat.

"I'm Charissa,"

Those tapered ears perked to my name. "Charissa…just Charissa? No last name?" he questioned, and my mind boggled.

I had always known myself as only that, and there was nothing more to my bloodline. Not anymore, I feared.

"I don't…I don't think I have one,"

"Nothing to be ashamed of. When some people come here, they leave their old names behind for a better one. I figured I'd ask since we're working on what to do with you."

"Huh?"

"Oh, uh, nothing." He cleared his throat. "What matters is that you're still breathing. If my sister and I didn't find you out there, you would have really been pigfeed." He mentioned, only reminding me again of the horrific memory that lingered. Seconds away from becoming mincemeat, something else intervened in my fate: the white figure.

The shape aligned, and once my fears subsided, it only occurred to me that my savior was right there. "Wait, you're the one that rescued me?"

"Yeah, believe it or not. We were looking for somebody else, and the last thing we were expecting to find was—"

The door creaked open once more, and deep down, I hoped it'd be someone with skin coming to my aid, but instead came another being of fur. Rather than the white-canine doctor, a woman stepped inside.

"Bea, there you are," Kyran called out. As the other stranger closed the door, my grasp of what was real and what was not slipped.

She nearly matched the male jaguar's height, but her figure was far lither and nimbler. She possessed pantherine qualities as well, except her features bore a softer shape. Dark fur and splotched rosettes too covered the woman, a deep navy blue rather than the male's onyx black. With her midnight hair curled in wisps, all pulled back in a tight bun, she wore a white coat and a lanyard, a buttoned shirt, and matching pants with flat shoes. A pair of clear, mono-block glasses framed her face, radiant with a glowing trim that matched those aquamarine eyes.

"The nurse told me what happened. Handled things rashly from what I could tell, but I was happy to hear our special guest was up." She conferred with her supposed brother, and I only gawked as she shifted her eyes to me, growing wider as the situation sank in. She approached me with a wide grin, whiskers waving as she leaned for a closer look.

"This is…incredible. How are you feeling right now? What is your name?" she asked, a starstruck glimmer behind the frame of her pristine glasses. I was at a loss, to which the keen feline took notice. "Oh, my apologies. I didn't even introduce myself. I'm Dr. Beatrix Rhodes, Head Scientist of our Biological Department. But you, my friend, can call me Bea. I assume you and my brother have been getting along?" she glanced between me and the man.

"I was going to ask her some questions myself, but I don't know if we should just yet. Might be best to quarantine with the state she's in. Showing her what's out there might make it worse." He intervened.

"Kyran, we've already talked about this. Her condition is stable, and her fears are only caused by the change of environment. Let her settle in, and she'll adapt just fine. Besides, there's no reason to still suspect she's a *fanatic*, if that's your bigger concern," she insisted.

"That's not what I meant." Kyran drew a deep sigh, stepping up and kneeling to my level so that my face met his. "Charissa, I'd like you to talk with my sister here. She just wants to know a little more about where you came from, and why you're down here. So long as you answer honestly, it'll give us all the more reason to trust you and know you're not part of the *wrong people*. Is that okay with you?"

Albeit frightening at first, and still warranting suspicion, he did save me. Given everything that had transpired thus far, I couldn't find fault in his stance, and in a way, I owed him. Plus, If I wanted any chance of crawling from this hellscape, I needed to be true and compliant.

"A-Alright," I said.

Kyran nodded, standing and tilting his head to the door. "I'm going to relay this back to the Reverences and hang around the courthouse until you're finished. If she has another outburst, don't let the doctors use any sedative on her. She's clearly no *berserker*."

"To that, we can agree. The last thing we need is to scare our guest, so I'll be sure she's not given an unwelcome stay. As many of us say, a little kindness goes a long way," she suggested, only baiting a groan from the irritated feline.

"No need to remind me about the one of the thousand proverbs from my training days. I'll radio you later." He turned heel, walking out the door and giving it a gentle shut on the way.

Bea took off her glasses, palming the embarrassment from her face. "He and I never intended to frighten you," she expressed. "You must be terrified, I'd imagine. Anyone would've been traumatized by what you've witnessed thus far. You've been out cold a while."

My fingertips jittered, sinking into the bed. The pacing notion of my sister's state drove me to a frantic despair. If my unconsciousness had lasted for days, I assumed the worst possibilities for her. Could she still have been alive, or did the abomination devour her? Or was she left to rot? "Doctor…Bea? Listen, I need to get out of here—"

"Slow down, slow down. I understand you're in unfamiliar territory and want to leave, but you're better off here than you are out in the rest of the city. Not many places are as hospitable as ours."

"What are you guys going to do to me? Are you going to hurt me?"

She waved in dismissal. "No, of course not! We've been keeping you well cared for. There's no sense in harming you in any way. I know all of this is a lot to process, but take a few deep breaths, in and out."

At first, I didn't want to take her advice, but the sooner I recovered and escaped, the sooner I returned to Narissa. I inhaled a full breath, letting it go, and repeated the process a couple of times over. "Okay…okay. So, why did you guys bring me here? Why help me?"

"After my brother and I found you, we took you back here to our town. There was no way we'd leave you, or anyone out there on their own." Given what I witnessed her brother do, I doubted her legitimacy.

With lethal, sentient creatures, I had to cooperate.

"If I answer your questions, will you answer one for me?"

"No doubt you have a lot to ask, so of course."

I crossed my legs. "What do you want to know?"

"Many things, but I'll try not to ask too much of you. What I want to know most is who sent you. We've spent years down here, with a lot of us hoping someone from above would come, but to no avail. We all thought the rest of the world forgot about this city."

Unfortunately, I had to bear the bad news.

"I'm sorry, but nobody. Before I came here, I lived on the island up above…Vinea, I think it's called. Found this pit out in the forest, my home. I've lived there my whole life."

She lowered her head, but it lifted with a renewed outlook. "So, nobody sent you, but you were rather closer than I thought. If you don't mind me asking, how long did you live on Vinea Island? Did you happen to discover it and become stranded, or…have you really lived your entire life up there?"

Truth would only further convolute my side, but lying to her was too dangerous. "Yes, but I was never allowed to leave. Tried finding some answers, and it all began when I came across this pit. My sister wanted nothing to do with it, and now I see why."

"Wait. Your sister, you say?"

"Y-Yes. Her name's Narissa."

"Now this adds a lot more complexity to the picture. Are you saying she didn't come here with you? Where is she now?"

My heartstrings tore. "I…I don't know. I think…they killed her…" I struggled to say, only causing Bea's pupils to thin.

"Who are *they*, Charissa?"

"The monsters. They wore the same cloaks you did, but their faces looked nothing like yours," I said, and Bea sat by my side.

"Can you describe what you saw?"

The twin horrors singed my conscience in unforgettable scars. Just like Narissa's screams. "Their faces were all messed up. Flesh melting off, they made the most terrifying sounds. They were like insects covered in meat and skin, giant claws and throats covered in teeth; even had these disgusting maggots in their bodies."

"The Ferecite," she gasped.

"What did you say?" I leaned in, but she averted her eyes in silence. "Bea, if these things murdered Narissa, I have to know who they are, and why they would do this to her. To me."

"I'm—I can't tell you. Not because I don't trust you, I want to, but I'd be incriminating myself and the well-being of our—"

My inner turmoil bubbled, spilling forth.

"If you're not going to tell me what I want to hear, then the least you can do is let me go," I snapped, to which Bea slid away.

Ears folding, she said, "Charissa, I know you're upset, but—"

"No, you don't know! They took the one person that mattered to me, and I can't sit here knowing her body could still be up there, or worse! I need to get back up there and see if she's—"

"There is no way up."

The fire in me burned out, as did my hope.

"N-No, but I have to—" I muttered, but with her firm stare, she did not lie to me. The hairs on my body stood. "That can't be true."

"Believe me, all of us tried to find some way to the surface. If we did, we would've left this city behind, but we're condemned here." Her voice lowered, as did her spirit. "I'm sorry for what happened to your sister, and I don't know how those Ferecites got there. If that's the case, then I'm afraid that my predictions might come true sooner than I expected." Bea got up from the bed and headed for the window, resting an elbow on the grates as she peered through for light.

"I don't understand…"

"This disease we all inherit. It'll be the death of us, and perhaps all of humankind as the world sees it."

"What disease? And who's we?"

Bea motioned me over to the window, and I stepped next to her. She twisted the knob nearby to shift the grates away, and the soft light gleamed through, the gaps offering a sight to behold.

Through the dusty glass, ambition had never glimmered so brightly. Outside were colorful lights, all crossing one another from many levels, but I didn't get to see too much from the murky window. Structures of stone, steel, and iron stood so tall, with *people* wandering among makeshift bridges. Everything outside appeared so alive compared to what I first witnessed upon descending into the city. Voices spoke in harmony, and they were all good ones this time, benevolent and cheerful.

"Everyone out there, including myself, we are *hybridian*." Bea's mention of her kind illuminated her spirits. "The symbiosis of animality and humanity."

Staring into the muddled vision of the community shifted my apprehension. "Hybridian. You're like people, but not quite." I said, my breath nearly taken away. "So this disease—is that why you look the way you are? To bear the face and likeness of an…animal?"

The longer I stared at her, the more the humanity in her visage showed through those otherwise bestial features.

"Yes, and if it were to spread from Misera to the rest of the planet, who knows how the future would look?"

"Misera?" I asked.

Her claws scraped along the edge of the grate, discontent. "Pietas used to be the name of this city. But ever since the sky-sphere shut off decades ago, where the projection of the sun, the stars, and weather disappeared for good, we as a people felt it deserved a different name."

"Because…"

"This place lost its worth being called 'the city of human devotion.'" she mumbled, closing away the grates and eyeing the machine above the door. "It's getting late, and most of us will have to leave the labs in about an hour. Since we have time, I'd like to take you down to our biological labs and show you what we're all about."

"Why's that?"

"Well, I'd rather not keep you in this room forever. If I'm to gain your trust, then that'd start with telling you more about myself and my work. So, what do you say?" She asked, and in a decision between staying in this box and leaving it, the choice spoke for itself.

"Okay."

"Excellent, then let's get started. Right this way, if you please." She directed me to the door, and I followed her tail. When I expected myself to open it, Bea held it for me instead, her gesture taking me aback.

"Um…Thank you."

The feline hummed. "You're very welcome."

Leaving the room, the stark contrast of the space became apparent. Heavy bricks slabbed the walls, chipped in a matte white finish. The hazel clay showed beneath, making the whole place feel ancient, yet still far more advanced than I'd expected. Lists of framed regulations lined both my sides, while faint beams of light resonated above. The artificiality of their brightness could never compare to the sun I once rose for every day.

"We'll go and take the scenic route this way. Oh, and feel free to look as much as you'd like." Bea headed down the linear path, her footsteps echoing off the clean floor. Keeping close to her, the coolness of the tiles seeping through my slippers. Walking again made me feel better. As we wandered through the corridors, Bea would bring her hand up to the device on her chest, like the one that the white-dogged scientist had. She'd whisper into the machine's webbed compartment, and I kept an ear on her communique, though without eavesdropping.

"That thing is a 'radio,' right?" I asked, causing her to finish her interaction with an abrupt click of the button.

"You're absolutely correct. Every lab worker and Virtue is equipped with one. You used it before, back on the street."

I got chills reflecting on that encounter. "I didn't know what I was doing. I was scared for my life until you and your brother came." I shuddered. "So that thing, and all those…other things, that were in that room…the bright ones. How do they all work? Do they need fire, or?"

Bea couldn't help but chuckle. "We use electricity and all kinds of energy down here. Actually, let's see how the power grid is doing." She put me to a stop, turning the next corner, where she brought me to a set of wide doors. Her fingertip tapped away at a pad, displaying a series of numbers before flashing green. The metal doors slid apart, and she led the way into a dark room. Ominous at first, a white glow shone through the obscurity. Many windows lined the space, as well as weird vines covered in a soft material. A couple of people in one-piece suits tended to the strange-looking vines using metallic apparatuses on their arms. Ahead, the biggest window showed a mishmash between the alphabet and more numbers, though above it all, the text in bright hues displayed a point of interest. *NEPTUNE HYDROPOWER* : *CONNECTED/ONLINE.*

"This is where we maintain our energy supply, as well as keep in touch with the hydrologists at the city power plant. From there, they're able to harness the oceanic momentum outside the island's core, providing enough energy to prevent the city from going lights-out. Without the sea beyond, we wouldn't have enough ventilation and temperature control to keep us all from boiling alive." she explained nonchalantly, taking me to one of the machines to display another glass-framed contraption, accompanied by a tray that had little squares in several rows, almost invitingly touchable. "These computers keep track of where we resource our power throughout town, and we try to ration it out accordingly. If we try to use too much, we risk burning out our systems as a whole."

"Computers…so that's what you call these things. And are you saying that this isn't the only safe place in Misera?"

"There are other communities, but…let's just say that they either don't have good intentions, or rather keep themselves isolated from the rest of the city. We're one of the safest, especially for outsiders," she answered, but it was difficult for me to listen, as the glowing screens entranced me.

"Uh-huh. And what're *they* doing?" I glanced at the two suited beasts, one with a reptilian head and the other with barbless quills. In their palms, the web-like metal apparatuses sparkled as they worked. From fingertip to shoulder, these devices emitted surges of power from their hands while they diligently worked on the strange tethers.

Bea dragged me over. "These're a couple of the lab engineers, and their main job is to maintain the connection to Misera's southeast sector. Looks like they're repairing some faulty cables." She waved them over. "Hello, you two! I see we're getting plenty done. How're we doing?"

They lifted their blue-hued goggles. The bearded dragon had huge, bugged-out eyes, as the spike-covered fellow had little beady ones.

"We're doing mighty fine here, Dr. Rhodes. Ooh, who's this?" beamed the one with glistening, sand-colored skin.

"If you told us you'd be bringing our special guest for a tour, I would've tidied the place up a bit more!" the mammal added, and it took all my willpower to not bolt from the room.

"Her name's Charissa. I'm showing her what we all do here, but I knew you'd both be excited to meet her," Bea said.

The two men stepped forth, tall and daunting.

"I'm trying my best to contain myself, but wow! Didn't think I'd ever see a human in my life!" the reptilian whooped.

"Chill out, don't make her feel like some kind of otherworlder. It's a pleasure to meet you, madame." The spiny man clicked his arm, the metal latches unhinged as he pried the machine off his limb. His bare, keratin-covered fingers reached out. I didn't move an inch.

"Or I suppose not." He retracted his mitt.

Bea intervened. "She's still settling in. After all, she's never seen anything like us before in her life. Don't try to take things personally," Bea told him, and the mammal's face brightened.

"I didn't quite think of it like that. Well, regardless, glad she can get a chance to meet us lab rats." He guffawed.

The wet-skinned man joined him. "Guess dreams do come true, huh? Come on, these cables aren't gonna fix themselves. Annoying little things." The engineers gave me their warm smiles, returning to their work, and Bea escorted me out of the room. The two metal doors slid together, and my face washed in a wave of roses.

"Don't be embarrassed. It's not easy meeting new people—let alone people that're nothing like you," she sympathized.

I kept my stare on the floor. My stomach tingled, as did my hands, almost jittering too. "I've always wanted to meet people, but...I just didn't picture it anything like this," I admitted.

"Given what you told me about your past so far, I can't blame you. You've only known one person your whole life."

Again, I reflected on Narissa. She'd robbed me of a life of connection, yet, what tore into me more was that I could no longer connect to her.

"Do you need a moment?"

I shook my head. "I'm okay. What else can I see?"

Bea led me further down the corridors, and more wings passed us. Geological Sciences, Climatology, Pharmaceuticals; the departments went on. Each one had a large glass pane spanning between the hall and the inside, where scientists performed their tasks using the same apparatuses that the engineers in the power room did. One had a radiant beam cutting through rock, another projected fire and ice, and the last one crafted the tiniest tablets with minuscule precision. Although it was hard to tell the purpose of their work, to witness such technology enthralled me no less.

"Have I really been missing out on all this?" I breathed.

"These're some of the more important areas we cover. Frankly, these scientists are what make keeping this town feasible compared to the rest of Misera. Our town prides itself in its laboratories, infantry, and hub life."

"Amazing! Those strange gadgets on their arms, what're they?"

"They're called *Catalysts*, arm-bound machines once used by Pietas' geniuses. There are various models with different intentions, whether it'd be surgery, altering one's strength, or spewing water to put out fire." she explained. "They're able to use a wide assembly of tools or cast various projections from their hands. Each one was built with a specific purpose, for better or worse…here, we use them for good."

"Kind of like magic?"

She laughed. "I suppose in a way, it is."

"How come you don't have one?"

"Oh, I do! But they can get quite uncomfortable after long periods of usage. I'll show you once we get to my station. In fact, there's a few labs on the way you might like."

An ecstatic rush filled me.

Leading me further, it came down to which window I should investigate first—Agricultural Development or Marine Farms? The decision made itself when I caught the distinct smell of dirt emanating beyond the pane, reminding me of home. Through the seeing glass, the vast room reached high, where the fluorescent lights beamed brightest as rows and columns of green growth surrounded the area, nearly touching the ceiling. Lab assistants on their ladders went high up with their Catalysts, weeding through and tending to each plant with nurturing care. Cucumbers, tomatoes, onions, and even some I never knew the names of. To think that such things could only be grown outdoors, but to witness such magic being made in even the darkest depths, left me believing anything was possible.

The more I stared, however, the more the shattered feeling in my chest lingered again. Yearning, my palm rested on the transparent barrier. I should have been amazed to witness things so astounding, but the urge to flood my eyes left them fuzzy.

I looked at Bea, chattering with her radio again. Because I didn't want such waters to fall, I ran to the other wall of the hall, gazing into the dreamy deep blues. Rushing waters called beyond, where the walls within lined with fish tanks and deep, netted pools surrounded the floor of the room. Ladders accompanied each circle, large enough for me to climb down and fit inside. Each "pond" held certain kinds of sea life: catfish, tilapia, trout, and other fish I had never seen from my days at the rivers and lakes. The people inside tended to each mini habitat, reaching in and sprinkling in food, or making their catches.

Without a noise, rivers ran down my face.

As Bea conversed with the device at her coat, she lifted her head to see my state. Panicked, she stepped close to me. "Charissa? You're crying…I'm sorry, I was just making some notes."

I wiped my tears and continued down the hallway. "It's nothing. Let's keep going," I assured her.

"Very well, let's conclude the tour with my lab."

We continued to the end of the corridor, where one more set of doors remained. Bea punched in the right numbers, the metal parted, and what little magic in me siphoned out. Apart from the desks accompanied by computers and equipment, there was a series of tubes lining the room, all of which contained a naked mutant. The transparent liquid kept them afloat, each bearing differences in their physicality. One mammal, one reptile, one avian, and multiple other variants. Upon closer examination, there was no essence of life within their vessels.

"What is all this? What are you doing to them!" I yelled.

Bea was quick to step in front of me. "It's not what you think. These people donated their bodies to us after they passed away of natural causes. This is what they wanted."

"They *willingly* wanted this?"

Bea brought my attention to each tube. "We keep them in suspension so that we're able to analyze their bodies for a plethora of reasons…the conditions of each animal kingdom, understanding every degree of our mutation to its fullest. The Transmutative Omnifauna Virus." She glid her fingertips to the cold glass. "However, there's one half to the ailment I've never been able to study."

"What's that?"

Holding a long stare inside the tube to the half-woman, half-feline suspended in the surging water, Bea faced me. "The opposite side of this synergy. The human factor. That's where you come in."

"I don't think I get what you mean,"

"Although we've only just met, I feel as though we can help each other. You're not obligated to do anything for me, but would you be willing to hear out a proposition? One that can benefit us both?"

This could be trouble. "I guess so."

"If you do happen to stick around and there's ever time you can spare, some samples of your human genes could tremendously benefit my ability to tackle this disease at a microscopic level. I don't need much more than traces of hair, saliva, and blood to get somewhere. Simple and sufficient, and I'd get results that would save me years of research."

My apprehension held, but I leaned in.

"…What's in it for me?"

Bea contemplated for a minute, looking at the floor.

"You need closure for your sister…" She tapped her fingers, then perked up. "I can't guarantee it, but I have some connections. I'll contact them and see their whereabouts when it comes to Ferecite. I'll take any information they can give me, and hopefully get you the answers you need, if not more."

Could she have answered the thousands of questions in my mind? Perhaps not, but the closure I yearned for most must've been apparent, and if she could help me, I'd take what I get.

"What I want to know the most is why it had to be her. Why they would kill her. And when I find out who put them up to it…"

"You have no idea what they're capable of. They're a fatal kind of evil. One you should never trifle with."

"Either way, I want answers."

Bea nodded. "I'll do everything I can for you. I know I can't deliver much right now, but you have my honest word. I promise."

For now, I had to give her a sliver of confidence. A fragment of possibility brought promise, and knowing I had nobody else to trust down here, Bea might've been my only way. "Better than spending the rest of my life wondering why. Alright, I'll help you, but I expect some kind of answer. You better deliver on your promise."

Bea put her hand forth. "We have a deal."

"I…What now?" I stared at her open palm.

"Ah, right. Here."

She reached for me, taking my hand, and bringing it to her own. Once they met, our grasps held together, and she lightly shook with firm pressure. "This is a handshake. It signifies trust, and sometimes, new beginnings. Perhaps this is the start of a friendship, even."

I started to understand what it was like to be a person—to make connections. Except as I held her, it was bizarre. She had a palmar pad like a wild cat would, her fingertips padded with gray epidermis. A strange sensation, to say the least, but her touch had a welcoming warmth, and I was curious how our *friendship* would work.

"Then it's a deal."

A blinking button came from Bea's radio, and she politely withdrew to answer the call. "Hello, Kyran?" She paused, listening in. "Yes, we're in the biological laboratories…wait, what was that? She's on her way here now? Right now?" Her brows rose, pupils dilating.

The doors behind us parted, a remarkable red figure standing in the frame. The stranger walked in, with her talons scraping against the cold floor. "Good evening, Bea. I'm here to take Charissa."

The assertive voice belonged to a well-poised cardinal, and about the same height as I was. Bearing feathers that burned in sanguine vibrance, she had sapphire eyes to pair with her fiery plumage. Several gilded, decorated badges pinned to the chest of her dress grays slated from shoulder to ankle. On her back strapped a scoped weapon of blue-silver alloy. Her presence naturally imposed. "Ah, you must be her. Are you ready to go?"

"Me?" I blurted.

Bea lit up. "Well, hello, Aliya—oh, apologies, *Chief Morales*. This is unexpected. I thought Kyran was supposed to be the one coming back,"

"High Reverence Constance asked me to come here personally for a first impression, as well as to take her to the courthouse once you were done spending time with her." The woman spoke to Bea, then turned to me, the edges of her beaked maw curving. "My name is Aliya Morales,

Chief of the Reverian Virtues, and rank-holder of Righteous Virtue of Patience. It's my honor to meet you, Miss Charissa."

Her charisma dazzled me. I put my hand out to her, and when she saw my palm, she took it with a firm grip, her feathers soft on my skin.

"I'm still new to this. I hope this is right."

"You're doing just fine, ma'am. It's good to make your acquaintance. Come with me, I'll take you to meet High Reverence Constance herself. Her courthouse isn't far from the labs here." She stated, and I looked to Bea for her permission.

"Go right ahead. I'm going to do some last-minute protocol here, but I promise I'll be seeing you soon. Oh, and thanks for letting me show you around." The jaguar grinned as she headed back to the cadavers in their tubes, and I still couldn't help but gawk at the sight of those things, willingly abandoning their legacies to be studied.

"Stay by my side while we head over. I'd like to know more about you myself." The chief gestured to the door, and I pried my gaze away from the tubed coffins, haunted by their lifeless, mutated forms.

The chief escorted me through the facility, the halls quiet as most of the scientists and engineers had gone. Once we took a series of stairs downward to the first floor, she took me to the main lobby, the space accompanied by benches, faux plants, and machines that displayed pictures of food. The setting would've been calming, if not for the large portrait that hung on the furthest wall. Contained in its steel frame, a picture of a hybridian stared at me, elderly and bearing sable-like qualities. Photos tacked alongside the centerpiece, as did an array of false flowers and material possessions. Each capture showed many of the scientists and citizens, sharing the moment with the man of the painting.

"Who's this?"

As I took in the glazed eyes of the mammal, the chief clasped her hands, finishing a silent prayer. "Dr. Nobu Kutsuki, director of this facility. Came here fifteen years ago, and fifteen years here did he make Reveria the haven it is. Even with Virtues, this place wouldn't be the way it is without his scientific contributions."

"But I didn't see him around here anywhere."

She reached for one of the stills, a memory of herself and the doctor. "He's no longer with us. Last year, he left this world on his own accord."

I closed my eyes. "So he's gone?"

"Gone, but not forgotten. The most we can do for him now is pay the respects he deserves." she bowed to her former colleague. "And it was my utmost honor to be one of his associates. Let's move on."

Bringing me to the front doors, the lights inside grew dimmer as the laboratories shut down for the evening, but whatever awaited beyond the building left me curious for more—though also fearful.

"I don't want to go out there," I told her, and although we shook hands, the tension with her strained in comparison to Bea's company. The natural aura she gave off promoted more anxiety than cordiality.

"There's nothing to be worried about, amiga. Once you're outside, you'll be just fine." As she accompanied me to the front doors, I took another deep breath.

"I'm ready."

We went outside, and the mesmerizing lights greeted me in person. The initial blur caught me off guard, but soon, all became clear. An entire town held together by metals and stone; the luminescence fueled the entire settlement. Ahead was a rail guard, and running to it, we were higher than expected. A system of bridges and stairs articulated below, with cubic and rectangular constructions unifying with one another. Although the individuals did not match the ordinary people I'd imagined, they were lively. Not even the dark, hollow sky could've snuffed out such fire. What I found before me was camaraderie.

Order in the chaos.

"You're in the safety of Reveria."

"This is nothing like how I first saw things. Everything out there was all falling apart. Dying. How is all of *this* possible?"

"Those ruins you saw when you first showed up here. How did it make you all feel?"

Despite the glamor of prosperity, the hollow ruins of Misera remained beyond the giant wall ahead. On the other side of the border, the skyscrapers harbored the distance in desolation. Even with all the jovial voices of the townsfolk, the city's null echoed in my head.

"Lost,"

"Reveria is meant to be a guiding light, built to protect others from the terrors that inhabit Misera's ruins."

"Being a Virtue—is that what you do? Protect others?"

I admired the badges on her uniform, especially the biggest one. A gilded aster flower substantiated her role.

"Virtues are peacekeepers, sworn to guard the well-being of others. I have to set an example for them. To be one of the two *Righteous Virtues* is to sacrifice, and that means putting others before myself, always." Her passion glimmered in her speech. "These people deserve calm lives, and I make sure of that. And someday, we can leave Misera for good."

The chief led me away from the rail. Up here, at the highest level, there weren't any mutants wandering about. Given the time of "day," I figured most would be asleep, though the rest of the town seemed so alive amidst the perpetual dusk. The subtle silence biting in the air, the cardinal did well to keep it astray as she continued to converse with me. "Tell me, Charissa, what did you think of Dr. Rhodes?"

"Well...Dr. Rhodes—I mean, Bea was nice to me."

"I'd expect nothing less. She's one of our best scientists. Frankly, ever since she showed up here, it's given me hope that she'll be able to change our way of living."

"What're you talking about?"

"She asked you to help her out with her research, I assume. I feel like with you here now, she'd be able to make her dream possible. Well, her and her brother's. They both share the same ambition."

"That Kyran man?"

"Incredibly talented soldier, he is. They both came here to start anew, and so far, they've done an exceptional job. Everyone that comes to Reveria is given an opportunity to begin anew. You're no different."

"I'm not sure about that,"

"You just need to settle some is all, and you'll warm up in no time. Speaking of, we're going to meet Kyran for your induction,"

"Induction? Where is this going?"

"We're about to find out in just a minute."

Confused, everything unfolded when we approached the front steps of the courthouse. From there, everything in my future would be decided. The architecture had a prominent dome topping its structure. Pillars of quartz kept the structure stable, as the polished diorite made up its construct. Above, where the gigantic rotunda resided, ten raised ribs divided its foundation. Each rib consisted of a different alloy, glistening a unique sheen. At its speared peak, a triad of gemstone doves connected, spiraling upward towards the sky; one each of ruby, emerald, and sapphire. A series of pristine stairs led up to the grand display.

"This is…" My loss of words caught the chief.

"Quite a sight, isn't it? Wait until you see inside."

Upon arriving at the last step, we came to a grand set of arching bronze doors. The cardinal opened one, and from the inside, a begrimed glow beckoned us, and thus we drew ourselves further towards the faint glimmer. Ahead was a large podium fitted for three, overseeing the space from above. At the center of the ceiling, the massive rotunda shone a warm light down upon the enormous room. Dust swam through, where rows of empty seats accompanied the place of high esteem.

"Let's head for the back," she told me, bringing me around the rounded space until we came behind the massive podium, where a wooden door led to our next destination. Holding it open for me, the chief took me inside. With a carpeted floor and an encircling light above, the room had a quietude that called for diligence. In the middle of the room was a large, round table of diorite, with ten chairs encircling it.

Though nobody filled the seats, Kyran stood at the far end, sorting through objects scattered on the table's surface. Next to him was a woman, whose weathered feathers were as gray as her eyes, matching her ashen robes, a sapphire begonia on her chest. Upon seeing her, she reminded me much of the exact harpy eagle I once witnessed.

An embodiment of what opened my eyes.

"There you are, Righteous Virtue of Patience. You've brought the girl with you too, just as I've requested. Let her have a seat here," she called out, having the chief bring me over. The tension in my shoulders rose the closer I got, especially when Kyran took his attention from the items, which turned out to be my own possessions. I got to the chair, sweat already pooled on my scalp and the seat below.

"With the girl now here, we can begin the assessment of her background and qualifications. I, High Reverence Constance, allow the both of you to undertake this process as deemed necessary."

Kyran wasted none of his superior's time. "Yes, ma'am. Let's begin with—"

"One moment, High Reverence Constance. Shouldn't our other two Reverences be present for this as well? This is an important evaluation being held, after all. Alden and Mikhail should be here," The chief interrupted, and the other avian woman lifted her esteemed chin up.

"You'd be most certainly right, Chief, but their initial opinions are unfavorable of the human's position. However, it's ultimately my opinion that will matter most here. They needn't be present for this."

"Very well then," she complied, allowing Kyran to continue.

"Now that all the formalities are out of the way…Charissa, while we do respect the privacy of everyone in our town, we had to check your things for safety. We found a few concerns worth talking about."

"You went through my stuff?"

"When you sound nervous, it gives us suspicion that you're trying to hide something. Is there something you want to say?"

"Kyran, that's enough," the chief demanded.

"I'm not trying to threaten her, I just want an honest answer,"

If it meant moving things along, I would comply. "No, I don't."

"I figured as much." Kyran hummed, dragging forward the first set of items front and center. "Let's start off with this weapon here, an archery bow along with a set of arrows. Seems very old-fashioned, nothing you'd really find here. Where'd you get this kind of equipment?"

Tears tempted to return. "It was a gift from my sister,"

"Bea did briefly mention that fact over the radio. You have a sister, but she's not here with you. Said she was killed by the Ferecite. Would you mind telling us where she's located now?"

My hands clenched. "She's still…up there, where I'm from."

"High Reverence." his lips tensed. "I'm not certain she's telling the entire truth,"

"Kyran. Stand. Down," the chief intervened.

"But there's clearly—"

"Don't defy my orders."

"Enough, Virtues." Constance demanded. "Charissa, if what you're saying is veritable, then that brings a greater revelation. Do you swear that what you're telling us is nothing but the honest truth?" She spoke without a blink, able to throw my life away with her power if I gave anything but my earnest word.

"Yes," I told her, as firm as I could deliver.

"Then please raise your right hand, and solemnly swear."

To her command, I rose and avowed it.

"You may continue the assessment," Constance granted.

"Next we have this." He slid over the leatherbound book. "Pietas kept an entire database of their residents and visitors, but they also maintained physical track records of people that immigrated to the city pre-outbreak. Why did you have it in your possession?"

"I found it near the pit up above the surface, hidden away in some kind of station of sorts. I wanted to know if these people were really down here, and why they were. I didn't think I'd find…"

"Beasts like us?" he finished for me. "Your story's barely plausible, but considering the value of this artifact, we'll be holding onto this in the instance any facts contradict themselves."

"Physical immigration records could only be found at that sole entrance both ways, Rhodes. Based on protocol, they kept a copy of all citizenship files in a book both above at the surface level, and down at the offices—not far from where you found her. You've been through that area multiple times and haven't seen any other books like this through there, have you?" the chief mentioned, stumping him.

"No, I suppose we haven't."

"Because any records down here have been long since destroyed or lost. Up on Vinea though, if nobody else but Charissa and her sister were there, somebody else would've found them by now. If Charissa's story aligns with Bea's relay, then I feel it's believable."

"With all due respect, Chief, it's unwise to always see the good in people forefront."

"It's more so giving credibility where it's due. Are implying that Charissa might've come here with ill intentions?"

He paused, glinting at me. "It's unlikely, but possible."

"Regardless, the book will be kept in our care. I'd like to examine it again, remark such history." Constance professed.

Kyran circled back to the matter at hand. "Well other than some inconsequential possessions, there is one last thing I'd like to know about." He brought forth the series of photos. "I'm assuming these're photographs of the island this city is encapsulated in, Vinea. Not to mention, you have a shot of a Ferecite cultist. Multiple shots, even. What can you tell me about this *Anastasia?*"

"I'm afraid I know nothing about her. All I can tell is that she left all these behind at the…Resort town, I think it was. I had no idea of its existence until a few weeks back," I told him.

"Did you happen to recall the name of this town?"

"Commoneo."

Constance leaned in with intrigue. "What else did you find?"

"Most of it was covered in overgrowth, but I found these photos in the library. There were statues of five people. The one that stood out had a name I couldn't figure out…" I delved deep into my memory, recovering the fragments. "I think it was something like Ar—"

The door ahead brisked open, and there stood two tall figures, sharing identical robes of slated, velvet grays.

"Alden? Mikhail?" Constance uttered.

To the left, an average-shaped man that had the facial features of an equine with pale white fur, a pink nose, and dark, thin eyes—a species I had only seen in pictures, but seeing the real example threw me a bit of disarray. He bestowed a ruby peony on his left pectoral.

To the right, a muscular reindeer with large antlers and wenge-colored fur. His coat was covered in white dots, his face tarnished with gruesome scars and evident wrinkles beneath his wide, clouded gaze. On the brawn of his chest, he bore an emerald statice.

They were all unlike anybody else I had seen yet in Reveria, and their resonant voices substantiated their high esteem.

"Figured it'd be best to take part of this preceding." The stallion said in a clear, concise tone. Grace and respect resonated with his stature.

"Alden, I've already made it clear to you two, that your bias would've compromised the welcome of our recent arrival." Constance brought up.

"Keep pretending like you could leave me out of an important matter such as this." Spoke the caribou, whose thick words came from an unrecognizable background. "We've come to see who she *really* is."

Listening to him clearly now, it became apparent who this man was. He was the opposing voice during my prior limbo.

The chief and Kyran saluted once the two men approached closer, and the chief spoke out. "Reverence Alden, Reverence Mikhail, this is unexpected, but we welcome your presence, nonetheless. We were just about to conclude our questioning with Miss Charissa."

"Oh, she has a name, does she?" The antlered elder surmised, stepping closer to me. My hands gripped the chair when he leaned down, his snout inched from my face. "This girl may as well paint a target on our back. If you think we'll benefit from keeping her here, you're wrong."

"This is exactly why I didn't want you to partake in this, Mikhail." Constance wiped her forehead. "Fine then. Let's all hear your opinions."

"He has good reason to be suspicious of someone like her," Alden said. "Having a genuine human being amongst our walls? All of our greatest enemies would do whatever they can to get a hold of her."

"Which is why she should remain here. We have the means to protect her. A foundation, weapons, and Virtues to use them." She stated. "Ever since we've built this place, we've had our oppositions. This human won't make a difference in the fact that we're still a force to be reckoned with."

"Constance, to keep this human being here would jeopardize our standing, more so than we already have to anticipate. Surely you must recognize that we can't let her reside here." Mikhail tried to reason.

"You act as if she isn't sitting right there." The chief defended, the eyes of everyone falling upon my shuddering, sweltering self.

"We simply cannot take the risk of granting her safety at the cost of our own." Alden surmised. "It's just not that simple."

"…What could I do to earn your trust?" I mumbled.

Mikhail's body shadowed me. "Leave."

"That's enough," Constance interrupted. "If you think that keeping one individual in our care is detrimental, so be it. I'd rather take the chance of letting her stay than let her be another victim of the very dangers outside our walls. Give her time, and she'll earn our trust."

"My thoughts exactly, High Reverence." The chief concurred.

"So, you'd be willing to throw away everything we built for this one woman?" Mikhail stood up to Constance. "Would you be saying the same thing if the Ferecite decided to arrive and ruin everything?"

"When will you learn that not all outsiders are here to defile what we've made, let alone associated with those cultists? Reveria earned its name for the pride of bringing those together, not tearing them apart!"

I sat there with sweat seeping through my garments.

"Because no outsider here is a human being! We wouldn't even be having this issue to begin with if Virtue Rhodes didn't bring her here." Mikhail's oblong stare tacked onto the panther. "Just what did you think you were doing with your chivalry?"

Kyran's throat clenched. "It's always been my duty to help everyone, even outside of Reveria. I only did what was right at the time."

"And now you realize the potential consequences?"

To that, Kyran didn't answer. The room fell silent.

I shifted in my seat. "I can leave."

"No, stay put." Constance prevented. "We have three Reverences for a reason. Mikhail, it's blatantly clear where your stance is. But Alden, are you certain you'd rather have her go? Tell us what you think."

"Yes, Alden." The reindeer turned to him. "What's it going to be? And you can't be the middleman here. It's either my side or hers."

After contemplating, he spoke up. "...I might not like it, but perhaps there's worth to what you've said. If one of our adversaries got hold of you, we'd be losing a great asset. We shouldn't squander this."

Mikhail bared his teeth. "Are you mad? Everyone will know of her presence, and that means the Ferecite! You've seen what they're capable of. Capable enough to shape a 'human' like this to breach our walls!"

Kyran's lips tensed, staring at my possessions.

"Not again with these conspiracy theories." Constance pinched her brow. "You and I both know having a human here is the last thing they want. She's not directly involved with them, don't be disingenuous."

"All the more reason to keep her out of Reveria." Mikhail firmed.

"There's clearly more to this, isn't there?" The chief accused.

The elder retracted. "You're all making a grave mistake. Alden, even you agreed with me just earlier. How could you change your mind now?"

The equine man gave me a brief look, until he took a glance to the light above. "Despite my initial thoughts, we should all be viewing this from an unbiased perspective. It's always been our belief to grant everyone who comes to Reveria a new leaf. We can't exempt her from that."

"We've denied people before. We still can here." He did his final stretch. "Letting go of one human isn't going to be the death of us."

"It doesn't matter how our capacity situation is, or anything." Constance planted her hands on the table. "We do whatever we can for outsiders. No other place has what we have: a haven. I know we can't accept everybody, but we can't refuse *her* now. No more arguments."

"Fine, let's just welcome everybody that comes here from here on out then!" The caribou turned tail, heading for the door. "See how long this principle can hold up. You'll come to regret it. Every one of you."

With a slam of the door, silence thickened the tense air again.

"We better get on with this before he tries to make this any more difficult." The harpy tilted her head to the panther. "The forms?"

Kyran stepped away, only to retrieve some papers. He placed them in front of me. "The forms as requested, High Reverence."

"Excellent. Now, collect the artifacts and sort her possessions accordingly. Afterward, wait outside the courthouse for new orders."

The panther's head lowered. "Yes, High Reverence," he accepted, sorting out the valuable keepsakes, and putting my other belongings into my old backpack. Once finished, he took my sack and stepped out—not before giving me another glance.

"As for you, Charissa, how well can you read?" the stallion asked.

"More than able," I answered.

"Then please, read these documents for me. Once you're done, sign below." He reached into his pocket, offering me his own pen.

"What's all this for, exactly?"

"Isn't it obvious?" the elder said. "It's like we said, we cannot afford to let you leave. On top of that, Dr. Rhodes requests that you stay for research reasons—which is why we're granting you passage to our town. A visa pass, but you'll remain here in our foundation."

"You heard what he said. Wouldn't I endanger you all?"

Constance's beady eyes widened. "Surely you can't give into Mikhail's front. If you left these town grounds, you'd have only yourself to depend on. Frankly, you'd perish before finding anybody else that'd help you, if you could even find one good soul in this city. There are fates worse than death."

The chief stepped in. "High Reverence, this is her choice to make."

"Well then, Virtue of Patience, please try to help her make the *right* decision. She might not be a citizen yet, but the longer she stays in our walls, the more she'll stand out as a model resident like all Reverians." Constance retorted, only for the chief to kneel to my level, and try to reach through to me with her own genuine honesty.

"Charissa, although this is all new and unnatural to you, we're your best shot at keeping you alive. If there's any hope you, I, or anyone can leave this city for good, then we need you here. No matter how much it'd be a risk to us, I, and all of us will keep you safe. Will you stay?"

After making the mistake of stumbling upon this forgotten city, my likelihood of survival had bottomed out. No matter how much I wanted to escape, it was inevitable that I'd get nowhere if I tried. Somehow, I'd stranded myself worse than before. Only now, I no longer had Narissa by my side, and instead the accompaniment of beast-faced strangers, more than capable of putting my means to an end if they turned to their inner animal. Once my name was made onto the line at the bottom, I could never crawl from it. Not unless I lost my right to live another day. If I ever wanted to see my sister again, even just to see her body, I had no other choice. I signed my name, doing it like she once taught me.

Alden's snout beamed. "Welcome to Reveria, Charissa."

As did Constance's beak. "We're honored to have you."

***

Out of my gown and into a pair of my old spare clothes, I stood in the bathroom. The pale, chipped porcelain walls left me frigid. I saw myself in the frame of the clean glass mirror, disassociating from my new reality. This strange room alone left me in awe. These fascinations made it feel like a dream from which I hadn't yet awoken. But after witnessing such creatures, and signing away my future to them, my destiny had been sealed within the earth. They took into account everything I told them about my past, took a photo of my likeness, and inked my handprint in the process. All the papers had been sorted, and no longer was the forest considered my home, but this community, which instilled both new promises and meanings of fear. All my life, I had never known such a place like this existed outside my once small world, let alone *underneath* it.

The chief pushed the door open. "Are you doing alright in here? We've been waiting for a while, and Constance told me to check on you."

Breaking from my trance, I tore my gaze from the mirror. "I changed my mind. I'd rather try and make it out of here on my own."

She stepped inside. "You've only been awake here for a few hours. There's time to have a look around town, get comfortable."

My hands gripped to the sink; the cold ceramic hummed. "The more I think about this, the more I think that Mikhail might be right. If those *things* knew I was here... What would happen to me? To you?"

The cardinal came to my side. In the frame of the mirror, we co-existed, and we couldn't have been any more different. "No need for speculation," she said. "Rest assured, you're fine. We all are. No matter what happens, don't give into any paranoia. We're here for you."

I took her word for the time being.

"Thanks, Chief—"

"Oh, you don't have to call me that. Aliya's fine." She smiled.

"Alright, Aliya," I corrected. "I guess I can't really hide in here any longer." Before I made for the door, she stopped me.

"Just a second. While Kyran was sorting through your things, he dropped this." Aliya dug into the pocket of her dress grays, pulling out the bandana. "I recognize the marigolds. My bisabuelo once told me they grew everywhere back where he came from. Figured you'd want to wear this out. Seems like it's something meaningful, special even."

The way the flowers bloomed made me wish I hadn't discovered what I did, back at the library. Had I not known of what horrors awaited in my future, I could have been blissfully content.

"It's not mine," I told her, but she persisted.

"Whoever it belonged to might've wanted you to keep it. It was in your possession, after all." She noted, and I continued to ponder.

Anastasia, what brought you here? Were you still here?

"I suppose."

"Here, let me try something." Aliya went behind me, taking my hair in a soft tug. Brushing my red strands with her feathers, she tied the cloth around my head in a delightful bow off to the side. "There you go, perfect. It looks like it was meant for you."

Seeing myself in the reflection brought a sense of belonging. Somehow, a simple cloth pieced me together, holding my hopes that one day, I'd reunite with Narissa, and do what I could to make ensure her life had purpose. Her condemners couldn't be forgiven.

"Yeah, you're right," I huffed. "I'm ready."

Once we left the bathroom, somebody had been standing on the other side of the door. With his arms crossed and his stature high and mighty, Mikhail waited for the right moment to corner me.

"So, you'll be taking residency here."

Unable to speak up, Aliya did the talking. "We've all come to the agreement for everyone's best interest, she's better off with us."

The old man scoffed. "You keep telling yourself that, but you'll see that this *Charissa* will be more trouble than she's worth."

"What're you trying to say?"

"I'll tell you this once, Chief Morales." He took another step, leaning over her. "Whoever comes knocking on our door, don't be surprised why they're here. Will you still be so inclined to do your job to keep this human safe, or will you think about the betterment of this town in the end? Think about it: one little life, or thousands more."

"Nobody knows of her presence here, Reverence. There's no need to keep indulging in your self-delusions."

"We'll just have to wait and see, will we?" He stepped past her, only to close in on the space between him and me. "One little life."

Solidified to the floor, I remained silent.

Nothing more to be said, he headed back for the room behind the podium. No longer in my sight, his presence lingered like an ill omen.

"Don't let him unnerve you. He's just trying to get under your skin." Aliya took my shoulder, guiding me to the bronze doors. She opened them, only to reveal perhaps the second-to-last person I wanted to see again: Kyran, holding onto my things.

"Everything okay?" he directed to me, only for his attitude to shift for Aliya. "Chief, I don't know if this is what's best for her. Shouldn't she stay at the hotel? One of the apartments?"

"We've already discussed this, Kyran. The town's on the verge of maximum capacity as it is. The hotel's for traders and visitors, and the apartments…I think putting her in a coffin-sized box won't make her stay any better. You can provide her a good home," she retorted, only leaving me confused as to what they were entailing.

It clicked.

"I'm staying with him?"

"Bea actually requested you'd stay at their home since the beginning, but someone protested that idea." She side-eyed Kyran.

"It's not exactly easy to let a stranger into my house."

"You found her; the least you can do is provide her a roof," Aliya countered, baiting a low huff from the panther.

"That I did."

"Try to make her feel welcome. It's not only your duty to protect all citizens and visitors, but have them right at home." She concluded her business with Kyran, and her bejeweled stare went to me, offering a softer approach. "If you ever need to find me, I'll always be around. Take care, Charissa. Have a good stay." Aliya smiled, bowing her head to Kyran afterward. "I'll see you tomorrow back at the station at noon sharp. I've got assignments for you."

"Yes, Chief Morales." He saluted, and with that, Aliya made her way down the diorite steps. With Kyran and I alone again, he snapped his focus back to me. "I suppose we're stuck together now. Don't worry, I'll be sure you get yourself settled in just fine."

"Did I do something to you?"

He paused. "I don't think I understand."

"Back in there, you didn't seem to fully believe what I had to say."

"I'll level with you." he glanced at the bronze doors. "I don't think you have bad blood, but caution is a healthy trait to have here. It's natural for me to be alert about a lot of the people that walk into this town. Never know what they're truly here for."

In a way, I understood his concern. "You have your reasons with me. I can see that."

"Right. Besides, if I looked soft in front of the Reverences, I wouldn't be so deserving of my title. Got to act a little tough so they don't think I'm losing my touch," he said, heading down.

"Can I at least carry my stuff?"

"You've got a lot to manage as it is. Let me take care of this."

I didn't argue with him from there. Although I'd rather handle my own things, I let it be until we got to his home. Once we left the courthouse, we passed by the laboratories, most of the lights within shut off to conserve power. To think one building could contain such innovative phenomena: *Kutsuki Experimental Laboratories.*

During our walk, Kyran clicked into the radio on his chestpiece. "Bea, we're right next to the labs. You ready to go?" he spoke, his ear twitching at the scramble coming out. "Still finishing up? Yeah, I'll be sure she gets home fine. See you back at the house."

His device clicked off, and he kept going.

"Why did Bea tell you guys about me? Was she just being nice to get something out of me?"

"No, if anything, I asked her to tell me what she can so I can connect some pieces. My sister's not the manipulative kind. Hell, she's always working seven days a week to help out everyone here."

I envied his pride in his sister.

"I see. Also, I never really thanked you both for saving me back in the city streets. I'm glad you guys were there."

"So were we, but…" he grumbled. "Still wish we could've found a trace of *him*."

"You mentioned that in the labs. Who were you talking about?"

Thinking about it, he refrained. "It's just personal Virtue business. Probably not the best to disclose anything to you, if that makes sense."

"I get it. Still, thank you for what you did. I hope I won't cause trouble here. Maybe I'll get out of your hair once I'm able."

"We'll see about that. Given how much Constance wanted you to be here, I'm not sure how it'll all work, but we'll figure something out."

We passed by the rail guard, heading down a structure of stone stairs leading downward to the common levels. The infrastructure of this town was interesting, meeting heights that reminded me of the mountain climb

I'd once made. Each home and building were cubic in their shape, and almost patterned in their structures, like grids and building blocks. Throughout the series of bridges and the rest of the town's complexes, many faces walked along the pathways.

Not a single human soul.

Passing by the other residents, my nose was hit with various aromas. Mostly earthy and odiferous, but some pleasant notes swam through. Through their natural smells, I caught whiffs of roast, some flowers, and warmth. In comparison, I stuck out with a different kind of scent among these people. Or rather, mutants, with the heads of animals, walking in the bodies of people. It was almost as if I were in the forest once again. A primal nature resonated among all of them, though it seemed to take many individual forms. Each one reminded me of animals that I had seen, ones I read about, and several species I could have never imagined in my dreams. Despite their differences, the disease they shared brought them all together. Not to mention that every single pair of eyes in the were all on me, with some folks exchanging hushed words with each other, or catching my fragrance in their midst.

Their whispers left me anxious.

"How many of you are there?" I mumbled to Kyran, feeling as though a million beasts were tempted to hunt me.

"Little over a thousand. Might seem like a big place, but we can only have so many here. Don't let them overwhelm you; you're a resident here like anybody else."

"Constance and Aliya mentioned something about a capacity problem. Seems like there's a decent amount of space." I eyeballed the streets below. Bustling, sure, but it had room for more good souls.

"Yeah well, lately, we've been getting a lot more requests for residency here." He directed to the border wall far ahead. "That world out there is full of all kinds of unspeakable things. It's no surprise that many come to us for safety, given everything that's been going on lately."

"Does it have something to do with the…Ferecite?"

"No no, they've always been a looming danger. Recently it's been…" He shook his head. "Well, it's nothing you have to worry about now."

Briefly looking at those that passed by made me contemplate just how terrible Kyran and everyone else I'd spoken with made the outside sound. In my position, I found more fear with these *creatures* as it is.

Benign, I'd say, but they wouldn't give me personal proximity.

No matter how hard I tried to keep to myself, their attention grappled with my attempts to keep any sense of composure. All of the ice broke once someone took my arm, and my blood froze.

His hooved fingers brushed against my skin.

"Oh my…such a beautiful face! That nose, those eyes. I don't believe it! A real, genuine human in our town!" the elderly pigman trilled, but it only petrified me further. Soon, everybody on the bridge began to crowd. Touching my skin and hair, they babbled their fascinations at my presence. An intense heat brewed from my innards, spreading to my head and toes like fire.

"Those specks on your face, what're those called?"

"What's it like to have skin? It looks so soft!"

"Don't you feel cold without any fur? Well, I guess it can be a little hot down here…"

Kyran could only do so much fending off so many. He had to stuff the bag in my arms, shooing them away. "Back away from the girl! You're all going to make this bridge collapse!" he yelled, causing the crowd to disperse, some walking away with frowns.

"We didn't mean to disrupt things. We're just so amazed," one said.

"Listen, now's not a good time. Please do not intrude on Virtue protocol, people. Go back to your own business," he ordered once more, causing everybody else to leave the bridge.

The pig stayed behind. "I'm sorry, it wasn't my intention to—"

Before he could finish his words, I clenched tighter on my bag and bolted. The adrenaline in my legs kicked in. Kyran hurried behind me, picking up on my trail once we left the bridge. It took him no effort to catch my shoulder. "What's gotten into you?"

"He was going to—" My fears couldn't speak out.

"Look, nobody in this town is going to try and kill you, alright? We're different than the pig you saw out in the city. We're not *berserkers* like he was." He eased his grip on me.

"None of this makes any sense."

"Guess Bea didn't explain the other side of our disease. Keep walking with me." He continued his pace. Reluctantly, I followed by his side. Any people that passed us kept to themselves, as Kyran gave them a warning eye. "That man in the streets. He wasn't like us."

"But he still…"

"Looked like an animal? Right, well, this mutation is unpredictable. You know what made him different from everyone else here?"

"Apart from being insane? You all have…restraint."

"Exactly. See how we all seem fine? Just people trying to live? Well, not all of us are exactly born to go out peacefully." He brushed his thumb across his exposed wrist. "The virus, it does more than make human and animal genes code together. No, it was manufactured to make people turn into full-blown monsters, but there was a flaw to it."

"And that is?"

"We still have human consciences, sentience. Without it, we'd really be wild animals." He stared at the ground. "We're all human on the inside, no matter how we look. But our minds, they're still animal to their core. And when that feral switch clicks, we're no longer ourselves. Instead, we're the beast we were born to be." His face turned solemn.

"What suddenly makes you go…berserk?"

"It's different for everyone. Maybe a carnivore like me tries eating another person, or someone loses their will to live. The moment you give into your beast's temptation, then it's too late. You're inherited to become an untamable psychopath." The grit in his speech softened, crumbling.

"So everyone will become like him," I mumbled.

"Not everyone. A few are lucky to live their lives naturally, be it old age or natural means. But if I'm being honest, even a bullet to the brain is more peaceful than being a berserker." Kyran shredded a layer of his tough skin. Or fur, rather. He paused, lifting his chin. "We're here. Wipe your feet and let's get you inside."

The front of a well-maintained house greeted us, its structure intricate in its design. All the houses next to his were nearly identical: one door, a strange unit attached to the window, and a metal box standing close by. Kyran fished out keys from his pocket, going in and picking at the door's mechanism until it clicked, pushing the mass of steel. I noticed the welcoming carpet beneath my boots. Wiping my soles and spreading them apart, the wool beneath said: *Welcome In, Pals & Confidantes!*

Going inside, a far bigger room welcomed me in indeed. In contrast to the air outside, I was greeted with a clean, light mint breeze. A wide rug covered the metal flooring, with a three-cushioned couch and a small table in front of it. Beside the couch were two end tables, one having a knife and sharpener, while the other had a chrome rectangle with black glass embedded within.

What drew the most attention were the decorated walls. Along the shelves, knickknacks and novelties filled the environment, such as geodes, mugs, glass bottles, and other relics of earthly history. Pictures framed the walls—some were portraits of more beastly people, the panther siblings themselves, and some even had photos of Reveria's sights. The size of this home made the treehouse feel tiny, but despite the extravagance, it brought no welcoming comfort.

To me, at least.

"I'm going to get out of my work clothes. Been too long of a day." He unstrapped his armor as he entered one of the lone doors. Four accompanied the large space, and at the far back was a kitchenette. The sight of it brought a vague remembrance of my happy place. "Make yourself at home. I'll be right back."

"Okay," I said, and he shut the door with the pull of his foot.

Holding onto my belongings, I took in this new way of living. The warmth of wood would have made me more content than the coldness of this iron box, but it brought security. Taking in my surroundings, something else offered the familiarity of my old home. A bookshelf was collecting dust, stocked full of old, but tangible reading material. I looked over towards Kyran's room, and the rustling sounds behind the door made me believe he would be busy for a while. My inner curiosity got the better of me, and I reached for the shelf, seeking the most compelling title. Instead, I found myself holding a framed picture. Two elderly panthers and two more younger ones, holding a pair of dark-furred cubs so lovingly. Despite being in rags, they were happy.

A large mitt took hold of the still-moment. Kyran took me by surprise, a tattered tank top and sweatpants now covering his broad physique. "Been a long time since I've picked this up," He spoke softly, taking the photo from my hold. "A little too long,"

"Is that your family?"

With solemn eyes and a stiff maw, he slid the photo back where it Nothing more was said, only for my stomach to interrupt the tension with a growl. I had forgotten that I had eaten nothing since I woke up.

Kyran's ears perked at the sound. "Should've picked something up on the way. Bea should be home any minute. She'll get you something to eat and show you the room you'll bunk in." He headed for another door, but I noticed something else missing.

"Where'd you put my bow?"

The fur on his back stood. "Right, about that. We're holding it back at the courthouse."

A red hotness took over my skin. "But it's mine."

"It's out of my power," he shared a tinge of regret in his throat. "Constance said that relic should be preserved, and I've been ordered to not allow you any weapon here. It's been a firm regulation that anybody on town grounds isn't allowed to open-carry until they've visited or lived here for more than a year. I don't make the rules, the Reverences do."

My fists balled tight, nails digging into my palms.

"I'll do what I can to make sure it's rightfully returned to you, but until then, I'll make sure you're safe around here. You might not be armed, but you got a Virtue to watch your back." He glanced over his shoulder, his golden eyes sparing guilt. "I have some work to do in here. You can sit down on the couch and get comfortable. Just knock if you need anything, and…yeah."

He was gone again, walking into the door labeled *Office*. I did what he said, backside to the couch, creaking to my weight as the fuzz on the fabric itched my skin. The frustration didn't stop building up. Tempted to leave the house and fetch it myself, I decided that being thrown back out in those streets wasn't worth the risk. I didn't dare to try and double-cross the authority here. Instead, I watched the device sitting on one of the end tables, glowing in a green hue.

21:47

All I could do was wait.

22:14

Creaks and groans came beyond the wall, and I stared at the ceiling in the meantime. Thinking of home gave me time to imagine, to escape. The crisp winter air, the stars above, and the ocean tides lapping at my toes. Everything I missed about the surface came crashing down, and the longer I reflected, the more regret sank into the sand under my soles.

The doorknob jittered, breaking my immersion.

In came Bea, with her full hair flowing and her glasses hanging from the collar of her shirt. She held a clipboard, along with a burlap sack in the other. Upon seeing me, she chirped, shutting the door behind her, and strolling in.

"Ah, hello! You're still up; that's good. Why's Kyran not with you?" she asked, heading past me as she unloaded her stuff at the rounded table near the kitchenette. On the surface, there was a checkerboard with little wooden pieces, as if someone had carved each one with care. Whatever game they played must have been left on pause, because a couple of the pieces were toppled next to some dirty plates and emptied glasses. Putting her things away to gather all the dishes, she took them to the sink.

"He's in the in the 'office,' I think it's called."

"Ah, he's getting some finishing touches in, then. Suppose I can do the dishes until he's all done." She hummed as she turned the knob to the sink. A strange, glowing light dimmed near the faucet.

2.1 / 5.0 GALLONS LEFT

With bare paws and steaming hot water, Bea took a soft-looking bar and scrubbed at the ceramics. Curiously, I stood up so that I could learn more about the strange intricacies of this world. "I've seen that before. It smelled good. What is it?" I leaned in.

"Why, this is some soap—locally made, in fact. My good friend at her general goods store sells it." She lifted the soft bar, the bubbly water running down to her wrists and soaking her rolled sleeves.

The aroma of lavender hit my nose, bringing me back to the days of spring. "And the 'sink,' it's called. Where does all the water come from? And that little line thing?"

"This is a water-use meter. Despite the seemingly limitless supply from above, we ration daily so as to not cause any disturbance to the local pipe systems. Nearly every sector of the city has plumbing connected all the way from the surface. From what I know, they siphon from the lakes and rivers above. You're familiar with them?"

"Yeah. I miss it all already,"

"I know it's not easy, but after a while, you'll understand every little intricacy that we have to offer." She shook off any excess water from each dish and set them on the toweled counter.

I picked one of the glasses up, blown away by the diamond shapes embellished in its solid form. "I hope you don't mind me asking about everything you guys have."

The jaguar chuckled. "It's great that you want to ask questions. I was worried you might've been too afraid to want to know more." She turned off the water and dried off her hands.

"Well…" I refrained from being truthful, as I'd rather much be anywhere than this caustic din. "It's never too late to learn."

"That it is, indeed! Speaking of learning, have you ever been taught how to cook?" Bea returned to the table, digging in her bag.

"My sister taught me everything I know, really. Cooking happened to be something we really enjoyed together," I reminisced, the ache in my heart turning prevalent.

Bea stopped pulling her things out.

"I've lost some of my own before, a couple of times over. Many of us have. You're not the only one in that regard." She resumed bringing out a few canisters, and a couple patties of protein in a glass container. "With how hectic the day's been, we never had the real privacy to speak. Would you feel better talking about her?"

After she made that suggestion, I gave a silent nod. She pulled the meat from its clear confines, bringing a pan out from the cupboard, placing it on a flat top that a giant, clunky appliance.

Pietas-Kitchenware: Electric Blacktop Stove.

"Never been so far away from her. The whole time I was asleep, I was trying to find her, but I couldn't. I feel lost," I confessed to Bea.

The white ring on top of the stove burned with a radiant blue.

"What was she like?"

"Always kind to me, and the creatures around her. Every day was perfect whenever we spent time together. But I took that all for granted. Everything had already been falling apart before she was…" The strength to finish failed me.

"I promised we will find out why the Ferecites took her away from you, and you can count on that,"

The void in my chest found a sliver of fulfillment, but 1 wouldn't feel whole until they paid for what they did. "I know, and I appreciate it," I told her, watching as she dropped the protein into the iron pan. The searing sizzles of meat hit the air and enthralled me with their savory scent. "What about you? How come it's only you and your brother?"

As she reached for the hanging utensils on the wall, she grabbed a tool with a flat paddle on the end. Bea scraped and divided the contents in the pan into a grounded mix. "Back when we lived in the northwestern sector of Misera, we didn't live the way we do now. We spent a lot of years in a shack house, as did many of my neighbors," she recollected, dashing in spices.

"Was it anything like Reveria?"

"Not at all. Here, we have a well-versed community, but back where we used to live, everyone was driven by avarice at the *Lion's Den Resort.*

Most luxurious place you could find in these wastes, but we lived in the impoverished outer region of its lavish walls, *The Ditch*."

Heavy steam clouded the kitchenette.

"I spent most of my life in that shack with my parents, Grandma and Grandpa, and Kyran of course."

"What happened to them?"

Bea turned down the heat, clearing the air.

"Grandma and Grandpa died of old age, thankfully…Mom, though, her health got her. Didn't go berserk, but even things like an infection can get the best of us. As for my dad, well…" Her breath drew still. "He wanted us to leave him behind so Kyran and I could find a better future here," she explained, idly scraping at the pan.

"I'm very sorry, Bea."

She wiped her snout with the sleeve of her lab coat.

"Death is simply something we all have to endure, but it's not something you have to go through alone. Finding the means to move on and let live, that's another thing." Bea rested the utensil in the pan, heading for an even larger gadget nearby.

Refrigerator Fascinations: Industrial Stainless-Steel XL

"Sometimes it's just best to distract yourself or spend time with the people in your current life. Hmm, have you ever tried rice and red kidney beans before?" she asked, bringing out a cold plate.

Her advice could've helped me as well.

"I've grown beans before, but rice? That looks a little like…" I gawked at the white bits as she came back to the stove.

"You're not afraid of bugs, are you?" she humored, dumping the leftovers into the pan and heating them.

"I've grown up eating the things, but worms…never been a fan," I mentioned. The more we talked, the unease in my body dwindled. Having someone to speak with helped take my mind off things.

For now.

"Hmph. Never been fond of roaches myself." The invisible barriers I once had around Bea were breaking down.

Despite my initial worries about what she was, her humanity continued to show through. For the first time, my wish for connection came true. "Looks delicious to me. Have a seat; I'll make your plate," she told me, and with the grumbles in my belly getting louder, I took a chair with ravenous haste. Bea dumped the generous meal on two plates, setting one in front of me, and the other on her side of the table. She fetched a couple of the glasses she'd washed, taking a pitcher of iced water from the fridge, and filling my cup.

"Oh, by the way. Is the water here, you know, safe?"

She gave a rumble as she filled her own glass, putting the pitcher between us. "The plumbing I mentioned earlier? The purification systems still work to an extent, and we have a small team that stores and maintains any runoff. No need to be scared, it's not poison; we boil it for a little extra measure," she attested, and I took her word for it.

I downed my glass. "May I have some more?"

She couldn't help but snicker. "But of course. Just don't forget to eat, too." Her white teeth gleamed in her grin as she stabbed her fork into her meal, eating in little bites. I poured myself another glass of water before I went in for my own food. The scent of garlic, onion, and paprika only accentuated the decadence of the…mystery meat. Scraping up a forkful of rice, beans, and protein, I savored my bite.

Delicious, absolutely delicious.

I indulged in my appetite, taking in mouthfuls as the salty flavors left me wanting more. I cleaned my plate while Bea was only halfway finished with her own, causing her to break out laughing.

"I see that the newest cultured meat is a hit."

"I meant to ask, what sort of meat is this?"

"You know how I showed you our agriculture and fish farms? Well, we have many ways for obligate carnivores to have more variety in their diet, without having to go through…barbaric means, as animals typically would. We can't necessarily digest plant matter like herbivores can."

"Oh, right…" I mumbled.

What community would this have been if people were content with eating each other? I didn't have the stomach to think about that prospect, but was curious about their methods.

"So, you see, this meat was actually grown in the labs, thanks to animal cells and amino acids—"

My belly sank. "Wait. Are you saying this is like, *fake* meat?"

"I suppose you might see it that way."

Then it dropped. "Could've fooled me with the real thing."

"For us carnivores to keep social peace with all hybridians, we all do our best not to indulge in our carnal appetites, lest we become savage beasts destined for insanity." She stared blankly.

"Are you okay?"

She didn't say anything, but instead gathered her leftovers, setting them on the stove. "We all make do with the burdens we're born with, but I'm content with what I am. To be alive is the best gift I could have." She gathered my clean dishes, putting them away in the sink.

I wasn't certain what to say to that. "Bea."

"Hmm?"

"…Thank you for taking care of me."

It was all I could muster, but enough to make her frown disappear.

"Nothing but the best for my guest. Oh shoot, that reminds me, there's something I have to fetch for you. Wait here, I'll be right back." The panther hurried to her door, only to pause and point to the sink. "If you'd like, you're welcome to take a try at washing the dishes. Just try not to scald your hands, and don't use too much water."

"Oh alright, I can do that. I think." I turned to the sink, already intimidated by its elaborate design.

"Red means hot, blue means cold. You got this."

Once she was gone, I got up from the table and inspected the sink. Its complexity threw me off, but I went for the red knob, turning it with caution. Warm water came rushing out, and picking up the bar of soap, I went to work. I scrubbed off the bits of caramelization from my plate and fork, setting them aside on the toweled counter.

I couldn't help but smile. What else could I learn?

"Watch how much you're using," that gruff voice called.

Jumping, I turned off the water. The surprise frightened me, as well as the water-use meter. *0.1 / 5.0 GALLONS LEFT*

Kyran approached, his fur gleamed in a light sheen of sweat. The prospect of an animal "sweating" was nothing short of strange, but he was supposedly half-human. The whole concept of hybridian nature still seemed a fantastical illusion.

"Phew. Saved me from paying the overuse bill." he gave an awkward chuckle, clanking the pan from the stove, and clinking a fork in. "Tomorrow, I'm going to be showing you around town. Do me a favor; try to get plenty of sleep. It'll be a big day tomorrow." He scraped the rest of Bea's plate into his helpings.

I dug my nails into the bar of soap. "Will do."

"I'm going eat the rest of this in my room. I'll be expecting you up at eight in the morning sharp."

"…What does that mean?"

Confused for a second, he caught on. "Oh. Just keep an eye on the clock from now on. You'll need it to know what time it is." Taking the pan, his heavy weight creaked over the floor, heading for his quarters. "Anyway, uh…. hope you have a good night."

He closed the door, silence biting the air again.

A clock. My focus drifted back to the end table. 22:37. So that's what that was.

Hearing the door close, Bea hurried out of her room, holding an object behind her back. "What was that? Did Kyran just come out?"

"Yeah…does he not like me?" I scraped under my nails.

"Oh no, he's just not used to having company. I'll be sure to have a talk with him tomorrow, make certain he won't cause you any trouble."

"It's not that at all, he's just…I'm not sure how to feel about him."

"It's because you're not used to men, I'd assume?"

That was one thing about him that daunted me. "I mean, I've read about them, but I guess there's more to them that I have to understand."

"Can't say I quite get them either." she jested. "Trust me, he's got a good heart just like everyone else here. No need to fear him. Come, I've got your room set up in here. Grab your bag and come look inside!"

I snagged my possessions from the couch, following her lead. When she held the room open, four walls of metal closed me in, with a floral rug covering the floor. A rusty bed with a mattress in one corner, a bent-up desk with a rolling chair in the other, a vintage wooden wardrobe and a cracked mirror beside it made up the interior. Fairy lights strung the edges of the ceiling, giving the whole room a gentle, whimsical atmosphere, and providing a strange sense of relaxation.

"I know there's not much. I had to pull out all my equipment and buy some things from the pawn shop, but I did what I could to provide a comfortable place for you to stay in." Bea twiddled her index fingers.

In a way, I was grateful, but bittersweet about it all. Being there only reminded me further of what I'd thrown away coming here.

"You didn't have to do all this for me."

"Well, I couldn't have you sleeping in an office chair and keeping your clothes in the filing cabinets. I wanted to make it all cozy for you."

I stepped further inside, basking in the cool, artificial air breezing through the duct. "It's wonderful." I let her believe my half-lie.

"Really? I'm happy to hear that! Kyran picked out the bed and hauled it here himself. Even got you some cotton bedsheets, see?" Bea beamed. "On the way back, I even got you something special to help make it feel more like your old home. I hope you like it!" With that, she brought out her present. A yellow bird, or rather, a dead one attached to a wooden stand, encased in a spotty glass dome.

A canary.

"You don't really see any real birds around here, but I've researched on them and how they flew all over the world. Reminded me of you. Taxidermy is a strange science in itself, isn't it?" She commented, as I remained speechless. My palms open, she placed the gift there, with my petrified eyes latching onto the bird's plastic pair.

"…Thanks," was all I could slip out.

"I'll let you get yourself settled in. If you need anything, though, my door will have the lab coat hanging from it…Welcome home." She closed my door gently, and I stood there.

Still lost.

I should've been happy, being provided shelter and food, and especially people. To belong elsewhere and to find others like me was my greatest ambition, yet…all this did not fulfill that dream, if not stretching it further from my reach. Did these creatures really have souls, or had I been deluded into thinking they had slivers of humanity? Despite everything that I'd learned in such little time, being introduced to things far beyond my wildest imagination, it only made me afraid of what more awaited me. As I stared at the canary, I thought: Narissa was right. I should have left this all alone, buried away.

***

My hair got stuck in the brush.

An odd tool, but for once, my head didn't resemble an untamed bush. Seeing myself all nice was…well, nice. That, and a breakfast of fresh scrambled eggs helped, locally provided by…some of the avian residents here. The prospect in itself left me with an indescribable feeling.

Bea mentioned that today Kyran would be showing me around town, but after my first impressions of him, I didn't know how an entire day with him would unfold.

Staying under his roof was already strange enough.

"Excuse me. I need to brush my teeth." He knocked, and I finished getting my clothes on. A flannel shirt, denim pants, and my old boots. To tie it all together, I knotted the bandana into the same bow Aliya made for me. Wearing it had brought me a sense of contentment the day prior, becoming my beacon of self-assurance.

A promise I'd go back to my true home one day.

"Sorry, getting out now," I called, stepping out. Kyran stood by the doorway, strapped into his leather armor, and bearing his gold badge.

"Morning, Charissa. You look…" He scratched his jawline. "You're looking good today. Once I get cleaned up, we'll head out," he told me, politely stepping past me.

At least he treated me fine.

Bea came from her quarters, tying her hair back in that same tight bun and grabbing her lab coat. "Are you excited to see what goes on around here?" she asked, and despite the somewhat good morning, my expectations for what the day would hold stooped at a low bar.

"Yes, very much." I tried to sound convincing, and she took my plastered smile as a genuine one.

"You'll fit right in, I'm sure of it. Just remember to be kind and don't be nervous. After Kyran's done showing you around, you both can do a little shopping down at the plaza!" she trilled, as if spending time on frivolous pursuits was more of a delight than getting my answers.

"Sounds great." My smile grew wider, more fake.

"Oh, and come visit me at the labs when you get a chance. I'd like to begin our research together right away."

That notion improved the prospect of the day.

The bathroom opened, and out came the big panther. Draping back his locs and rolling his neck, he eyed the clock. "Alright, let's get this show on the road," he said to me, glancing at his sister. "Going to need some grocery money before I head out. Can't get pickings short-handed, not when we can't have as many leftovers anymore."

"Kyran." Her pitch went stern.

"What? Oh, no no, what I meant to say was…I need a little extra money so that we're able to have enough for our friend here," he huffed.

"That's more like it." Bea reached into her coat and pulled out a small cloth bag. Jingles resonated from within as she placed it in his hand. He opened the little sack, humming with a toothsome grin.

"Oh yeah, I think that'll be a decent amount of *marbles* to get us everything we need, maybe even a little more."

When he mentioned marbles, my interest piqued.

"You mean the ones you play games with?"

Kyran gave me a curious glance, while Bea bumped her elbow into his shoulder. Getting that confused look off his mug, she reached into the little bag and pulled out a couple of little orbs. One of them had a gray exterior, and the other had a copper surface.

Both barely shone with soft, dull finishes.

"*Miseran Marbles* they're now called. The metal of money. It's what we use around here for trade and many other things. Just giving Kyran a little bit extra so we can afford more rations for the next couple of days," Bea explained, and I got the gist, somewhat.

What exactly was…money?

Kyran stuffed the bag in his pants. "Get excited, we've got a lot to look forward to."

He went to the rickety coat rack, taking off a couple of burlap bags from its arms, and headed out the front door. I hurried for him. Bea waved me off in my haste, and I gave her the courtesy of waving back before heading out. "Well, see you later,"

"Hope you have a great day!" She beamed.

"Yeah, I'll try." I gave my goodbyes, shutting the door.

What in the world was I getting myself into?

Back into the scenery of Reveria, its livelihood peaked in its waking hours. As I stepped to the rail-guarded sidewalk, the bridges and stairs bustled with mutants, overwhelming me. To bear its grandeur from between buildings fifteen stories tall left me with the desire to keep inside the quaint house I had only been in for a night.

Kyran pulled me back from the rail, his claws barely grazing my flannel. He could've easily torn through if he wasn't careful enough. "Watch it, don't want you falling over."

Taking my distance, it finally settled just how high up we were. He picked up his pace, and I followed closely. My hope was that nobody would care about my presence, let alone notice me after the initial introductions I dealt with.

But I was mistaken.

While walking along with Kyran through one of the bridges and going down a giant set of stairs, everyone couldn't help but to stare at me. Longer than I realized. Whether they'd be black beady eyes or colorful gazes, each one of them had never been so astonished by the sight of me. While it should have been a pleasant feeling to receive such attention, it was rather uncomfortable to have so many faces all directed my way. I was fresh meat to them. The only saving grace Kyran brought was fending off anyone from getting too close, brandishing his gladiolus like a repellent. If anyone tried to approach, he'd simply look at them, and they'd get back to minding their own business.

"…This is all so unbelievable."

Kyran chuckled. "Think so?" He eyed the citizens looking our way. "This isn't going to be easy. Just keep low while I show you around, and I'll make sure none of these people get in our way."

Going by his orders, I did what I could to keep my focus on the ground, watching his tail not to lose him. Although the sensation of a thousand stares made it difficult not to lift my head, terrified by the monstrous faces greeting me, each bursting with toxic excitement.

"Oh my, is that a true, pureblooded human? Remarkable!"

"Wonder where she came from. The sky, perhaps?"

"Hey, you, tell us about the sun! You've seen it, right?"

Being a walking spectacle only made me feel more alien. I couldn't even pay attention to the constructs that the jaguar showed on his tour.

"We got the schoolhouse there for the kids, then there's the town's marble bank and the community center. Got a laundromat and local bath house too if you need to get yourself or your clothes cleaned. But now we're heading for our pride: the plaza." He pointed at various things around, but with the tension getting to my head, I got distracted. "Hope this isn't too much so far—wait, what's wrong?" Kyran turned to me.

"They won't stop bothering me," I told him.

He sighed. "They'll learn to mind their business the longer you're here. I'd try ignoring them for now." He retorted, and once we turned the corner sidewalk, the next street led to a bazaar that'd leave anybody either bemused or overstimulated.

Tinges of spice, fish, and burning wood floated around the marketplace. Storefronts were illuminated by artificial lights, bringing brightness to the broad dark. Whether in one of the buildings or from the streetside counters shaded in sheeted shingles, each owner made what they had work. Every merchant put their own personality out there, but one thing they had in common? They all brandished a sign, whether on a sheet of steel or projecting from a digital screen, boasting about their daily deals. Buy one vintage smartwatch and get another free. Used sonic screwdrivers and automated tools on sale. The incentives worked well, as much chatter fluttered throughout the plaza. Exchanges between sellers and their buyers, people making hasty decisions, and some trying to figure out what they would eat for dinner. Had they not worn the fur, scales, or what-have-you of beasts, they could've easily passed for true people—yet to me, they were still monsters.

"Reveria's probably the best and only real place in the city to do trading. We always get travelers from other communities coming here, but we're always careful on *who* we let into town…" Kyran leered at a couple of suspicious perps, but swiftly snapped the bitter look off his mug. "How about we look around and get you something nice to keep. Call it a little welcome gift on me."

"That's…nice of you."

"Go on, check things out, and I'll be right behind." He bared a grin, and I went by his word. I tip-toed around anybody in the way, only to be greeted by awestruck faces and even more curious eyes. Looking past their glances, each business provided a unique service.

One building housed a walk-in boutique, where the beastpeople inside specially tailored clothes and shoes for anyone walking in. Accommodating for any shape and size, they sewed and seamed together old clothes that otherwise wouldn't work for their current physicality. Some even got themselves sheared, having their stray fur caught in baskets, and used to make new attire and accessories.

The Community Closet & Carpentry

"Think you got plenty of clothes." Kyran hummed.

Another store had an array of weapons, the same kind that Kyran had strapped to his back. Inside, a camel man at the counter took a customer's marbles, taking them in the back and smelting them into odd little tapers.

Reveria Public Weaponry & Ammo Dispensary

"I don't think you'll be needing bullets," Kyran added again.

"I'm not really sure what I want,"

"Hmm…I got it. How about I take you to the general goods store? Or pawn shop, rather. They got a lot of stuff there." He took my wrist and threaded through the busy street. Any vendors who spotted me from the crowd did everything they could to draw me in.

"Excuse me, hello? Hello! I've got a free sample for you!"

"You should come by my shop; I'll give you a discount!"

"Human! Human! You'll love these sunglasses I'm selling!"

It was hard trying to not break down right then and there, my senses nearly overloaded. Compared to the serenity of the forest, the bustling disorder of this street life made me lose my footing. Kyran noticed my imbalance, reaffirming his grip and making me stand straight. "Charissa, what's going on?" He fretted, and I lacked the ability to utter a word. Dragging me away, we hurried from the crowd.

Wading through the townspeople, I finally caught a breath on the least busy sidewalk. The inquisitive looks of the mutants continued to deter me, and while I tried to look them in the eye, my only solace came from keeping my focus on the dirt road instead.

If I ignored everything, it'd all go away.

Drowning out the voices, I prayed that any second, I'd wake up from this dream and be in the comfort of my leaf-bed, and no longer be confined within the island's core.

My hopes were extinguished once Kyran spoke to me.

"You look like you're doing a little better now."

"I'm fine. You don't need to treat me like an inconvenience,"

He gave another confused glance. "What do you mean?"

"You don't have to feel like you're obligated to watch over me. Feels like I can't be around here on my own."

"That's not it at all. There's just a lot you don't know about, and I'd rather not have you getting lost or messed with."

"Is that it, or do you still not fully trust me too? Like Mikhail?"

"Again, I'm just trying to do my job."

"Which is it then? Are you trying to be my friend, or are you just doing what you're told?"

"Charissa, I do this in and out of uniform. I might've only met you yesterday, but it's still my duty to protect you like I would anybody else. Both as a Virtue and as a regular man. Don't take it the wrong way."

Maybe *his* paranoia brushed off onto me. That, and being in a new environment, rattled me. I held my reddened face. "My mistake."

He looked at the people passing by, keeping to themselves. "It's overwhelming, I get that. But if you're going to be here, you need to learn how to fit in." His stare returned to me. "I'm not saying it's an easy thing for you to do, but it's necessary for being part of a community."

"I know. I still have a lot to learn."

"Hey, keep that chin up." A click of his tongue followed. "The morning's not over yet. Why don't you take a look at this?"

Taking my sour stare, he showed me another marvel.

A tall and prominent building entranced me. Concrete stairs cased from the pavement to the entrance, with a dim light shining through the stained-glass window of the front door. Perhaps the largest store I'd come across thus far, and probably the only one in the town made from brick. *Joelle-Of-All-Trades* was spelled out in scrap metal and held itself up with iron bars, the lightbulbs flickering along the edges. Next to the big construct was an extension to the store, with a heavy garage door that opened halfway. Sparks flickered within as *Otto Parts* beamed above in fluorescent lights.

"Biggest shop Reveria could offer. Hate it, though; it's always cluttered with junk," he grumbled. "You know what, maybe this'll give you a chance to be your own Reverian."

"What're you talking about?"

Kyran dipped his fingers into the little sack and withdrew about five copper marbles, pocketing the rest of the stash. He took my hand, placing the dull orbs into my possession, making my fingers hold onto them. "Take these marbles, get whatever you want."

Befuddled, I reluctantly took them. "Are you sure?"

"You're right about one thing, I can't be always over your shoulder all the time. I'm letting you get your feet wet, see what it's like to be another citizen."

I fiddled with the marbles. "I mean, I suppose I can try."

"That's the first step at anything, isn't it?"

My palm grew clammy. "What if I do something wrong?"

"Charissa, there's nothing wrong with making mistakes. Even if you mess up, nobody's going to laugh at you for trying to be somebody. How are you going to learn otherwise?"

Although his apprehension back at the courthouse rubbed me the wrong way, I attempted to move past that. Or rather, learn what it meant to be another citizen, as he said. And to give him a chance.

"That's actually some good advice."

"Let's just say I've done a lot of learning myself coming here. If I can do it, you can too."

"I'll see about that." I stuffed the marbles in my pocket. "And thanks, Kyran."

"You're welcome. Have fun shopping."

He spotted a vendor across the street, selling something on a stick. It was some small roasted, four-legged little creature. Hungry, he wandered to see what was on the menu. I made my way up the steps, getting closer to the wooden door with the colorful window. Jagged shards of hues connected to the circular frame, appearing kaleidoscopic. Underneath the mosaic of glass, a sheet of metal hung by a nail, reading out "Barter, Trade, Buy, or Sell!" in white paint, though there was also red underneath. *"Stealing will cost you. Don't try it."*

On turning the crystal knob and revealing the inside, a shining light greeted me through an arched entryway ahead. I wandered into a tiny corridor where little charms on strings strung across the arcs above, clinking together to create a harmony of peaceful clinks. Posters hung on the two walls beside me, all of them had wear and tear, with huge rips through the sheets that were taped together. One displayed an advertisement for new *androids that can manage your calls and messages*, the other an *A.I. powered vacuum cleaner* that guaranteed to pick up all dust bunnies on its own. Another showed a promotion involving the *new home-grade tool for the modern Pietan, the CataLyte, where any common citizen can cook and do personal repairs* with utmost ease.

So many wonders that I could never fathom.

I continued further into the hallway, the finely made carpet, woven together in washed-out colors, took me up several more steps where the light shone. Once I reached the top, glowing bulbs swayed in their strings from the wooden-beamed ceiling. They stretched from one side of the space to the other, creating trails of incandescent specs, dotting from one point to the next. Almost appearing like fireflies frozen in time, intertwining with one another, they shimmered warmly, and everything became clear. Hundreds of shelves welcomed me inside in their organized mess, each one holding up a particular array of objects and curiosities, putting everything in its place. Pots and pans, drinking glasses, hats, soaps, magazines, used books. The walls even had stuff put on display. Mattresses, paintings, mirrors, and old clocks. I imagined this would have been where all the angels made all their *miracles*, even if that proved to be a lie long ago. I stepped further in, lost. The shelves on the plank floor were arranged in such a disorientating way, turning into a maze with people cluttering the aisles as I tried to squeeze my way through. Several were kind enough to make room as others wanted the time of my day, but I ignored them as I focused on figuring my way around, until I found myself in the center of the massive room.

A large pillar was centered, with glass counters surrounding the beam by its four corners, and behind the display cases, someone rummaged around. Inside the transparent containment, jewels and treasures were brandished in their grandeur, with little slips of paper taped to each trinket. *500, 870, 930;* the labels had an array of numbers for every gem. Approaching to admire the glamours, the stranger behind the counter caught my presence, perking up and turning tail.

Quite literally.

Sunshine in beastly form faced me, with big sienna eyes glittering at me. She showed the striking features of a wild dog, with golden fur that made her glimmer in the bright lights above. The dogwoman had the widest smile and the whitest canines, with silky hair on her head tugged back in messy twin tails. On her full-figured body, she wore a pair of overalls and a white shirt underneath, both of which were tattered with holes. Her approachability showed in her excitable nature, but I was uncertain of how she would genuinely perceive me.

Maybe the smile was only for show.

"Well, howdy there! Word caught on that there mighta been a new face here in town! Though I was on the fence when I heard that it'd be a real human…But lookee here, the human is right in my shop!" Her enthusiasm sparkled with joy, but she finally returned her whimsical attention back to me as I stood there. "Ah, sorry, I'm so starstruck! It's kinda like seein' a dream come true is all. I'm Joelle! I run this market of merriment here, and I'm sure you must be tryna find somethin' in particular if you stumbled in my parlor. Got a name, hon?"

Her voice was cheery and eccentric, and it made me more comfortable talking with her, although it tested my nerves.

"Charissa. If you're the one running this place, how are you supposed to find your way around here without getting so overwhelmed by everyone, and well, *everything?*"

"You sorta find your way through the more you visit! Then again, it can get a lil' hard keeping track of everythin' that comes in here…includin' the customers. True, this place can be a little tricky to worm around, but you'll always find what ya came here for!" Joelle chirped with thrill. She leaned over the glass counter, elbows resting on the polished surface. Her hands propped underneath her chin as her fluffy tail wagged. "Don't mind me asking, but what're ya huntin'?"

"I can't really say I know. I only have about five of these things, but there's so much stuff here that it's hard to decide."

Joelle tilted her head curiously. "Hmm…Thankfully for ya, I have a selection of things for affordable prices. Just look at the tags and you'll easily find a treat suited to your taste," she suggested, but gawking at the prices of the jewelry alone, I was stumped.

"I'll try my best, then." I wandered to try and find something, but everything in this store seemed so expensively out of my grasp.

"When you get what yer' needin', come back here!"

There was so much junk around that it was difficult to find anything I liked. I skimmed through aisles of old scrap, raggedy dolls, and other dusty wares. Though as I made my way through the cramped aisles, something stole my eye as it sat there on the edge of a shelf, alongside other metallic, musical keepsakes.

A harmonica.

The shimmer on its cover plate reminded me of my own back home, and once I took it in my hold, thumb to the holes, it compelled me back to a simpler time. Taking a breath and closing my eyes, I brought the instrument to my lips, playing a short tune of brass notes. The more I went about my song, the visions of my past surfaced in a starlit sea. Tranquil nights at the treehouse, the singing voice of Narissa, the smell of fresh air and the memories of spring.

After the melody, it left me empty.

Opening my eyes, glossed with a couple of tears, I feared as though the more I remained here, the more I would yearn back for everything I threw away. Though with this simple, manmade wonder, it gave me a sliver of peace that'd never let me forget the memory.

I lifted my head, only to scramble back to find Joelle's bright face peeking between stacks of plastic disks. I almost bumped into the shelves behind me, and even screamed!

"Oh, I'm sorry! Did I scare ya?" she blurted.

"Gah! No, you're good…you're good."

"Yer song was just so gorgeous, I had to come by for a closer listen. Never took ya for a virtuoso, but ya got some real talent!" she praised, withdrawing herself from the shelves. "I can tell ya found exactly whatcha wanted. How about I go on and check ya out?"

Joelle directed me over to the same spot where I last found her, and she and I went back to the center of the store, where I went and placed the harmonica on top of the glass counter. However, there was one crucial detail I overlooked with it. The little label: 5o.

"Is this really that expensive?" I pulled out my marbles.

"Hmm? I don't get whatcha mean!"

"I mean, it's amazing and all…but fifty?"

She remained silent, until she couldn't help but burst out laughing.

"Girl, that ain't a zero! That symbol stands for the marble. Because they're both circular, ain't they?" She wiped her wide grin and still chuckled a bit more, which only caused my face to turn into a big, bright tomato. "My bad, my bad. It's funny because we're all so used to it. It's normal for us to all write zeroes down with the lil' line through it too. Though, yer new here…I didn't mean to make fun of ya."

"I get it now. So, it'd be five marbles for this, right?" I corrected.

"You'd be right, hon! Y'gottem?" She reached forth; her hand covered in golden fur. Her palms and fingertips had epidermal pads colored black, with a set of dull claws polished in pink sticking out.

"Yeah, I do. Here." I handed all the marbles I had to her, leaving them in her possession. Again, the sensation of touching a strange animal-hand, paw, *thing* left me bemused, but she closed her palm and shuffled down behind the counter, retrieving a pad of yellow paper and an old-fashioned pen.

"Alrighty! Our receipt printer's getting fixed up at the shop next door, so I'm gonna write down your transaction here and that'll do it!" She tore off the little sheet and gave it to me, which I skimmed.

Charissa

(1) Harmonica

Total: 50

Thanks for your business! :)

"S'been nice meeting ya. Hope to see ya again real soon!"

With that, she returned to her business, tending to another customer who perused the novelty bracelets nearby. Taking my treasure, I retraced my path to where I came from, eventually finding my way out of the chaotic maze and stepping back into the grand 'outdoor' scenery.

So, this was society. To be human. Or pretending to be.

Kyran sat at the bottom of the stairs, and when I walked down to speak to him, he turned with about two—no, four skewers of meat-on-a-stick in his hands. I could not tell what it was, apart from being the charred carcasses of something, and Kyran ripped into each morsel from their wooden skewers with his sharp teeth. Upon seeing me, he swallowed his big bite and licked his chops.

"Didn't think you'd make it out of there alive," he joked, before standing and digging into his next nibble.

"Bea told me that you guys eat lab meat…what is that?"

He scarfed his next nip. "Ah yeah, we do, but you sometimes find vermin that breed like crazy and make for easy meat. Anything that isn't lab-grown is considered gourmet to a lot of folks here."

To my astonishment, animals lived down here too, aside from these talking beasts. *True animals.* Seemed only reasonable to believe, but during my brief time here, I had not seen a single creature that didn't walk only on two legs. But what four-legged thing was he…eating?

"You didn't answer my question."

"This? It's rat. The vendor over there breeds and cooks them for a living. Not a bad thing he has going on if you ask me."

I couldn't judge.

"If you say so," I replied, and showed him what I bought. "Anyway, I found something. Take a look."

"A harmonica?" He hummed. "Neighbors wouldn't appreciate you playing that at nighttime, but so long as you keep that in mind, then it's alright. Anyway, let's get going; Bea is waiting on you," Kyran tossed his skewers into the nearby trash can and headed for the concrete steps ahead, and I loomed behind. I had no idea what to expect from there.

***

Going through the pathways and stairs of the town, we arrived at the laboratories within ample time. With the lack of any daylight down in the hollow city sky, the only way time could have been told was from the large clock upon walking in. Ahead of the front desk, 11:53 showed on the digital display, near where a large-toothed receptionist tended to his computer. Spotting Kyran and me from his seat, his tiny ears perked.

"Good day, Virtue of Courage. And hello to you as well, Miss Charissa. Dr. Rhodes left a note saying to keep a lookout for you lot," the marmot informed us with a quaint accent, clicking the little letters on his...keyboard, if I recalled correctly.

"Right. I'm just dropping her off and then heading to the station for my shift. Try to make sure she stays out of trouble, doc."

"I'll escort our guest to the biological department in a minute. Let me just inform Dr. Rhodes that you've arrived," the man said, rolling back in his chair to radio Bea.

"I'll let you take it from here, my good man. Take care of yourselves now," he called out to the marmot once he finished his call.

"Happily, Virtue,"

Kyran patted my shoulders. "I'll see you back home. Don't stress, Bea's the best," he said, heading for the glass doors.

I had to try, for his sake.

"If you'll follow me, I'll take you right to Dr. Rhodes' quarters."

"After you, then,"

The white-uniformed male led me to a strange chamber in the wall. After pressing a few buttons on the nearby pad, two metal doors parted, leading into a tight-fitting box. "Aren't you coming into the elevator?"

"We're not taking the stairs?"

"It'll be faster this way. Fret not, we'll be just fine in here," he tried to reason, and unwillingly, I complied. Stepping into the odd mechanism, the steel closed together, and the box shifted. Or "elevator," I suppose, far smaller compared to the one that brought me here. I lost my footing in the cold confines, flashing back to the night of the midnight storm. To be in this chamber only brought remembrance of my descent into darkness, but the marmot pulled me out before I could delve into the mental recess.

"Your skin's turning pale. Is that normal?"

"Just nervous," I spat out, to which he stepped out with me once the machinery stopped its momentum.

"About your time with Dr. Rhodes? There's nothing to worry about; she's quite exceptional with her work. Come, you'll feel more at ease once we're at her labs," he said, escorting me down the corridor. I followed him, but the gnawing thought of that elevator…the one that brought me here. The compulsion to return to it grew stronger.

Going through the familiar halls that I'd witnessed a day prior, the fascinations they bore turned to regrets. The greenery, the fish, it all clung to me. Even the newest discoveries made me wish I had never known of them, and content I would've been to be ignorant of. All my worries were put on hold once we made it to the biological department, where the rodent brought me in to find Bea observing one of the test-tubed cadavers, making notes on a piece of glass in hand.

"Charissa's here, doctor," the clerk said, and Bea nearly dropped the rectangular device upon hearing his voice. She spun around, setting down her things on her desk and coming up.

"Apologies, I was so focused I lost track of the time. Thank you very much for bringing her up,"

"My pleasure. If you need anything else, just call me," he replied, stepping away. With only Bea and I alone, it brought some semblance of peace, despite the room's dreary tones. The cold walls and the humming tubes of the deceased unsettled me.

"Your timing couldn't have been more impeccable; I was just getting things ready for you. Have a seat in the chair, and we can get started." She directed me to the desk where her research remained. I wandered over, my backside supplicant to the comfort of the cushion. Bea went up to the computer at her station, clicking the keys in rapid succession. "How was your tour of the town? Did you and Kyran have a good time?"

Instead of the same fickle smile I put up from the morning, I shared my real one. "Yeah, I'm glad we got to shop together,"

"Good, good! I was nervous he'd scare you, but I'm happy to hear that my talk with him paid off."

During our conversation, my gaze drifted to an object at the corner of her desk. A chrome frame, with a full-colored picture changing each second. In every still-moment, it was her, and a familiar face.

Dr. Kutsuki.

"I recognize that man, the one from the lobby."

Her ears perked, and it took her a second to process. Those focused eyes tore from her computer screen, and the light on her face faded. She reached for the digital memento, putting it in the drawer of her desk. "Didn't realize that was still there, sorry," she returned to typing.

"Oh, I didn't mean to…"

She dipped her fingertips under her glasses, wiping her eyes. "No, you did nothing wrong. It's just…still hard for me to move on, even after enough time's passed."

"Aliya told me he meant a lot to the people here."

"He did." her mouth thinned. "I was his assistant when I first came here, and he taught me more than anyone and anything that a database could provide. He was like everyone's father. I miss him every day."

"I'm sorry."

She said nothing more in that regard. When she finished readying her computer, she pulled up another chair and took her seat. "I'd like to ask for your consent. Are you alright with our logs being recorded?"

Confused, I agreed regardless. "Yes."

She clicked one of the keys, clearing her throat. "November 18th, 2174. Before we begin any testing, I'd like to ask you, Charissa, for your permission to partake in such research, which you can decline if you wish. Do you feel safe and comfortable proceeding?"

"Yes, that's okay," I said again.

Bea typed at the keys, only for the nearby wall to slide open, and a metal plate extended out. A metallic apparatus clung to the frame, which the jaguar picked up. Rolling up her sleeve, she fastened the strange device to her arm, and the machine whirred to the movement of her fingers. Like a second skin, it radiated a warm heat.

Catalyst-O: Constructed by the Abundantia Association

"I'm going to take these tweezers and pluck a hair sample, if that's alright with you. Just a gentle prick," she told me, coming close. From her fingertips, tweezer-like extensions protruded as if she sheathed out her claws, taking a pinch of me. "I'm going to count to three. Just let me know if at any point you don't feel well, alright?"

"Okay." I gripped the chair, clenching my teeth.

"One…two…" Pluck! "Three…how are you doing?"

"I'm alright, don't worry," I reassured her.

She placed the piece of hair into a shallow dish, closing it with her metal-clung digits and bringing out another. Along with that, she brought some kind of…

"I'll be taking this swab and collecting a saliva sample. Open your mouth for me; I'll try and make this quick."

I nodded, prying open my lips, and letting her do work. Bea leaned in, taking the soft stick, and putting it in my maw. The palm-center of her Catalyst projected a concentrated light as she dragged the cotton stick along my gums and under my tongue. Once she got her sample, she dropped it in the second dish, and retrieved a third and final one. A needle-like extension came from her fingertip as she loaded a glass vial into the bulky compartment of the Catalyst next.

"Lastly, I'll need a little bit of your blood. You might feel a little twinge, but I promise it'll be a painless process. Are you okay with going forward, or would you like to wait another day?"

I drew a deep breath. "Let's just get this over with,"

With a firm nod, she took a band and wrapped it around my arm, keeping it tight around my muscles. She laid my arm out on the desk, spraying a chemical-reeking liquid from one finger as the other prepped its needle. "I'm going to count to three again…look to the ceiling and take slow breaths; it'll be over before you know it."

My eyes on the fluorescent lights, I tried to find my inner solace. *Breathe in, breathe out. Breathe in, breathe out.*

"One. Two." The needle went in, freezing me in place. "Three. You're doing good. Just stay still for me." She hushed, and I continued my soft inhales, up until she pulled out. With haste, her fingertip gelled a substance on my arm, rubbing it in. In mere seconds, the red dot on my skin faded. "Didn't think it'd be easy drawing blood from you. The lack of fur and scales certainly helps, plus your patience." She trickled a few drops of blood into the final dish, clipping the vial out from her Catalyst.

"What do you need all this for, exactly?" I rubbed myself.

"I'd like to closely understand your genetic mainframe from several angles. Humans and animals might be different, but they share more than we know. I want to figure out how you compare to hybridian DNA." Bea retrieved another device from nearby. "Let's put your samples underneath the microscope for evaluation."

With that, she grabbed her samples and slid them into the contraption one at a time, peering into the pinhole scope. Turning the knobs on the side and humming to herself, she sounded satisfied with whatever she saw through the lens.

"Fascinating, truly fascinating…hair and saliva looks promising; now let's just look at your bloodwork," she mumbled, sliding the red-pressed glass in. Her smile dwindled in an instant.

"Is there something wrong?"

Bea clicked her tongue, withdrawing her head. "Oh no, I just forgot something crucial. Let me run a scan really quick."

Tapping at the small screen of her Catalyst, she raised her palm at me. A faint cone of light projected from the machine, the rays casting over my body. My eyes fluttered to the brief intensity, causing a couple of tears to well in my lids. After a moment, she retracted her hand, looking at the glass pane on her forearm. Her puzzled face remained unchanged.

"What's the matter?"

After a long stare, she shot her head up. "Oh, it's nothing! The screen says you're the picture of health. Suppose you were well-off having pure oxygen up at the surface world for your entire lifetime, I'd imagine," she assured me, tapping her arm-fastened tool.

"If you say so. Are we done here?"

"You've given me plenty to start with, I'll admit. But we might have to do more tests later. Several."

A soft heat ran through my flesh. "There's still more to do?"

"What you brought me is exceptional. If I'm able, I'd like to work further with you, so that I may be able to fully comprehend your being."

The strain in my arm tingled the more I warmed up.

"Are you telling me this because I can genuinely help you, or is it because you can't keep up with your promise?" I accused her, but she rolled back to her computer, typing at the keys.

"I've made contact with a few people out there in the wastes, but they haven't seen anything. I told them to keep me updated if they find any Ferecite activity going on, but with how rare their encounters are…" She ceased her clicking, fidgeting her fingers. "It might take a little more time than I'd like. I wish I could do more for you."

"So how many tests will we need to do?"

"Maybe just a few more, but I assure you that you're doing me wonders by being here, and I will do everything I can to fulfill my end of the deal we made. I won't let you down."

All I could do was seethe in my seat.

"If it means I'll be able to atone for Narissa in the end, I'll keep doing this." The grief that burdened my conscience lingered tenfold.

How much longer I could live with it?

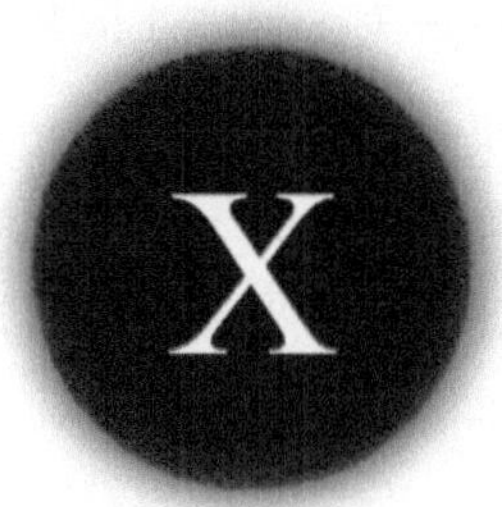

A few days turned into a few months. *February 17th, 2175.*

I became desperate to see the sunlight. To wake up to the songbirds and their morning serenades, having the same soft sand beneath my feet, smelling the fresh air breezing past the ocean, and even find serenity in the treehouse I once considered too small. I yearned to go back to my old life—though that was impossible. I'd never intended to stay longer than a night, and even if it was once a dream to find a place where I *belonged*, being here only turned my fantasy into a sham. After giving in to Bea's plea, it solidified my place here. I still had no idea how she convinced me, considering how much I wanted to leave…but maybe the desire to be *wanted* mattered to me.

To matter at all.

I began to resign myself to what she'd told me the first time we met. That we could never escape. I could do nothing about it, other than to be stuck. Despite being introduced to this unusual way of living, I had grown to adapt and comprehend the fascinations offered in this town. I explored all the "human" advancements that were sheltered from me. Relics of the past I never had became a slow infatuation. The labs introduced me to such intrigues, but the longer I remained in Reveria, the more I learned about the artistry of cameras, the entertainment of televisions, the wonders of music contained on compact discs. Marvels like buses and cars, despite their lack of function, and even tablets and cellular phones, regardless of their connection to the outside world. After months, I became acquainted with the tools the wilderness lacked. The creations that humanity left behind continued to besiege me.

"Dammit!" that baritone voice yelled out.

Jumping in my seat, I turned back to the wolf working on a broken-down vehicle. "What happened?" I called out, midway through cleaning off the other parts he'd handed me.

"Killed the alternator by accident. Coulda made some good outta that," grumbled the utility-suited lupine man, Otto.

Sporting an oily gray mane with white fur trailing from his chin downward, yellow eyes, and a muscled frame, his body showed the arduous work required by all the machinery he had to deal with in his everyday life. Otto did well to keep most of the engineering in Reveria functional, communicating with the laboratory engineers to ensure things in the lower levels of town functioned. When he had no big jobs to do, he would tinker next door to Joelle's store, and sometimes I would visit after my shifts to see what he was up to.

"My bad, didn't mean to get all barky."

"It's all good, Otto. Mistakes happen." I assured him, at which he dropped his tools to the concrete.

"Yeah, but I can't make stupid-dumb whoopsies like this. Think I've been workin' a lil' too long today." He went for his rag, doing his best to wipe the oily grime from his hands. The years of experience left the fur stained a smoky black.

"Maybe you need a little break. Plus, I think I got all the parts cleaned up," I mentioned, wiping the muck off my own palms.

"That right?" He moseyed over to the worktable, delight revealing his many teeth. "Well look atcha! They looked like they were built just yesterday! Yer a real doll, Char."

"It's nothing, really. Joelle knew you had a lot on your plate this afternoon, so I'm glad she sent me to your garage." I wiped the sweat from my brow, despite how minimal my work had been compared to a real individual's profession.

"Well I just appreciate ya helpin' a greasedog like me." He took the parts and sorted them into a crate. "I'll see if the folks back at the labs or any of the plaza need these here."

The special thing about Otto was that not only did he have a jubilant glow like Joelle, but he gave back to his community. Doing much of his work for little to no pay, he'd disassemble salvageable parts and scrap, donating the fruits of his labors. Passionate about his work and neighbors, he could only be deemed a good man.

I could see why Joelle married him.

Speaking of, she barged in from the side door, connecting from in between her shop and his big garage. She had a tote bag over her shoulder. "'Scuse me, mister! You can't be shoutin' while I got customers here!"

Otto's tail lowered. "Oh, I'm real sorry, hon—"

"Otto! I'm just givin' ya crap. Just try to keep a watch on your volume, alright?" She scurried down the doorway's steps, coming to peck her beloved wolf on the cheek.

If he could blush, it'd show through. "D'aw. Can do, babe."

Joelle's bubbly face turned to me. "Oh, Char-dear, thank ya so much for givin' him a hand. He needed the help more than I did."

"No problem. Thank you for painting my nails…but I think some of them already chipped." The yellow finish at my fingertips had cracked and peeled at the edges. Orange flowers glossed over the gold.

"They still look great on ya!" She giggled, fiddling with the strap of her bag. "Say, I've got a real big favor to ask ya."

"Sure Joelle, anything."

"I've gotta run to the ammo dispensary a little ways down the street and give 'em some old iron and copper scraps that've been collecting dust. Do ya think you'd be able to watch over the store while I'm away?"

A peculiar rush swam from my head to my toes. "You want me out there by myself? I'd figure Otto always took charge when you're gone."

"You've been working here a while now, know yer' ways around. We trust ya enough to make sure things stay in tip-top shape." He waved off. "Besides, got a few more jobs I gotta do in here. You'd be doing both of us a service, big time."

To handle such responsibility, it was an honor, yet a nerve-wracking duty. My mouth took control of itself. "Yes, absolutely! I'll do it."

"Thanks a whole lot, 'sug! I won't be gone no more than an hour, might make a couple stops on the way. If ya need anything, holler at Otto and he'll be able to help ya." She patted my back. "Be back in a bit!"

Joelle headed for the garage door, lifting it up and slipping under, only to slam the metal mass shut. On the digital clock above the workbench, 18:41 blared in its bright green. An hour? *I can do this.*

"Better get a move on. Don't work too hard now, Otto." I waved him off, making my way for the staircase leading to the store.

"You too, Char!"

***

I should've been grateful, to have a part in a real community. I no longer had to imagine it from the pages of a book, confabulating what it was all supposed to be. Like the books, it nearly gleamed with prosperity and hospitality, but it was far from the pictures I had once seen. *Here,* I was introduced to the cruel reality of it all. To be part of a myriad of bound souls, to never know peace. Not to mention, even after all this time, I still got treated like a walking spectacle. The mutants here tried everything to be my friend, but not for the right reasons. My humanity was what they desired from me, and it made me feel more alone. Every day, it was stares, questions, or blabbering. The more I lived through it, I figured out that I was in Hell all along. Yet another endless cycle of monotony, much like in my old life. Looking back, though, I had truly taken what I had for granted.

In Misera, it was far worse. There was no fresh air. There was no fresh fruit. No rain and nothing to gain. There was nothing here but the pressure of the earth and the subtle stress of its heat. Some days were bearable. Most days were insufferable. But every day was—

"Um, excuse me?"

I surfaced to my senses.

"Can I have my receipt please?"

Taking a moment, I returned to the present. I blanked every so often, or rather, once every couple of days for my weeks here. It had gotten worse since, and the fog in my mind tried to make me forget I was ever in this city. Yet every time, I surfaced and found myself in the same life.

In the middle of bagging up a customer's items, an old silverware set with a few cracked, ceramic plates, I had blanked longer than I should've.

A lot had happened going forward from the first day I stayed in Reveria. I couldn't go anywhere else, not until Bea delivered on her promise. Every day I asked if she'd heard anything, only to be given a regretful apology every time. Each night as I went to sleep, I contemplated how I would find Narissa. To escape this city and give my sister a proper burial. Even in my waking moments, she always came to mind, as I tried to contend with the horrible prospect that she had to be gone. I gave myself a little peace by telling myself she was dead.

I had to accept the facts.

"Yes! My bad, it's been a long day." I said to the donkey fellow, clicking at the keys of the receipt printer. Yellow paper whirred from the machine, and tearing off the strip, I handed it off to him. "A cutlery set and some plates, you saved twenty marbles on the damages."

He took the slip and his bag of contents. "Can always count on Joelle to have the best accommodations. Glad she's hired someone too."

Although every night I sulked, I had to keep myself up during the day. Bea encouraged me to pass time by helping those around me, despite my dissatisfaction over having to remain idle here. I helped the folks with their deeds, simple things at first; deliveries, lifting heavy crates, and cleaning windows. Bea told me the best way to earn trust with the people was to tend to their needs, but after a while, she told me I could earn more respect if I found a career contributing to the community: a job.

Of course, many businesses wanted me to work for them after I put myself out there. Though really, I knew I would have simply been an attraction to rope in more customers. I declined everybody that tried to bait me in, but there was one person who made me content with my efforts, not based on looks: Joelle took me in without a second thought.

Her can-do attitude brushed on me some, and because of that, I'd built an ethic and drive, finding something to find a sliver of happiness for. But even then, a crumb of fulfillment came at a cost. Living was expensive, after all, but while I was thankful to already have a roof given to me…I couldn't spend my time here for free.

While my human resources were of Bea's benefit, Kyran continued to help me blend in with the society here. He introduced me to the ways of the common man, and learn how to live like one, especially when it came to income. Anytime I came home with any marbles at all, he'd ask for them, said he'd keep them at the bank for me. He didn't necessarily use my earnings, but he assured me he wanted to keep my funds in a safe hold, said it'd build up over time. Although he was doing what was best for me, it made my daily efforts almost meaningless.

Would keeping all my earnings saved really make a difference?

"Hey, just glad I can work here. Anything else I can do for you?"

"Yeah." He looked over his shoulder. "Make sure you don't let that troublemaker break anything. He's been a nuisance since I walked in."

Once my latest customer made way for the maze of shelves, my attention directed to the miscreant touching all the glass items. Every time, he dared to push those fragiles off to get a rise out of me, knowing I'd have to clean up anything that broke. He came every Friday night, always up to no good: Shank, a stupid moniker for an even stupider man.

"Not this again..." I muttered to myself.

Without Joelle around, it was my duty to make sure everyone got the service they needed, even if some didn't deserve it. Stepping from behind the counter, I headed for the glassware to deal with the lizard.

Approaching the bony reptile, Shank ogled me. What set him apart from most Reverians was the chrome on his body. Making himself out to be some downlow "gangster," each of his fingers had been replaced with metallic appendages. Where he came from, everyone willingly parted a piece of themselves in exchange for the feeling of social and physical prestige. Something that was useless here.

I granted him my obligatory smile. "May I help you?"

"So nice of you to ask, skin." The greasy lizard smirked. "Turn that little backside of yours around and get outta this town, slag."

My grin wavered. "Is something wrong?"

"Yeah, something's wrong. The last thing we need is your high n' mighty ass wandering around town, thinkin' you're better than everyone,"

"I'm not sure what you mean by that."

"Course you don't." He hissed. "Jesus, can you just fuck off? I'm tryna to look around and you're naggin' me."

"Of course, sorry to bother."

Turning around, I returned to the front counter, knowing all too well he wouldn't buy anything, as usual. While I did my best to keep my eye on him, my long stare went to the mantel and analog clocks sitting on another shelf ahead. 19:57, they ticked. Where the heck was Joelle?

"Hey, you gonna help me?"

Shank appeared right in front of me, having a circular mirror in his hand. To my surprise, my fingers instinctually typed on the receipt printer.

"Just the mirror for you then?"

"Nah, I just wanted to ask you something." He lifted the glass, my frown showing in the reflection. "How much for this piece of shit? Surely, I could get a discount if I bought something so ass-ugly."

Shank laughed, and my cheekbones ached as the blood rushed to my skin. "There's no need to be rude, sir. I'm just working."

"Oh, enough of the fuckin' act." He bared his glossy teeth. "I've been hearin' some things about you. I know what you're *really* here for,"

What was he even talking about?

"Please don't make me call Joelle."

"What? That fat blonde bitch? Do it then, call for her, see what happens." He leaned over the counter. "Let's pretend she's here to help you. C'mon, you're such a strong girl. You can take me by yourself."

"O-Ott—"

"Aw, now you're gonna try to cry out for her fuckmutt? Damn, you've got no balls, don't you? Instead of being a lil' pussy, how about get your scrawny ass out of—"

A series of stomps came from behind him, and over his shoulder, Joelle came to view. "What did ya just say to her?"

He zipped his maw, slowly facing her. "N-Nothing, Joelle."

"Don't even! Yer' foulmouthed kind ain't welcome in my store, not when ya speak to a woman like that. Especially to my Char." She pointed for the exit. "If ya don't leave here in the next minute, I'm calling the Virtues. And if ya ever step foot near my store again, I'll make ya sorry."

He shuffled in his boots, furrowed brows on his hideous mug. "…You have more respect for this skinbag than your own kind? You're just a suck-up, like everyone else in this shit-town." Shank looked right at me once he took the mirror, crushing it to bits in his stainless-steel fingers. "Better keep an eye out for me, girl. You won't like it when I find you."

With a twisted grin, the lizard left.

"I'm so sorry, Char, I shoulda banned him a long time ago. I'm gonna contact the chief myself about this," Joelle grumbled, careful not to get her toes near the shards. Out of instinct, I grabbed the nearby broom and dustpan, stepping out from behind the counter to sweep the mess.

"Maybe I deserved it."

"Don't say that." Joelle took hold of my back. "Doesn't matter what or who ya are; nobody deserves to be talked to like that."

Finished cleaning the broken glass, I did my best not to frown. "I appreciate you for standing up for me. Don't think I could've asked for a better boss." I mumbled, only to have her dig into her overalls, handing me a small cloth bag brimming full of metal marbles.

"And thank ya for being a good worker. If anything, ya deserved every commission ya earned today. Nobody sells like ya do."

I returned a soft grin, stashing the evening's pay in my own pocket.

"Looks like my shift's about to end,"

"Do ya want Otto to walk ya home?" she asked, but I shook my head, wiping the excess red from my cheeks.

"I can handle my own."

"Are ya absolutely sure?"

"Yeah." I faked a wider smile. "I'll be okay."

"Alright hon', if that's what you want. Please stay safe out there. I'll see ya tomorrow, alright?"

"Will do." I dusted myself off, wading through the maze. Stepping outside, I flipped the open sign to *close*, walking down the stone stairs. Back to the "great" outdoors of Reveria. Another day, another ache.

The plaza brimmed with beasts, as usual. Citizens fiending for the Friday specials and relishing the side street vendors for their snacks. It was so baffling that they still enjoyed ordinary lives, even as the world outside the town limits fell apart in front of them. After living here a while, observing and understanding the creatures with their habits…it made me realized that all of this was simply an interruption from the bigger, scarier picture. Businesses? Money? Why did any of it matter?

At its fundamentals, it didn't, but having things like shops and overall community helped bring people together in a time of crisis. Even when the future looked so bleak, the folks of Reveria peered through the lenses with rose-tinted gazes and hopeful hearts. Something I wish I could do instead of dragging my feet, but I just couldn't find the answers to why they could be so blindly content. I thought to give it a try.

Although it was Kyran's advice to give him the money I made for safekeeping, I decided to break from the norm, as I once did, hoping I wouldn't repeat history again.

Buying something for myself couldn't change my fate.

Perusing the marketplace made good deals call to me. What allured me most? Streetside cod-bits on a stick; pairs of discount sunglasses? Or maybe a new pair of shoes with those fancy cotton laces? The material possibilities were limitless, so it seemed, and I drifted to make a choice.

A grip took my shirt collar.

Pulled into an alleyway, I stumbled until I was thrown against the stone wall. Slumping to the ground, my vision blurred, returning only to find Shank above. I tried to pick myself up, but he was quick to shove me down, leaning down to overshadow my face.

"Wh-What's going on…" I mumbled.

"Don't got your bitch-boss to help you out this time, huh?" he cackled, taking me by the hair and yanking. "You know how this goes.

Cough up your money, don't say shit, and I won't tear that lil' pretty nose off your smooth face."

I was quick to dig into my pocket, throwing him the sack of marbles. "There. Can I please go?"

"Good girl, but this ain't gonna be enough. After the shit you pulled back there?" He let go of me, my breath growing frantic. From his pocket, he pulled out a toothed tool. "Been wanting to do this for too long."

"Y-You don't have to do this."

"Nah, you've been asking for this. I'll make some hella marbles off those two front teeth. Give you a bit of a makeover too!" he cackled, and my eyes went to the alleyway. The beastpeople were too busy to notice. With the lizard's slimy grip on my jaw, he forced my mouth open.

"Say ahhhh…"

In he went, bringing the pliers closer to my mouth. Not a single peep escaped my tense throat. Only my cries of agony would hint at my fate after the pain came rushing in…

"Stop right now!" a voice called.

"Shit! It's the chief!" he yelled.

From the end of the alleyway, a marksman rifle aimed down. The thug backed away against the opposite wall. Through the dim glow of the alley signs, Aliya came to my aid with no hesitation.

"Did he hurt you?" she stressed, and in a panic, I rushed behind her. "What the hell are you doing? Answer me now!"

He tried their best to conceal the pliers, but Aliya was quick to pin the lizard to the wall, prying the tool from his mitts.

"I was just…" He struggled to spit out any excuses. "I-I promise I won't mess with her again!"

The cardinal jammed the jaws of the tool to the wall, right next to his muzzle. "You aren't going to get yourself out of this one! First it was vandalism, then extortion, and now you're going as far as to try and harm a resident? You aren't in *Carpe Noctem* anymore. What makes you think these crimes are okay here?"

"P-Please don't kick me out of here…"

"We've given you many chances. We've tried to help and offered you rehab. But each time, you've thrown every offer away. I'm convinced that you don't want to clean up your ways. *This* is who you are."

"You can't send me back there! They'd kill me if I went back!"

His desperate act wouldn't fool her this time.

"Eddy, you still hold that fake name like a trophy. We welcomed you here when they kicked you out, and this is what you do? You have done nothing but let your fellow citizens down."

"Wh-What're you going to do to me?"

"I don't intend to evict you from Reverian grounds, but you've left us no other choice. You're going straight to headquarters." She clicked her radio. "Prep a cell at the station. I've got an arrest in the making."

***

Aliya escorted me and Shank back to the police station. The looks we received weren't the usual ogling and obsessive friendliness, but rather of concern and morbid intrigue. Anybody in the streets could watch as we made our way to the highest echelon of the town, past the laboratories and the courthouse, heading for the sanctuary of the Virtues. A foundation of brutalist concrete that held itself for its pride and sense of protection, it served to be one of the many symbols that Reveria stood for: Salvation.

Reverian Virtue Headquarters

Once inside, no questioning was necessary, given everything Aliya had witnessed. Shank was thrown into his isolated cell of iron bars, given the proper treatment he deserved. As for myself, I sat there in the main lobby, watching as the mutants in their leather armor came and went, each one looking at me like a sad puppy. Although I did nothing wrong, I wasn't proud to be there. After about an hour of protocol, the digital clock at the front desk blinked *21:38*.

"We should've acted from his very first offense. Ever since he moved here last month, he's been nothing but an issue." Aliya argued from around the hallway corner. "You know how those Nocturnes can be."

"Much like everyone that's migrated here, he's no different from having a rough past he's trying to leave behind. Had I known just how severe his misdeeds were, I would've advised you to arrest him sooner." Mikhail spoke in his same, callous tone.

To hear his voice brought an aggrieved weight to my back.

"We knew very well of his background and where he came from, yet the three of you were still fine to grant him entry?" She retorted.

"Don't question my authority, Chief Morales." He scoffed. "Ever since we've allowed that human here, we decided to give more people chances at entry. You should be happy our capacity's been expanding by a couple of dozen, let alone have any more room at all for them."

"Still, we allow most here within *reason*, your Reverence."

"Eddy still deserves a new start; we just need to be more patient with him. I'll speak to the boy myself and set him a higher bar. Hopefully, now that he *has* to be rehabilitated, we can shape him into the model citizen that Reverians come to be."

"Very well, but he's on thin ice. After what he tried to do to Charissa, a man like him warrants the probation he's given himself."

"Give him time, and he'll become a new man."

Mikhail stepped out from the hallway, spotting me sulking on the bench. He gave no courtesy to speak to me, instead heading for the front doors and leaving the station. The familiar cardinal that had saved me from bare gums came to view, taking a seat next to me on the bench.

I remained quiet ever since we left the alleyway.

"He won't be causing trouble for a while. Once he's out, he'll be put on watch. You've got nothing to be scared of anymore," she sighed. "How come you never told me about what he did to you?"

The slight pressure gave my voice a push.

"Just never wanted to be considered anyone's enemy…if I fessed up, he would've—" I choked.

"He wouldn't have done a thing if you told me sooner. Thank God, he didn't leave you disfigured. Suppose having no weapon doesn't help."

"No, it doesn't,"

"Since Mikhail isn't here, come with me to the firing range. I have something to show you. Perhaps it could make you feel a little better," she offered, getting up from her seat and extending a feathered hand.

I took her hold. "Yeah, maybe so."

Coming down the gritty corridors of brick, we entered a separate room, a vast indoor playground surrounded by gray walls and weapon-tune stations. Just the two of us and a set of crimson targets lining the back, sectioned off by individual spaces. Although the place was empty, given how late it was, we went to the furthest end of the range.

"Having no firearm makes you an easy target anywhere you go," Aliya mentioned as she went to the steel lockers lining the sidewall.

"Kyran told me I haven't been here long enough to warrant one."

"That might be a regulation that the Reverences instilled for everyone, but you're at greater risk than anybody else."

"But what if I hurt somebody?"

"Any rookie is bound to make a slip. But you're no rookie."

"I don't know. What would Kyran say?"

As she opened her compartment to fetch her equipment, nervous tension and clammy sweat came to my hands. The same as the last dozen times we practiced together.

"I don't care if he thinks this is a mistake. This is necessary."

I stiffened. "You told him about our sessions?"

"He talks about you a lot, always concerned about you. But when I mentioned having a word with the Reverences about letting you open-carry, he turned very apprehensive. He might not want this for you, but this is my call. So do me a favor and take this. Call it a late Christmas present," she said, pulling out a small, articulate pistol. The weapon was impressive, made from "carbon fiber" as she told me, and built to her specifications. Plated on the slick black surface was the name of the standard issue, *HORNET.* "Here we are, a carbon copy of one of my favorite Pietas Militia classics. Now you no longer have to ask for mine, because you got your own genuine article. Treat that fine piece of metal well, amiga."

Aliya handed me the weapon and a magazine, both of which I held anxiously. When I brought it closer to inspect the details over again, like I did every time, such a lethal impact in a small design scared me.

"This is very generous of you, Aliya, but…do—do I really have to use this thing?" I strained, and to my dismay, she snickered.

"No, I'm afraid archery has been a long-outdated practice. Down here, gunpowder and a spark are your best friends. Here, put these on. Got to keep those ears of yours intact." Aliya reached into her pocket before giving me a pair of metallic earplugs. I wedged them into my canals, and while our conversation was maintained through the noise filters, the droning of steel lingered in my head.

"But still, why would someone make something so…terrible?" I asked, nervous as I gripped the man-made menace.

"Well nowadays, you need something terrible to fight the *more terrible.*" Her sad truth etched itself on my mind as I inspected the chamber of the weapon before I did anything else. Like she'd taught me, I made certain that the safety remained on while I loaded it carefully.

"What exactly were the Pietas Militia fighting off?"

"Before the outbreak, the old city military was always afraid of terrorism and outside forces to uproot the success here, so they made a plethora of weapons for every situation. Pistols, turrets, mechs…List goes on and on. Point is, the military is long gone, and now it's up to us to bring a little law to this hellscape with their special tools."

The sweat on my palms grew colder.

"Didn't think they'd go so far."

"Unfortunately, it's how we still have to live." Aliya's gaze reflected off the gunmetal. "Nearly every major settlement out there has an arsenal to keep themselves protected. For Reveria, Dr. Kutsuki collaborated with the Reverences to ensure our protection was of the utmost quality. Had he not been here, *anybody* would've found a way to undermine us."

"I thought he was just a scientist?"

"I'm about to sound like Beatrix, but there's a science in *everything*." She grinned. "Kutsuki's greatest work went into not only our wall, but our foundation, weaponry, and armor. He was our greatest legend to live."

To think one man could do so much for the hundreds here.

"He's clearly earned the recognition." I couldn't shake off the uneasy trembles. "Now that you bring all that up, the guns scare me kinda bad…I don't think I could ever use one in a real problem if anybody broke in."

"You're a quicker learner, Char. You've done a fine job at handling that gun, and you'll know how to solve any problem with ease. Just know *why* you're pulling that trigger. In this city, you'll need to learn all about your *right-hand man*. Let's get reacquainted with him," she encouraged me, and I became a little more secure once I made my stance at my target. I waited for Aliya to take her place, loading up her own HORNET.

We aimed and focused on our marks.

"Three…two…one!" she counted before we pulled our triggers. The crackling sound was voided out through the earplugs, but the feeling always left me frightened. Our bullets tore through the air and pierced our targets. Hers landed on the edge of the bull's eye, while mine was a little further away than intended. Almost had it.

"You're getting better," Aliya commented.

"Still not used to this thing. It's complicated,"

"I guess you really do miss your old bow," Aliya remarked as she prepared for another shot, and I followed along. My forehead grew hot just thinking about the fact I couldn't get back what belonged to me. The only real memento I had of Narissa, kept away.

"Every day," I muttered, counting. "One…two…three." We both fired, and she managed to reach her target's dead center, while my bullet scored the concrete wall in the further back.

My mistake didn't miss Aliya's impeccable sight.

"I know you must miss everything. Though you need to focus on what's happening now, not what's in the past," she told me as she readied her grip again, and I fidgeted. I could have never found composure like her, for she was so much stronger than me.

"Like how you did?"

"I learned to become who I was meant to be, but I will never forget where I came from. I chose a name for myself, and wasn't going to let anybody else decide on that," she stated, and the struggles she once told me about came to mind: her journey to discovering who she was.

"Wish I had the strength to be you. Your own woman. One who doesn't let others get the better of her," I confessed, and as she was about to count down, she leveled with me.

"Becoming a woman was hard, but now, I can be *Aliya.* Life's never easy, but you need to find your inner pride in who *you* are and use it like ammo for your future. Don't let your what-ifs soak your bullets."

Aliya had been through so much to become who she was now, and I needed to learn from her example. To be able to move forward and find the strength to deal with what was in front of me. But the yearning for the past was difficult to part with, connected to my very being.

"It's…hard, not to always want to go back to the life I once knew. I want to live it all over again." I readied myself again, and Aliya wanted to console me more. But as she observed me prepare, she braced for her third shot with me. We handled our grips tight.

"I understand where you're coming from, but you know that you can't dwell on what's been done. You can't go back to a past that's long gone." She drew a deep breath. "This is your new life now, and you should make the most of it, as you did with your old one."

Maybe she was right.

I had to find the ability to embrace what would come forward rather than lean toward the past, and I needed to face the paths that fate gave me. But I had to choose my road: take everything in stride or struggle to adapt? I focused on the red dot, and Aliya counted again.

"Three…" This was my new life.

"Two…" I wanted to keep turning back, but...

"One!" I needed to focus.

We took our shots, and simultaneously, they punched into the center of our marks. All the oxygen left my astonished body, and Aliya clicked her tongue in proud delight, throwing her fist into the air.

"There you go, sharpshooter! Let's keep that momentum up!"

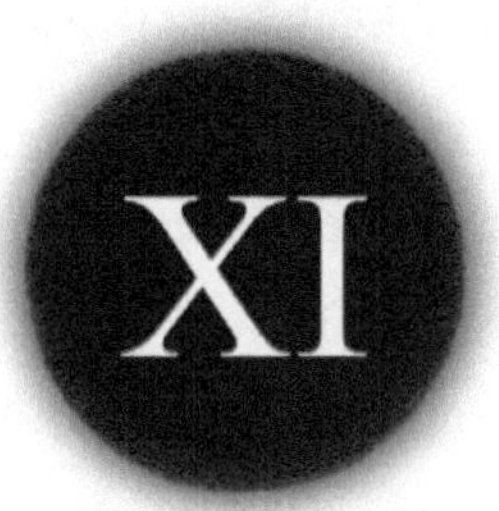

After much-needed time off, Aliya and I spent the rest of the evening emptying our magazines before she walked me back "home." She took me up to the same house I stayed in, and we peered briefly at the town of Reveria, pausing our conversation as we stared at all those lights and the people accompanying them.

A sight that I had grown to loathe, unfortunately.

"Well, this is your stop."

"Yeah, so it is," I replied, reaching for the concealed gun at my side. "I don't think I should really hold onto this."

"You need it more than you think. Just know when to use it. I promise you won't regret having it when the time comes."

"If you believe I can, then I suppose I will too," I huffed.

"Lighten up. Tomorrow we can do some more practice, maybe grab some elote after. Know a guy down at the plaza who makes the best out of that lab-grown corn. How's that sound?"

"Sounds great…thanks, Aliya." I humored that idea. Despite her rank and prominence in this town, I saw her as an equal I could confide in. When her smile grew wider, mine did as well, but not for long. "Actually, can I ask you something? There's just one thing I don't understand here."

Aliya rested an elbow on the rail, leaning in to lend me her attention. "What's going? You look worried."

I took hold of the metal beam, gazing at the jubilant crowd. For my months here, it made me question: "How come every day, you always keep your head up?"

"Well, I've got plenty of things to help keep it up. My career, the family that still loves me back home, and friends like you," she reasoned, but that didn't wipe off the frown that stuck to me.

"Sure, but…every day, you and these hybridians seem to live as if nothing terrible is happening just outside the town's walls. You all worry about what you'd rather eat, what you wear—you don't even need to wear clothes. Why focus on such little things but ignore the bigger problem?"

Aliya's gaze dropped.

"It's like what I told you back at the station; making the most of your current life." She too stared at the hundreds of innocent lives below. "If you have nothing worth holding onto, then there's no point in living, no matter where you are. There's a reason we all choose our own purpose, even when it seems like the end is bound to come."

I lifted my stare to her. "Because ignorance is bliss?"

She shook her head. "Without a purpose, we'd all become berserkers. You lose *yourself*, you lose your soul. People are afraid of them as much as they are of becoming one." Her eyes met mine. "These *little things*, like enjoying your favorite food, or wearing clothes that you love, are what make us still human. To you, this might all seem ordinary. Or perhaps simpleminded. But to everyone, this is their only way of keeping sane. To still be a little human in an unforgiving place."

"I see…" I mumbled. "Well, goodnight, Aliya."

She patted my back. "I know you've had a long day, but it'll get better from here. Nobody else is going to mess with you, so get some sleep for me, yeah? Hasta mañana." Aliya waved to me as she parted.

Was living for Narissa my only motivation?

It had to be more than that…it had to be.

Yet, I couldn't make the most of my new life if every day meant having no answers, and knowing my sister was still up there meant my prior life's purpose had been left to rot. The image haunted my thoughts. I shook away at the prospect as I approached the front door to my current *welcoming*, high-above-ground home. My hand went for the handle, but my inhibitions to turn it paused after hearing voices from the other side. Kyran and Bea's words were muffled through the metal.

I leaned in, ear to the cold steel.

"I am not doing this."

"Kyran, please, I made a promise to her."

"We gave her shelter, gave her a place here. Does she really need anything else?"

"Charissa's given me so much more than I imagined, and I owe it to her to fulfill my end of our deal. Just go to the downtown hospital and see what you can find. If the intel I received was true, there should be Ferecite activity there. We've both dealt with—"

"Bea, the Reverences would be outraged if I went off on a limb to meddle with our greatest threat."

"But—"

"But nothing! Some people have been talking about her, you know, and I can't help but think the same way. Think about it: why would a human come down *here* on purpose? What if I've been right all along?"

"Again with this, Kyran? Do you seriously still believe she's some spy for the Ferecite? She's shown no reason to warrant suspicion."

"Really? She sure does seem to try her best to appease everyone, snoops through our stuff like she's *curious*. Oh, and let's not forget what that gash she left in that berserker's skull. She's not exactly harmless."

"Now you're just being paranoid. You're trying to make something out of nothing. What has *he* been trying to tell you?"

"She's not as dull as she makes herself out to be. There's a good reason I made sure she never got her hands on that bow, or anything on that matter. All I know is that the rumors about her are spreading outside of town, and frankly, I'm terrified of what'll happen to us. I've been tired of playing pretend with her for the past few months now. So no, I am not risking my life for some girl's fake sob story of a dead sister!"

"Well how would you feel if you were in her position…?"

"Don't even try to—what would I even be looking for?"

"*Iris* said the Ferecite have been bringing some of their gatherings there. There's a possibility that Charissa's sister could be a victim."

"Even if you think Charissa's telling any bit of truth, she said—"

"Those fanatics don't just kill their prey outright. They find use for them, one way or another. Not trying to give you any ideas, but—I'll feel better if you can find anything."

"…You're seriously making me do this."

"Even if you don't find what I'm asking for, any information against the Ferecite is necessary. You understand that it'll be crucial for what I've got planned. If I'm going to make it happen, we need to commit."

"Fine, if that's the case, what else can you tell me?"

"*She* told me that a victim crawled from a seventh-story window. Plummeted. I'd imagine that's where the activity is coming from."

"…Okay, I'll look but won't make any promises. When's Charissa supposed to be home? Didn't she get off work a couple of hours ago?"

"I can't say. She's probably at Joelle's still."

"Well with how late it's getting, she should be here any minute. I'm going to get my gear ready and try to be out before that. But no matter what, don't let her know a thing. Alright?"

"…I won't say a word."

The hairs on my neck rose.

I'd accepted the fact that my sister was gone, but to hear that she could still be alive? In the hold of those demons? Trembles ran through my knees, and a wave of fire washed through my blood. Was this fear, rage, or a mesh of both? And not only that…

But these people I considered my friends only showed their true selves when I wasn't around. To think that Bea would undermine me about the true state of my sister, using me long enough to get what she wanted. But it was another thing to have someone like Kyran put on a false persona in order to make me complacent, to make me feel like I mattered to him. After all this time, I believed them with blind faith.

I couldn't calm myself, but I put on my normal face, preparing to head inside and confront this all at my own will. If neither Bea nor Kyran could be true to me, as Narissa couldn't, then the blind indignance that took control would have served better. Betrayed again, lied to again.

Not anymore.

I opened the door, walking in plain and nonchalantly. My arrival stunned Bea, but that caught-off-guard look on her face was quick to flip back to the soft and earnest one she'd always given me. For all I knew, that could've been part of her trickery.

Everyone's kindness could've contributed to a bigger deception.

"Oh, there you are! I was getting worried you might've forgotten the time again. Did something happen at work? Are you alright?" she asked.

"Fine, just decided to help Otto in his garage after my shift," I gave her my own deceit, and she gave into my lie with seamless belief.

"You know, your efforts really have been showing lately. The people here have been very thankful that you could be—"

"Have you heard anything yet today? Anything at all?" I interrupted, and the mentioning drew the gladness away from her face.

"Oh—I'm afraid that I haven't heard any news, but I'm still doing my best to relay with my contacts every day…I'm sorry," she told me, as she did nearly every time I confronted her.

"It's okay," I repeated the cycle, except this time, I saw through her. She would not so easily manipulate me like my sister.

No matter how much Bea had done for me, it was no excuse.

"I know it'd never make up for it, but I've been trying to discuss things with Kyran, and I think I convinced him to—"

Speaking of the devil, he came walking out of his room, draped in that white robe from our first meeting. Except this time, with my senses crystal clear, I saw that the mask of a porcelain swallowtail concealed his face. He bore the same automatic assault rifle in his grip as he did that fateful day, *TAIPAN* embellished its scale-like, beige gun metal.

"Charissa…I didn't expect you home so soon. You doing okay?" His falsely concerned words were barely muffled through the haunting guise, but I kept my silence. I continued the usual routine, digging into my pocket and tossing my bag of marbles on the coffee table.

"Oh, thanks. I'll be sure to get these deposited at the bank, but right now I have to go on a quick expedition. Don't worry, I'll be back in a bit," he said, passing me and somewhat distraught by my lack of response. He glanced at me before he left the front door. "Okay, what's going on? You're only the quiet type when you're reading."

I shook my head. "Just hope you make it back safe."

With an uncertain huff, he turned the knob. "Yeah, me too." Like that, he disappeared. With only me and Bea in the living room, the brief quietude held a noticeable weight.

"Charissa? You really don't seem like yourself tonight. You know you can tell me what's wrong." She loaned her ear, but what could I really tell to someone that'd withhold information from me?

"I think I just need to sleep; been a long day."

"Oh, I see. I was hoping we could stay up tonight. I decided to take the day off tomorrow, so I thought we'd make something special! I might not be a good cook like Kyran, but how about we whip up some 'banana pudding'…hm?" From her door, the lab coat on the hook buzzed. Bea rushed to fetch the radio, answering the signal. "Hello…? Wait, say that again…? Are you serious? Of course, absolutely, I'll be there right away!" She beamed, putting on the white cloth and quickly tying her hair back.

"What's the matter?" I asked.

"One of the closing scientists discovered something at the laboratories. Said it's so important I had to be there now. I'm going to see what's happening, but I wanted to make sure before I leave…" She draped her lanyard around her neck, fixing her uniform. "Are you okay staying home on your own for the evening? I won't be long."

For once, fate decided to shift the events in my favor.

"Sounds good; I'll be in bed anyway."

"Okay, but tomorrow morning, let's make it about us. No tests, none of that; just a day for relaxation and good times." She granted me another one of her soft smiles. "Sleep well, my friend."

Without wasting another second, Bea scurried out and left me by my lonesome. If she wasn't going to give me the peace I'd needed from day one, then it was up to me to find it myself. I went to her room, her space littered with notes on the walls and her office equipment cluttering my way in. If Kyran kept his disguise in his own quarters, the same had to be assumed for Bea. I was careful not to move any of her things, but adamant about finding what I needed. Resorting to the last place I'd look, I went under the bed, only to pull out a box. I peeled away the flaps and discovered the same white robe she once wore, as well as the porcelain mask of a tiger moth, a massive crack fissured through it leading to a jagged hole in one of the eyes. What had to be done to get such possessions from a twisted creature, I couldn't tell, but I'd seen the demons before.

I intended to exact my vengeance.

Stealing the disguise, I hurried to my room, got my old backpack, and stuffed the robe and mask within. I only wished I had more time to prepare a rather hasty plan, but this once-in-a-lifetime shot could not be missed. I gathered everything, bracing myself for what possibly awaited beyond the town gates. But how I'd get past them was yet unconsidered.

Locking the door and closing it shut, I left the house, keeping watch for anybody passing by. With it nearing midnight, not many wandered the bridges or streets, encouraging me to move forward. I made haste from the railways, hurrying down the flights of stairs and ignoring anybody who tried to get my attention. Never had I been so motivated, nor driven by my own blinded temper, even more than when running away from my old, true home.

Past the houses, plaza, and community buildings, I took the time to hide away in an isolated alleyway. Fishing out the robe and mask, I put them on, concealing my body head-to-toe in a veil of white. I might've not stood the same height as Bea, but from knowing her for the past few months, I could find my way around. Once I was finished getting ready, I stepped out once more, making my way to the point of no return.

Ahead stood a massive gate, supported by a tall steel border, circuitry tethered to the diamond frames covering the construct. Next to the gate stood two guards in leather armor, holding rifles with their senses on high alert. They bore canine features, resembling stray dogs that had seen the worst that life had to offer. Mustering a false confidence, I stepped up, doing my best to pass through without trouble, but the guards lifted their brows as well as their guns.

"Bea? Looks like you've lost some inches since the last time I saw you," the Alsatian shepherd joked, and the sweat pooled in my boots.

"Hrm." I choked on the spot.

"Quit it. She's been working hard at the labs day and night. Clearly, she's having back troubles," the pitbull mentioned, directing his focus to me. "Your brother didn't leave long ago; you should still be able to catch up to him," he said, and I nodded his way.

"Hm, guess you got a point…alright." The brown-furred dog slammed his fist to the gate. In seconds, the heavy masses of metal creaked and slowly parted to show what was beyond the barrier of the town.

"Kyran said he was going to do this thing of his solo, but I'm glad you're deciding to watch his back. Keep him safe, Bea."

Without a word, I passed them and the gigantic gates. As my scent wafted through, the shepherd sniffed at the air, stopping me in my tracks. "Just a sec. Your tail between your legs or something?"

Shit.

I stood there, unable to make an excuse. The only saving grace was the pitbull bumping shoulders with his fellow guard. "If you had a human living in your house, you'd smell different too. And for Christ's sake, she's scared for her brother, can you blame her? Those damn *scavengers* have been going around more than usual. You'd feel the same if—"

With that, the shepherd backed down.

"I get it." He turned to me. "Whatever you do, just bring him back in one piece. You two know your way around Misera best, but still, never know who or what you'll find out in that damned city, especially right now. Good luck." the full-coated dog finished, slamming the gates again.

They withdrew into the city limits, and the masses of metal closed once more. I was safe from suspicion, but no longer was I safe from the desolation that haunted the metropolis. Beyond the salvation of Reveria, abandoned homes with crumbling walls formed a shattered wake, leaving an ocean of broken debris and rubble in the vast graveyard. The streets that lined the neighborhood went downhill, going forth into the distance toward that same unnerving smog that obscured everything ahead.

The buildings of the broken city called to me. My veins constricted as I became immersed in its false, hollow atmosphere. A shattered oasis with no hope, no future, no redemption. As the lamb here…should I stay with these wolves, or fight the bears out there? No, turning back wasn't an option for me, not when I'd already gotten this far. The crumble and ash on the street were marked with Kyran's boot-prints, leading out towards the subterranean wasteland, illuminated by dying lights.

Here I come.

***

The humid, feculent air clung to me as I followed Kyran's trail, exactly as when I first came here. The streetlights offered little solace, for they only signified the industrial decay. Broken walls of building materials collapsed on the fissured roads and sidewalks; such destruction couldn't match the dread that lingered in the darkest shadows. With every step, I found more cries for help written on the structures that were left unanswered. The many constructs that once stood so proudly were now shells of lost history, left as mortal reminders of those who suffered the fate of this city. But this drive of mine suppressed my fear. I was alert, and determination kept me going despite my self-preservatory instincts.

As I continued to tread among the treacherous streets, tracking each fading footstep, it occurred to me that I was now preying on Kyran, reversing our roles. Far ahead, he was the size of a little ant, taking his stride without fear. He had been here all his life, and he probably faced the worst of it all. I could not have envisioned that he ever lived his life afraid. Not when he'd faced atrocities since birth.

But I saw his every flaw.

Ever since I knew him, I understood his patterns. Always looking over his shoulder, knowing he was being watched. I hid in the shadows at every instance, him being none of the wiser. I'd get what I needed.

Coming close to the street intersection, my body stood still. For what reason, I didn't know. The answer pattered to my ears. Bare paw-pads to the concrete, erratic and approaching. The sounds came from my right coming straight in my direction. Unable to turn back or move ahead, I hid around the street corner's building, waiting to see what'd come my way, hoping to evade it.

With the sprinting came screaming.

"Help! Somebody help me!"

Danger. Taking what little control of my body I could in the tension of the moment, I peered past the concrete inches from my face. In the distance came a flighty catman in tattered, unkept clothes, clinging to a broken arm. Despite his frantic nature, he couldn't have been a berserker.

"No! No! Stay away!"

In the distant shadows, another figure ran after the fleeing feline. The stranger reeled back, only to throw an object. Swirling right for the crying man came a bola of razor-lined tethers. Another series of yelps escaped the helpless victim once he became entangled in the crude snare, dropping him to the ground and unable to break free of the restraints.

The assailant approached their captured prey, coming in view underneath the nearby street pole. From head to toe, black garments dressed the figure, adorned with plucked, bloodied feathers. Face covered in rags, the only distinguishable features were the spotted tail that followed the marauder, as well as the feminine voice that came through.

"If only you'd fucking listen to me the first time. Hurts, doesn't it?"

"I didn't do anything to you…Why me?"

Boot pressed to his back, the woman ground her heel to his spine, making him writhe in further agony. "Because you'd make for better merchandise. Try anything again, and I can make this so much worse."

In his struggle, he lifted his head, welling eyes spotting me.

"Y-You! Help! Help me, I'm begging you!"

By instinct, I dipped my head away from sight and solidified to the wall. A moment of silence passed until a loud crack of a gun followed. A bullet zipped past, hitting the walk sign. Breath at a standstill, I clung to the wall behind me once those daunting footsteps neared the corner.

"I know you're there. I can smell you. You're scared."

Silent, my eyes shut tight. The crunch of her boots came closer, and once she caught me, there's no telling what'd happen next.

"Aha!"

I flinched, another gunshot cracking the dying air. With that came a bloodcurdling cry from the catman. "A-Agh! I-I can't feel my leg!!"

The feather-covered female stomped away from my vicinity. "You think you'd be slick, trying to worm away while I'm not looking? Let's go."

Daring not to look again, the wails of the pitiful were enough to paint the scene. The dragging of a body, the razors that scraped across the asphalt, the remorse in my chest ran rampant. I couldn't do anything.

"D-Do something please! D-Don't let her take me! Please! Please!"

His wails faded in the distance, as did the tension in my ribcage. The volition in my heart overtook whatever regrets tried to tear their way in.

I had to move forward.

Picking up back on Kyran's trail, an hour passed. Cautious in my steps, he led me right where I wanted. *The Miriana Memorial Hospital.*

The power still buzzed within the seven-story building, its rows of windows either draped with curtains or broken out. The flickering light poles revealed the parking lot, reduced to a cemetery littered with mechanical and hybridian remains alike. Some were skeletonized, and some were fresh, instilling the danger of what was contained ahead. Dead bushes and trees lined the hospital's outer walls, a circle of twig husks. Near the front entrance, Kyran ignored the warning signs, evading the large vehicles with *MMH Ambulance* painted on their sides.

Fragments of the lost could not sway me, for I walked through the lot with nothing but unstoppable intent. Past the fallen doors of the hospital, silent in my approach, I entered the dead lobby. Empty chairs were knocked and abandoned weapons were scattered all around the dirty floor, the television screens on the supporting columns smashed in. Ahead, there were two hallways on either side of the front counter, possibly leading into the inner sanctum of the hospital. In the center of the waiting lounge, a defaced statue was fixed to the floor. An angel welcomed me, bowing her head with sleeping eyes and clasped hands. Grime covered the intricate crevices, as did scratch marks and deliberate cracks. On the stand where the winged girl rested in heavenly peace, words of remembrance were chiseled in its crumbling stone.

To my daughter whose fire faded too soon.
May God give her a future of rest in heaven.
As I dedicate this place of healing to her name.
Let her light be found here in Pietas once more.
To Miriana, my only beloved child, I love you.

\-   Yarilo Borisyuk

There was something else behind the podium. Glowing paint smeared to form an ominous symbol. An eyeball, with flower petals blooming from its center. The soft violet it emitted gave me the suspicion that beyond this point lay imminent danger. But I cared not for what was ahead. I wouldn't leave here without the peace of knowing if Narissa's murder proved true, or if hope still lingered.

Footsteps echoed from the right passage.

Peering from around the corner, Kyran made his way to a metal door at the far end of the hall. Once he went in, I crept out. Along the way, I passed by a number of rickety doors, most of which were closed. Of the few that were open, disasters lay within: collapsed hospital beds and advanced medical equipment broken to smithereens. Many were etched with the remains of victims, from intact skeletons to dismembered parts, or mere splatters of bodily fluids. The numbers on the doors marked each personal torture chamber.

Caring not to see anymore, I hurried to match Kyran's fast pace. Making it to the stairwell, I headed inside. Holding onto the guardrail, I ascended, an unsettling bleakness swallowing the heights above. The cacophony of steel moans resonating throughout could not drive me away, and instead, I sought relief in the fluorescent lights that beamed above each door with its designated level number. It was a long haul until I discovered the cold door that led to my destination.

LEVEL 7 / Birth Center & Maternity Services

I walked inside, finding myself in the right place. Wandering the halls, keeping an ear out for any noise. A creak came. Peering around the corner, a set of doors swung back and forth. Kyran must've been in there. Sneaking along the wall, I went inside, the desks amess with lab equipment. Milk bottles, empty little beds with newborn names, and more computers accompanied every station.

The panther was nowhere to be seen.

Stepping into the faint darkness, I searched for him, but didn't see a trace. The steam from my breath fogged the mask. Uncertain where he could've gone, I tempted myself to turn and leave. That was snuffed once a pair of hands grabbed my arms, pulling me back. A gasp escaped my throat, as I was brought into the shadows. When I was forced around, my hood came off as my guise slid to the side.

Kyran caught me in a broken leer.

"I knew something was following me. I just didn't want to think that it was really you," he yanked me closer. "Should've known this was all part of your plan. You finally decided to take me out, huh? Knew those fanatics would be here so that you could corner me into this trap?"

He had nowhere else to go.

"I'm here because you and Bea know something I didn't. My sister isn't dead, is she? You can't hide anything else from me."

"Just stop. It's over." he let me go, fist clenched to his weapon. "I truly wanted to believe you, but now that you're here…you almost played me a fool like everyone else. You might've convinced them all, even my own sister with your sad story and that innocent little act you had, but I would've never bought it. You can't deceive me."

The glow in his eyes dimmed. My own stare tensed.

"Don't think you're any different. You played me the whole time, and I was stupid enough to think you really cared. That you were my friend. Now that I know what you truly are, you can't hide anymore."

A short, shuddering breath left him. Gritting his teeth, he pressed the barrel of his gun to my chest. "I never wanted it to come to this."

The air from my chest drew still. "What are you doing?"

His grip couldn't keep straight, his shaky eyes clinging to my own. That finger edged closer to the trigger. "Give me one good reason why I shouldn't kill you, because there's no way I'm letting you kill me. I have people to live for now, and someone that still needs me. And I need *her.*"

…Did *I* have much other reason, than for Narissa? Was she the only thing that truly kept me going? He was going to kill me, and I couldn't stop him. To some degree, I almost hoped he…

"I—"

From outside, a cry clamored the hall. We both drew our focus to the wails as the cries came closer to the doors. Kyran withdrew me in the darkest corner, covering my maw with a clawed mitt as someone barreled into the room with us and crawled under a desk.

"Don't come in here, don't come in here, don't come in here…" The cowering hare spoke, and even in the dark, he bore the twisted deformities of a berserker. Tumors bloated his body, his wide eyes flooded with bleeding tears, and his blistered lips foamed. "Not me…anybody but me."

Kyran and I froze in our places, watching the man struggle to remain still. From outside again, clicking and crawling seeped through the air. As it drew closer, it cast shadows through the window. In that instant, goosebumps riddled my skin. That feeling. It was unforgettable.

The doors slammed open, and two Ferecite cultists crept in. Despite their angelic veils, the foul stench of decay and their domineering presence flooded the room. It didn't take them long for them to seek their victim, crawling under the desk and clamping a jagged claw on the lapine male's ankle, snapping his bone.

"No! No! You can't *feed* me to it! I'll do anything, please!" he pleaded, the abominations dragging him out. The claws of the hare screaked the tile floor as his helpless cries shattered the hallway, only to fade away.

Kyran let go of my face.

"We can't stay here," he told me, taking hold of my arm. He dragged me off to peer into the door windows, seeing nothing. When the coast was clear, he tried to sneak us out, but I yanked away.

The way that stranger wept…it was so human.

"We can't let them do this. We have to help him."

"Trust me, if we could, we would…but he's gone berserk now. We can't do anything for him. He's long gone."

But if that wasn't enough to convince him, I had to know one thing for certain. "Then I'm not leaving until I know if they had my sister. I'd rather learn she was killed than to be *fed* to…I don't even know,"

Despite everything he believed…Kyran, for once, gave me a sincere chance. "Just stay behind me," he demanded, keeping close to the desperate claw marks and the slime trail streaking the hall.

We erred on the side of caution, keeping close to the walls as we edged the corner. Turning it, we were left perturbed by the distinct, meaty growth crawling through the hall. The fermented biomass dripped in rancid juices, fouling what little oxygen there was. Not letting the crawling, clinging flesh deter us, Kyran and I pursued the source of the widespread rot. The closer we got to the end of the infested hallway, the more a repulsive tingle lingered in my body.

Neonatal Intensive Care Unit

We approached the twin, grimy doors closed tight. With the lack of a knob or keypad, it was unclear how it could be breached. Our worries grew tenfold as the screams of the hare pierced the steel.

"There has to be a way in. We need to hurry."

"I'm going get us in, just hold on." He dropped his gun, digging his fingers into the mushy seam.

"What're you trying to do?" I hounded.

"A door's whole job is to open…so do your damn job!" He gritted his teeth, forcing the metal apart. Strings of fleshy matter stretched between the doors. With his claws tainted in gunk, he wiped it off like it was nothing, picking up his assault rifle and taking aim at whatever lay within the dark, murky chamber. Flashing on his tactical light, he illuminated the humid room—and its unimaginable horrors.

Every inch of the space was drenched in creeping, organic matter, squelching as the light cast on its gloss. As Kyran shone the light around, the fresh remains and severed parts of creatures meshed with the ever-present decay, as if the room itself was barely alive, nauseating me. At the back of it all, I witnessed the twin cultists gripping the struggling hare as they forced it down into the gullet of a hellish atrocity.

A giant, pulping mass of flesh, an amalgamation of arms and legs, with different bodies all entwined into one being. The face of a mutt, the head of a gecko, and even the mien of a sheep. So many mouths, noses, and eyes. The blob of oozing meat groaned as it caught sight of its unwelcome visitors, but it didn't stop consuming its latest offering, whole and alive, gurgling as it did so.

"No! N-No, I don't want to die!" were the last words the hare could fathom, only to be inevitably digested, becoming one with the coagulation.

When the cultists spotted us, their crustaceous bodies clicked in disarray, fading into a white mist. We were now left alone with the insatiable hunger that gargled at us with its gaping maw. As its body pulsed, so did my vessels, my limbs shuddering to their rhythm. If what Bea mentioned might've been true, could it have been…

My sister, connecting to me?

"Narissa…?" I muttered.

The howls of a thousand beasts roared, and with a restless vigor, it tore itself from the wall it was attached to, using its many claws, limbs, and tendrils to come for us. In its fit of rage, an intense pressure crept over my skull as my stomach twisted in a gordian knot.

This thing…it had no trace of her.

"Angels above!" I shouted.

Kyran's grip faltered, his breath struggling to sputter out. His brave front met its limit. "Run like hell!" he yelled, throwing me out into the hallway, lunging by my side. I shook off the tension and sprinted as the palpitating vessel slurped out from its chamber and for the back of our necks. The force in my head strained my brain.

"Don't stop! We can't let that thing get us!" he screamed.

As we headed for the stairwell, Kyran slammed to the grimy floor, his gun flailing from his grip as a violent yelp escaped him. One of the creature's vile cords slung to his ankle, dragging him away. The jaguar kicked, digging his desperate claws into the floor, but even with his size and strength, it was no match for the abomination.

"Sh-Shit! I can't!" He tried to resist its pull. "I-I can't…!"

My conscience had to act.

Whipping the HORNET from my cloak, I aimed, but…my hold jittered as the panther came to the edge of death. The gun rattled; my arm struggled to keep straight. *Something* within me wanted this to happen, like my internal drive refused to let me act.

My body couldn't allow it.

"Grrah!" He screeched out as his foot slurped into that mushy mass. In seconds, he'd be fed. In my hesitance, the fear in those amber eyes cut straight through me. In his silent plea for mercy, it was like his soul touched mine. *Don't let me die.*

I could never forgive him, but it wasn't my right to let this man's fire fade. Putting all qualms aside, everything in my instincts ignited. Aliya helped me find the reason to put my finger on the trigger. He once saved my life, and I had to save his. No more resistance.

I tore away these internal forces.

With my aim in a nervous shake, I fired my shots. The devourer's size sponged up my sporadic bullets. Smoke left the barrel as the magazine clicked and emptied in quick succession. 9mms of copper soared through the decaying haze as each one pierced through all that meat and mass. The creature unwrapped its tendril from Kyran's leg, spitting him out. It screeched in agony, and the pain it felt…it soaked me.

I screamed at the sensation, like needles swimming through my veins. Head pounding, the teeth-gritting feeling was excruciating, otherworldly. My balance nearly stumbled. But through the pain, before the window could close, I rushed, stretching my arm out to the jaguar as he struggled to get up.

"Ch-Charissa…?"

As I was about to grab his hand, the sentient mass flailed, thrashing itself against the walls as its wounds sputtered out with white larvae. The integrity of the hallway gave in. Cracks formed everywhere, and the floor beneath collapsed. The heinous monstrosity plummeted, and as it succumbed, the needles in my bloodstream disappeared. Yet as the tiles all crumbled, they fell apart under Kyran, and he joined the beast. Desperate, I reached out for him, and even when I barely managed to get a hold of his hand…his glove slipped in my grasp.

He faded, out of my sight. Kyran was gone.

Unable to save him, I scrambled to escape before I too fell. Rushing into the stairwell, I scampered down the flights, clenching the rails as I fled for my life. I did not look back as debris and chunks showered above. As the entire hospital began to lose itself, my own blood pumped faster than ever.

I returned to the first level, down the hallways, and into the lobby. I couldn't stop sprinting, desperate to make it out of the parking lot with my life. Every fiber in my muscles screamed while the entire building crumbled, all once-proud seven stories falling to smithereens. Misera howled as one of its grand constructs became dust.

This weakness would haunt me forever.

***

Aimlessly, I kept running, empty gun in my hand. The bleak hues of the streets became even more desaturated as I trespassed among the architectural husks and the corpses slumped beside them, deprived of sane life and thought. The city's stench forever engraved itself into my sinuses, with the scent of decay infesting the bare semblance of oxygen. The longer I sprinted through the desolate avenues, the sinking actuality of despair crawled into my flesh. Misera defiled my spirits as I was exposed to her streets, and the only solace I could find was in hiding.

Streetside stores gaped open to tempt travelers along the way, left to unfixable disarray, with the insides ransacked for nearly anything usable. So many desecrated venues. High-end fashion boutiques, titanium jewelry departments, and electronic shops. At the corner, there was a primitive sort of restaurant. "Retro," as people in Reveria would call it. The fluorescent bulbs coursing along the windows and signs were long-busted, and *Deanna's Diner* had lost all its color and charm.

It lured me in.

Through the shattered door, torn-open red leather seats accompanied the grimy, checkerboard tables. Far ahead in the lobby was a jukebox, and a ruined bar lined with cushioned stools. There was even a whole kitchen in the back, with ticket orders pasted along the open window and plates of moldy food on the edge of the sill. I cared not for the smell, nor disgusting atmosphere as I crawled underneath one of the booth tables, balling myself up, gasping for air. Pathetic of me, perhaps, but I could only handle so much. Tearing the mask from the side of my head, I clenched my eyes, trying not to cry after what I just witnessed. Kyran's death was now on my hands. First Narissa, and now him…

Was I a walking omen?

Though I was tempted to go back to Reveria, that seemed impossible. Even after all the disdain I had for that town, it was my one place of safety—but I had thrown it all away, just like my old life. Leaving in secret, going against everybody's wishes, and being the reason one of their most resilient Virtues was dead.

His glove was still in my possession. Bringing it from my pocket, I saw his name stitched into the thin black leather belt around the wrist. Funny how little things like that seemed negligible at first, only to become the most memorable details. How I wished I could've done better, but now, this was all I had left. Slipping it on my own hand, I tightened the mesh glove to fit.

I was alone again.

Drawing myself from below, I seated myself at the booth. Untying my bow, I held the cloth over my face, wiping away the sweat and muck, balling it up, and stashing it in my pocket. I peered outside, beyond the dusty, broken fragments still attached to the window, and kept wondering what I was going to do. Being alone had already given me nothing but paranoia, leading to chitters constantly resonating in my ears. That same crawling sensation shivered through me again.

Did that *creature* follow me? Did it somehow live out of spite, just to consume me? All of it sank in again.

A cockroach scuttled across the table. I slammed my fist. The dishes on the table rattled to the impact, and the bang rumbled throughout the little diner. I couldn't live with this guilt.

I had to go back to him.

Despite all the mistrust, he was right. He had people to live for, a purpose, unlike me.

I didn't even know if my sister was dead or alive, but it amounted to nothing at that moment. I had to redeem myself, and to be rid of the culpability that'd otherwise torment me for my waking moments. I needed to see if Kyran was truly dead.

Clink! Clank! Clack! Noises came from the kitchen.

My heart stopped beating, and my fight or flight kicked in, screaming at me to flee the scene, but my fear left me fixated on my seat.

"Who's there!? A customer? Shit—shit! We haven't had one in years! Deanna, get out there and give them a fresh mug!"

Yells and coughs came from the inside of the dark kitchen, and it sounded like an older man with a wheezy voice.

Someone had been there the whole time.

"Deanna! Deanna! Oh, you good-for-nothing—fine then, make me do all the work! I'll bring it to 'em myself."

The kitchen door creaked open. Flies buzzed from within, a lanky figure lurking in the shadows. A weathered man with the face of an opossum. Grime covered his body, while his naked tail layered in scabs and pus-ridden wounds dragged across the messy floor. Boils and burn marks scarred his arms, with an apron, pants, and hat draped over his bare-boned body. Roaches crawled from underneath the fabric, but he did not even care. With a malformed face, his jaw barely held together below bag-draped eyes that sank into his skull. There was nothing but black in his gaze. He wheezed a bit as he stepped over, a mug in his hand and a pot of coffee in the other. The tar-like substance clung to the murky glass. He gave me a genuine smile, exposing his sharp teeth as drool puddled from his sore, festering lips.

"Ah, it is so nice to see someone finally…anyone…come into my diner, eager for a breakfast they could never forget! Make yourself comfortable, miss!" he gurgled, rumbling my eardrums. "Mmmmmh, it smells heavenly, don't it? Freshly brewed in the pot. We always welcome our guests with a fresh cup on the house. Lemme know if you'd like any cream and sugar!" He stepped right up to the booth I sat in and poured me a mug. The black substance within the carafe slugged down into the cup until it splatted to the bottom. The "coffee" curdled, steaming with a sour, stomach-churning smell.

"I can tell from the way yer looking at it, you definitely prefer your coffee black! If that's so, what can the chef cook up for ya this morning? Chocolate pancakes? Good ole' fashioned bacon n' eggs? You name it, sweetheart, and I'll whip it up!" He hunched over the table, one hand planted next to the mug while the other gripped my seat. His jagged, unkempt nails dug into the leather, and a couple of roaches crawled from his sleeve and right next to my shoulders.

I had to play along.

I eyed the menu that was encrusted into the table, pointing a finger toward one of the specialties without thought. He glossed over the selection and gave a coarse chuckle.

"Listen, lil' lady. Yer gonna have to tell me. These old eyes aren't like what they used to be. So y'know, make my life a bit easier for me…say whatcha want," he spoke, chattering his teeth.

I physically couldn't say anything to him.

"Say it, you twit!"

He slammed his fist onto the table, causing it to rattle loud and heavy, nearly breaking from the metal stand below. I flinched and tried my best to hold back from crumbling, glazing over the menu again and muttering out the first thing my eyes darted to.

"B-Blueberry muffin, please."

I said what I "wanted," and he gave me a cheery laugh, stepping back. "Oh, excellent choice, missy. We just made a fresh batch not long ago. You're going to love this, I assure you. Be right back with your lil' treat!" he cheered, erratically making his way back towards the kitchen, and despite my breaking point, I was still on the impulse to escape.

About to take that chance, he shot it down fast.

"And don't you *dare* leave. No no. I haven't had business in a long time. This is the comeback I need! Do not ruin this for me! This restaurant is my dream! My life!" He waved his finger and glared at me before going back into the kitchen to get what I "ordered."

I could not stay any longer.

When the coast was relatively clear, I turned to the window, seeing how I should have dealt with the large fragments of glass still panned to the frame. Should I have kicked the remaining slabs of glass out so I could make my escape, or discreetly leave through the entrance? In my predicament, I hesitated again. Before I could take my opportunity to leave, shuffling feet scattered behind me. I quickly seated myself as I turned to face the far-gone man, holding a black… "Muffin," covered in an unpleasantly green fungus speckled with the rotten eyes of rats. He had the most crooked smile on his face, his bleeding gums on full display. He did not catch on to my plan to escape, but I had to keep playing pretend.

"Here we are, ma'am. A fresh one!"

He moseyed over while I had my hands folded over the dirty surface. I played my part, trying to be a polite "customer," but my anxious smile held a tremendous weight as he stared me down. He placed the inedible muffin right in front of me, and my grin grew wider, along with the terror.

"My beautiful wife makes these herself. She hasn't seen another lady in a long while. I'm sure she'd be delighted to meet ya. Ohoho, I bet you two would love to do girl talk." He cackled, but managing to notice the pile of dirty dishes on my table, he grumbled under his breath. "Grr…I was so pleased to make your acquaintance; I didn't even see this mess! My thick-skulled busboy's on break, that oaf. I'm so sorry about that! Lemme get these out your way."

His greasy, slender arms reached and gathered the nearby plates. The fetid smell so horrid that my lungs shrank, but I kept that saccharine smile up. When he faced me, giving me his biggest grin, it shifted once he noticed something else was off.

A tear trickled down my face.

"What's the matter, sweetness?" he asked, and I tried to be inconspicuous. I smiled even wider, even showing my teeth.

"Nothing, sir." I gave my soft answer.

He squinted before he stood up "straight" with the plates in his hands. Averting his gaze to the muffin and coffee, it went back to me, and he refused to blink. "...Go on. Enjoy."

I didn't move...he did not either. I had to make an excuse.

"I get nervous eating in front of people."

My answer did not make him budge. His grip on the dishes grew tighter and shakier. The plates rattled violently in his hands, as if he was tempted to throw them at me, but he calmed down, snickering it off. "Heehee…well, don't let me scare ya off now! I'll just–"

His scarred ears perked, and he turned his shoulder. More crawling…only to be followed by painful groans. Past him was yet another horror of the madness. Some*one* crawled on the checkerboard floor—a jittery monster, practically skin and bones. He whimpered, dragging himself from the kitchen and through the muck. The wailing victim was a sheepbeast with gray fur, more horrendously burned than the man only a few feet away from me. Underneath his clothes, his body was scrawny and weak. Rope burns covered his palms, while his hooved fingers and horns were scuffed. Through that mop of long and messy hair, riddled with bits of char and dead bugs, I could see past those strands and into those oblong pupils, desperate for help as they quivered. Despite his injuries, there was sanity in his stare.

He couldn't have been berserk.

The sheepman glanced at the chef, only to see the door. Immediately, the victim went into a frantic spiral as he attempted to escape for the entrance. Before he could get close, the chef bombarded him with the dishes. The frail man cried out for every filthy plate that struck him, writhing as his bones cracked under the onslaught. Once the barrage of ceramics stopped, I saw that gashes now adorned the incapacitated lamb, his pale flesh showing through. He balled up and covered his head with frail, fidgety hands.

"What the hell did I tell you! I told you to stay in the back! You're supposed to be on break!" the chef yelled.

My opportunity struck.

I kicked the rest of the glass out of the window, and the impact caused the whole frame to lose its structure, the noise loud enough to resonate inside the diner and to the outside. The risk could cost me my life, but I had to get out.

Now.

"What the hell! What was that?" the opossum screamed, and unthinkingly I glimpsed back at him, about to get his mitts onto me. "You! You're gonna have to pay for that!" he raged at the top of his lungs, and it struck me.

The coffee.

I grabbed it in a hurry and hurled it. The mug broke on his forehead, and the tar-like substance splattered on his malformed face, with the coffee scalding his flesh until a visceral screech erupted from his putrid maw. "It burns! It burns!" He staggered, clenching his tearful, sunken sockets as his skin seared like melting butter on a hot skillet.

I leaped out of the window, careful not to slide on any of the broken glass on the sidewalk as I bolted. I managed to get a head start, but the marsupial came barreling out behind me. Stomping on the pavement, his face sizzled with more gnarly blisters and burns, disfiguring his already unrecognizable features. Engulfed in a bloodthirsty rage, he did not let up. I kept running as fast as I could, but soon he would catch up. "You dirty little dasher! Get back here!"

The corner of the street came closer, and I dipped around the corner. With my fleeting time, I hid behind the brick wall until his pattering neared. "Where do you think you're going!? Don't you—"

The opossum managed to turn my way, and I stuck my foot out. In his stumble, he slammed head-first into the concrete. His entire body fidgeted until it went limp, and a wheeze hissed out of him.

He was dead. *I* killed him.

That guilt cored into me again. Comprehension of my sins washed over me as he lay there lifeless. Leaning over his corpse, I checked to make sure he was truly gone. If my sin was truly substantiated.

His scab-ridden tail coiled around my skull, trying to crack my head open. I gasped as the slippery pressure was on the verge of crushing me. "Y'think you can rob me!? I don't think so, missy! Hold still while I crack ya like an egg!" He violently thrashed, attempting to throw me off. Hands clenching to his tail, the grease on his skin made it impossible to pry away. Fissures were about to form in my cranium, the mask to my side crackling to the force, I feared my next breath would be my last.

Misera would make me one of her own.

He tried to clench onto my head tighter, but his strength ceased. The crunch of bone tore through the air, as did a series of gurgles. Once that grease-ridden tail fell from view, I saw that the marsupial's skull had smashed into bits and pieces, brains running like orange yolk. A clawed, steeled foot dug into the mash of flesh, belonging to the most gruesome woman imaginable. Her shadow cast me, and I took her in. Bearing rusted armor and armed to the teeth with belts of ammunition, she wasn't berserk. No, far more threatening. I scrambled to the concrete, cowering before her.

The stranger stared at me, bewildered by what she saw.

"Kakogo cherta?" she spoke. Her words made no sense.

As she stood there, I crawled back, trying to keep my distance. Shaky eyes on her, fearful that I'd be next. The battle scars and light machine gun in her sharp-clawed grip ensured that my rate of survival dropped to the single digits.

"St-Stay back…I'll– I'll…" I whimpered to her.

She approached me, the scratching of metal coming from below as blood grazed in her trail. Up to her hip, she had a leg comprised of mechanisms engineered and mended seamlessly with her flesh. The machinery creaked as she came into clear view of the streetlight. An older woman: half polar bear, half machine, entirely ruthless. Sporting muscles on her strong bones, she was a tank. "Zdravstvuyte. What're you doing out here?"

Once she leaned down to my level, I couldn't talk back. She could have easily torn me apart if she wanted to, and I submissively tried to appeal to any hint of mercy she could give.

If she had *any* at all.

"H-He was going to kill me, I swear. I wasn't trying to—"

"Bah, don't cry. You didn't die, so why so sad?"

Her stern nature took me by surprise.

"I don't want any trouble."

She reached for my cloak and the moth mask that still hung around my neck, and like the concrete sidewalk, I stilled to her touch.

"Wearing this costume? You're trouble walking. How'd you get it?"

"I found it. I was hoping it'd keep me safe." I fretted with her.

"Pfft. You are nothing like *Blessed*. Too small, too frail. You couldn't convince a mouse." The polar bear chuckled, letting go of the bloody white veil. "You're the human from Reveria, no?"

"You...know who I am?"

"Hard not to. Everyone in this city has heard of you. The question is: what brings the likes of you down to these parts? It's not safe to walk these streets alone. Don't you know what'd happen to someone like *you?*"

"I'm from the surface. I came down here on my own, hoping to figure things out."

"Well, that was a very unintelligent thing to do."

"Yes, well, I left Reveria not long ago. I've got nowhere else to go."

Lifting her head to the empty sky and squinting, she hummed as she entertained my unbelievable story. "Devushka, what's your name?"

"Charissa. That's who I am," I stated, wary of her next move.

"Okay Charissa, you twisted my arm. I have space for you. Let me take you back with me."

This had to have been some kind of trap. After my experience with everyone, and *everything* I had previously met, I averted my eyes.

"I think I'm better off–"

Before she allowed me to say anything more, she grasped my forearm and dragged me away. "Nyet, I insist! Let's go now!"

The polar bear was eager to take me elsewhere, despite my evident refusal. I struggled in her fearsome grip, but her strength was threateningly strong. If I kept up my resistance, the results would not be pretty. I stopped trying and stumbled behind her as she led me through the sidewalks, all while she held her LMG to her shoulder.

"Where are you taking me? Who are you?"

The polar bear escorted me through the perils of the atrocious roads. In her presence, the streets were emptier. "Oksana Garina. I will take you back to my *home*."

My steps clammy, she took me away to who-knows-where. Was she going to take me someplace where nobody would hear me scream, or was it going to be far worse than that?

I would have to live to find that out.

Oksana brought me somewhere deeper into the center of the city grounds, downtown: a death sentence. My blood pumped with dread as she dragged me towards my final destination.

Doric columns kept the stone and gravel structure proud and tall. The shades of once-clean white on its exterior were stained with decades of desolation, showing how this was yet another relic turned into a casualty of Misera's relentless tragedies. Despite the visible damage it suffered, the foundation still managed to hold itself together with its durable walls and firm infrastructure. The building stood two stories tall and centered to the front above, there was a large clock frozen in time. Right beneath the timekeeper was the construct's name in faint, aged serif lettering.

The Pearl Bank of Pietas

"We're here."

She directed her attention to the twin, concrete front doors. There was a metal bar twisted around the makeshift handles, and she bent it with ease. Opening the way, Oksana tugged me to the inside of the vast bank, forcing me into a dark corridor. My heels scuffed along the marble floor as I resisted her.

"Wh-Where are we going?" I muttered.

"For your information, there's no pearls, marbles, or anything left here. We already checked. But this place made good shelter and has handled plenty of fires and bullet storms. Strong walls, durable and resistant. We're heading for the lobby."

As we stepped inside, the walls beside us led further toward the inner sanctum of the treasury. Flags lined the space, framed and organized alphabetically. Brazil, Sweden, Egypt, United Kingdom…each one called out to me. Had I *truly* spent all my life on a forgotten island? I would never have known, in my position. At the glass doors leading inside the main hall, there was a series of boots, shoes, and other footwear sat nearby.

"Take off your shoes," Oksana ordered me as she slipped off her lone boot. Confused by her request, I complied in taking off my pair. Discreetly, I left my handgun in one of them, to no longer be a threat once further inside. If I wanted to be shown any sort of pity, I needed to lose the only edge I withheld, even when I had no bullet to spare. "Spasibo. Time for you to go in."

Beyond the glass entry was the spacious lobby of further forgotten history. As I got a better view of the inside, everything was still somewhat preserved. The interior was built to a professional standard, and the decor remained mostly intact. Paintings, vases, and even furniture had been restored. The surroundings here were nearly untouched, if not lightly covered in dust or wearing age.

A couple of people were also in the lobby—another polar bear messed with the light fixtures, as a reindeer beast swept the floor. They both turned their attention to me once I was brought in. Their frightful mugs left me frozen in place. My eyes shifted between them both, to the warlike scars on their bodies, and the weapons each one carried. Sweat collected beneath my soles; each droplet made my stance unsteady. As the two beasts grinned, and I clenched my eyes shut…

They *knew* what they were going to do to me.

I braced for the worst of what they had to offer…

"Dobro pozhalovat domoy!" they howled.

Befuddled, I opened my eyes. Why were they waving and laughing? This had to be some kind of elaborate ploy. "Wh-Who are you people?"

"This is my clan. What did you expect? Go on, make nice." Oksana pushed me to meet them, and they continued to observe me. They stopped their work to approach me, inspecting me up and down.

"Kozha…Chelovek…?" the reindeer man said. He wore an olive trench coat with an off-white button-up and slacks underneath and a belt of heavy ammunition. On his back, he carried a bullpup assault rifle. Standing a few inches above my own height, minus the antlers, he could've been about my age, if not just a smidge older.

"Woah…" The younger polar bear was about my size and shared the same features as Oksana. More gentle in her demeanor, a frilly blouse and a flowery skirt covered her body, a handgun strapped to her calf with a spare mag at the other.

"Ona odna iz nikh?" the young male asked.

"Nyet, Igor. This girl is Charissa. She is too tiny to be part of *Blessed*...And didn't Oleg teach you manners, boy?" she instructed the reindeer, and he huffed, bowing his head my way.

"Sorry."

"Where'd you find her, Mama?" the lady observed. Her teeth were so sharp, they gleamed when she spoke. She could have easily sunk those killers into my neck.

"One of those psychos tried to crush this girl's skull, and I found her before it was too late. Nearly became varenye," Oksana remarked. "Check her for any wounds."

The woman's eyes lit up. "Of course. Let's see what we're dealing with." Lada reached out with her clawed hand. Taking my face, the woman examined my features, squinting as she did so. "No injuries, but she needs a little cleaning. Perhaps a bath, if we can spare it."

Oksana nodded, rubbing her black nose. "She needs it, she reeks of filth. But for now, get that grease taken care of, and make sure she's not hurt elsewhere too, pohzhaluysta."

Lada took my arm. "I can do that."

"As for you, Igor, wait for Oleg and Nikolai to come back. Keep watch from here while I go tend to your Baba."

"Da, mem. I hope they bring some good stuff," he commented, keeping watch at the front doors while I got hauled off.

"Come with me," Lada told me, and I followed, afraid of what sort of hell they intended to put me through.

Staying with Lada, nervous every step of the way, she led me down to one of the halls in courtesy. Why were they acting like this? They were welcoming to someone they barely knew, and there was no chance they had any kindness in their hearts.

Strangers out here could have never been this nice.

Lada took me into a bathroom with mostly clean, baby-blue walls. As she brought me to the sink, taking off my cloak and Kyran's glove, she ran my dirty arms underneath the rusty water. Rubbing her black-palmar fingertips against my skin, she cleaned my palms, checking for any wounds, humming an entrancing melody during the meanwhile. "Hmm…hm…everything seems fine."

I remained silent the whole time. My uncertainty was obvious to her from the way I blankly stared into the sink hole. I still found it all too unrealistic that these people I'd never met would willingly help me, a stranger tainted with a berserker's blood.

"Charissa, they say the quiet ones are the most dangerous."

I found myself in her stare, stern as her mother's. "S-sorry."

"You know, we've taken in wanderers that never meant harm to us before. I've been used to this for a while,"

"…Why are you doing this?" I asked.

She turned off the faucet, took a towel from the hook, and dried off my arms. She handled me in a way that was caring and considerate. "Mama taught me to treat the kind with kindness, and the cruel with cruelty. A simple lesson to be learned, no?"

Her words seemed reasonable, but she had never met me. There was a fault in trusting someone forthrightly without knowing their past mistakes. And I'd made many.

"But you didn't know what I did."

"Well, the cruel never feel fear or remorse like you, and I always trust my mama and her judgment, bringing strangers here. Besides, not like you're any real threat. Just look at you."

"...Lada, was it? I'm sorry. I didn't expect any of you to be...not hostile. It feels like an unlikely outcome with what's in those streets."

"You make such a habit of apologizing, do you? Pft. I can understand why you'd be wary of us, but now you're in good hands. You're from Reveria, da?" Her accent had a strong presence in her voice, much like the other clan folk, though her speech was the most fluent and well-spoken.

"Everyone really knows about me?"

"Many say you might've come from the outside on some kind of rescue mission, among other things. People make anything up."

"Well, they're wrong. One thing's true though, I came from the island, far up above the city. I know it's hard to believe, but—"

"It's not hard to believe, with you wearing *skin*. I've known of your kind before, but never knew I'd see one in my life." She finished patting my arms dry.

I kind of wished everyone I met was not so taken aback by me. Whether good or bad. I did not want to be an outcast, yet I did not want to belong here. What did I want anymore?

With another glance at the tiger-moth mask, Lada inspected its detail. "Foul creatures. They come in many shapes. You're not Blessed, yes? But why would you wear their repulsive veil?"

"I was going to...It's complicated. Let's say I've met them, twice. They...I never understood why they'd take victims, and I tried to figure out why. Tell me, what's the purpose of it all?"

She traced one of her claws along the porcelain paths of the guise. "Ah, they took someone from you."

No use denying it. "Yes."

"They harvest the undesirable and twist the worthy to their own agenda. To cull us like true animals." she elaborated nervously. After witnessing what they'd done to the hare, it made me dread *what* they were feeding. "Many make their own theories as to why, but we all believe this is all some cruel punishment, a result of this generational plague. The Blessed, or Ferecites as some call them, they're disciples of the disease, carrying out the will of its creator and His devoted loyalists. They say if you speak of His true name, you will be next to *reap*."

Again...why Narissa and me?

How come the zealots came all the way to the wilderness, going as far as to hunt away from their own city? Were we both meant to be harvested? Or *twisted?* Thinking about it further made me imagine the most horrid outcomes for her condition, if she was even still alive...

"The strong. What do you mean they twist them to their own kind?"

Her caress of the mask faltered. "If they find you worthy, they'll turn your strength into their power. The cultists you see, each Blessed, used to be like us—now converted to perpetuate His order."

So, my sister wouldn't have been dead…but one of *them*.

The blood in my veins froze, and my will to live evaporated. Not when I was thinking of the thousand terrible things that my sister must have been going through. I kept my crestfallen eyes in the mirror, seeing my reflection. Grime and sweat covered my face, obscuring me with the muck of the city. "If what you say is true…then I've got nothing left."

Lada set aside the mask, clasping my chin. She directed my face to hers. "Surely you have something worth fighting for, do you not?" She took a new rag from a nearby dispensary and briefly wetted it under the faucet with some soap, only to wipe the dried sweat and dirt off my cheeks.

Again, my sister flooded my mind.

I would always cling to the memory of her. But even so, I could've never imagined her being a corpse, let alone one of those atrocities. *Or a torture victim of the Ferecite. Or somehow worse.*

Without her, I had no other purpose.

"I—I just don't know anymore…"

"That's fair, you needn't say more. Here, take a look."

She wiped my forehead, and as the last bit of residue left my skin, I shifted my gaze back to the mirror, where Lada viewed the reflection too. Side by side, we were polar opposites, yet somehow not too far apart from each other. I grinned briefly, but it faded fast.

"Thank you for taking care of me. But listen, I don't think I should overstay my welcome here,"

"After how mama brought you here? I think it's best you stick here, at least for the night. Reveria, da? Few of us could take you back there tomorrow morning. Little distant, but no trouble."

No matter what, I could never return there. I was a deserter. A murderer, to make it all worse. Kyran's demise weighed down my conscience, and if my face were to ever be seen by the people that he swore to protect—the people that looked up to him? They'd punish me. I put the glove back on, unable to let go of his memory.

"I can't go back."

"But where else will you g—"

The door opened. Oksana stepped inside. "Lada, everything good?"

Lada rang the rag over the sink. "Da, Mama. We were just talking,"

"Go ahead and keep Igor company. I need to speak with her,"

Lada did her mother's bidding, wishing me goodbye and leaving the bathroom. Now, it was me and the den's mother. Turning to face the tall woman, she held the handgun I left behind in my boot, cleaned of any blood and filth. "Where'd you get this?" she inquired.

My hands balled into fists.

Although it had only been hours since I saw her, Aliya would've been so upset, knowing I squandered the faith she instilled in me. Thinking about how I left her behind, my regrets piled higher. "A woman I knew during my time in Reveria."

"Ahh, podruga?"

"I'm sorry?"

"Was she a friend of yours?"

"She was. I had a few friends, actually. I don't think I could ever go back to that place…they'd never forgive me for what I did."

"What could a little thing like you have done?"

The now-pristine gun in my hand, I clenched it "Too much."

"Regardless of what you did, perhaps time away would help you,"

As much as I'd like to believe that…time might heal wounds, but it couldn't bring back the dead. "We'll see."

"Anyway, gave your gun a proper spa day and I went ahead and loaded you with a new mag. Looked like you didn't have any ammo to spare. Speaking of: are you better at loading mags, or making repairs?"

"Er, why do you ask?"

"Well, if you're going to bunk with us, you need to at least put in some effort. Think we'd let you stay here for free?"

From that insinuation, I had to refuse. In my sensible conscience, I could not remain here. Anywhere I'd go, I was a risk one way or another. I wouldn't do the same with these people.

"What makes you think I want to stay?"

She scoffed. "You'd be an imbecile not to take a roof over your head. Besides, we both know what happened back at that street corner. Do you really want to go through that again? Be picked off like a little rabbit?"

That was what Lada meant. Like her mother, they knew I was incapable of defending myself. On my lonesome, I was helpless, but to put a semblance of faith in these outsiders would've been no better. I had no knowledge of these people, and I didn't couldn't become a liability to them. It was already burdening to be in a town of many, and it'd be worse to do it to a group so small. Besides…

What would they do to me, once they knew what I was?

"Sorry, but I don't think I should stay here."

"Why do you insist on being on your own?"

"I wouldn't want to—"

"It's just for the night! Not like you'd be eating up all our food and power. You've got nothing to prove trying to be a big brave girl."

As much as I wanted to refute her claims, especially of *their* nature, I couldn't manage a way to ease out. She was right: I couldn't survive on my own, even if I tried. "Alright, I'll stay. Only for the night." I accepted, feeling déjà vu once again. "And I've had a little experience with an engineer once. Only a little, though."

"Good, the men could always use an extra hand. Speaking of, my husband will be home soon, along with Oleg. Come, you'll have to meet them if you want to stay," she demanded, and as she went to hold the door open for me, the mask and cloak left on the sink caught me. I grabbed the garments and left the bathroom. As they tainted my hands with their abysmal influence, I prayed my sister was somehow safe.

Wishing and hoping desperately that she was still herself.

***

We headed back to the lobby, where Lada and Igor conversed on the patched-up leather couch, a laundry basket nearby as they folded clothes on the coffee table. While they passed the time, there was another stranger keeping them company in her wheelchair. An elderly polar bear, knitting a lengthy quilt of pastels. She bore a wrinkled smile on her face, her eyes clouded in cataracts. On her frail figure, she wore a cotton sweater and pants, and a headscarf that had daffodils patterned on its dark blue fabric.

"Who's that?"

"Moya mama. She might not look like it, but she's one hell of a survivor. Been here ever since the days of living on the island above. When I mentioned you, she was excited to see if you were real, ha!"

While I met a few older folks back at Reveria, it was uncommon to see any elders. If her mental fortitude was enough to prevent her from going berserk, and able to live a long life without getting entangled in Misera's mortal thorns, then I wanted to meet her. The grandmother heard my approach, and those graying eyes brightened up. That frigid smile stretched wider, but before any words could be made, the entry to the lobby burst open.

Everybody's attention went to the doors.

In came walking another white bear and reindeer. They were the largest in the pack, both showcasing a strong physique as they hauled bags inside. One had bits of rice trying to leak through the packaging, and the other was a tarp sack full of perishables. Oksana grinned once they arrived, taking me by my arm to bring me over, and the imminent dread nearly led me to the brink of a fleeting sprint. They were big men, terrifying ones at that—with large, sharp teeth and daunting mugs. Once they caught me in their line of sight, their eyes clawed right through my body. The two males frightened me more than Kyran initially did.

"Kto eto?" the age-worn caribou asked, putting down his bags and coming close to me. He stood several feet taller than I did, with a chunk of his upper lip missing and antlers big enough to mangle.

"Charissa. Found her in the streets," Oksana answered, and as the reindeer was about to try and touch me, she smacked him away. The man retracted his mitt and winced as the mother bear pulled me back.

"Don't touch," she threatened.

He huffed and picked his bags back up, hoisting them over his shoulders. Igor came rushing over, sharing a big grin. "Papa! Dyada Nikolai! You're both finally home!" he whooped, hugging his father at his side. The mature reindeer brought him in, heartfelt to see him.

"Privyet, kid. Do me a favor, take Nikolai's bags, and help your old Papa take them to the kitchen. Got you plenty of ingredients." the scar-worn man told the younger caribou.

The picture of this group became a little clearer, but it was still foggy. Before I could make any more assumptions, Igor grabbed the polar man's bags. "Spasibo ogromnoe," the white-coated beast said.

Shades of gray covered his thick fur, as though he wore the ashes of the city naturally. He waved off the young man and patted his reindeer compatriot. From my initial impression, they had a close connection, comfortable with one another. Igor and his father parted ways, taking their found food elsewhere.

"That's Oleg?" I wondered.

"Igor's father, yes. Man's been a friend of ours for years. It's just him and his son now, but we treat them like family," Oksana said.

"That man's been my best friend since we were both boys, and I've known this beautiful woman here for half my life." Nikolai chuckled as he approached Oksana. The two of them exchanged a couple of words in their foreign tongue, only for him to lean in to share a kiss.

Pink roses washed over my face. I had to cover my eyes with my free hand, and they both couldn't help but snicker.

"Charissa, it's only a little kiss," Oksana humored.

Frankly, it was something I was unused to. The concept of romance struck me as odd, but intriguing. I had never delved into the idea of love before, especially down here. As much as the prospect of seeking out somebody, anybody, incited promising daydreams, such a thing mattered so little when I already became so "intimate" with the terrors that had already crept their way into my heart.

"Ech, she is still young, don't tease her. Charissa, da? Good to meet you! Pleasure's all mine!" Nikolai greeted me with a boisterous cheer, reaching forward with his bestial paw.

Uncovering my eyes, I brought my hand forth with caution. He had no issue grasping my palm, nearly on the verge of bone-crushing, though he eased up upon seeing me wince. As he shook it, I tried to be firm with my grip. Once he let go of me, I made sure my fingers were still in their right places, if not shattered.

"Same to you." I shared a nervous laugh.

He guffawed once more, only to shoulder his wife. "Podarok?" he murmured, and her eyes went to the cloak and mask that I kept to my side.

"Nyet, she was wearing it. I did not ask her to bring a gift—"

"Here, take them," I offered them the disguise.

They both directed their attention to me as I held the folded robes, the porcelain guise resting among the white. Nikolai, further intrigued by the "gift," took them, pleased by my gesture.

"Hmph, pretty trophies! Good gift," Nikolai commented.

I was doing both of us good, now that I did not have to carry that eyesore anymore. They could have taken it as a way of showing that I was not an enemy to them, but even so, I was still unsure of where I stood. They turned out to be a friendly bunch, but the arms they wore would bring carnage wherever they went.

Nikolai closed one eye as he held it up and humored himself as he tried to use his artistic vision. His gaze met mine again, and he offered a wholesome smile across his otherwise carnivorous, menacing mug.

"*The Claws* welcome your visit, Charissa!"

Pecking his wife's forehead, and exchanging a couple more words, he headed to one of the glass display cases nearby, trying to find a good place for the new prize. Next to the trophy shelves was an immense wall full of collectibles and memories, holding a substantial treasury. These individuals held outstanding pride, and it showed in every one of them.

"So that's what you call yourselves."

Oksana motioned me over, bringing me to the wall of various portraits, photographs, and mementos pinned to the drywall ahead. Akin to Dr. Kutsuki's memorial shrine.

"For you, yes. But in our tongue, we are Kogti."

"What can you tell me about yourselves?"

She was more than delighted to share.

"Our mark was made here long after Vinea was founded in '60. Moya mama was one of the first citizens to be invited a little over a decade after its discovery, becoming part of Commoneo and its former greatness. But, for her to do that, she had to leave her home country to ensure a promising life for her future legacy. It's her blood that fuels our drive to persevere in the Devil's paradise."

Vintage pictures of their homeland were pinned to the wall. The country where they originally came from. The frames held landscapes of their flower fields and their grand architecture. There were fuzzy images of people as well, but to my surprise, they were human.

"Who're these people?" I pointed to the photos showing their faces, and Oksana unpinned one of the pictures to bring it closer.

In the photo, there was a young man and woman, sitting on a bench in a park as they held hands and posed. They even had a little girl between them, and through the black and white, I could tell that they were a happy family with candid love. "Ded. Babulya. My grandparents."

I compared them to the ursine woman, unable to tell that they were family. "But they're human,"

Oksana bared a soft sigh, brushing her thumb delicately over the photo, careful not to damage it. "They met in the Motherland. When that little girl in the picture grew up, Moya Mama? She met my Papa, and they were sixty years together. It was only a few years ago that he passed away." She pointed to the coffee table in the distance, and the picture became clearer. I gawked at the elderly polar bear, almost blasphemed. The same little girl in the picture was her was once human? Like, *skin and all?*

"When she and Papa had me amid the outbreak, all we had was each other. But when I turned twenty-four, Oleg, his baby son, and Nikolai were just a group of boys trying to survive, like my family. It was then that we formed a pack that'd never be broken." she trailed off.

"Has it always been those three men together? What happened to *their* families?"

She unpinned the next picture. A colored image of a family stilled the square, all mutated with reindeer features while a white polar bear stood apart from the rest. A young adult Nikolai and Oleg were present, as well as two elderly caribou, an adult doe, and two reindeer children that couldn't have been past their toddler years.

It all made sense.

"Oleg's family is no longer with him. His grandparents, wife, Natalya, and only daughter, Mila, were victims of this city's wretched fiends. Oleg and Nikolai, no matter how much they fought for them, they were already gone. Igor was the only lucky one to have escaped."

"So, Igor's all he has left."

"Poor boy suffered as much as his father. Nikolai told me once he saw his best friend, with a gun in his mouth. Had he not been there, Igor would've lost everything."

"Oh…Oh." I lost my words.

"My husband's like the brother he never had. Though you know, Nikolai was no stranger to loss, either." She took another photo. In the jaded colors, an ursine father had a young cub at his lap, sharing solemn faces. Dragged in the bowels of hell, covered in scrap armor and warpaint, they shared the characteristics of true pillagers.

"Where are his parents?"

"Hmph. Mother was raider scum, his father an unwilling participant. After everything she did, her husband had to end her wrongdoings, then took his life after. Nikolai realized without his parents; he'd forever be raider property. He was only eight years old when he ran away and found Oleg with his mama and papa…you know what happens long after that."

Such tragic pasts wrenched my chest. "That sounds horrible."

"So you see why Nikolai couldn't have the same happen with his only friend. Those men have been through it the worst." A sympathetic sigh parted her lips. "When me and my parents found those boys, after our pack formed, Nikolai wanted to take my family name, and we've been together for a near twenty-five years of hell and back."

My attention was directed to their daughter.

"Then you had Lada," I connected.

"She's another reason why I want to preserve my legacy. Doesn't matter that we're hybridian now, for we're still human deep down. Even in the bowels of hell itself, my family will live on, and once we all crawl from its clutches, we will see our Motherland."

I reflected on the wall; Oksana took a deep breath as she basked in the pride of her heritage. In the center of the entire memory wall, a massive flag draped wide amidst the artifacts. The colors of their nation. Their country, pride, and blood.

White. Blue. Red.

Further drawn to the letters right above the tapestry, I didn't recognize what they said, given that they were in a different language.

"What does that say?"

Oksana crossed her arms, a profound smile of pride on her face. She read the proverb written above with all her passion.

Бережёного Бог бережёт.

"God keeps those safe, who keep themselves safe."

Amid the revelation, Nikolai swooped from the hallway, pacing to Oksana. "Oh love, I've got some bad news for you,"

"Water pipes break? The stove's out of juice?" Her guesses piled on.

"No no, kids just asked for a couple things and neither Oleg nor I could find them. Igor some flour, Lada a nail file, and—oh, right! Mama's running low on yarn, and she's going to want to make a blanket for our special guest," He listed off, and she hummed.

"You know her so well. Well, if you couldn't find anything like that, it'd be best to find someone who might have what we want." She went for her LMG, kept in a trophy case when it wasn't in use.

"I've got a feeling you're referring to our long-limbed friend."

"Been meaning to pay him a visit," she cocked her gun to that notion, and the follicles on my neck stiffened.

"You're not going to kill someone, are you?"

Nikolai's mouth went agape. "Nonsense! We'd never kill our favorite trader! Ugly face, sure, but very nice guy!"

"I'm just going to do some barter with him, then be back." she gave her frightful grin. "You'll come with me."

The hairs couldn't have stuck up straighter.

"You want me to go back out there?"

"I saw what happened earlier, yes, but the first lesson you'll learn from me is that you can't let Misera's vermin frighten you," she stated, heading for the entrance. "Ready that gun; we're going now."

With a tense stare, I glanced over to a shrugging Nikolai.

"She's the leader, and what she says goes," he reasoned.

No matter where I went, there was no room for me to have a choice. As long as I was visiting the mother bear's cave, her rules had to be followed. Pulling my pistol out and checking the mag, it was fully loaded with ammo. I put it back and took Oksana's tail, keeping close as we left the safety of the bank and back into the boulevard of death.

***

About a half-mile down the street, we went, and all was quiet. The avenues, seemingly hollow, didn't let me stop watching my back. Ever since the diner, it became apparent that anything could be lurking in any shadow or structure. With the polar woman's company, it was reassuring to have someone by my side who had survived in these ruins all her life.

"Recharge station should be down at the corner here. Keep low and watch out for any danger," Oksana told me.

"Do you think he'll have what we need? Out in these parts?" I whispered, to which she looked left and right, turning to me.

"Nothing's ever guaranteed. You either try and hope to find something, or die doing nothing."

With that, we neared the street corner, going up to the abandoned mart and its parking lot of fizzled, electrical car chargers. Back in the day, people would come here to regain energy for their automobiles, if not to enjoy whatever commodities that the store close by offered. From the inside, wooden boards covered the windows, and posters that once advertised all-organic groceries and neo-beer were tattered along the panes. The building's foundation was falling apart, bricks crumbling, and graffiti along its dead walls. Despite its wear and damage, I could've once envisioned this quaint place to be a pleasant stop. But *Charge & Go Convenience* was nothing more than a shell of its past prime.

"It's all planked up. How do we get in?"

"Follow me; I know the way," Oksana instructed, taking me around the other side. In an alleyway, desecrated with bullet holes and dried bloodstains, a dumpster blocked the backway of the store. With minimal effort, she pushed it aside. The metal door was covered in slash marks, dents, and all kinds of desperate efforts to get inside.

"First place most look for anything is stores. Little do they know most of the stuff inside is long gone. But this one is special." She fished underneath her armor, taking a set of keys from her pocket. She jangled the right one, putting it into the rusty lock.

"It seems like you've been here before. I'd imagine you took everything left,"

The mother bear snickered. "You've yet to see the special part, darogaya." She clicked, and the way was open.

I still didn't know if I should've trusted this woman, considering the short time we'd been acquainted, but I took her word for it. Once she locked the backway, I powered up the tactical light. The musty darkness proved unwelcoming. Planchettes and shopping baskets were scattered about; ants crawled throughout the space as the tiles were covered in splinters. At one of the damp corners, a clump of mushrooms grew. The humid tinge in the air only downgraded my hopes of anything good left.

Or perhaps Oksana would unveil her true intentions here.

"Aim the light over here for me," she ordered, bringing me to the corner space. A staircase, leading to another metal door. Going down the steps, it somehow felt colder once she cleared her throat. *Knock knock.* The polar bear leaned her ear in. Confused, I wasn't certain what she was doing, but Oksana waited until the right moment to call.

"Theraphosidae."

Jittering followed from the door, as did a pleased smile on Oksana's mug. As she pushed it open, a dim light shone through. Once it cleared up, a fierce barking came to my feet. *Woof woof!* A dog covered in patchy fur ran to me on its four legs, pinning me against the wall with its barks.

"Hush, boy!" a voice called out, crusty and crickety in its pitch. Dragging my eyes from the animal, yet another horror overcame me. Of the many hybridians I met, this one was nothing like the rest.

Two jewel-like eyes, followed by six more. A set of legs below, two arms from his shoulders, and four more sprouted on his back. Holding a pump-action shotgun in his tapered fingers and clicking his huge fangs together, the tarantula set his sights on me. Before I had any chance to react, he retracted his gun upon seeing Oksana. He even dusted off his raggedy jacket and pants with his many fingers. The mother bear dapped the arachnid like a brother.

"Garina? It's been a while since you paid me a visit," he joshed, only to set his strange gazes on me. "And you brought…the human? I heard she was down here, but *you* found her?"

"Met her just today. Says she came from the surface island. Same one that my Mama once saw long time ago," she mentioned.

"Thought they were just a made-up story for the longest time. Guess you always come by with new surprises every time, eh?" the tarantula said, glancing at the dog. "Seems like Beau likes you, too."

"Huh?" I bumbled, only to feel a wet lap on my hand. The dog had been licking me, and I was too awestruck to notice. "O-oh, yeah. Didn't think I'd ever see a, well…animal-animal here."

The well-armed man gave a discontent grunt.

"Found him in the jaws of a berserker, rescued him. He's a part of my life now, and it wouldn't be *Bern* without Beau." He chuckled, and with his spiderlike visage, it was hard to tell his emotions.

With a nervous chuckle, I tried to calm myself. "Well, it's good to meet you. Sorry, I just never really met…" I didn't know how to best put it. During my stay in Reveria, I'd never had any resident with more than two arms or eyes cross my path.

"An arthropod?" He finished it for me. "Don't blame you. Many like me hide away and fend for ourselves in the darkest corners. Not easy sharing the face of those white-dressed parasites."

The mother bear expressed a solemn frown.

"Shame, really. Folks like Bern here are easy targets, in any street or settlement. Not only for their looks but like his pooch here, they're hunted for easy food." Oksana bumped shoulders with her friend. "Wish he'd take my offer to stay with me."

He couldn't help but *pshaw.*

"Answer's still the same, Garina. I just have a better time with me and my little man. Plus, all these beautiful wares."

His hideaway was lit by dangling lanterns and tea candles. The shelves were stocked with a plethora of both junk and useful goods. Racks of clothes, books, kitchenware, and tall bottles with strange liquids filled the space, ranging between soups and booze. He even carried weapons and apparatuses of the cheaper variety on his wall. Some spare gun parts, barrel mods, and such piled on the racks. As for the CataLytes, they were run-of-the-mill and rusted, like the ones Reveria's bizarre offered. Low-quality ones, like *CataLyte-L*, which only served as glorified flashlights.

"Ah yes, you and your excellent selection. I've come to do business."

"With pleasure. What're you looking for?" he chirred.

"Don't suppose you might have flour, yarn, and a nail file? Pack's in need of a few things."

The merchant tapped his chin with one hand, as his many others reached around the items. He didn't even have to look to find what he needed. "Luckily for you, I've got everything that a mother and her family needs," Bern chittered, bringing up everything she requested.

"Chari, hold onto these." Oksana nudged, and without much thought, I took the goods. It was difficult, though, as the pooch was pressing his paw at my leg, whimpering for attention.

"Don't bug her, Beau," Bern humored, at which the dog huffed and trotted to the big, single-man mattress at the far corner, lying down. "Now comes the hard part. It'll be about seventy-five marbles' worth for everything today. Have enough to cover that?"

"Afraid I can only carry so much, but I got something else you might like." Reaching for her set of keys, she unclipped one with a grocery cart keychain. "You know that old *Melior Groceries* some distance from the downtown library? Heard it's a dead zone. Might be able to look for some extra supplies," she enticed the trader.

"Ahh, now that's certainly worthwhile. Been meaning to break into there, but it's always been a pain in the ass to finesse my way in. I don't even care what's there. I think I'd be able to bunker in that place instead," he fantasized, happily taking the key from her.

"Just be careful whenever you do make your move. Never know what might be inside." She warned.

He chortled. "Appreciate it, beautiful, but no need to get all worrisome for ole me. Where'd you get the key though?"

With a stern face, the mother bear disclosed her secret. "Picked it off a thief. Shouldn't have come near my territory, that slag."

"Oh? Tried breaking into the bank?"

"Tried but failed. She didn't expect *me* to come back home, that's for sure. Anyway, the key's better in your hands than mine. Call it a token of gratitude for all our years of good business."

"You know how to make a man blush, huh? You both best head out before any berserkers or…Erg, *buzzards* pass through these streets... They know to strike at night when many are none the wiser."

"Will do, and me and Nikolai will come visit you at your new place if you decide to stay at that supermarket. Come on, Charissa." She held the way open for me, and I nodded.

"Alright…you know, Bern, you're not so bad as I thought," I said, his fangs jittered with a pleasant hum.

"Well thank you, my friend. I just hope we see each other again in the near future." He wished me well. "As for you, Garina, best to your family, and better keep that head on your shoulders out there."

"You better do the same, my friend." She grinned at her old colleague, bringing me out and shutting the door. The lock clicked, and as we made our way out from the convenience store, Oksana blocked off the backway with the dumpster. I reaffirmed my hold of the items.

"Never did I expect anybody nice out *here*," I mentioned, only for Oksana's content grin to twist to a solemn one. She passed by me, and I followed her lead back into the trenches of the urban abyss.

"For every good soul you find, there's twenty more wicked curs lurking. Thousands more."

Heeding Bern's advice, we managed to return to the bank's solid walls before any more monsters, whether insane or corrupt, infested the streets. Oksana and I went into the lobby, and she locked the entrance tight and pushed a heavy bookshelf in front of the bullet-proof glass doors.

No such thing as extra security with these mutants.

Apart from my first time stepping in, the lobby lacked any waking souls, except for one near the couch and in her wheelchair.

The grandmother.

Upon hearing the ruckus, Nikolai arrived from the hallway to greet us from our brief trip. "Ah, my love. I'm glad you both made it home with not wounds but presents."

"Heh, you're too sweet. Everyone else is in bed?" Oksana asked.

He gave a wide-mouthed yawn himself. "It is past midnight, but Mama wanted to finish her little project before she got to sleep too. I was just waiting here to make sure the both of you got back,"

"Well, no need to worry anymore tonight. Here, take these and put them in the kids' rooms. They'll love a good morning surprise." She handed him the flour and nail file, and he spotted the yarn.

"Ahh, you even found some material for Mama. Want me to give that to her as well?"

"You're doing plenty. I had someone else in mind." She turned, holding out the cotton string bundle. "Charissa, give this to her. The both of you didn't get much of a chance to speak."

Tension riddled my lips.

"Oh, well…" I couldn't find an excuse this time. "I guess I could. I just don't want to be a bother to her, is all."

"Hush." Oksana piled the yarn into my hold instead. "It's one thing to be scared of monsters, but to be scared of a babushka? Heh, just be yourself, and she'll accept you."

"Okay, I can do that,"

"Me and Oksana are going to rest up, but Lada said you could bunk together. You have a sleeping bag waiting for you."

His faith warranted surprise, as did Oksana's. "You're both serious? I thought this was all some trick,"

"You haven't shown a bit of deceit, but don't think we won't be keeping an eye on you. So long as you continue to be true to us, you won't get your head blown off." He emphasized.

After all my assumptions about their group, at least they didn't kill me outright. Instead of being a wandering exhibit, I warranted caution by these folks. It was best not to test the sliver of faith they loaned to me.

"I appreciate the chance."

"You only get the one with us, so use it well," Oksana warned.

"See you in the morning, sladkaya," Nikolai said, and they both headed for the hallway, holding each other all the meanwhile.

Only the older woman and I remained in the lobby, and it was up to me to close the distance. With a deep breath and steady stance, I made my way to the couch and got myself a seat as the elder focused on twisting her yarn into an intricate sheet. The delicacy in her pace and cataract-clouded vision made her progress impressive. For a minute, I watched as she turned simple cotton into a work of comfort. Time must've passed a little too long because, amid my awe, she paused in her alpine stitching to show a near-humane smile.

"Hello, milaia." She settled her project on her lap.

With her breaking my mesmerized state, I panicked.

"H-Hey. Oh right, this is for you." I presented the yarn, trembling some. "We didn't get the chance to talk earlier."

"Ah yes, my little girl was dragging you around, wasn't she? Heh, it's just nice having someone new to speak with." Her shakier hands went for my own, and she took the offering. "Very kind of you to go with her and fetch this for me. I always feel better knowing she has someone with her. Would you like to tell me your name, rebyonok?" she asked, and although her accent was stronger than her daughter's, the softness in her voice spoke volumes from that kind-hearted spirit.

"Charissa, ma'am. What's yours?"

"I've been called many things. Mama, dedulya, babushka, little lady, and more." She gave a wheezy laugh. "It's been a long time since I've been called a *lady,* though. No, I'm all old, wrinkles and fur now."

I offered a bit of a giggle myself. "You've been through a lot, I bet. Oksana said you were one of the first people to set foot on Vinea once."

The older woman drew a soft breath, setting the yarn and her work in progress in the basket nearby, relaxing in her chair. "Would you believe that I was human once too?"

"I've seen your photo on the wall when you were a girl, but I don't think I could've imagined what it felt like to turn into…"

"A monstrosity?"

"I wouldn't call you that—"

She guffawed again, patting my knee with brittle fingers. "It is what it is. Can't change what I am now, but it's true. Once in my lifetime, I was just a woman with a loving husband, given a chance at a better life, at the expense of leaving my homeland." Her milky gaze went to the ceiling as she reminisced about her better days.

"What was it like when you first came here? The island, this city…was it really beautiful once?"

At that, the elder brought her soft stare to the wall of memorabilia ahead. She brought her fingers to the control stick of her chair, the wheels spinning in a gentle motion. As she moved, I got up to follow.

"When I just became an adult back in 2071, I was an average young woman. Hard to leave my parents and country behind, but I knew with my love, we'd have a better life at Vinea Island." She trailed on, drawing close to one of the display cases. Within its confines, a tattered book collected dust. "Me and him didn't know what to expect. When I received a letter from the Abundantia Association, we figured it was just a prank. But after being given an all-paid cruise, full of many other people, we took a leap. And when we came to the grand opening of Commoneo..." She paused, her still-sharp claws clinking to the glass. "It was like we left our troubles behind."

The way she reflected, telling it like it had happened yesterday, I had to listen to every detail she unearthed. "So, you really did show up there."

"It was an unforgettable moment for me. Skyscrapers, a beautiful mountain, monumental technology, and friendly faces you'd never be tired of. The island was everything anybody could've wanted and more...and for no cost. All we had to do was find a way to make our new home a better place, being a beacon for humankind."

I glanced at the pictures of their homeland. "What did you do?"

"For forty-two years, I was their historical photographer, assigned to capture Vinea's legacy in the making. But there was something that always disturbed me," she speculated, bringing out the memory book. Those fingertips brushed along the near-ancient, peeling lamination of its cover. "While I stayed above, people around me were invited someplace else...somewhere better. A future ten kilometers underground. I thought I was just either unlucky or good enough at my job to stay put at Commoneo. More people left for the 'heart,' more people came to the island, but nobody departed beyond the sea. Made me wonder what was truly down below."

"Well, what made you come down here?"

"2123…a year that'd change everything. It was a cloudy night when it happened." She flipped through the pages at the further end, unveiling the dark photographs. Fires at the seashore, humans running in horror within the town's once-safe light, and ghost-like apparitions chasing them into the forest. "Nobody knew what to do. Everyone fled into the trees, hoping to find salvation in this city's lights instead. My husband and I joined them. Otherwise, we wouldn't have been breathing to this day."

The photographs…No, it couldn't have been.

"And when you got to the bottom…"

"All of us barreled into the city, gates willingly wide open. But when we were locked in, we could no longer escape, nor the disease it offered. Within minutes, all the air that pumped into the city turned into toxin, and the projections in the sky-sphere went dark for good. As night and day disappeared, one by one, each of us fell, and we all writhed, until suddenly…our bodies changed." The next series of photos were frames of people, altering in different forms. The tearing eyes, the cries of anguish, and the impending madness were captured in every instance. "It didn't take long for me to succumb. But through all the pain, I took these, so that one day…someone from the outside would see what went down here and be able to unveil all the horrors that happened to us."

…Could it have been?

"You really did live through hell itself."

"Hmph, still living through it. But even though I could no longer do what I loved; I have other things to be grateful for. Even with Dmitri gone, I still have Oksana, my zyat', my vnuchka, and those Morozov lads. No matter how much you lose, you have to find something else worth holding onto."

"I have to know, baba…what is your real name?"

Even beyond the hollow sky down here, the stars above aligned. No twist of fate could've led to this moment. My whole world came to a standstill. The library, the photographs, the note…

"Anastasia. Anastasia Garina."

She was the woman who left them to my discovery.

"Anastasia…" For a moment, my breath ceased to flow. "Your photos, the ones in the library. You were the one that left them there?"

"So, you really did find Commoneo." Anastasia, too, figured it out. "Yes, I am the one and only. I prayed one day that whoever found Vinea Island would save us, and that if they did…I'd be able to return home to die where I was born."

To meet the individual who'd changed my life, for better or worse, struck me like the stars out of reach. Was it worth this anguish to get closer to the truth behind my existence? My reason for being here? Coming face-to-face with the fire that had started my own was worth it.

"I can't believe it's really you," I stammered. Reaching into my pocket and taking out the marigold bandana, I bestowed it on her, thumbs draping over its long-lasting fabric. "This must belong to you, then."

She lit up, touching the cloth. "Ha! You even found this. My old bandana. My favorite one from when I was a child." Her astonishment was short-lived. "But why, devushka, would you come here? You must've seen the pictures. Didn't you read my note?"

Despite her warnings, I went against them. It seemed impossible for me to leave, not only to seek others like me. Narissa had warned that to leave Vinea would've brought scars along the way, and after witnessing the atrocities that Misera and its history had to offer…she had been right all along.

"My entire life has been made up of lies, and I just wanted to find one truth in it. That had to be down here," I told her, my regrets heavy. "As much as I should've heeded your warnings, I had to know my ties here. My home."

Anastasia couldn't believe her ears. "You're saying Vinea was your birthplace? That this is where you truly came from?"

The deepest dwellings of my memory could not fathom a different alternative. My roots tethered to Vinea's, and from there, I accepted that fact. No longer could I deny it. "Someway, somehow, it would seem."

The elder closed the book, placing it back in its case. "Perhaps you're the miracle that Misera needs,"

"…What do you mean, baba?"

Anastasia wheeled close to me, taking my forearm, and trailing her palmar tips to my skin. "Look at you. Lada said you lived in Reveria, for months even. Yet here you are, still the picture of human excellence," she observed, staring into me. "There's something within you that refuses to succumb to Misera's miasma. Something that nobody else here has."

"So, you're saying that…"

"That perhaps you, Charissa, are immune."

That couldn't have been true. Impossible, it felt.

"But I've been told that this virus affects all human life."

"You're a sole exception, a *miracle*. Exposed to the island your whole life, and not once have you bent to the will of the beast. Perhaps destiny brought you here for a reason, as mine would be to meet you."

Once, I was so indebted to the prospect of fate and destiny, but through my stay here, that belief dwindled. Meeting the woman who led me here, the spirit link, begged the question of how our paths finally intertwined, and how it was possible.

The marigold tethers brought us together.

"Maybe *She* wanted me to give this back to you." I brought up her lost bandana, parting with the piece that led me here.

"I think it's meant to be yours now." She refused, closing my hands with hers. "You've found it for a reason, after all."

"…What reason do you think?"

Her trembling digits firmed. "That someday, you'll bring change."

***

A little over a month passed, *March 26th, 2175.*

Initially, my stay with The Claws was meant for the night. But after the incident at the hospital, and the diner, the idea of having to fend for myself out there in those streets further frightened me. In a desperate plight, I offered my assistance with anything they asked, allowing me another night after another. While they never kicked me out or asked me to leave, they still knew when to keep their distance. I still remained more like a recurring guest than a family friend. Even if I did not share the same blood as they did, we would have meals together and tell stories, and they even let me take part in their games.

It was better to be with them than to be a corpse.

I counted my days here for every one Oksana checked on me. She'd ask if I'd like to be taken back to Reveria, but I declined each time. I couldn't continue holding onto this family as a crutch, but I also couldn't confront the issues that drove me here. Until the time was right, I was allowed under her roof, so long as I earned my keep.

But to say if I deserved to ever set foot near Reveria was difficult.

While it was nearly alienating to be treated with too much, they still had a place for me in their community. The longer I stayed here, the more I wondered why Bea didn't reveal her knowledge of the Ferecite to me, nor the remote facet of immunity. Whatever the case might've been, my reasons for finding answers on my own were blinded by rage, and it only made me regret parting ways without a word. And if I did return to her, how would she feel, knowing that I abandoned her without a word? That because of me, I *killed* Kyran.

I never could've been ready for that confrontation.

"Pick that one," Lada called out.

"I know," I said, holding a pair of clippers and a small plastic bin. At the bottom held three strawberries, a dozen less than what I collected a couple weeks prior.

"Not a lot, but we'll be able to make it work." she mentioned, plucking the rest of the turnips and adding it to the rest of the gathering.

I did what I could as to not be a freeloader. Assisting Nikolai with the bank repairs, giving Igor a hand in the kitchen, and being another travel body with Oksana. But every Sunday morning, I'd join Lada at the earliest hour and help her tend to the indoor garden at the second level. The first time around, we managed to get a basketful of produce. Though ever since I'd been sharing the same roof as the Claws, the produce ran out more than it could grow.

"Has the fertilizer been working right?" I asked.

"No, it's got nothing to do with the fertilizer," she answered. "We'll just have to see if we're lucky enough to come across a trader that happens to carry fresh food. Any food for that matter."

Unfortunately, it didn't take much of a hint to understand. No matter how much I could've contributed to earn my place here, it wasn't enough.

"Right."

"You look troubled," she noticed.

"Oh, it's nothing." I wiped the look off. "Just hope I'm not overstaying my welcome."

Taking off her gloves, she dumped her dirty tools into her box. "You've been doing your fair share of work around here. Not like you're being a leech."

"Doesn't seem like it."

"You're fine, Chari. We're fine." She hefted her supplies, taking the basket of produce on top. "I'm going to wash these in the bathroom, but you should go ahead and finish up here. Breakfast's almost ready."

"Yeah, I'll be quick."

Once she left, I did the last steps. After powering up the integrated humidifier, I turned on the incandescent lamps that loomed above the clinging viridian. Pots lined the walls and hung from the ceilings, but even with the added fertilizers and extra seeds we bought, not much improvement had been made to the green growing from them. There was only one pest I could think of that was affecting the well-being of these plants. With shame, I shut the glass door to the greenhouse room.

I rushed to the lobby, intending to scrape by whatever was left. There, everybody else finished their plates at the large, round table in the waiting lounge. I got there and snatched an empty chair, and everyone there greeted me. There was Oksana and Nikolai, with Lada just joining them. Next to her, of course, was Grandmother Anastasia. *The Garinas.* Then, there were the *Morozovs.* Oleg, sitting alongside his only son, Igor. Determined hybridians whose Russian lineage never seeped away, colleagues I looked up to.

"There she is! We saved you some syrniki and pirozhki. They're still fresh and warm." Igor sang, getting up from his seat to bring a plate holding a single cheese pancake and a couple of mushroom-filled pastries to me, kind enough to pour me a half-mug of black coffee too. Every morning, I showed my thanks for a delicious breakfast and fresh brew, no matter what the portion.

"The food looks beautiful as always, Igor."

He took my appreciation with a hum as he went to take the finished dishes to the kitchen. With my posture upright and my elbows daring not to touch the table, I was about to dig into his cooking.

"Charissa, do not forget prayers," Oksana interrupted.

I put my utensils down. "Of course," I replied and clasped my hands, closing my eyes and softly reciting the prayer they taught.

At every meal, giving grace was one of the many rules.

Narissa had introduced me to the idea of religion before, but Christianity was never made a staple in our lifestyle. She told me that there was an afterlife and that there was a place of damnation. The good were rewarded, while the evil were punished. The idea of eternal life and suffering was my moral compass for the longest time in my youth, but now I was not certain where my beliefs were. I never became that familiar with the aspect of God, until the Claws showed me. Back in the wilderness, I always thanked "the sky and its angels" for my life. But now that I was in tune with the fact that there could have been a higher power, I acknowledged how people here needed a way to look up from this hellscape. God was a figure that some people here could find faith in. I was not certain if I had complete faith or not, but even so, He brought hope to those who needed it most down here.

I admired that.

Regardless of my beliefs, I paid Him my respects for the meal and unclasped my hands. I helped myself to the small plate of food that I had been granted.

Oleg finished his coffee and excused himself from the table. "Oleg, we need to check the cables downstairs. Make sure they're ready for our new toys." He told the mature caribou, then turned to me. "May need your hand again with the tools. So be ready for any mishaps."

I sipped the last of my brew. "Sure thing, you can count on me."

Oleg hammered his mug, getting up after and staring at me. "*Da*, big job. We'll let you know. For now, poka, everyone."

The two fathers parted ways from the table, but not before Nikolai showed some love for his wife. After their morning kiss, Oksana seated herself next to Lada and Anastasia, planning.

"Oh Mama, me and Baba were going to stitch up those old dresses you and Chari found at the boutique the other day. Was there anything you wanted me to fix for you?" Lada asked.

The oldest bear let out a wheezy chuckle. "Lala, my little girl's never been one for dresses, or even skirts. Ever since she was a baby, she liked pants, and now armor's her new phase!" She laughed harder.

"Dresses don't prevent bullet holes, Mama," Oksana smiled. "No need to save anything for me; just fix up those rags and we can trade them with one of the merchants. They'll know just who to sell them off to…God knows we could use more coffee, and food."

I would have been lying if I said watching these women be so content with each other didn't make my heart ache, not being able to have someone of my blood anymore. Missing my sister, like I had time and time again, unable to part from the past. Having a sister was one thing, but to have a present mother? A grandmother?

How different could things have been if I had either.

"Will do, Mama. Say, Chari? Would you want to help me and Baba again today? You have a better time holding needles than I do,"

"Actually, I need her to help me with the turrets up top. It's no race, so you and Baba can take your time seaming those clothes."

The young woman nodded to her word.

Only a few days ago, Oleg managed to install a quartet of security machines on the bank's rooftop. They concluded it was about time for more protection in the event of a raid. It was bad enough for this place to get attacked nearly every day by raiders, but according to rumors of traders and fortunate wanderers, there had been more break-ins involving different settlements, mainly smaller groups. Abduction, they continued to bring up, not done by your typical bandits. With that and the amount of bullets the outside walls of the bank have handled the past week alone, The Claws couldn't risk the possibility. For Oleg, not again.

"Oh, good thinking. Well then, Chari, don't get your hands too dirty!" Lada gave me her goodbyes, taking Anastasia's wheelchair. "Come on, Baba, let's get to work. I'd love to fix that old romper."

"Bah, alright. Hope *my* hands don't get too shaky," the elder bear humored as the two of them went to the sofa, getting comfortable as they prepped and threaded their needles.

It was just me and Oksana.

"Charissa, are you well? You haven't been so happy. It's been showing on your face for a few days." She took the time to sit in the chair close by, leaning in.

Her daily check-in.

"Just thinking about the past, like always,"

It had been one of the more intrusive trains to my track of thought. The same kind that had been harboring in the back of my mind late at night, keeping me restless and unfulfilled.

"About Reveria, or about your sestra?" she pressed.

"…Can it be both?"

"Of course, devushka. But holding onto your regrets will drag you down with them. Not much can be done for *her* anymore, but as far as that town goes, we again have no problem taking you back there. Can even be today if you wanted." She told me once more, as she proposed many times before. But again, I struggled to face the prospect.

"I still need time." Why couldn't I just let these burdens go?

"If that's the case, let's put you to work."

Working would have been better than the incessant dwelling on what-ifs. So, I pushed myself out of my seat and got mentally prepared for the rest of the day. "I think I'd like that."

"Well get yourself dressed proper and meet me on the rooftop. Don't keep me waiting." She headed out, and it was my turn to do the same.

Going back to Lada's room, I got myself dressed up and brushed my hair, keeping it neatly done in the same headwrap Anastasia parted with. Again, my remorse nagged. I needed to go to the rooftop to put my mind on other things. After cleaning myself up, I went towards the stairwell at the back of the bank. Upward about two flights, I went through the metal exit. The passage was always kept locked for obvious reasons, but with

Oksana expecting me, I had no issue stepping out into the high ground. There wasn't anything worth mentioning about the rooftop, other than it gave a view of the barren streets below and the railways accompanying them. During the night, one of The Claws kept watch, "as the most opportune time to stab someone in the back is in their sleep," or so Nikolai once told me. But with turrets installed, everyone here could have slept better.

All they needed was a little more maintenance to function.

Oksana hunched in the distance, working on one of the gun machines at one corner. Having four to work with, I went to see how things were going as she checked the circuitry and if enough bullets loaded the chamber. Whatever unfortunate intruder that happened across the fortress would be in for an unpleasant welcome. I was still fascinated by this piece of old tech, and they were supposedly hard to come by. From what I learned, back in the day when Pietas was in development, they had these machines in the event of potential invasion or terrorism. Anything to protect their city.

Though the truth was, that the real *enemy* was inside all along.

"It really is a miracle that Oleg managed to find all of these. They're impressive," I mentioned to Oksana, and she gave a content *humph* as she closed the back panel with her oil-drenched hands.

"These are truly some beautiful machines," the mother bear remarked, finishing her checkup with the turret. She and I made our rounds with the other few, keeping an informal conversation going as we talked about how thankful we were to find the things we needed.

Whenever we went out for searches, we did not have to worry about coming back hurt, either. The Claws had taught me a lot in the short time I stayed with them: to be resourceful, tenacious, and keep a level head, no matter how trivial or dire the situation.

"Cut seems like it's doing better. We need to find you a knife that you can keep yourself," she commented on the healing stitch that webbed my arm. The berserker that left it might've done damage, but Oksana made certain that the injury he received was *fatal*.

"Lada did good with her stitchwork, but is it okay if I ask you something?" I sat down beside her.

Oksana finished setting up the fourth turret, and when she closed the panel, she knelt to my level. "What's on your mind this time?"

"Tell me, why have you been so nice to me?"

She gave me a chortle. "Because hospitality is standard with us."

"I mean, why were you so willing to go out of your way to help me? On the street, you took me in your arms without question; on the first night, no less. There must have been a reason for that, right?"

Peering from the rooftop and down at the railway tracks between the buildings, I constantly reminisced about the evening that I came across their group. After my experience in Reveria, a sliver of good nature seemed to be a hidden gem out here, rare and unprecedented.

"Well, two reasons. One, because you were too small to be a threat to any of us," she stated. I was not expecting her to jab at my size, but granted, she was an immovable mountain.

Next to her, I felt like a sand pebble once again.

"Secondly, I must admit, you reminded me of my own girl. When I saw you, I saw Lada. I knew I couldn't let you be out here by yourself."

"Are you sure about that? I mean, she's so much stronger-willed. Like no matter what happens, she's always calm and collected…hell, I still get scared whenever this place gets hit,"

She bestowed a deep breath. "Chari, you remember how I told you the story about that raider and his group of pals that ambushed Nikolai and me coming home? Tossed a pipe bomb at us, and I had to shield him with my life?" The vivid imagery of that tale never went stale.

"That even though you lost your leg, you made those scum suffer?"

She glanced at the mechanical appendage. "You imagine what that was like in your head…but Lada didn't have to imagine anything when she saw me come inside with one leg. She's been through some of the worst with me, and you've only been down here for a short while."

The steel on her leg echoed her visage.

My reflection showed too. "I forget that a lot of you have lived your entire lives down here. Makes me feel weaker in comparison, I guess."

"Weak? *Weak* is bringing others down. You still have plenty of time to keep growing, but you're no baby." She pinched my cheek. "You shouldn't spend all your youth beating yourself up and worrying over little things. Heh, who knows, maybe you can become big and strong like me!" She let out a burst of exuberant laughter, an infectious one at that.

I giggled back, and like she always did, she uplifted my woes. "You're like the mom I never had," I confessed, and her expression softened. I was being honest though. She filled the void of that role in a short time.

Oksana made me feel like the daughter I could've been.

With a sputtering whirl, the turrets shut down, tilting downward. Oksana leaned over to the machine next to us, opening the panel with tense eyes. "Strange. Everything's all in order," she mumbled to herself. The door to the stairwell burst open, and Lada came running over towards us. With a flashlight in her hand, her fur was somehow whiter.

"We have a problem! The bank's power has been cut!"

My own skin paled too.

"Figured as much. Well, let's not waste any time standing around. Let's get everyone to the vault," Oksana commanded.

Down the stairwell, back to the first floor, it was pitch-black within the building. All of it reminded me of when I first found myself in the dark, and when the voices tormented me every second. My breath became shakier with every step through the oblique halls. The only saving grace was the light that Lada held, and it was perhaps the one thing that kept me from freaking out.

She led us through the halls until we came across a giant vault door. Back before the outbreak, inside this massive space of steel, was where most of the town's pearls, or marbles rather, went for safekeeping. Whenever it came to emergencies like these, the Claws would use it to their advantage. Now was the perfect time to use it.

Nearby was a dull combination pad covered in an unbreakable plastic case. Oksana pulled out a key to unlock the lid and shifted the numbered wheels until the inner mechanism clicked. When she got the code right, she grabbed onto the vault door and turned it over several times, opening the enormous safe. Inside, there were plenty of beds and large canisters of both food and water. Weapons and firearms stocked the steel drawers, with ammo stashed inside, while all the other supplies were stacked and organized together during times of crisis. Everyone else memorized the procedure, with Igor making his way with Anastasia, but Oleg and Nikolai were nowhere to be found.

"Are you kids alright? Mama?" Oksana stressed.

"I'm fine, sladkaya," the elder reassured her.

"Right in the middle of doing the dishes too. What's happening?" Igor wondered, all while I struggled to keep my composure.

"We're not getting attacked again, are we? Are we going to get kidnapped?" I panicked to Oksana.

"Nyet. If it were that, we would have seen them outside. This must be something else…" She pondered, only for heavy footsteps to come from outside the safe. Nikolai and Oleg managed to get back to us, their hands dirtied in grime and irritation.

"There you both are. What's going on?" she asked them both, as they were still wiping the grease from their mitts, breathing heavily.

"It's the bank's power cables. Wires must have fried trying to connect with the turrets. Should be fixable, but without the parts or a proper Catalyst to repair the damage...we have no other way to connect back to the city's energy grid," Oleg told her.

"Pieces of shit were bound to be cut short eventually. We need to do something right now. With how things are, anybody could strike," Nikolai demanded. Oksana devised the next course of action, giving everybody a role during our untimely circumstances.

She turned to Lada and Igor. "Kids, make sure Mama is safe, and don't leave this vault."

Her eyes darted to her beloved, Nikolai. "Watch from the rooftop, lyubov. Nobody gets in."

Lastly, she faced Oleg and me. "The three of us will find what we need to fix our mess."

When everyone had their task, they did not hesitate to get to their positions. Nikolai and Oleg gathered their assault rifles from the metal drawers nearby, racking up ammo on their bodies. I checked my own gun, preparing my mind for another expedition on the line. This trip was the most important one I had to be ready for, yet my nerves still jittered, which did not go unnoticed by Oleg's keen eyes.

"What are you so afraid of, devushka?" he asked me.

Nikolai came forth. "If you'd rather stay here, you could swap with Igor instead—"

"I'm fine. A little overwhelmed, but I'm good,"

"If you say so. Good luck, you three." Nikolai rushed out, heading for position up top.

"Since you're still in this, you're going to need some extra firepower. Like I've told you before, if that little pistol runs out, it's best to use a backup. No time to reload." Oleg searched through one of the drawers and found a better weapon for me to use. Before he handed it to me, he checked its intricacies to make sure it was safe to handle. When everything met his standards, he handed me the firearm.

Something he made me a little familiar with.

I was given a standard-issue, 10mm pistol that was a little heftier than I'm used to, but still easy for someone like me to manage, labeled *POLISTES* on its slide. Fourteen bullets in its mag. During the past few scavenges, he taught me how to use it if my other, weaker pistol failed. On top of the lessons Aliya ran me through, The Claws had given me extensive experience in armaments.

Every day with them was a lesson in gun school.

"Still remember how to use it?" he asked, and my palms dried up. The sweat on my hands dissipated as I cleared my head. Although he checked the heavy pistol, it was necessary to always do a double take. Clanking the chamber out, I checked the mag, clicking it all together, and made certain that the safety remained on.

"It hits harder than how my usual does, but it never hurts to have a backup, right?"

"It's one thing to sound like me, but don't act like it. You need to stay behind Oksana and me when we're out there. If we get into any firefight, you take cover and stay out of it."

Distraught, my grip firmed on the second weapon. "Then what was the point of everything you taught me so far?"

He pinched my wrist. "Polar bear and reindeer skin is thick, plenty of fur too. You? You're thin, like tissue paper. Bullets would pass through you, and when they do, Oksana and I can't do anything about it. We can't get this done if you get hit even once."

Another lesson I learned? Not to disregard an elder's advice.

"I'll stay out of the fire then."

"As you should. Are we good, Oksana?"

Nearby, Oksana gave her child a farewell kiss on the forehead, a pat on Igor's scalp, and a gentle hug to her frail mother. Once finished, she reassessed her light machine gun, her signature weapon. She told me once that she pried the trophy off the hands of her first kill, and that she stuck with it ever since. A weapon of red brass and formidable power, *RHINOCEROS-LMG* plated its gunmetal.

"We've got no time to waste. Off we go."

The three of us set off from the vault, heading back down the dark hallways until we passed the lobby doors, fitting our boots before we went for the front entrance. Stepping outside, Nikolai surveyed them from the rooftop, keeping hold of his five-round burst AR close.

Spotting us, he waved us off. "Better be back! Can't lose my brother-in-arms and wife in one day,"

Oksana cupped her hand to her maw, hollering back. "Worry not, *milyy*, we'll be back before you know it!"

All of us marched around the side of the bank, and Oksana led us down the alleyway as we kept our senses peeled for anything. The stains of past assaults desecrated the grays, too many I lost count. It might have been incidental, having the generator and its parts malfunction, but we never let our guards down for a second.

Beyond home and within.

"What place will have what we're looking for?" I asked.

"There's an elementary school some distance away, used to be raider den. Heard some rumors saying now it's ghosts. Could be worth checking for any good loot and parts," she proposed, and while the idea might have been feasible, Oleg had his frets about her judgment.

"How could you be sure they have what we need?"

"School like that required a good amount of power. Bound to have what we need and plenty more." She mentioned.

"I know you've got a vendetta against them, but what if they're still there? What if they already took the parts we'd need?" He worried.

Oksana cocked her gun back, a cold tone in her throat. "If we find raiders, they'll all die. If we don't, we'll track them down and take what we need. Give them what they truly deserve."

"How much farther is this school?" I asked.

"We're expecting another half-hour's worth of exercise. Do you think you can keep up?" Oleg teased.

"I used to walk miles and go mountain climbing. Maybe someday, when we leave this place, we can all go do that together."

"That'd be wonderful, Charissa."

"Hush now. Don't want to be too loud." Oksana reminded us.

"I doubt we'll find anything good there. Especially functional parts, let alone a proper Catalyst. Not around this sector." Oleg murmured, and admittedly, I continued to have my doubts as well.

"Oh, come now, my gut's usually right."

"It's just…"

"Oleg…what're you *really* worried about?" she pressed.

"What would happen, if say, Charissa got grabbed and we couldn't do anything about it? What then?" Oleg mumbled. "Natalya, Mila, Mama, and Papa…every day, I fear we'll lose somebody, and I don't want these expeditions to repeat history for me. I know we're strong, but are we strong enough?"

Oksana paused, causing us to stop in our tracks.

"You did everything you could, Oleg, but what's done is done. We still have each other, and that's what matters now. Besides," she softly assured him, putting a hand on his shoulder, "your family could still be out there. There's no guarantee that they're truly gone."

"That's what hurts me most," Oleg choked.

To see a man show his sorrow was a difficult sight to bear, but he had the right to be *human,* to be able to know loss. The anguish though.

Nobody deserved that.

"You're not alone," I told him.

His face shifted to me; a light trickle of tears streaked over his scar-worn face. Through the waters showed comforting blinks, followed by a sigh of ease. "Thank you. Both of you. Let's not dawdle here any longer; we got a family to get back to." Oleg wiped away his grief.

"Alright."

"Let's keep our heads up high, you two. We've got a little more ground to cover. After this, we can play *Durak.*" Oksana offered.

Playing cards once we returned home brought enough promise to keep us going. But it was hard not to brush off what would happen if— or *when*—I disappeared from their lives, one way or another.

After my time with them, I would've only added another scar.

***

Ahead in the distance stood an immense foundation of red brick. A barbed wire fence bordered the property, and faux grass was planted beyond the steel. The fake lawn maintained its vibrantly verdant color but offered an eye strain among the grim hues around. The blue-colored benches and lunch tables were covered in empty beer bottles and abandoned weaponry. The brick walls of the school were covered in grime and vandalized in graffiti, with the windows destroyed and covered with blankets. The playground had been modified for torture, installed with belts and spikes on the equipment while rusty nails and glass shards were left in its sandpit. Ahead there was a flagpole, where an old and desecrated corpse had been left to hang. A rope lingered around the neck, with the wrists and ankles tied. The school had been ransacked, and the warning signs would have driven anybody away. Sane people, at least. But for raiders, this grim sight suited them well. Other than the single corpse at the flagpole, there was nobody else on the outside. No guards. No bodies, even. It would be one thing to see a trace of life, but to see nothing was as concerning.

If not for the mass devastation, I could have envisioned this as a place where the most ambitious of kids had their chance to learn. Something I never had. Now, it was every child's worst nightmare.

"Anyone that was here must've run off. We should look somewhere else. A repair shop could be better," I suggested.

Oksana shook her head as she went to examine the fence with a hole cut out from the prickly wire frame. "No, most auto shops were picked over for parts long ago. We should still scope things out before we change our plan and go elsewhere."

She carefully gripped the fence and tore it open wider, creating a larger space for the rest of us to move through. Oleg made his way onto the forged lawn on the other side with ease. Thus, I became obligated to do the same. When the soles of our boots crunched across the imitated grass, we waited to see if we would be greeted with an ambush, but nobody came. We kept close to one another as we surveyed the school building, watching for any surprise hostiles.

Nothing.

Whatever came through here had driven the previous tenants away, because there was not another living soul in this place. At least, that was what all of us hoped.

"No trouble yet but stay on your toes. We're going in."

By Oksana's direction, we went up towards the archway of the building, holding the entrance underneath the grand curvature. The kids that once attended here would have been welcomed by words of steel fixed on the rounded span.

Little Futures Elementary School

"What happened to the children here?" I mumbled.

"Sometime before the impending outbreak, they shut down the schools when kids became ill. They were hoping it was only the flu, but that's when…worry not, we won't find children here." Oksana granted me an ounce of relief.

No child should ever have walked the perilous avenues of this city.

We walked to the front doors to see how they fared, but when Oksana tried to turn the handles, they would not budge. No locks from the outside. However, a card reader was close to the entrance, where a little red light buzzed from its mechanism.

The power within lingered, so it seemed.

"Maybe we go through the window?" Oleg suggested.

Oksana dismissed the idea. "If there's anybody in there, that'd be too noisy, and every door probably needs a card. We need to find one."

"Where? No chance there are staff cards lying out here." I grumbled.

"The body there. I think I saw one on him when we got here." Oleg pointed, and Oksana and I directed our attention his way.

"Then get that thing down and come back here after. I'll see if I can do anything with these doors until then." Oksana sent us off as she continued to do her work. If all else failed, brute force would be our card to get inside.

Oleg and I went to the flagpole, standing high from the ground. Even from ground level, the hanging corpse leaked with its stale, decaying odor. Tethers of rope bound it to the beam, as if the body was meant to stay where it was. A grisly reminder for those who trespassed. He settled his assault rifle on the grass and pulled out his knife, trying to cut the rope that layered around the pulley of the sick, twisted system. "Bound thick and tight. This might take time," he grumbled.

I had a thought. "Boost me up; I think I can grab it."

"Very risky for a small girl like you, but…" He shrugged and sheathed the knife in his holster, cracking his neck after. "Just be very slow and steady, okay? Easy does it."

He squatted and offered his shoulders for leverage. Holstering my handgun, I gently stepped onto him. Once he boosted me, I clenched onto the pole and my legs clamped around the roped beam, with my eyes glued to the jangling card above. The smell gripped my throat.

"Bud' ostorozhen," he called, prepared to catch me.

Breath held tight, I scooted my legs further, reaching upward to clench higher onto the beam. Sweat drenched my palms, and I nearly lost my grip.

"Der'mo!" Oleg panicked, but I managed to grab hold of the cold steel again. My breathing shuddered.

I've been through worse. I got this.

With a huff, I continued to climb. Pacing my way, I got closer to the body. Finally, within reach, the card dangled to be taken. With one arm holding out and the other clinging onto the pole, my fingers got to the lanyard. But as I tried to pull it, the corpse would not budge.

"What's going on up there?" Oleg hollered.

"It's stuck, but I almost got it!" I gritted my teeth as I concentrated, giving one harder yank, hoping to have the lanyard break off from its owner…only for the spinal cord to snap, causing the entire corpse to fall, along with me, crashing down. My screams broke through the air and my blood raced, bracing for the impact.

Before I could become one with the ground, I landed in Oleg's arms. We both let out a deep breath.

"You're a lifesaver."

He placed me back on my feet, dusting me off. "It's nothing. Let's see what he has for us." Approaching the brittle remains, Oleg ripped the wrists off the corpse, untying the lanyard.

"Think it'll work?" I questioned.

"If not, we're in for a long day. Let's go," he ordered.

We returned to the front entrance; Oksana stopped in her attempts to break off the bolts to the door. "What happened over there? I heard you scream and saw you in Oleg's arms."

"It wasn't a big deal. We found our way in." Oleg held up the lanyard in his hand, with the card hanging from its loose end.

Oksana glanced at me. "You remembered what I told you, hm?"

She taught me a lot of proverbs, and many of them I recalled, but one that stuck out to me was… "She who doesn't take risks doesn't drink champagne?" I guessed.

"That's right, kukla. Just be a little more careful, da?"

She pinched my ear, making me pout. The caribou handed her the card, and Oksana went to the door. She picked up her gun first before approaching the access panel nearby, bringing the staff card up to the sensor. Red to green, the light went. Grabbing the handle, she pulled slowly, and it opened with relative ease. Peering inside, it was still dark within. "Power might be on, but it's pitch black. Stick close."

She stuck the card inside her pocket and flicked her tactical flashlight on, Oleg and I doing the same with our weapons. With caution, we stepped inside the school and into the main hallway. The haunting whispers of the academy's dead moaned through the dark space, as there was no visible light to be seen. As we went further in, we caught a lingering, rancid stink that permeated throughout the air. Traces of struggle accompanied the detritus of mayhem. Garbage and casings scattered the colorful tile floor, the walls adorned with bullet holes. Among the heaping junk, a massive pile of desks and chairs blocked off one of the major halls. When I searched for anything that could help us navigate our way around, I found a large map posted on the brick wall, covered in mucky stains and crude vandalism.

"Over here."

They gathered behind me. The map had a concise layout of the entire school building. There were many classrooms, given their own numbers and subjects. Anyone could have gotten lost in here without this guide. Or lights. I was not sure where to begin when it came to the idea of finding spare parts, but Oleg pointed out a particular spot. At his fingertip, a large box indicated a cafeteria, with the extending rooms of a kitchen and basement/boiler linked to it.

"Basement could have what we're here for. Let's go."

We collectively agreed as to where we needed to go, but turning for the hall leading directly to the cafeteria, the heavy barricade of school equipment proved formidable. No way we could have torn it down without making too much noise. Oksana went back to the map for reevaluation. "We'll loop around this way, but let's be careful. Check every room we pass by. If you see anything, say something."

We pathed towards the next hallway we could access. Debris obstructed our path, and we needed to tread lightly. Oksana shined her light forward, while Oleg and I kept watch from our backs. We approached each room, peeking in and scoping out any signs of life, but we found nobody. Nothing but crackling chalkboards, more desks toppled to the floor, along with broken bookshelves. Every classroom was left in a mess, but still, they were dead inside. Even so, we could not let our guards down for a moment. While slowly wandering the halls together, we could see a twin set of wooden doors further ahead. From the promising sight, we hoped that might have been where we needed to go. I kept behind everyone, watching our flanks, only to stop.

A creak came from one of the doors we passed. A glass one that had been mangled for entry, which led into the gymnasium. I peered inside, the space showed pitch-black, but a subtle dissonance came from within. I was going to ignore it, assuming it was a rickety fixture. About to catch up with everybody else…the noise became more distinct. A faint, recognizable whisper came to my ear.

"No no, not here…It's too cold, steer clear."

Goosebumps riddled my skin, and I pointed my light toward the door again. Panicking, I called out to the rest of the group as they headed down the hallway. "Guys, wait a second."

When they caught my distress, they came back to my aid.

"What's wrong?" Oleg asked, and they peered through the shattered pane next to me.

"I heard someone."

Oksana grabbed hold of the metal handle, prying the door open as she leaned her head in. Oleg readied his firearm in case anything came out from within, but the space was so large and convoluted that in darkness, it was difficult to tell what lingered within the shadows.

"Knew I smelled something off. Let's look," Oksana suggested, and she yanked the door wide for us.

We kept our alerts high as we entered the gymnasium.

The vastness of the expanse could be found in how high the windows went, with bare illumination peering through from the outside. The floor's wood had suffered much surface damage after years of wear, where a continuous scuffed streak of white paint lined from corner-to-corner to the room's surface area. The metal beams creaked above us, and when we directed our flashlights toward it, we came across a crackled board of glass, with a netted hoop attached. Other than the interesting design of the gym, bleachers accompanied the left and right sides. I was suspicious that whoever made the noise might have been hiding away beneath, and so we checked for ourselves.

"Oleg, go over there and scope out any unwelcome company. I'll go over here with Charissa," Oksana ordered.

The reindeer went to investigate the further side of this sports room. Meanwhile, I kept close to the mother bear. We searched the bleachers, only to find blankets and pillows among the several rows of splintered seats. From what I could tell, this school must have housed many raiders. Although, I could have never been certain as to why they would leave this all behind, given the durable structure. Not to mention the amount of usable room that the institution provided.

I could have only imagined how much potential the children had here, given so many possibilities. Now, it was nothing more than an old den defiled by scum, all left to fall apart into rubble.

After finding nobody hiding around the bleachers, we came close to the opposite end of the gym, as Oksana and I were about to meet up halfway with Oleg. Once we approached the large and lofty end wall, an impressive mural that once embellished the gym captivated us…but it was certainly strange. In the center of the whimsical artwork, past the defiling marks made by the previous tenants, a comically characterized kangaroo jumped in the air in front of a bright blue sky. A decorative rainbow arched above with bubbly clouds in the pretty-painted background. Despite the marks and slurred words, in comparison to the rest of the stark atmosphere, this was a speckle of glitter left in the school's abandonment.

Jump and reach for the sky, Joeys!

"What's this all supposed to be?" I gawked.

Oksana scoffed. "Used to be silly art to inspire the youth. Pfft. *Joeys.*"

A utility closest creaked nearby. The door blended in seamlessly with the white paint on the rest of the wall until the crack showed through.

"Well, I found nothing on my side. What's going on here?" Oleg asked when he came back, catching Oksana with her eyes on the ominous clue. From the entry, a wet substance streaked on the floor.

Blood.

She brushed her bare finger pads onto the speckles of deep red, and when she brought her hand up, the ichor was still freshly wet.

Someone passed through these parts recently. Too recently.

Promptly, she stood up, hefting her lead-spitter as she came closer to the door, signaling us to prepare for trouble. Without hesitation, Oksana slammed her shoulder into the utility closet, barreling inside and pointing to whatever lay within. In the room, it smelled reminiscent of one of the Miriana hospital rooms. My nostrils tingled to its staleness. Following her lead, we were greeted by carts of deflated sports balls, with other equipment toppled to the concrete ground. But beyond the clutter of gym material was a grisly sight at the far end of the closet.

On the floor, a blue mat had been spread out, with a lifeless body left on it. The back of the corpse faced us, balled up during its last few moments of life. A profuse amount of crimson trickled from it, lying in its lake of tainted essence. I could not discern the beast at first, because I was distraught by the familiar clothes the corpse wore. Upon closer look, it was unmistakable. The black garments, the bloodied feathers that adorned the body, and the spotted tail.

The marauder from the streets.

"Good ears, Charissa," Oksana praised.

"I've seen her before."

"You have? Where?"

The memory overcame my conscience. The howls of the poor catman, the way he was entangled in razor tethers, and the same woman that snuffed any semblance of freedom. I could've never shaken off the regret of doing nothing but to hear him get taken away to his demise.

"Back before I met you all, out in the city streets. She took someone…If she's here now, I wonder if he's here too."

"So, you've seen how *Vultures* work."

"You mean the abductors I've been hearing about for months?"

"Same disgusting pigs that took my family." Oleg spat on the corpse. "She deserved a far worse death. If this school became one of their newest hideouts, they must've been collecting for another delivery."

Right there, I became acquainted with a brand-new fear.

"But what could've killed her?"

Before we left the equipment room, another clue loomed above. Not far from the floormat, one of the ceiling panels had been left on the concrete. An intrusive hole opened the plaster, large enough for someone to crawl through. Oksana stepped over the body to shine her light into the dusty space. Fibrous particles faded through the light, but there was nothing in the ceiling.

"Now I see why this one was murdered in her own quarters. Not only do we have Vultures here, but another threat's with us. We've come this far; we can't be cowards now. Keep your eyes sharp."

Oksana walked off the mat and we followed her out from the sports closet, sticking ever closer to one another. We returned to the hallways, not too much further from the cafeteria. The grip on my weapon remained firm, though I kept my finger off the trigger until I needed to use it. Without that voice lingering in the dark, the air was quieter than ever, and only our breaths trembled through.

A new noise stifled the hollow space.

It was swift and near silent, like someone ran on the tip of their toes, but I was afraid that I might have been the only one hearing things again.

"Do you all hear that?" I whispered to them.

They both turned my way; the silence froze the air. We held our breaths as we tried to listen more closely. A soft groan came from above, and we prepared ourselves, aiming our arms, and *crash!* It fell to the filth-ridden hall floor. Another one of the ceiling panels had fallen out. Oleg approached the foam-filled rectangle, only for nothing to be above. The entire place was falling apart, and this damned school put everybody on the edge. "Who the hell else would be here?" Oleg hushed.

There was running once more, and it came from the end of the hallway near the cafeteria. I trod on my own, trying to figure out who was with us, or if it was all the figments of my imagination.

"Charissa…! What're you doing?" Oksana called to me, but I could barely make out the words she spoke.

My mind trailed to the sounds, as did my feet. I could not have been the only one hearing these things. I had to find out where the noises came from. My ears rang, as the same voice from before made itself known again. But that woman was dead... so, why? Why was she back? We came across her body only a minute before, so why was she speaking? Did I hear her ghost? Out of nowhere, her voice came to me, overlapping with several more. Three of them whispered to me.

Mocking me.

"She doesn't know."

"She'll miss the show."

"But soon she'll go."

The voices flooded my eardrums.

They rattled my skull, overwhelming me once again as I listened to their laughter amalgamating into a boisterous vortex.

They all started crying.

Suddenly, they screamed into my ears.

It hurts to hear them.

Their screeches made me fall to my knees—only to follow with derisive giggles. What was so funny? Why did they all laugh at me? I wanted them to stop, but they continued to torment me.

Stop…I've had enough of this! Stop! Stop! Where were you all hiding!? Get out of my head! Out! Don't laugh at me! Stop laughing at me! Please stop!

"Charissa!"

Oksana grabbed hold of me.

"I was hearing things again. S-Sorry." My speech trembled, and Oksana glanced back the way we came. Never had she seen me like *that* before. *I* had never seen myself like that before either.

"Maybe you and Oleg could keep watch at the entrance."

I wiped the sweat from my brow and kept moving towards the cafeteria. "I'm fine." I didn't blink. I could not let my head get to me.

"Charissa." Oksana tried to reach through to me.

I was fine.

We continued until the double doors faced. Stickers of various foods clung on the wooden surface, with their happy little faces and adorable little eyes carved out by a knife tip. Vinyl signs were adhered nearby; scratched and picked at, but still legible.

This is your lunchroom! Help keep it clean!

The cafeteria held more than rotten food, for the whole area was left a calamitous mess. Crushed beer cans and broken booze bottles littered the lunch tables, along with plastic trays that crawled with ants and mold. The paint on the walls and the coverage on the ceiling peeled off into a state of decay, and the rancid, gut-wrenching stench grew thicker. While nausea crept to my stomach, we were not too far from the kitchen now, and thus closer to the basement. Closer to getting what we came here for. However, at the kitchen doors, we found a morbid memento on the pocketed floor. A severed arm, covered in more plucked feathers. The cut was brutally done once again, leaving the tendons and bone torn through. A blood trail of retreat, along with smeared footprints, led through one of the kitchen doors. Oksana approached the lone appendage, reaching down to touch the fresh river of red. This too, was left here recently.

"Another one? Eto piz' dets," Oleg mumbled.

"Looks like whoever got attacked ran into the kitchen. Let's get in and find them before we get what we need."

Oksana and Oleg tried to get the single kitchen doors open, but each of them was blocked from the other side. Whoever was inside must have tried to barricade themselves in.

"We can't budge it. Hmm, how about this?" Oleg pointed to the window counter nearby. He pulled it upward, and it cracked open. A dozen flies escaped through while he tried to yank it back down to give it another go, but it stuck completely in place.

"Don't think we can get in like this. Maybe we can head outside and find a backdoor to the kitchen." Oksana contemplated.

"I think I can make my way in," I volunteered. "It's small enough for me to squeeze through."

Oksana's wrinkles strained. "Charissa, you haven't been doing too good, and it's too risky. You shouldn't be doing this."

This had to be done. I didn't want her to treat me like a kid.

Just like Narissa did. Just like Kyran did.

"The moment I get in, I'll find a way for the rest of you to come through. I promise. You have to trust me."

She seethed out a deep breath. "If anything happens, you must crawl back through. Don't make me regret this."

Hoisting myself, I managed to worm my way underneath the shutter. Into the kitchen, my boots squashed into chunks and muck. Shining my flashlight around, more buzzing horseflies surrounded the fetid, pitch-black space. The veins in my neck constricted.

Bloody utensils accompanied the desecrated kitchen: bone saws, meat hooks, peelers. The dismembered bodies of raiders scattered across the tables and floor, cored of their innards and their bones stripped of flesh. Maggots crawled over their fermenting carcasses, with jars of offal and flayed meat filled to the lids. The mesh of smells permeated my senses. Clasping my mouth, my efforts to restrain my esophagus were outmatched by the festering pigsty. Stomach acid spewed between my fingers, running down my arm. I uncovered my mouth, and the rest of my breakfast splattered into the lakes of biofluids.

"Charissa, what's going on?" Oksana called out.

I wiped my lips. "N-Nothing."

Unbelieving of my words, she let it be. "What about the doors?"

Doing my best to ignore the pigsty, holding my breath, I took notice of the doors on both sides of the serving window, barricaded. An entire fridge dripping with red blocking one off, while the other had a rolling shelf loaded aplenty with massive aluminum cans.

"One of the doors is blocked off by some cart, but I'll move it."

Holstering my gun, I got straight to work, grabbing onto the roller to pull it away from the door. I strained my back and shoulders, but with a little more force, I managed to get the whole thing moving. To my dismay, one of the large cans toppled over with a loud clang. Juices spilled out onto the peppered floor, along with their fruity contents.

"What happened? Did you get hurt?" Oleg leaned in, trying to fit his head through the shutter door, but his antlers prevented him.

"I knocked something over. It's only—"

There was something with me.

Soft, delicate footsteps trailed around my vicinity like falling snow. I hurriedly pointed my gun toward the obscured figure that appeared at the corner of my eye…only to find nothing there. I could not have been going crazy. Someone had to be messing with me.

They were *there* with me, but where?

A faint light flickered in the dreadful dark. A cracked door led directly into the basement, where the boiler must have been located. Possibly where the parts could be. As I was about to turn around and inform everyone about what I discovered…someone spoke out to me. That same, velvety whisper returned to haunt me.

"Help us, please. We need release."

It came from the boiler door once more, and my skin crawled with thorns. On the floor, the fresh trail of blood led directly inside, making me stumble back. In a jittery fright, I hoisted myself back onto the counter. About to get myself underneath the rolling shutter, a screw came loose. The shutter slammed down with a startling crash. Desperately, I latched my hands onto the handle, trying to pull it open.

It was stuck tight.

"Charissa!" Oksana and Oleg called.

As they tried to pull the rolling door up from the other side, it refused to move. I tried to lift once again, but my efforts proved futile. The basement door cracked further open, and the flickering light inside grew brighter, flashing faster the more my adrenaline kicked in.

The whispers only grew stronger, more controlling.

"We can't breathe, we can't see. Come to me."

I could not contain my *own* breathing.

Back at Deanna's Diner, where I ran for my life, I almost lost myself. Except here, there was nowhere I could run, hiding was futile. Narissa came to my vision. To see her crystalline eyes left me shattered, only for Kyran to come into view. It was like reliving the same moment twice. The amber of his soul cracked too when all I did was watch him plummet to his demise. All I ever did was run away. I could not live as a coward.

I wasn't a child.

These irrational fears could not consume me, to drive me away from everything. I had to face my nightmares head-on. The footsteps? The voices? Whatever was down there in that basement? I was going to see for myself. Pushing off the counter, and readying my weapon, I slowly approached the basement door. The barrel of my gun aimed inside; the stairs of concrete led down further. Cobwebs stretched above me, and the steps below had blood smothered in a downward trail. I took a deep breath, before I took my path forward, prepared for anything that I would find at the bottom. Slowly I went, repressing the anxious tethers that tried to pull me back into weakness.

I'm not weak.

I stepped into the basement, the busted pipes that coursed through the bleak confines crawled with rust and leaked with perspiration. A faint mist flooded throughout the tight space, but it did not faze me. On the floor, cleaning supplies were toppled over. Brooms, mops, and heavy-duty sprays spilled out, and amidst the mess, that river of blood led further in, until it disappeared around the corner. The fluorescent lights above incessantly clicked on and off, and bullet holes scattered into the walls that threatened to close me in.

None of it mattered.

I stripped off any last nerves, and cautiously put my back against the pocketed wall nearing the corner. Teeth bracing myself for what was to come, I turned over ready to fire.

A horrific display scarred my mind.

More bodies. Three of them, grisly gashes decorating their flesh in the sharpest, deepest cuts. Their spilled organs muddled the dark, feathered clothes they wore, the exact style of the marauder from the gym. Rags torn from their heads; their faces were disfigured. Their eyes gauged, maws torn open, and their throats fileted, they were unrecognizable.

Whatever came through here lacked any humanity.

The bodies had crudely plated guns at their sides, with bullet casings that accounted for every hole in the walls. What caught my attention other than the rusted chains clinging to the bricks and torturous tools beside them were the strange objects that stuck into the fermenting bodies. Throwing knives, but their shapes were abstract and handmade. I reached over, plucking one out, and the disgusting squelch made my ears tremble. The dagger was tapered into a lanceolate leaf. While examining the fine craftsmanship, something moved. In a blink, one of the carcasses shifted. The way it twitched and writhed…I dropped the dagger, aiming the sight of my pistol down at the gurgling body. Reanimated, it began to laugh.

"Angels above…Wh-What is this…" I muttered to the corpse.

He became dead-still again, turning to face me. Eye sockets empty, his grotesque smile somehow stretched wider, as slobber sputtered from those crackling lips. "Oh, oh, little lass! If you're looking for laughs, look for the star, and you'll go far!" The gargling words hacked out from those dying lungs as his body finally fell limp. There was no way it could have still lived, not when he lost his last breath…

When I brought my attention upward, something came to view.

Lying beside a large machine, a fourth corpse with her spine splayed out from her back. On her bandaged arm was a Catalyst-M model, the power surging in the metal webbing remaining on her lifeless limb. Before her demise, she must've been working on…a generator! I scrambled, checking to see if the massive device still had function. The mechanism appeared impressive, with *Constructed by Pietas Militia* overlaid on its side. Power still surged through it at a low capacity, with plenty more charge in its system, cables, and functional parts to spare. Exactly what we needed.

Now I needed to get out.

Before I managed to get away, there was something else above me, taped to the wall. When I stood up, another map introduced itself to my eyes. Not for the school, but instead, for the entire city. Everything in my body tried to tear me away, to make me run, but there was a strange pattern about the layout. There were trails and circles made in marker, as they had routes leading around the metropolis. There was a red oval made around here, the school, which led directly to another location. Above it, a star.

Fruor Falls Amusement Park (Main Pick-up Location)

My gaze roamed sporadically, picking up the trails, names fitted the pattern, given a certain number. Caelus Commons, Carpe Noctem, Florence's University for The Gifted, and other communities. 2,000 captures, 750 captures, 300 captures. A shock overcame me. On the map before me, there was one last location, branded for malevolent pursuit.

Reveria. 1,000 captures. Pursue.

The bulbs burnt out above.

Darkness surrounded me once more, and I dared not to move an inch. Those muffled footsteps made themselves known again, the same ones from the kitchen. Soft, gentle breathing accompanied them, making my spine shudder. Every exhale hushed behind me, steadily approaching as those nimble soles stepped into the lake of blood. This was not just my imagination, and I was not going insane. Everything that happened around me…all of it was real.

The nerves in my skin screamed to panic, but instead, I took control of them. Pistol tight in my hand, fingernails digging into the gunmetal, I clenched my teeth tighter. Slowly, I turned around and aimed for whatever crept behind me.

Nothing.

Until I lifted my head.

A black figure held onto the wooden beams across the shallow ceiling. Its four lanky limbs stretched above like a black widow. Those sharp eyes widened when our glares met. Illuminated in a bright, penetrating green, they tracked my every breath, unblinking. The fibers in my muscles constricted, and we continued to eye each other, for but a split second.

Impulsively, I followed.

The bullet soared; the shadow quickly pounced until it landed behind me. A sharp pain shot through my body once he caught my wrist, pulling on my arm and causing me to fall to my knees. Pistol clanking to the floor, the flashlight managed to cast a blur of brightness over the silhouette now on top of me.

The figure pinned me down, trying to shank a thick, shorthand blade right into my neck. I screamed for help as my fists clenched onto its arms, struggling against its strength, and doing everything in my power to resist. My attacker stared into my soul as it exerted a deadly force. My eyes clenched, I could not think, but my body reacted. Before he managed to skewer the knife into my esophagus, I shifted my head to the side, and the blade gratingly clanked into the concrete.

The shadow's effort faltered.

I found enough strength to throw my opponent off, causing the assailant to stumble over into a pipe, the rust snapping it from its screws until the beam dropped to the ground. A haze of moisture seeped from the waterways. Obscured in the light mist, the shadow stood on its feet, ready to slaughter me. Taking a stance, I picked up the cold, busted pipe, lunging to bash his skull.

As I was about to bludgeon the shadow, its short blade sliced through the dark towards me, and the metals clashed. We both grunted as we met each other at an impasse. While our weapons hissed like vipers, I struggled to bring my attacker down. In our stance, he clicked at his handle. From his blade, microteeth sheathed from its edge. Spinning with lethal speed, the pipe shattered at my fingers, and my broken poise caused the both of us to trip.

In a state of hysteria, I tried to reach back for the pistol at my side instead. Another wave of pain swam through my flesh, more excruciating than before. The shadow left a gnarly gash across my shoulder, and my muscle fibers shredded, causing me to screech out again. I slammed against the concrete wall, clenching onto my fresh wound.

The dark form rushed for me once more. I briskly evaded the shank from his bloodied chain blade, and the tip of his buzzing knife drilled into the wall this time, causing it to cease function. With the gun light cast, I scrambled for it. In his moment of weakness, I twirled to get my aim on the illusive menace.

In that split second, the tip of his stiff, teethed blade barely pricked against my neck. While he had me at knifepoint, the barrel of my gun was at his chest, and we were both at a standstill. If either of us made the next move, one of us would have been dead. Or neither of us would make it out of this alive. As we stood before each other, panting for air close to the rugged wall, my assailant broke the ice binding us.

"That glove."

A soothing male voice came from his wrapped garments.

"Don't talk. Make a move and you'll regret it."

"Then maybe you shouldn't have given me a weak point."

In a swift motion, he spun around right in front of me. I tried to fire another shot, only for him to duck to my side with little effort. Grabbing hold of my arm, and twisting it to submission, the assailant disarmed me once more. He swept my ankles, making me collapse. I scrambled to the floor, finding myself in the worst spot again. Cornering me in, he gripped my wrist, bringing my palm closer to his eyes, and his tongue clicked as he witnessed me cowering in his hold.

"Where did you get this glove?"

My fresh injury strained to his force. The gash was not deep, but it hurt like hell with every little movement. I had no clue who I was dealing with, but considering I had no position to run or be deceitful, I resorted to being honest for my life. "A man I knew. He gave it to me."

One hand nearly crushed my bone, the other brought out his blade. He leaned in and pressed the sharp teeth on my neck. A single click of a button would've torn me apart.

"Give me your name before I take your life instead."

I bit my tongue. I clenched my eyes shut, with my jugular so close to being severed. All that self-convincing of not being afraid. Of not being a scared little girl. All of it blanked out the moment I was on the edge of death to ruthless hands. "I-I'm Charissa. The man, the one from Reveria. P-panther, has a sister named Bea…The Rhodes."

His grip alleviated, and he pulled away from my throat before sheathing his metal. He stepped away to the map on the wall, barely visible in my hazed vision. "So, you know him. Very interesting."

He glimpsed over his shoulder at me, and I grasped my neck, where the littlest cuts had painted my skin. With my body on the ground, his mercy left me in shock. "W-Wait. You're not going to kill me?"

"I thought you might've been with these abductors, but seeing as you have that glove, and you're the *human*, killing you would not do any good. At least I hope."

I picked my gun up. Getting back on my feet, I managed to get distance between us. "So, you're the one who did all this."

He turned around to me, his movements phantomlike.

"I'm making a difference, unlike those politicians in their sophisticated courthouse. They don't have the slightest clue what's coming. Look at the map, and you'll see why I'm here. Why I did what I did. You'll understand."

From above in the kitchen, there was a loud smash. Oksana and Oleg had managed to break through the door and were about to come to me. I turned around, as their footsteps trampled toward the basement.

His soft voice came again. "If we ever cross paths, remember who spared your life."

Before I could face him again, he left with parting words.

"The Rogue Virtue."

He was gone, vanished into thin air.

"Charissa!"

Oksana and Oleg came rushing in, their flashlights pointed at me. Their faces stretched with immeasurable distress for my well-being, only to soften once when they witnessed the dead bodies on the ground, gasping at the slaughter amidst their feet. Oleg examined corpses, mortified by the severed limbs and disemboweling left behind.

"Blyat', I've never seen Vultures get a taste of their own medicine. These bastards got what was coming." Oleg scoffed, albeit perturbed.

"That's not important right now." Oksana ran over to me once she saw the damage to my arm, her grip grew tight and overprotective. "We knew something was wrong when we saw the state of that kitchen. Who did this to you? Where did they go?" she demanded, and with how fast everything happened, the impact made me lose my tongue. Oleg walked over, showing one of the leaf-shaped daggers to Oksana. Her gaze lit up once she took it in her hand. "That fox. No wonder it was nothing but ghosts here…must've had a score to settle with these vermin."

"Who are you talking about?" I mumbled.

"Ever since news of hybridian kidnapping and trafficking started to stir, so did the word of him. For months he's been labeled as a slaver-hunter, and not even those he saved know his face, nor his name."

"I just can't believe he let me live..."

Oksana's grip on my arm grew tenser. "And what did you think you were doing, acting like an idiot? Why would you try to do this on your own? You should've gotten the door for us right away instead of doing something so stupid. We could have helped you."

I sulked, unable to answer. There had been many instances where I should not have lived, yet here I remained.

What was fate trying to tell me?

"Wait a minute, is that what I think it is?" Oleg moved past us and knelt, unshackling the metal apparatus from the dead body, and inspecting the plating. "Sure is. A mechanical engineering-issued Catalyst! Let's see what she was working on." Opening the panel to the generator, he gave a pleasant snicker, shutting it confidently and fixing the gadget to his own arm, only to use its multiple tools to work at the machine.

"What're we working with?" Oksana asked.

"Well, I'll be. This generator's made by Pietas Militia! We really hit the jackpot here! I'm going to pick out all its good stuff, yank its cables, and we'll be out of here." Oleg beamed as he got to work fiddling with the generator's extensions, unplugging everything and prying out what he could. Oksana continued to stay by me. With her umber stare, there must have been another lesson I had to learn.

"We're going to talk about this later, but for now, I'll be thankful that you weren't left with any fatal wounds." Instead, she would spare me until we returned to the bank. "You handled your own, and we got what we needed. But still, you can't do whatever you want. You can't take on every battle alone."

"...I disappointed you."

She brushed her thumb gently against my wound, trying to wipe off the trickles of blood seeping from the gash. "You haven't disappointed me yet, Chari. You only worried me, was all. I understand you wanted to be brave, but it's alright to have people by your side. In this world, you're nothing without allies."

I should have taken her words to heart.

"Got everything?" she hollered to Oleg.

With handfuls of mechanical wealth, along with a new toy on his arm, Oleg stood up, eager to put everything we found to better use. "All that and more. Ready whenever you ladies are."

Oksana lit the way for him, and I was about to follow along after getting over my own self-troubles. Turning to the wall, shining my light on the map still taped to its surface, I reconsidered the words that the rogue had told me minutes before. I had to understand why Reveria was a target for these slavers. It was too critical to leave behind.

As the two headed up the stairs, I peeled the map off the concrete, folded it together, and stashed it in my pocket. And when I hurried my way back to the group, I went to the slain bodies one more time, plucking one of the leaflet daggers. Picking my up pace, I caught back with Oksana and Oleg, keeping my head low. I had made the same mistake, again.

The first time, the night of the storm.

The second time, at the diner.

Thirdly, right here in the basement.

How many more times would I repeat it? These consequences were never worth the risk of attempting to gain something on my own accord. But to add to all that…Those Vultures, and that enigma.

It substantiated an ominous outcome.

Despite the long haul, we managed to return to the bank successfully, without any more cuts or danger. From our arrival, the worst we came back to was a berserker in the street, who got put down by Nikolai before she stepped foot near the bank. After bringing back the fruits of our labor, the turret systems became functional thanks to Oleg's handiwork, and the electricity substantially improved. The fixtures were brighter than ever, and plug-ins no longer made the outlets burn. Even though our emergency expedition turned fortunate, I went astray in more ways than one. Not from my bizarre findings, but lost in thought and mind.

"Chari? You're still playing with us, right?" Nikolai asked, and once I snapped back to focus, the cards on the coffee table beckoned.

"She's just thinking of her strategy, don't push her," Oleg added, holding his own cards. Nikolai had no more cards to spare, while Anastasia paid no care, leaving hers out in the open.

Granted, she only had one left.

"Not too much further from *Durak*. Come on, Chari, you can beat this old zhopa." The elder snickered as I glazed over the game.

We were playing a traditional card game that Anastasia was taught in her youth. For as long as the Claws lived, Durak was a family favorite that'd inspire good times. For me, however, it was only a distraction from the bad ones. "Right." I huffed, placing my ten clubs to attack Anastasia. Able to defend herself, she placed her own queen of clubs.

"No more cards for me. Now it's just you and Oleg," Anastasia said, as he and I were the last ones with numbers. Hiding his own, he only had two, while my maximum of six remained.

It was inevitable how this went.

With no words between us, he attacked. King of diamonds to the table, I defended with my king of hearts. Attacking me again with his king of spades, no more cards were in his hand. The last player that remained with a deal ended up the loser, or otherwise…

"Durak! Haha, that was fun, huh Chari?" Nikolai bellowed, declaring me defeated in this match. I'd been the last one standing in this game several times, but tonight, the title sank into me more than usual.

Truly, I was a *fool*.

"Very good game, well played," Oleg commended, noticing the sore strain on my lips. "Huh? Devushka, are you okay?"

"Now look what you boys did," Anastasia grumbled, reaching over to take hold of me. The skin under my eyes puffed up.

"You know I never mean it, Chari. It's all in good fun," Nikolai said.

There was something off inside of me. I couldn't figure it out.

"Dinner's ready! Borchst is nice and hot! Enough for everyone, finally!" Igor called out, and while the other three got up from the table, I remained on the floor.

"Come on, milaia, it's time to eat," Anastasia told me, but with my gaze on the carpet, I stood up.

"That's alright. I'm not hungry tonight," I said to her, making my way past the men.

"Chari," Oleg tried to reach for me.

"I'm just going to get some early sleep, don't worry about me,"

Heading into the hallway and up the stairwell, I stormed off to Lada's room on the second floor. Alone at last, nobody to bother me.

A creak came from the doorway, as did a cast of the hall light. Oksana's shadow loomed over the sleeping bag I bundled in, her weight creaking the carpeted floor as she came closer, kneeling beside me.

"Nikolai told me about what happened. Are you upset that you lost?" she asked, and the nylon bag crinkled to my discomfort.

"No, it's just been a long day."

"You still think I'm upset with you. That must be it," she pressed again, unwilling to give any space until she got an answer.

"It's not that either."

"You said you were alright when we came home, but you've been nothing like yourself since we did. Tell me what's going on."

"I told you that nothing's wrong, Oksana. Everything's fine."

"Clearly not. You can't just get worked up and not let anybody help you. Don't you remember what went down at the school? Or our talk after?" She scolded me, and the tough love didn't help either.

"Can't you please leave me be? Just go away," I snapped, and to that, a sigh parted from her.

Standing up, she headed out. "Acting like a child will get you nowhere. You better figure out what's turning you into one." The door closed—not with a slam, but with a disheartened groan.

Burying myself deeper in the blankets, the warmth enveloped me, as did the inexplicable anger. From there, I shut my eyes in a desperate attempt to sleep off all this inner conflict.

***

Trying to sleep did no good.

Tossing and turning in hot sweat, there was no rest for me. In my half-slumber, warped visions deluded my conscience. Many questions flooded my mind that needed answers. The intent behind that map suggested a terrifying ploy, and if those Vultures were up to something vicious, I had to learn of their scheme. One prospect welled the pit of my stomach deeper the more it riddled me.

Reveria.

They planned to make their next move on them. With that damned fox leaving me with no direction, I had to find my own. I had to understand what he meant by *looking closely* at the map. The constant idea of it all made me so gutturally anxious that I couldn't drift off. The prospect of those beasts in that town, only for the worst things imaginable to happen. Innocent people taken, enslaved, slaughtered, or consumed. Even if I had left them on a whim, they still deserved to be safe in the place they called home...

Home.

This inner ultimatum was bound to come soon or later. Should I go back to warn everybody of the imminent danger they would soon face? Or did I stay here, with the ones that made me feel like a human, rather than an alien...while I watched those faultless lives become victims of a horrific onslaught not yet fulfilled.

I needed to get up.

Slipping from my sleeping bag, I checked to see if Lada was asleep, but she was not anywhere to be seen. I sat there, my entire body soaked in perspiration, waiting in the darkness, wondering if those voices from before would come back, even if they were delusions that came and went during my moments of frailty. I needed somebody to tell me what I should do, yet there was silence. Why was it so quiet now, of all times, when I needed guidance? It dawned on me. Instead, I needed to listen to my *own* voice telling me what I should have done long ago.

I had to go back.

Rising up, I made my decision—a better one. I knew what to do, but I had to tell somebody first. Lada had to hear my intentions, but I wasn't sure how she would react. She and I had developed a solid friendship compared to everyone else in the clan, but I always knew deep down…I was not part of their group, lineage, or history.

I was simply a visitor. Like a proverb they once taught me, "It's nice to visit, but it's better to be home."

My feet drifted off into the hallway, an electric lantern in my hand. I stepped out further, where my bare soles pattered the cold tile until I stood out in the lobby. I spotted Lada lying on one of the couches, reading the same book about advanced medical practices. I did not want to interrupt her, but her open heart would have been willing to hear me out. In my approach, she caught me in the corner of her eye, showing a soft smile.

"Couldn't sleep either?" she spoke quietly. "I'd imagine making my mama sad made you upset too. Why else didn't you show up to dinner?"

I knelt beside the couch, only to rest my back against it. Nestling the lantern by my side, I made myself comfortable on the frigid tiles. "Haven't been myself since today."

"You should consider apologizing to her, you know,"

Wiping my face, I winced at the thought. "I don't know how I'll tell her, but I will." I turned my head to her. "What're you reading about?"

"Same medical assertations, nothing new."

"As usual. Listen, I need to talk to you about something. It's what's been keeping me up at night." I asked, and Lada slipped her bookmark in between the pages. "You know how I've told you about Reveria, why I left, and how those people viewed me from the beginning?"

"Isolated but surrounded, driven to find your lost kin, leaving all that safety behind and leading you to where you are, with us."

"Despite everything I thought about them, back when I didn't know better, there's something I need to do." I took a moment to breathe before I went on. "When your mom and I went to the school earlier in the day, something happened there. I found something important. Even if it doesn't seem like it, Reveria needs me. I think we both knew this day would come, but…" My teeth clamped together before I finally said it.

"I want to go back."

Her gaze drifted off as she sat herself up and invited me to sit beside her. I took the open seat, and she sighed softly. "You want to go back?"

"Yes,"

"…If this is because you feel guilty about our food situation, it's okay, we've still been managing. Or, have the assaults worried you?"

"There's a lot more to it than that."

She tapped her claws together, ears folding back. "Call it selfish of me to say, but I was actually hoping you would have stayed here a little longer. I know everything here isn't so pleasant, but every time you mention your sister…it's nice to think I was like one to you."

The doubt poured through again. Was I really ready to part with these people? No, I *had* to be. For every attack this bank has suffered, and the lack of food made by me came a revelation. No longer could I be the reason for this family's imminent downfall. "Lada, I have to do this."

The soft frown on her maw refused to budge. "I know. It's just—"

As she was about to speak, something rolled out from the shadows. Wheels came out, and we were surprised to see a familiar face emerge from the shadows. Anastasia approached us in her chair.

"Baba? What're you doing up this late?" Lada asked.

Anastasia's wrinkles bundled up when her lips arched in that pretty, genuine smile. Rolling closer to us, she sipped at her glass. "I was getting some water, Lala, then I heard you two talking. Is it true that you want to leave, devushka?" Anastasia questioned me.

"Yes, Baba, it's what I want. Even if it's not my real home, even if they're not really my family…" I continued asking myself why I wanted to return, and there had to be more to it than helping them, but I did not understand the sensation that lingered in my chest.

Anastasia reached into her garb, and after she dug around, she pulled out what appeared to be a locket. When she opened the small pendant, two little oval photos were on each side—one of her father and one of her mother, from the memorial wall.

"You already know this, Chari, but my Mama and Papa had a hard time letting me go. They didn't want to see their baby go away on that boat. Before I left our country with my love, they did everything to make me stay…but I had the right to make my own choices," she affirmed, brushing her thumb on the photos.

"And that you wished you went back."

"Yes. I still hold my regrets for leaving them. Nearly every day, I wondered how my life would have been had I stayed behind in the Homeland. To know that they're gone, and that I can't see them."

My condolences grew tenfold. "What else do you remember about them? The memory that always comes to you first."

"Before I set off, they said to me…" She took a long breath. "'You're a woman now, and you should be able to see the world…but never forget where you come from. Experience what life offers and continue the honor of our name. Share the gift of our family with those you were destined to meet, but pave life the way *you* see fit.'"

Tears welled in her eyes, doing nearly the same for me. Lada had been silent the entire time, sniffling from the sentiment. Anastasia chuckled and clasped her granddaughter's hand.

"Chari, when we first met, we talked about how our destinies led us to that very moment. Well, whether you like it or not, you were *destined* to go back to Reveria. Fate has already decided that."

"But what if they—"

"You might've been wronged, and you might've made mistakes of your own…" she paused, and her eyes went to the dim lantern below. "But there's no good dwelling in the past. You move on. Because no matter what, you can always do better. Those people mean something to you. You might've not seen it then, but now, it's vivid."

Anastasia illuminated me, and she was right.

Deep down, I cared for them. Perhaps I had become too shrouded in judgment and spite in the past, but everything came to me through a new lens. Even if they were not Narissa, Reveria took me in from the streets when I needed somewhere to be the most. As I realized that, Anastasia offered me tender words. Another proverb to hold onto.

"Vy ne vybiraete sem`yu, oni Bozhiy dar dlya vas, kak i vy dlya nikh? The ones you first met…They're your family now."

Lada cried.

"Lada?" I asked.

Anastasia hummed as she handed me her locket. The emotion seeped through the silver. Lada faced me, and her words were the most profound moral I'd heard in all of Misera. "You don't choose your family. They are God's gift to you, as you are to them."

***

Shortly after my late-night conversation with Anastasia and Lada, I returned to bed with a little more reassurance in my choice. When the following day came around, I discovered a newfound confidence moving forward, but after everything she did for me, I needed to have Oksana's approval. She deserved to know of my intentions the most.

Once breakfast was finished, I asked her if she and I could sit down to have a more personable conversation and try and explain my situation. We sat with one another on the rooftop, with our legs over the edge and keeping our eyes on the streets and railways. The soft rattling of the turrets now accompanied the otherwise silent air. The whirs were calming, but I became tense as no words were exchanged. After how things went yesterday, I was afraid of speaking up to her. For the first few minutes sitting there, all I could do was keep my gaze focused on a plastic bottle drifting through the street. I could not handle facing her like an adult.

"Charissa, you invited me up here, no?" She attempted to get me to talk, but I did not have the courage to let my voice out. This reminded me about the time I tried to talk to Narissa on the night of my birthday, and how it went in flames. I didn't want it to happen a second time here.

But Oksana broke the tension for me.

"You're being awfully quiet. This has to be about yesterday." She huffed as she turned her focus to the dead sky, and there, I still could not confront her, for weakness took me over. "…When I was your age, I was exactly like you."

"…You were?"

"Mhm. My Mama sheltered me for a long while. She didn't want me to go out there, but I didn't like that. I wanted to do things my way and be the woman who could handle herself." Oksana's eyes locked with the void above as if she could reflect on her earlier days through the bleakness. "I never liked being coddled nor babied. I believed I would have been a kid forever, but…it turned out my Mama just didn't want to lose her only child. We had our cries, but eventually, she understood me. But she gave me one condition if I wanted to go out and be brave. You want to know what it was?"

"What was that?"

"'Be brave for others, and not only for yourself. Don't show courage to *seem* strong. Do it because you care about the ones you love and use that courage for *them*. Be the shield for the ones you care for.'"

"So, don't be strong to only act like a fool, but be strong for the ones you love, because you can?" I evaluated.

"Exactly."

"…What if the one thing you fought for was gone?"

"You find something else to live for, even if you can't let that one thing go." Her smile softened as she reached over, ruffling my hair. "Alright, Chari, what's this all about?"

Here, I found it hard not to cry, like I always did.

"Narissa was all I ever had. Without her, I feel like I'm all alone, deep down. Like nothing's worth surviving for anymore,"

Her sharp claws delicately brushed against my neck. "Don't say that. You might not know where your sister is, but you still have yourself to survive for. You believe that don't you?"

I rubbed my eyes. "Oksana, you've been nothing but the best to me, but…After what happened yesterday, it made me realize that I can't stay here with you guys anymore…Because I need to…" I wanted to explain further, but I fumbled. She stared at me intently, already aware of why I brought her to the rooftop. Like a mother, she knew these things.

"You finally want to go back to Reveria, and right your wrongs? Be able to have something to fight and live for?"

"They need me as much as I need them."

"And are you positive you're ready for whatever happens?" she questioned, and like in the school, I could no longer keep running.

"More than ready."

After our talk, it gave me the assurance I needed. Oksana helped gather everybody in the lobby for the news. Anastasia, Nikolai, Oleg, Igor, and Lada had their seats, as I stood there with Oksana by my side for her support. The women already knew of my intentions, and I only hoped the men would be as understanding as they were.

"What's this all about, Chari?" Nikolai asked.

"Hopefully this isn't about last night's game." Oleg worried.

"Not at all, it has nothing to do with that. Oksana helped bring you all here so I could tell you guys something, and all I ask is your understanding…this isn't quite simple for me to do."

"Well, we're all ears, friend. Whatever you got to say, we're here to listen." Igor permitted, and with that, I stood my straightest.

"I've decided that I'd like to go back to Reveria, but you all had the right to know before I left. So, in a way…I guess this is goodbye."

The men's jaws dropped as they rose from their seats.

"You're serious?" Igor gasped.

"Well, I suppose you had to go one way or another." Nikolai bore an honest huff. "We might be better without you, but this place will feel emptier, that's for certain."

Oleg seconded his colleague's stance. "Yeah, I'll admit, having nobody to load mags with is going to be a great shame. But at least you don't have to worry about getting shot being with us."

Anastasia waved her delicate hand to the astonished men. "Boys, boys, be glad that Charissa is doing what's best for her. And be even happier we were able to be here for her when she needed people most." To that, the lads eyed one another. In the end, they nodded their heads and faced me with content grins.

To witness just how much they've looked forward to my parting, as well as missing me, came as a surprise. Now that I no longer depended on them, they'd be able to live as they did before.

Destiny knew what She was doing.

"She's right. Although I hate to see you go, you've been a great guest. I wish you nothing but the best." Igor said, baiting a smile from me.

"You still got that gun I lent you yesterday?" Oleg asked.

In a blink, my lips tensed. "N-No, I could've sworn that I—"

He patted my head. "I'm just messing with you." He snickered, taking the POLISTES from his side and handing it to me, along with a box of ammunition. "Take good care of her; she suits you well."

Lada rolled Anastasia up, and although they were content with my decision, it was only right to properly part ways with one another. The young polar bear opened her arms, and nothing needed to be said for me to lean in and take her in my own, squeezing her tight.

"You ever pass by around these parts, we'll be happy to see you," Lada told me, and when Anastasia opened her frail arms, she deserved a hug the most.

After all, she'd brought me here, and for better or worse, this was the new life that had been given to me. It was mine to lead, and nobody else would decide my future, other than my very own fate. Leaning in and bringing the grandmother in my hold, she gave me the guiding light that I needed in this hollow, inescapable void.

"And you, Baba…I'm glad to have met you, especially," I confessed, and her old bones bestowed warmth and comfort to mine. Caring for me and seeing me in my own skin in a city of beasts.

"Just remember where *you* come from," she said. "Even if this city brings out the worst in you, remember that you're still human. It's all you have left at the end of the road…your humanity."

Once I finished my goodbyes, Nikolai stepped up. "I assume Oksana planned on taking you back by herself. Afraid I'm going to have to tag along on this one. Just one more trip."

"I'd love it if you came," I said.

"Well then, my love, shall we go?" Nikolai asked.

Oksana, remaining quiet, flicked the droplet from her eye before it had a chance to fall. "Yes yes, no more sad goodbyes. Let's make this a happy, final farewell together."

With that, I gathered all my belongings and was ready to set off for the horrors of the municipality. This time, however, it'd perhaps be the last time I'd ever see their faces. They helped me recognize how to learn that every mistake was a lesson, and to be able to move forward. I still had so much to understand and time to mature, but I had the willpower to rebound. I would never forget a single member of the Claws.

***

Despite the long distance it took, Oksana and Nikolai stayed by my side every step of the way and watched out for me as though I had always been one of their own. We talked to one another while we made it through the treacherous streets, and it reminded me how much I would miss them all. After several hours of wandering, we finally found ourselves far from the

Reverian gates. The incandescent lights of the town shone beyond, while the distant chatter between the citizens resonated in the otherwise dead air of Misera. I stood there, still a little uncertain how they would react once they faced me again.

"It's not too late to turn back if you need more time away from home," Nikolai told me.

"No, this is where I have to be. It might not be easy coming back here, but life's never gonna be easy. I have to face it." A sigh parted my lips as I approached the both of them. I offered my palm to Nikolai, who had been nothing but great to me, firmly shaking his hand. Like the first time we met, he squeezed my hand hard, and I found the strength to clench back with just as much might.

"Thank you guys, for taking me in," I said to him.

"We're going to miss you, Chari. Don't you dare forget this old man and his tales. I might have more to tell."

"Heh, how could I ever forget?"

I turned to Okasana. I still had a challenging time being able to go our separate ways, and she had similar feelings. Walking up to her, I offered my palm, hoping she would take it. From the way her saddened gaze stuck to me, maybe she was not so willing to see me go, and so I began to withdraw my hand. "Oksana? I hope you know that–"

She pulled me into the tightest, almost back-breaking hug she could provide. Bouncing me around, I became dizzy in her clutch, but a smile remained on my face as an even wider grin stretched across her muzzle.

"Oh, malyshka, why must you do this to a mother?" She finally let me back on my feet. "You're braver than you think, you know."

I couldn't take all the credit.

"I don't think I would have ever thought about returning here if I had never met any of you. I'll always mean what I said. Thank you for helping me, even if I started off as a stranger," I confided.

"It's nothing, truly. Before you go, I have a gift for you." Oksana reached into her coat pocket, pulling out what appeared to be a photo. When she handed it to me, it was a photograph of their entire clan. I was not sure how far back this was taken, but it had every face I had known from their bunch. "A little reminder that you're always welcome to visit us. If anything ever happens, we have an open door waiting for you."

Every face in the picture left me with a brighter smile. The greatest thing they'd taught me was that to face a cruel world, I couldn't do it alone.

"I'll hold onto this always. Goodbye, you guys, and I hope to see you all again. Please, take care of yourselves."

Facing Reveria once more, I approached the gates. As I walked up to them, my heart fluttered, and I gazed backward. The couple waved and hollered with nothing but best wishes.

"Udachee!"

"Da vstryechee!"

Their native words carried tremendous weight, as now, I understood everything that they said to me. *Good luck. Until we meet again.* I was destined to cross paths with them, for fate had it in store for me. Goodbyes were not always forever, and when the time came, our roads would entwine for another chapter.

I walked up closer to the giant gates. A patrolman kept lookout from the watchtower above, and upon seeing me, he yelled for the entrance to be opened. The slabs of metal grated together before they parted, and one of the last faces I had seen before I snuck away from Reveria came towards me. He walked up to me with a rifle in his hands, surprised to see the likes of me stumbling on his front door once more.

The shepherd's wide eyes were enough of a greeting.

"It's you, the human?" he blasphemed. "You snuck away under our noses. We all thought that you got yourself killed out there."

"It's true, but I'm back now. Alive," I said.

With a discontent hum, he signaled over to the other patrol officers, and they all nodded to his cue. He stepped aside, making way for me to come through. "Before we do anything, please hand over any weapons in your possession."

"All part of the procedure, I get it." I reached for my sidearms, handing over both pistols. When he took them, he handed them off to the watchman in the side window entrance. He gave me one last sniff to make sure I had nothing else on me, so as to not make the same mistake twice.

"Once we get this all sorted out, we'll make sure they're rightfully returned to you. But please, you must see High Reverence Constance at once. She'll want to know that you're still alive."

"I will," I assured him.

The first step beyond these gates was a monumental moment, even if small. I stepped inside the town, embracing the sight of iron foundations, and a community of over a thousand faces. The voices of the people coalesced into a melody of geniality as the lights glowed brighter than before.

I was *home*.

"Have a wonderful stay at Reveria. We hope you value your days here, as we value having you here. Welcome back, human."

Nothing had changed ever since I was gone. The plaza was busy as always, with crowds of beastfolk wandering the dirt roads as they bustled to get to the shops nearby. The smell of fresh food and good times swam through the jubilant air, calling to me. Although I was told to see the High Reverence, I had to find someone else more important.

I needed to figure out where Bea was.

She was the first person that had to know about what I'd found. With how much she cared for her people and her connections within the town, she would have an idea of what to do, but I was uncertain how she would react to my return…especially after everything I did.

Sneaking away, only to have her brother killed.

She could have been devastated, shocked, angry, or all three in between, but regardless, I had to show her the evidence I retrieved. If that fox was one of the Reverian Virtues, she had to know who he was.

As I walked down the street, those who happily enjoyed their hot meals and cold drinks dropped their wares to gawk at my arrival. The chatter in the air drifted into awestruck silence. Doing my best to ignore their stares, I continued to pick up my pace, with nothing but focus on doing what I came back here for. The shuddering doors of the local pub opened behind me.

Something grabbed onto the back of my shirt collar. Pulled and thrown down to the dirt-covered street, I found myself on my knees.

When I peered up, it was the bastard that nearly plucked out my teeth: Shank. My rough skin burned as that lizard at me. I tried to be the better person by wanting to forgive him for what he did, but he opened that foul mouth of his. "Man, I was hopin' you got killed out there. Figures a stubborn skank like you would come crawling back just to see me."

After what those city streets put me through, his putrid spit and mockery left no scratch on me. His hate-ridden chatter amounted to nothing. I got up from the ground, most of the passing folks stopping to watch the two of us. This was the last thing I needed right now.

"Shank, I don't have time for this."

I tried to get myself out of this predicament, even attempting to walk away from them, but the scaled prick ran in front of me and tripped me over. People gasped as they witnessed me kissing the dirt again. My indignant eyes went to that shit-eating grin.

My cheeks bloomed to sour, scarlet roses.

"You come back to town, thinking nobody's gonna bat an eye? Ain't happenin'. The shit you pulled weeks back at the pawn shop? Meddlin' with me is the last mistake you'll ever make," the lizard grinned wider.

The crowd gawked but didn't have the nerve to end it. I got myself back up again, brushing the dirt off my clothes.

"I'm not going to fight you." I took my ground.

"Yes, you will! After spending a month in that jail, you're going to regret putting me there!" He snarled, and I took a deep breath.

It was obvious why he wanted to do this, but the fact that he needed everyone here to make a point was embarrassing. If I had known anything about Shank, which was not much, it was that he was truly pathetic.

"You really want to do this? For what? You're just going to go right back there. It's how probation goes."

Evidently, I struck a nerve in his fragile ego.

"Heh. You're such a stupid bitch. None of the Virtues are strollin' around here right now, and frankly, I don't care if I get behind bars again, so long as I beat your ass to the ground. So, what're you gonna do, lil' girl? Where's your red-assed bird to save you?"

Shank wasn't going to leave this vendetta alone. If that meant I needed to win this stupid fight, so be it.

I took my bandana off and tied my hair back.

"Fine. Let's get this over with."

I accepted his challenge, and he eagerly rolled up the sleeves of his jacket and brought his fists up, stainless knuckles glinting. Taking off my bomber and backpack, baring my camisole, I retook my stance with him. The twisted excitement on his face barely made my anger simmer, and I couldn't let him get the better of me.

I was ready to fight him.

"Then let's go! C'mon, hit me!" he roared.

He jumped at me, but didn't make his first move. Instead, he'd bob back and forth, motioning to his mug. Taunting me, looking at his hideous features only stirred the temptation to make him disappear.

"I'm right in front of you, whore! What, too scared?"

The moment he opened his filthy mouth, my inhibitions no longer existed. I fell for his words, throwing out the beginning punch. Knuckles making contact with his jaw, I stunned him in place.

Quickly, he recovered.

"Oh, that's the best ya got? Let me show ya *mine.*"

He lunged forth, unleashing a barrage of punches my way. My arms blocked his blows, with my feet slid against the dirt. From his steel knuckles, fields of bruises embellished my skin, and he did not let up. He struck me in the stomach, and I flinched. Punting his knee into my chest, he launched me back until I found myself in the dirt once more. He snickered as I seethed from the searing pain, clenching my bosom. Everyone all around remained speechless, seeing me get put in my place, but I was not going to give up quickly. Not to the likes of him.

"C'mon! Don't got anybody to help ya now, do ya!"

I shook off his scorn and bounced back. I threw punches of my own when he least expected it. I managed to get a blow to his chest, but he would block my shots. He was stronger than I was, but he was never smart. I socked him in his jaw the moment another opening showed itself, nearly knocking him to the dirt. He grabbed his mouth, and blood ran from his chin, dripping down to the broken tooth on the ground; his prized, golden one. He scowled at me, engulfed in fury.

"Oh, now you fucked up!"

He ran to me with a thirst for my blood, and his torrent of punches flooded me. I tried to withstand every blow he dealt, but his strength was too much. His brutal attacks pushed me to kneel to the ground. I helplessly tried to defend myself, but he nearly fractured my arms. I had to let up, and when I did, his knuckles impacted my chin, throwing me back for the final time. I writhed from his brutal onslaught. I'd lost the fight.

Maybe I was never strong to begin with.

When he claimed his victory, he stepped up chuckling. When everyone set their wary eyes on me, none of them wanted to see my downfall. But being isolated from the real world, the Reverian citizens had no idea what to do when they relied on Virtues to keep peace.

Nobody could help me.

"Heh, say your prayers, skank," the scaled prick snickered.

He had the most taunting scowl as he brought his boot up, hovering over my head as he was about to stomp on me. Iron spikes embellished his sole. My eyes grew wide, and I glanced at the onlookers.

Everyone stammered.

Shank glimpsed back at the people, giving them a sneer. He cracked his neck as he was intent on proving his point, to the extent that he would want to kill me. He leered me down, and he became delighted to rub salt further into my wound of loss. "Y'know, I heard ya had a sister, right?"

The air in my lungs and time stilled. Why would he bring her up?

"Heh, that bitch got what was comin'!" With a burst of supercilious laughter, he brought his knee upward. Every pint of my blood boiled, and my nerves singed with an erratic stimulation.

He knew I already lost. Why was he doing this to me?

"Now, you get to eat the dirt with her. Rest in peace!"

Before he could try to crater me into the soil, I grabbed his boot.

My palms dug into those spikes, past the mesh glove. As I clenched onto his sole, the iron drove deeper into my flesh, and every fiber in my arms strained with an agony I never endured before. Everyone fell silent as Shank tried to kick me off.

"What the hell are ya doin'?"

My blood trickled from my hands as little streaks dribbled to my elbows and on my face. I closed my eyes tight, siphoning the horrid air to my chest with a newfound determination. I refused to let him win. I refused him to ever talk about my sister. He was not getting away with any of this. Something awakened in me. Something terrifying.

My eyes opened wide. All I could see was him, hazed in red, like he was my prey. I had to *hunt him* and *take him down.* Throwing him off, making him fall back, I got up back on my feet. I glared at him as he gathered himself, standing before me. He found amusement in my twisted anger; his derisive chuckles drove through my ears again.

"Aw, did I make the li'l girl angr—"

I made him silent.

My palm jabbed at his snout, stunning him. His nose cracked upon impact, throwing him to his knees as he clenched onto his snout. Blood dripped from his nostrils. I'd scared him into jitters, but I did not care about his emotions. I wanted to *break* him to pieces.

I wanted to make him regret ever talking about *her*.

"W-Wait! C-Calm down, skin—"

The words of a thug meant *nothing* to me.

I grabbed the lizard by his collar, raised my fist again, and struck him over. And over. And over again, until his breath fell short to my ears. The bones in his face ground together. I jabbed his cheek and went for his throat, all while he struggled to keep on his knee. I didn't stop until he had completely fallen to the ground, quaking where he lay. His shaking grew stronger. I stared at him with bestial, violent hunger.

"I-I was just kidding… I was only trying to—"

He tried to beg, but I was not *done* with him.

I kicked him hard. It made him cringe and clench his stomach. I kicked again, and he trembled as his ribcage shattered. Again, I punted him until he rolled on the floor, suffering under my touch. The crowd grew petrified as I made him succumb to his defeat. Again and again, the tip of my boot struck him. I wanted his insides to rupture.

I wanted to do worse. This was far from over.

"N-No…P-Please…"

Dirty hands could not wipe away his tears.

I got on top of him as I foamed at the crowd, too scared to intervene. Nobody did anything, and they could not. I glanced back down at the reptilian beneath me as he tried to push me off, but I dug my knees into him and clenched my hands. My blood pumped, hotter than ever, even rumbling through my veins. I would give him no chance for mercy.

I *would* teach him to be *afraid* of me.

"This wasn't supposed to—!"

I drew my arm back until I slugged him across his snout. My other arm reeled before it pounded him again. I was ruthless. I did not stop beating him, punching away until his skull fractured. I coldheartedly bludgeoned and battered him until he sobbed, begging me to stop. He kept struggling to get up, but I did not want to give him the chance to fight back. I blackened his eyes, made his maw pool red, and started to pant heavily. My knuckles became numb and bloodied as my palms burned. Lava bubbled in my body. A *primal beast* awakened in me…

…and it was making me do this.

The crowd was struck with absolute terror. Nobody could stop me, and I did not want them to. I was not doing this for my triumph. I wanted to *relieve* this world of one less monster. One less parasite.

I was going to *snuff* his flame. The *Beast* in me wanted to.

He was the loudest scream in my head, demanding to take what was mine. His demands attracted me the most. I listened to it, to my instinct to go in for the kill. My rose-hazed vision blurred as my breath became hastier. The noises all around me meshed. My ears rang, and my hands shook as the carnivorous hunger in my chest was left unsatiated. My lust for his suffering never stopped. I kept slamming my fists into him until he slowly became redder, and redder, and redder in my clouded sight. My heart pumped harder; my blows became deadlier. I screamed louder, my cries of rage bellowing out until boiling-hot tears streamed down my face.

Seeing him bleed? That was not enough for me.

Seeing him on the verge of death? I craved it.

The predator inside of me *thirsted* for this.

When I finished my barrage, my scarlet-riddled fists shuddered. I could see Shank struggling to stay alive, nothing more than a hazy red mash in front of me. I was blinded by the rage that had welled in me for so long. His racing palpitations came to me. *Fast. Desperate. Scared.*

Ruin him. Finish him. Consume him.

I had to feed *It,* and I was about to deliver. I grabbed onto my prey, knowing well that my next move would sever his life. I could not deny this euphoria inside of me. To sate my hunger, I needed to give a final blow…*one. Last. Strike.* My hands slowly rose once more, about to unleash the last bit of might in me, the last bit of howling rage that I had. I was about to steal his final breath. About to revel in his despair.

About to take what was mine.

…A pair of hands grabbed onto my wrists.

—No, no! What was happening? *Do not stop me!* I *needed* this! I needed to *erase* him!

I thrashed violently, screeching loudly, as I could not finish what I started. Unable to finish Shank. Unable to make him suffer more. My eyes glossed with rage; I became something else completely.

The Beast inside me begged to be free.

"Let go of me! Let go! Let go! Let go!" I kept screaming, but…

"Charissa! Stop this! Do you hear me!?" Kyran's voice called out.

No, it couldn't be. I had watched him die. So then why? How could he speak to me? Was this my last piece of sanity grappling for escape?

Ripping my red-hued vision from my prey, turning to see if eyes deceived me. They did not. He was the one holding onto my arms, grip tight and claws nearly digging into my skin. The boiling trickles of tears on my shameful face turned cold, as did the lava in my veins.

"Christ, look what you've done to him!" he yelled.

The sea of crimson dissipated from my sight, and as all the numbness subsided to be overburdened with agony, my reality unraveled once I witnessed the horror I'd committed.

Shank's face was unrecognizable, battered to a pulp. His broken jaw mushed as his shattered snout struggled to breathe.

He was unconscious, barely alive.

Once I calmed down, Kyran let go of me and glared at the crowd before us. They were all frozen in fear, having witnessed the atrocious act I committed, all stricken with dread and covering their mouths. With my hands soaked in blood, my regrets coalesced. It was not the same dark ichor of a berserker…this was the crimson of a person.

"Alright, everyone, get out of here! Nothing else to see here! I'll take care of this!" Kyran hollered.

Those who watched immediately dispersed. Moments passed, until the plaza had become empty. The emptiest this town had ever been.

I was the true monster here all along.

Shank lay there, unmoving. His chest barely expanded and eased, sputtering soft breaths. Kyran approached him, biting his own claws.

"Shit…Shit, what am I supposed to do?"

He turned to me; my nerves seared worse than before. It was one thing to beat a man to near death, but after weeks of believing he was dead, his demise being my fault—only for him to be alive and witness me become a monster…it was the worst pain of all. We kept our eyes on one another, and the soft breeze of the empty marketplace whispered by.

We did not move, nor speak.

Kyran bit his breath, approaching me. Instinctually, my feet drifted back, but when his palms clutched the sides of my head, my bones froze. He was shaking, claws dug into my hair. "It's…It's really you."

My lips quivered, and he could tell I was unable to make a sound. Blood trickled from my fingertips, causing him to grab onto my wrists. "I—God…let's just get you out of here." He picked up my things and wrapped his arm around my shoulders, taking me away. My feet absentmindedly strode along the voiceless road. I found myself trapped in my mind. Ashamed. Unspeaking. Unblinking. I returned here, hoping to do right for these people. To warn them of the dangers yet to come. But the first thing I did was show my true colors.

Everyone feared me. I was the *danger*.

Sitting there on the couch, back at the same place I had once stayed, I found that nothing had changed here either. Every object remained where it last was. The kitchen had some dirty dishes here and there, the fridge made that familiar low hum, and the television still didn't work. Kyran tried to turn it on and help me ease my nerves, but it would not have done any good for my foggy mind. I slumped back against the cushions as Kyran wrapped the last rope of bandages around my arms, palms, and knuckles. I winced when he got a little too rough on me.

"My bad, my bad...."

When he finished his handiwork, he closed the medical kit and wiped the sweat from his brow. Kyran sat there beside me, but I had not spoken since we were on the plaza street.

The air was tense, and he tried to break through it.

"I guess you deserve an explanation." Kyran stood up from the couch and started to walk from one side of the room to the other. "When that whole hospital fell apart, my life flashed before my eyes. I didn't think God would give me a second chance, but when he did, I ran out of that hospital. Fastest I ever ran." He paused, turning to me. "Fastest I ever tried looking for you…But when I couldn't find you anywhere. I believed that you died there, and that it was my fault."

He tore his eyes away from the memorabilia on the wall. His awards collected dust.

"When I came back, the Virtues tried to find you, but once I gave them the news, Constance took my badge, and told me to never leave this town again. And when Bea learned that you were gone…it'd been years since I saw so much hope leave her eyes. She blamed me for everything that happened, and she was right."

No matter how hard he tried to resist, he had to face me again.

"…Not only did I believe that you were gone, but every day, I looked back on the moment that *thing* nearly ate me. Right there, I accepted it…I was going to die, and you would watch it happen." He sighed, wiping his strained mug. "I knew you wanted me to disappear. Why wouldn't you, after what I was going to do to you?"

A scoff left his bitter lips. He came up to the couch, kneeling beside it and resting an arm on the cushion. Holding his head, his troubled stare kept to the floor. "But when you took your shots, and you ran to me…I had never been more wrong about anybody. Though even to this day, I still don't understand why you fired that gun. So, tell me, for my peace." His claws dug into the seams; he gritted his teeth as he struggled to get the words out of his throat. "Why did you save me?"

What was I supposed to say?

When I continued to keep quiet, he nearly ripped the fabric at his fingers. "Don't just sit there and say nothing, dammit. What made you pull that trigger? Just tell me, please!" he begged.

I jolted in my seat.

Kyran snapped me back into reality as I got lost in my own mind. The bandages began to stain ruby splotches, leaving me further discontent. Once I accepted the fact he was gone, the burden became a part of me, but now I had to realize that he was in my life again.

He deserved an answer while he was still here.

"It wasn't my right to let you go."

Even after giving him what he wanted, it wasn't enough. Bolting up from the floor, he demanded more. "No, I know there's more to it than that. After putting a gun right to you? No way you just pitied me."

He was right. It wasn't just as simple as pity. Remembering what he told me, I reminded him, "I thought about it. Unlike me, you had people to live for, *someone* even…I don't have that anymore."

Kyran was quick to refute that. "You can't say things like that. That's not true."

"Don't try and tell me it isn't." I laid my head to the side. "I suppose it's my turn to ask…were you really going to do it?"

He became stiff.

"…Back where I lived, I spent my life believing the wrong people. Wasn't until I came to Reveria that me and my sister found folks that wouldn't *use* us. When you came…I didn't want to make the mistake of being duped again. To have to start from the bottom again."

"So that's a yes."

"…No."

Confused, I shot my gaze back at him. "But you just said—"

He threw his arm out. "I was scared, okay? I couldn't think straight! I really thought you tracked me down to take me out!"

"That doesn't answer anything. If it weren't for that hare, we both knew what you were going to do."

"You're wrong!" he shouted. When the air froze again, he struggled to get his voice out. "I just…I'm tired of living in a world where you can never rely on the trust of strangers. There are only a few here I can trust anymore, and…I'd rather lose my place here than put a bullet in you. If I did, I'd be no better than the monsters out there. I might've made a lot of mistakes, but murdering you would've been my biggest regret."

"…I find that a little hard to believe myself."

Drawing a hand to his eyes, it draped to his maw. His pupils shivered. "I don't expect you to forgive me, but if it means anything at all…I really, really wish I could take it all back. Because if I did kill you, I would've lost everything again…and someone I should've put my faith in from the start. It would've been the worst thing I could've ever done. I'm sorry."

These were his true colors.

I never faulted him for his suspicions, but there was a flaw on his part for not delving into the prospect of giving me a chance. One, sincere chance. There was no reason to dwell on the past, and instead, grow from the good that could still be made from it.

"I don't know what all happened to you and Bea, and you don't have to tell me…But whatever you thought of me before, you don't need to worry. I've never intended to undermine you, this town, or anybody. This is who I am, and always has been. Do you finally get that?"

This time, he had no excuse to refuse my stance.

"…I do," he said, his stare unblinking. "Charissa, I'd like to try and do things over. I'm not going to ask to put it in the past, but for a second chance from *you*. I'd like to own up to my mistakes and be a better man, and a real *friend* to you...will you give me another shot?"

For the first time, his genuine sympathy showed, and I didn't have to believe it was some act. To say the least, this might have been the start of moving forward. One that we both needed.

"If you're willing to give me one, it's only right you deserve the same," I told him, a trembling grin spreading on his face.

"You don't know how much this means to me," he confessed.

I would see his words through, but there was a greater problem at hand than our past animosity. "Kyran, I can't believe you had to see me like that. I didn't mean to hurt anyone…I don't know what to do."

That grin shifted to a thin press of his lips. "After you went missing, Aliya thought that Nocturne drove you away from here, said he'd mug you, but you didn't say a word. Why?"

An uneasy breath seeped into my nose. "If I fessed up, he said he'd kill me, and he was about to," I told him.

Was he really going to…?

"So, you fought back. I get that…but were you any better, nearly killing Shank yourself? You battered him, even when he lost. I know what he did was inexcusable, though I don't get what went through your head to act like *that*."

That man might have done me wrong, even nearly killing me, but my actions were nothing but heinous. He begged for my mercy, my forgiveness. I did not want to give it to him either. I was unsure what to say. What could I even say? I was still dazed, remorseful, and regretful. What I did was brutal. Even inhumane.

What was my excuse?

"He mentioned *her*. Narissa. The moment he did, I became something else. Something…Scary,"

His eyes lit up.

"Shit, if he said anything about Bea, I would have done the same thing. But by now, someone's brought him in the clinic, and who knows if he'll even make it." He worried not for Shank's sake, but for mine. "You could either get jailed, or banished from the town if that man dies. I don't know what they'd do to you, and there's no chance you'll be pardoned."

I deserved what was coming for me. After what I did, I was no longer worthy of the privilege of life, because I'd almost robbed someone else's. Yet, I wasn't in control of my own body. Had the insanity of the city finally broken my mind, manifesting itself into a malevolent power to take hold of my conscience? No matter how Shank behaved, and how he'd wronged me, there was no justification for my cruelty. He did not deserve to be brought to the edge of death at my hands. What would have happened if Kyran never held me back?

"I shouldn't have come back here."

After admitting my guilt, he was a little taken aback by my words. "Charissa, we all got our inner demons. Yours got carried away, and you couldn't handle it. What's done is done." He extended his hand, his gloveless one at that. "No matter what happens, though, I've got you, just like you got me. We're friends now. Real friends."

He took me aback, and so, I took his open palm. Bringing me up from the couch, we held our grip tight, regardless of my hurt. I found some relief from the tension that lifted. To forgive was the first step.

"I'm glad we finally can be."

As we reconciled, hurried footsteps came from outside the front door. Someone fidgeted with the handle when they came close, only to slam it open. Our eyes darted once Bea stepped inside.

Quickly shutting the door with her foot, her hands were full of lab equipment and papers, and once she saw me, it took her a lot of willpower not to drop everything. "Charissa! It's really you!"

Bea hefted her belongings as she went to the dining table, seeing that it was still a bit of a mess. She needed to make some space, shoving things aside to have a spot to put her materials. "The moment I heard the news that you came back into town…I didn't know if I could even believe my ears!" When she was done, she turned back over to the both of us. "…Am I interrupting something?"

Kyran's eyes became wider, and he cleared his throat. "No, I was making sure that her arms weren't fractured. You probably already heard what happened out at the plaza." He stepped away, allowing his sister to come face-to-face with me. Seeing my bandages, a discontented frown stretched across her tired muzzle.

Her disappointment struck me the hardest.

"So it's true..." she mumbled, and it took a lot of grit to come look her in the eye, having to realize I wasn't the same woman I had been. I stood up, clenching up some when I had to confront her.

"I'm sorry, Bea. I-I didn't know what came over me. It all went blank, as it happened...I feel horrible for what I did," I croaked.

Simple words would not change the fact that someone was in critical condition because of me. However, a tear trickled down her face before she jumped, wrapping her arms around my neck. Blank-faced, I stood in her hold. "People were saying you got assaulted, and you wanted to save your own skin. I can't condemn you for wanting to stay alive. I'm—just glad you're back home." Bea sniffled, and before she released me, I mustered the decency to put my own arms around her.

I truly did miss her company. "I'm happy to see you, too,"

Releasing me, Bea sat herself on the couch, taking off her glasses to wipe her eyes with the sleeve of her lab coat. I had never seen her cry before. "Sorry, this is all so sudden," she apologized.

"No need to be. If anything, I should be the one saying sorry...for a lot of things." My back turned to them out of shame. "First I snuck away, then came back to this. Everyone's scared of me now. How am I going to fix this? What do I do to fix this?" I asked them.

When Bea finished wiping away her tears, she undid the bun in her hair as Kyran pulled up one of the chairs from the dining table, seating himself and hunching forward. "I might've believed your whole good-girl act was a trick, but seeing that this is who you really are, I know that those people will see you're no monster."

His confidence showed, and in a way, reassured me. Still, I had to take accountability, and in time, make amends.

"What happened to you? Where were you this whole time?" Bea had a catalog of questions, as she always did, but I would not have been able to answer all of them. I rubbed the back of my neck, thinking about how to explain myself and my endeavors.

"I'll tell you guys everything that happened, but I have something more important that I need to show you both," I said.

I reached into my pockets and first pulled out the map, unfolding it as I laid it out on the coffee table. Kyran towered over it. "A city map? What's this all about?" he asked, trying to make sense of the markings, while Bea's pupils trailed along the patterns. To make everything more transparent, I pulled one more object of interest from my possession. I brought up the leaflet dagger, and immediately caught his interest. "Wait, I recognize that knife." He lifted his palm, and I handed the dagger to him carefully. Taking the knife in his mitts, Kyran easily discerned who it belonged to, all while Bea was continuously enthralled with the crude nature of the map's marks and points.

"This seems like a plan, or rather, a slapdash attempt at one. Where did you get all of this?" She asked.

Kyran tracked the fine intricacies of the dagger's leaflike veins, the dried blood left within the crevices wafting into his nose. "Yeah, I'm real curious how you got your hands on this too. It's genuine."

Suppose it was time I told them my whereabouts.

"I happened to come across this school of sorts, Little Hopes Elementary. I found these…marauders, butchered and covered in those daggers. From everything I learned, they used the school as a hideout. They must've already kidnapped and sent off their captures, because I didn't see anybody else…Can't do anything about it now though."

Immediately, Kyran's ears perked. "And you went there alone?"

"No, I was with a group. Kogti— the Claws, I mean. They're a family clan that hides out in an old pearl bank—but they're good people, I swear they are. Took care of me the whole time, no strings attached." I reassured him, even pulling out the picture that was gifted to me.

His shoulders dropped. "Hmph. Yeah, I've heard of them, but don't know much about them, other than they can be as ruthless as they are neighborly. But, if they did you fine, then I guess they're alright."

"Vultures though…That's a greater dilemma." Bea trailed her claw to the school's location and followed the mark, leading to the same name that had haunted me the moment I laid eyes upon it. *Fruor Falls.* "What business do they have at that amusement park, of all places?"

"Your guess is as good as mine, but it's definitely not good," I said.

Bea resisted her nauseous urge. "It's no surprise. Most have to pass around the area to get to the settlements in the city. If those Vultures have been abducting victims and using a space that big for collection, then it only makes me wonder just how many they've got there alone."

"Why do they need so many?" I continued.

Bea's head shook. "Their macabre business is more widespread than you realize. The demand for labor and protein alike is unfathomable, and they pertain to a large, cruel clientele. Those slavers have been a threat to every settlement in the city, and places like Reveria make for good protection against them. Looking at your findings…They've been planning to take us down ever since last year, and the rest would follow."

"Ever since Dr. Kutsuki passed, you think?"

She remained still for a moment and clasped her forehead. "That must be it. The moment we lost one of our greatest minds, they've been thinking about how to best take control of our disadvantage. Without someone to improve our defenses, they'll find a way to easily breach."

"It makes sense, given everything he's done. Barely anybody to continue advancing our protection, our methods are outmatched." I bit my breath, gritting my teeth. "I'm starting to see what he meant."

"What do you mean? Who's *he?*" Kyran asked.

"I met a guy who was there, the one who killed those few Vultures. He left those daggers behind, and nearly got me too."

"This guy you met. Fox tail, right?"

"He called himself 'The Rogue Virtue,'" I confirmed.

Kyran stuck the dagger into the coffee table's edge, then lifted the map a little. When he reached under, rummaging through a pile of mail and papers, he pulled out a letter from the bunch and brought it up to show me its contents. "His name's Yuto Tachibana. Been here about a decade. He held the title of a Righteous Virtue. About a year ago, he left without a word to anyone but me and Bea…and the chief."

"So *he* was the one you were looking for a few months back."

He rubbed his thumb across the paper. "Still looking. He left us letters, saying that 'there was no justice here and that he'd make his own elsewhere.' Every day we just pray he'll come back home."

"What did he mean by that?"

"Unfortunately, it's not my right to say. Aliya could tell you, but…I'm scared about him. If he's messing with those sons of bitches, there's plenty of reasons to panic. And if he's still alive and kicking, we need to figure out where he is ASAP."

"Charissa, did he say anything else to you?" Bea asked me.

"Told me to *look closely* at the map, and I'd understand why he was there," I recalled.

"He must've been looking for something more than their hideouts. Information, perhaps. If he got what he wanted from them, there's reason to believe he headed for the city carnival. Though I wouldn't know why he would want to meddle with the monsters over there…" She trailed off into her own mental world, and that led to Kyran standing up from his chair and heading for the front door.

"Where are you going?" I asked.

"Going to talk to the chief—Aliya, about this. Might not be under her authority anymore, but she has to know what's going on. Maybe together, she and I could inform the Reverences of what you found,"

A familiar face that I hoped to see soon. I nodded.

"Let me know how everything goes," I told him. "Oh, and when you go see Aliya, tell her that…that I missed her." When he reached for the handle, he bowed his head, nodding back and even smiling a little.

"She'd like that. She missed you too." He left, shutting the metal behind him as he went to do his business.

Bea and I were left in the living room together. When I turned to her, she was still focused on the map. However, with only the two of us remaining, it would have been a good opportunity to talk one-on-one. I went to the chair that Kyran previously used and took a seat in it myself. I leaned over as I rested my elbows on my knees, trying the best way to go about this. Confronting her wasn't simple.

"Bea, you could already guess why I snuck off."

I tried to get her attention, and as she continuously attempted to connect the dots on the map, her eyes shifted to me. She quickly sat herself up and folded her hands in her lap as she gave me her focus. "I—I don't think I could," she muttered.

I wasn't surprised she'd want to deny it, even after everything.

"Bea, you knew something about Narissa this whole time but didn't want to tell me. We made a promise. Why go back on it?"

Her back hunched, avoiding my stare. "Because…" She sighed. "Because I knew you'd try and find her, and I wasn't ready to let that happen." Her nervous claws tapped her knees. "After our first session, I got the results I'd always dreamed of. Thanks to you, my research has never been so exceptional. I wanted to keep you safe in Reveria for as long as I could, you see."

I should've known she was deceiving me from the start.

"So, you were lying to me the whole time?" I accused.

The tension on her neck eased as she lifted her head. "No. When my contact, Iris, told me about her sightings not long before you came home, I was going to have Kyran investigate to relay what he'd find. But after I came home to you gone, and he returned to town, explaining everything..." She froze. "It was like the future had already been lost. I knew you must've found out, and my worst fears came true."

That name begged another curiosity. The night that I overheard the whole conversation, it never crossed my mind. "Iris. Who's she?"

Bea's lips stiffened, and she reached into her coat to pull out a pendant, a familiar symbol. An eyeball with flower petals surrounding it: the same one from the hospital.

"She may very well be the reason I know so much about the Ferecite. Wherever she goes, she leaves her mark to let others know where the cultists gather." Bea's thumb brushed over the alloy. "*Im Glück nicht jubeln, im Sturm nicht zagen.* Although nobody's seen her face, she alone has prevented many from being exalted or consumed."

Like many of the mysteries Misera held, *Iris* was another to add.

"When she gave me her intel, it was a difficult decision between giving you closure or keeping you safe. Your contributions were so essential that I was desperate enough to do anything to keep you unaware…" She brought her hands to mine, fur to bare skin. "And for that, I'm sorry. I broke our promise, and I have no excuses."

After using me as her guinea pig for months, I wasn't certain whether she deserved any form of understanding, let alone forgiveness. I ripped my hands from hers, unable to look into those once-trustworthy eyes and find a semblance of my supposed "ally."

"You're exactly like my sister, you know. Trying to do what's best for me," I scoffed. "Since we're finally being honest, I know what else you've been hiding…you never told me I was *immune*."

Her whiskers twinged. "How did you—"

"It should've been obvious from the start, but I'm not stupid anymore. What I just don't understand is why you didn't bother mentioning it. You didn't tell me immunity was even possible."

She couldn't evade it. "…It's true. You would've turned by now, had you not had some form of immunity," she admitted, only to add: "But there's more to it you *don't* know."

"Then what is it?"

The jaguar stood, heading for her room. "Actually, there are two reasons why I kept you here." She reached in, the clank of a shut file cabinet followed before she came out with documents. "It's true, your body is resistant, and because of that, your genes were exceptional. But even then, there had been some drawbacks to the samples you gave me."

With her fingers shivering on the papers, her urge to resist going further made me press. "What are you talking about?"

She shook up. "…You're still infected, Charissa."

"Wh-What? But that can't—"

"That day when I took your blood, there were traces of TOV in your cells." She handed me the research, with printed images of my bloodwork in splotched ink. Microscopic bodies of black amid the sample, the shock settled in. "Your physical form might be perfectly fine, but your mind, your soul…it's just as susceptible to the disease as anyone else's. I don't know how it's possible, but…it simply is."

No. There was no way. I had been fine for the entirety of my time here, ever since I set foot in Misera. I was still me.

Or…was I?

"So, what I did to Shank…that was because…"

"I'm afraid so. You're already changing."

Visibly shaking, my nails dug into my scalp. The idea alone was enough to get me crawling with goosebumps. "You're telling me I could become an animal? That I might turn berserk? That can't be—no, this can't be right. Please tell me you're just still lying to me; I refuse to believe that—"

"I might've hidden things from you, but I'm not a liar," she told me, holding the documents to her head in stress. "This is a first for me, but rest assured…you're still human. You're still sane."

Could I believe her at this rate? In *anything?*

"Am I supposed to trust you? After all this?"

Her ears lowered. "If I told you any of this, it would've only made matters worse…but looking back now, I made a terrible example of being someone to trust." She dropped the papers onto the coffee table, covering her eyes as she hunched over. "You have no obligation to associate with me for what I did."

She'd be right: she betrayed our promise, history repeated for me. Though when Narissa broke my trust, I denied her the means to redeem herself or to hear her out, for weeks. Would I perpetuate the pattern here?

Not this time. I had to take a different course.

"Just tell me. Was there something more to all this?"

She didn't take her chance for granted. "…Yes, there is." She drew a particular paper from her pile, a series of formulas on its off-white. "One of my assistants came to a consensus after gathering enough of your DNA, the night you snuck away. Because of you, I've already been able to begin undisclosed development for a solution that'll revert our abominable deformities into humanity…and freedom from this curse."

"You're saying that you could make a cure?" I asked.

I'd never seen her so passionate.

"I've dedicated my life to one day making it happen." The glint in her eyes shifted. "I haven't told the Reverences about it yet. I'd rather not get their hopes up if it's truly not possible. But I intend to make it so."

I didn't want to crush her dreams, but the damage that I'd witnessed warranted concern. The extreme degrees their mutations went and the deterioration they showed, physically and mentally—it all seemed irreparable. Hybridian to human? It was a dream many here shared, but to say that such an idea was feasible was hard to tell, especially since the circumstances had changed for me.

How could I provide any benefit?

"But I'm infected."

"Only partially. Part of you is still your pure, human self, and because of that…" Hope illuminated her once-somber blues. "I think I'm close to finding the answer. If we eradicate the malignant virus, our bodies could return to the human forms we were robbed of."

"But you were born this way…there's no way you could just turn human," I mentioned, but she wasn't one to give up an ideal.

"The beautiful thing about science is that nothing's impossible," she told me, her inner light refusing to dim. "If there's even a possibility that this disease could be purged, then I won't stop at nothing to see it disappear. Making an antidote is the only thing that matters to me."

Although what she did to me wasn't right, it was within reason. Did she use me? To some extent, but it was more than a petty pursuit. Putting the bitterness aside, I wasn't the narrow-sighted woman I once was in my old life. To embrace this new one meant adapting.

"I don't appreciate having things kept from me…but your motives were for the greater good. That, I can recognize," I said.

"Charissa, I don't deserve—"

"We all make mistakes, Bea." I continued, standing. "That's what makes us human. And if what I've done for you has already gone this far…" I reached out my hand. "Then I want to keep helping you until we make a cure possible. It's what everyone would want."

My gesture of faith brought Bea to her feet. She took my palm, holding it firmer than the first time we met. From there, our alliance reignited, as destiny had intended, for each of our sakes.

"…This matters to me more than you could ever imagine, my friend…but let me make you one more promise. One I'll hold to the end." She overlapped our clasped hands with another one of hers.

"Yeah?" I asked.

"No more lies. No more hiding. When this is all said and done, I'll make it my new life's purpose to be in your debt." Her inner flame crackled with a newfound vow to uphold. "You want to end the Ferecite? We'll find a way. If you want to just see your sister again? I'll do everything I can. What we have, you and I, is special. And I feel like together, we can turn this dark future bright."

Ever since I could remember living above the island, I would have never imagined that there was something more beneath my feet. When I got community, I took it for granted, refusing to embrace the cruelness that reality offered. Undermining the people that life gave to me, I was a fool to disregard them due to my own fanatical expectations. The books I once read glorified a simple life, but Misera thwarted that. This metropolis taught me that the human conscience, even in bestial bodies, was a temperamental vessel. Qualities and flaws: everyone had them, but to make the world better or worse was a sentient decision. While I still had a sane mind, it was my responsibility to use it to its fullest. I refused to contribute to the corruption that ran rampant and sought to be part of the little good that this perilous city still had.

These hybridians were human, and I saw them no less than that.

"Are you with me, Charissa?"

During my time here, I'd understood that nobody, whether good, evil, or berserk, deserved this horrid fate. If developing a cure could give them the peace they deserved, and one day be able to go beyond the earth's crust, as I once dreamed of going beyond the sea, then I sought to make their dream happen. "Until the very end," I promised.

A vow to myself, to hybridian kind, and our entwined destiny: I wouldn't squander the gift of life, and instead use it for the betterment of others. Together, we would see the light of day.

***

The dreadful stares of hundreds clung to me. Shank's screams haunted the once jovial air, and my fists burned red. Every gruesome detail crept into my nightmares, and no matter how much I tried to tear them all out from my memory, the visions of his unrecognizable face flashed from different angles. Mutilated. Irreparable. Barbaric. The bloodthirsty beast on top of him, with her face twisted in wrath and adrenaline…but through those bruises and boiling tears, everyone bore witness to a new kind of abomination.

Me.

There was not a single moment in my life where I had been so free, yet so possessed. Every ounce of rage that bubbled in my blood managed to let loose, but my mind had no control over the blows. When my body got controlled, a *monster* clawed into my brain, sinking its way into my conscience until I lost myself. The violent scene replayed in my head repeatedly, and I begged myself to stop as I witnessed everything unfold from above.

Stop doing this! This isn't you! This isn't...me.

Amid the mauling, my desperate pleas reached my possessed vessel. Everyone in the crowd remained frozen until all of them turned to meet my dream view. Every one of them had been left ravaged by my wake. Their flesh ripped apart, their bestial faces gorged, and their souls in shreds. As their corpses stared at my frail, ethereal self, my physical body lifted her head from her prey. When I gazed into my own self, I did not see a single semblance of *Charissa* in there.

It stared at me through my own eyes, hunting my spirit. The hands it took pried into her mouth, tearing her skull open to reveal the animal within. A vile body crackled out, talons torn through, blood searing its skinless form, my inner beast showed itself for what it was. In its unhinged maw, its hunger groaned, ravenous teeth beckoning to be sated as its hollowed stare craved my soul. The carnivore that was destined to seize control bellowed: **RELEASE ME.**

In the blinding white, my screeches woke me. The clock at my bedside blared 18:31...I lay still in hopes that it was all a nightmare, but my actions truly happened. Sweat soaked the mattress, and breaths struggled to escape my raspy throat.

Bea busted into the room to find me shivering.

"Charissa! What's wrong?" She rushed over.

"B-Bad dream…probably the worst I've ever had," I huffed out, clasping my neck. I had no idea what was happening to me.

"Everything's alright. Could I get you some water?"

With my throat siphoned off all its moisture, a drink would've done wonders. But I didn't feel safe in my own bed.

"Yeah, I'm thirsty…but can I come with you? Please?"

She wrapped an arm around my troubled shoulders and then helped me to my feet. She led me out of my room, slow and steady. "Yes, of course you can. Let's get you in a chair and cool off."

Bea brought me into the kitchen, where I sat at the dining table as she got the kettle going. Her lab work was confined to her own quarters, and that same chessboard managed to return to the spot where I'd first found it. Many of the white pieces had been taken off the tiles, and the black side was so close to victory. The Rhodes had been at this match for months, though it only reminded me of the war I waged with the Devil himself, and if I could ever escape his realm.

"Do you want to talk about it at all? I'll listen," Bea tried to comfort me, but still, I was shaken up. Instead, I took one of the outed chess pieces and fumbled it in between my fingers. I wished the black bishop could have purged me from such wickedness in my brain.

"No, I'm okay…how long 'til the water is ready?"

"Needs to boil for a little longer, but it'll be good to drink after it cools off. Got some ice only a few days ago too." She answered in between checking the stove and grabbing a chilled cup from the freezer. After boiling on the stove for a few more minutes, Bea took the kettle and allowed it to cool on the counter. While she fanned off the steam, she brought her attention back to me. "Did your dream have to do with what happened earlier? Because you weren't in the wrong for defending yourself." She added on, but despite her reassurance, I couldn't find ease in my tension.

"It doesn't matter. I never should have gone as far as I did. I don't think I'll ever get over this." I struggled to tell her, and she took a seat across from me, not letting up on my troubles.

"Survival is an instinct we all have. It's only natural to fight back. You can't let this eat away at you."

I appreciated the sentiment, but the impact lingered on me.

"I know…but for now, I have to try and process what I did, and hopefully I can make up for it. Somehow."

Her head tilted downward, where the dim light shifted to the frame of her glasses.

"I understand; you just need a little time. Plus, I imagine that you're scared for your own safety…but Kyran and I will always be here for you, no matter what. You can count on us." Bea gave me a consoling smile, fetching the kettle. She poured the cooled water into the frosty can, along with a few ice wedges. When she placed the drink in front of me, there were still a few bits of mineral ringing the liquid, but I chugged down the contents with contentment.

I managed to drink up every drop, and the desert in my throat became an oasis. After I set the can aside, I glanced over my shoulder, at where Kyran's room remained open. "Speaking of which, where's he at? I thought he was going to go visit Aliya, then come back,"

Bea's stare drifted to the front door. "I'm not sure…I imagine he might've gotten hungry along the way and got something to eat. Hopefully, he should be—"

Knock, knock! A series of slams clamored.

We were both taken aback by the noise, but when Bea and I glanced at one another, she went to figure out who the visitor was on the other side of the front door. Before she had the chance to peer through the peephole, the metal slammed open, and two Virtues stood at the entrance in leather armor and wielding HORNET handguns.

"V-Virtues? What's this all about?" Bea stammered.

"Dr. Rhodes, we've gotten urgent reports earlier of a possible berserker case, and we're here to take the suspect with us," the Virtue woman claimed, while the male guard spotted me.

"There she is! Quickly, get her restrained!"

The two sentries came to me. I instinctively jolted from my seat and backed up against the corner of the living room, cowering to the floor. The barrels of their guns aimed for my head.

"Wait, you don't understand! She did nothing wrong!" Bea pleaded, but they did not care for her cries as the Virtues pinned me against the wall. My cheek slammed against the metal of the house while they took my wrists, constricting them with handcuffs while I desperately tried to escape their clutches.

"You didn't see it happen. After what she did to that man, could people really consider that *self-defense?* Not a chance. This woman is a high-level threat, and she needs to be contained in a cell," the patrolman asserted, dragging me off by the arm.

Before I could be taken elsewhere, Kyran arrived. He stood there with his claws clenched onto the doorway, panting heavily, as it was too late for him to come to my aid. "What do you two think you are doing? I told you she had no other choice! Stand down!" he yelled at his former associates, but he had no authority. Not anymore.

"Move aside, Kyran. You can't do anything," the watchwoman said, and he aggressively stepped up to the guards, baring his teeth in a scowl.

"I'm not letting this happen."

They were unfazed by his display. Instead, they pulled out a document and handed it to him. "The Reverences demand that we apprehend her so that she'll be taken to a proper hearing tomorrow morning. You've already lost your badge, so if you do anything to interfere with our job, you're welcome in your own cell, or risk being exiled. Now please, step aside."

With that, Kyran fumbled the printed orders in his hands, gawking at them. Meanwhile, the Virtues hauled me off, and my feet dragged on the carpet in resistance.

"Charissa's not a berserker! You can't do this!" he shouted.

Right as they brought me to the doorway, I turned my head to the panther siblings…my friends. They could do nothing but watch as my fate was twisted out of control.

"Kyran, please! Don't let them take her!" Bea begged her brother, and he tore the paper into shreds, unable to interfere.

"Dammit…Dammit! Char!" he screamed out for me, but it was too late. They took me out of sight.

They kept their tight grips, nearly crushing my forearms in the process. Any citizen that was out on the balconies, bridges, or streets could witness me being taken into custody. The same hundreds of eyes from my dreams watched a former beacon of hope become a pestilence worthy of fear. "Wh-What's going to happen to me?" I mumbled.

Their unforgiving grips grew harder. "The Reverences will decide what to do with you. Better count your days of freedom, because you might not see many more soon."

I spent the rest of my night in confinement.

By morning, the word-of-mouth of my brutality managed to spread like wildfire throughout Reveria. After Shank's had been brought him into the clinic, it was no surprise they'd reported my crimes to the station. From there, nobody in the town found safety, not when I still walked the streets of their sanctuary. I had no means of saving myself from this situation, and although Kyran made every effort to stop my arrest, the Virtues had to do what they were told. I couldn't blame them for doing their jobs, but I didn't know what to anticipate.

Would the rest of my life play out in a single room?

The walls of my cell were cold with the wrongdoings of past offenders, and from my perspective, I was no different from them. My side remained on the steel bed as I stared into the white bricks that were only inches away. It was impossible to get any rest, not when I had the charge of assault and battery tacked to my head. That would be a label that followed me for the rest of my days, if I even had any left.

While I continued to reflect on my misdeeds, the iron bars behind me rattled, and I turned my head. A visitor showed up at my cell. When I got up from my hard bed to see who it was, Joelle stood there on the other side. The labrador held a set of clothes and shoes in her hands, along with a container. She was one of the last people I expected to see, but now that she saw me behind bars, humiliation came over my skin.

"Joelle? What're you doing here?"

She handed me an offering through the gaps.

"They gave me permission to come see ya. I wanted to give ya a proper set of clothes for yer trial." She huffed. "Even got you some food down from the ole' cafe, give you something better than jail food."

"I—I don't know what to say."

"…Listen, darlin', I ain't mad with ya for being here, but it kinda hurts to see ya like this. It's just a shame you had to go that far,"

"I think now more than ever, I could use a friendly face. Didn't think anybody would come,"

"What kind of *lab* would I be if I wasn't there for one of my best employees? Sure, we became buds through business, but even outside of shop hours, yer important, like anybody else here."

"You didn't have to visit me…but I'm so glad you showed up. Thank you for bringing these to me, although, these clothes are kind of fancy. And…is this a Scotch egg I smell?"

"Just some old business attire that looked like would fit ya, and some shoes nobody would buy, mainly 'cuz they'd ruin 'em. This is my treat, so don't worry 'bout payin' me back," Joelle assured me. "Otto and I will be there at the hearing for ya. Yer going to be fine, dear."

"…Thank you so much, Joelle."

"Always. We're gonna be rootin' for ya,"

She headed down the hallway.

My trial was scheduled to be in a little over an hour.

With what little time I had to spare, I got comfortable on my bed as I popped open the container. A salad of richly fried egg mixed with ground mouse meat laid on a bed of lab-grown spinach. I savored the meal, the flavors brought me back to better times.

After eating the moral-boosting breakfast, I took off the sleepwear I was brought in with and got myself changed into the new clothes. A white button-up shirt, with a navy-blue suit jacket and slacks. The shoes had flat heels with cross-over straps, and I was thankful they were comfortable. Although none of this was my style, I had no right to complain. If my chances with the higher-ups were to improve, I would have to appear at my most presentable best.

While I made sure everything fitted fine, another rattle came from the iron bars behind me. Between the gaps, there was a familiar face that I hoped I would never find myself in this situation, yet there was no escaping her.

Aliya stood there.

The flickering, beaming lights shone behind her, and those disheartened eyes twinkled through. She held a cigarette in between her feathered fingers, taking a long drag. I should have been relieved, or even happy to see her again, yet there was nothing but shame in my chest. When I hauled myself away from the corner, I stepped up to her, sulking the whole way through. No words that could be said for my part.

"Charissa. Look at me."

To her command, my chin lifted, and our bittersweet stares met. Her gaze remained solid, as mine became unsteady. "Aliya. I'm sorry."

My few words amounted to nothing. To my surprise, she brought her free hand to the bars, holding one. "You don't need to apologize to me. Kyran told me it was self-defense. I never considered you to be the violent type."

Despite where we stood, having her there meant mountains to me. It tempted me to smile, but I had no privilege to express happiness when there were so many sinful spears lodged in my back.

"Doesn't excuse what I did. I'm guessing you must've seen Shank. How's he doing?" I worried.

"Eddy's still alive, currently getting treatment at the clinic. Even after everything's that happened, I don't think you deserve to be behind bars."

Although she didn't want to see me in cold confinement, it was better for everybody's sake, including mine. As Kyran told me, *what's done is done,* but everything led me here. Even if it might have been some inner demon that took possession of my actions, it was *my* vessel that delivered the evil. "I don't know. What I did was unforgivable."

"You might believe that, but everyone has the right to earn forgiveness. That being said…you don't know how hard it was for me when I first heard the word that you left." She tapped the ashes of her cigarette off into her palm. Rubbing her thumb around the cinders, it finally penetrated just how much damage I'd wrought by abandoning her. Aliya was always there for me, but I squandered her efforts from my blindsided, past anger.

"I get it, you're right to be upset. I didn't expect myself to run away, but…I just wasn't thinking when I did. I guess I only made things worse by saying nothing again, didn't I?" I asked.

The sapphires in those eyes jaded.

"I kind of wondered what more I could've done to help you. I felt like I was doing everything possible, but I have to ask, Charissa." She gave a shaky breath, before biting her beak down. "Was it not good enough?"

I clenched onto the bars. "Absolutely not. I wasn't in the right headspace when I ran, and I didn't mean to make you feel like everything you did for me was meaningless." I told her. My grip on the iron grew tighter. "What you did for me always mattered."

Her stare followed the smoky wisps in the air, as the fluorescent tubes above buzzed to their fading dance. "I couldn't stop you if I wanted to. Kyran told me why you left. Family means everything, and I can't fault you for wanting to find your last trace of it. I just wish I could've done more to help you, but..."

I might've not been there for her in the past, but I had to be then. "Aliya, you've been nothing but a good friend to me. One that I needed most when I practically had nobody. I know that *sorry* probably doesn't mean much, but…I really am."

She remained silent after my confession, and it took her a second before she turned back to me. "I know you mean it. It's great to see you back here, but not so good that we had to reunite like this. I'm supposed to take you to your trial soon."

"Oh…well, I guess I'm ready to go."

Before I was about to step away from the gate, she brought her hand up. "Well, not so fast. I'd like a few more minutes to talk. I haven't seen you for about a whole month. I've missed our conversation."

Uncontrollably, a smile came to my lips, and I took advantage of the short moment we had together. "You've probably got a lot to ask."

Before we continued, she turned her head from left to right. She dropped her cigarette, snuffed it out with one of her talons, and quickly picked it up. With her arms crossed, she leaned her shoulder against one of the metal beams to my holding quarters. "I was kept in the loop about your time away from Reveria. Said you came across our old associate." She twiddled the cigarette butt. "Is it true then, that he was alive and well when you last saw him?"

Kyran already made me aware that she and the missing Virtue had a history, but the extent of it was beyond me. "Everything happened so fast, but by the end of it all, he was fine. I didn't speak much to him, but he gave me an idea of where he was heading. Fruor Falls."

She scoffed. "I really do hope he knows what he's getting into, that damn man. He went missing a long while before you arrived, and the Reverences have been nothing but desperate to get him back."

"Yeah, I heard he was a Righteous Virtue,"

"He was, except he was one of the best too. Though I can't blame the bigwigs for worrying about their wild Virtue. In fact, I think *I'm* more worried for him than they are."

"What do you mean?"

Before she could answer, her smile grew even wider, and she lifted her gaze to align with mine. "You'll think this is coincidental, but Yuto and I used to be a pair. A couple of lovebirds with big dreams."

Never in a million years would I have imagined a well-managed cardinal like Aliya to ever be matched with…well, *a ruthless predator.*

"Seriously?"

"When I first traveled from Caelus Commons ten years ago to become a Virtue, he actually happened to move here shortly before I did. He was the first to welcome me to town and we hit it off right away. First man who loved and accepted me, but things changed…"

"I'm guessing things didn't work out?" I pried.

Her gaze was fixed on the floor. "Both of us being Righteous Virtues, we were both selected by the Reverences to compete in the position of Chief Virtue. When I got the title, that wasn't what impacted him most…No, there's a strict regulation when it comes to the fraternization between a superior and a lower-ranked elite."

"So, you had to sacrifice your relationship to get where you are."

"I'm not proud of it, but Yuto said he knew this was what I wanted. Looking back now, I feel as though I would've rather had him than be responsible for hundreds here."

"And that's why he ran away?"

An aggravated sigh left her. "No, something in him clicked. I tried talking to him a dozen times over, but he'd never budge. He's been through a hard life, can't blame him for bottling things up. But I think when Dr. Kutsuki passed, when it affected everyone, it sent him off."

"We all process loss in our own ways. Can't say I don't get it."

"All I could figure is that with that, and our falling out, it was too much for him to handle in such a short time. Ever since then, we've sent out a Virtue or two to locate him, but to no avail. We can't have Reveria without two Righteous Virtues. I still have to grant my held title to another, and the other's plain missing. So, the moment we clear your whole situation up, I plan to go find him because of you."

From the way she stared at the floor, she still had deep-rooted feelings for her runaway lover, and it nearly tempted her hand to reach for another cigarette from her side pocket. I couldn't bear to see her in such a fragile state. "You're really worried about him."

The reach for her next smoke faltered.

"Oh, trust me, I'm *devastated* for him. But good things don't last forever, and frankly, I'm more stressed about *you* right now." Her gaze lifted to mine. I brushed my fingertips along the cold steel, shivering from either its chill or from the unknown of how my verdict would unfold.

"What do you think they'll do to me?"

She shrugged. "The handful of berserker cases that did occur here were handled discreetly before I was promoted to my Righteous title, so there's no guarantee what your sentence is, but I'll be there at your trial. Rest assured; I'll see to it you come out a free woman."

Even if my circumstances were grim, she managed to shed the faintest light on my otherwise hopeless misfortune.

"I can always count on you."

"If I could have changed everybody's minds about you, I would, but only one woman can do so much." The feathers on her head rose. "Do me a favor, and prove the Reverences wrong…Hell, *everyone.*"

"I'll try, knowing that you'll be there with me…but can I tell you something before you take me away?" I asked while she stuck one of her keys into my lock, opening the gate.

"Always."

"I'm glad we got to see each other again, whether it was your job or not. Really, I could have never asked for a better friend than you." To my surprise, she brought her hands to my shoulders.

"Por supuesto que sí…when this is all settled and over with, then maybe you and I could catch up on some lost time." A chortle clucked out of her. "You and I are here through thick and thin."

With that, I voluntarily turned my back to her, presenting my wrists. She didn't like it, but she cuffed me, took me by my arm as gently as possible, and escorted me out of the station. Aliya stood by my side—not solely out of authority, but because she believed in me.

Having her there, gave me a little flicker for my fate.

***

There were plenty of folks who wished to see me put to justice, along with the few who otherwise pleaded my innocence. When Aliya brought me through the highest peak of the town, many of its people crowded around the area, and all of them clamored the moment I appeared in their line of sight. The Virtues sectioned them off into two halves, thus creating a corridor of loathing that led towards the courthouse. Every Virtue from the station stood guard as they herded the citizens and did what they could to keep the peace.

Projector screens acquainted each side of the crowd, displaying the inside of the courthouse to broadcast my hearing. Although it fizzled by a filter of static, most of the visuals themselves were discernible, though the number of people that packed the sanctum became apparent. I wouldn't have been surprised if about every citizen showed up today just to see my case, as all the crowds brought their families, friends, and even enemies to see me perish. While one of the vendors made easy marbles selling his foil-wrapped maize, another sold out of his imported *Cobra-Cola* in minutes. There was even the otter paperboy giving away free newsletters as his father brought his old-fashioned camera to take pictures.

"You! The skin! Look over here!"

Instinctively, when my face lifted, a flash blindsided me. When the older otter caught my mugshot, my likeness blotted out in a square of film, forever engraving the town's history.

Reveria's First Human Turned Savage

"Reveria Publications! The first human to ever touch town grounds faces the Reverences! Read all about the gruesome details over here! Only one marble per sheet, people!" The young boy hollered out, everybody scrambling to get themselves an issue. Only so many people managed to see the offense take place, so those who never had the chance wanted their scoop. Through the glimpses of pages, there was a photograph of me at my worst, along with pictures of Shank in his clinic bed.

In black and white, he was barely held together, nothing like his past self. With tubes in his body and his entire skull concealed, the captured moments served no good for my case. As each of the citizens got a look at the horror, they screamed at me. Aliya did her best to protect me from any assailant, but that did not stop them from throwing balls of foil, glass bottles, and any other trash they could find. Not a single person held back from howling out their frustration, booing me down while I skulked to avoid the egregious embarrassment.

Whether fearful of my presence or enraged that I still walked on their grounds, they were in true unison when it came to my undoing. Their shouts swamped out my own thoughts.

"We used to trust you!"

"You'll pay for what you've done!"

"We never want to see your face again!"

The only instance my gaze lifted was when we approached the courthouse, and from there, the diorite stairs called to me.

"Are you ready? We can take it slow," Aliya advised.

"Please. I think I need to,"

She held me up the stairs, where I had to keep track of every step. My conviction could not come a second sooner, but I diligently took my time, so long as I could enjoy my short lapse of freedom while it lasted. Nothing could have predicted the outcome, but I was not ready.

I didn't want to be back in a birdcage.

Upon arriving at the last step, we came across the grand set of bronze doors that arched above. Now more than ever, would my life be decided beyond the twin masses. There were another two Virtues that kept watch on its premises, and when we stepped forward, they were swift in holding the doors open. From the inside, a begrimed glow beckoned us, and we drew ourselves forward.

The massive rotunda shone a warm light down upon the rows of seats that were packed with anticipating spectators. When they all took notice of my arrival, quietude lingered in the air. Aliya and I briefly eyed one another, and I assured her that I was ready, yet deep down, I was scared for my life. When we trod towards the center, the stares of everybody in the seats weighed me down, but I kept moving forward. I found myself standing under their emblem of unity.

Ahead, there were two screens that accompanied the tall podium from behind, where the video cameras tracked my every move. There was something disturbing about being watched through such lenses, as I was made further self-aware of my fragile reality.

When I glanced around, I spotted a few distinguishable faces in the crowds. Joelle and Otto sat together, as did other familiar faces I recognized. My worries only worsened, when Kyran and Bea were nowhere to be seen, and my face wrinkled with anxious tension that everyone could see through the cameras.

On the monitors, the cameras fixated on the court representative as he presented himself in front of the grand podium. Everybody's attention went toward him as he cleared his throat. "Good morning, everybody. Today is March 28th, 2175. We've gathered here today to witness the hearing of *Charissa v. Reveria,* on the charges of residential abandonment and berserker behavior involving the livelihood of a citizen. Before we begin, let us show our utmost honor to the founders of our benevolent home, as they will be the guiding light towards the judgment of the blackened...arise."

All the viewers stood up, bringing their eyes to the soft light of the rotunda, and they all recited unfamiliar words. I turned my head to them as they were all driven by the glow.

"Enlightenment be with us, as we show no different to the damned. May the Reverences of our sanctuary bring forth justice and purge the corruption we endure. Misera's chains will not keep us subdued, so long as our doves of diligence glide us toward the sun, we will one day witness."

Their words unified in a trance of respect and gratitude. In a moment of silence, the sound of opening doors came from behind the podium's stage. A trio of footsteps followed suit, as everyone seated themselves to be in the presence of their most valued figures.

Silence bit the air as the three revealed themselves.

They all wore robes slated in gray and made their way up to the tall podium. The pious individuals who were owed nothing but the highest respect stood before us, gracing the courtroom in their presence.

The Reverences.

"I, High Reverence Constance, grant the right to begin," the harpy of honor spoke.

"I, Reverence Alden, agree to begin," the equine stated.

"I, Reverence Mikhail, too, agree to begin," the reindeer concurred.

The fear of the creatures out in the city streets did not compare to what these individuals brought, but I did my best to keep composed.

"Charissa, first you abandoned the privilege of residing in our town, only to return to commit a crime. I had hoped to not see you stand before us like this, though it appears I've been regrettably mistaken,"

I bowed my head.

"Perhaps I've set too high of expectations of you," Alden mumbled. "After offering you salvation here, I wish you wouldn't have been so careless to abandon everything we provided. We're truly ashamed."

"I'm sorry, your Reverences."

Mikhail, the one who opposed me from the start and prayed for my downfall, stared at me with unforgiving eyes. "Does apologizing heal wounds? I'm afraid not. You might've had a pleasant upbringing during your brief residence here, becoming a greater part of the community that many would call their neighbor. But after your recent offense, you've betrayed the trust of the people. Something I've long expected."

I couldn't even take the time to soak in his scorn, as Constance had to face the evidence in front of her. "Indeed. Charissa, you stand here knowing well of your crimes. Everyone in this courtroom and beyond knows of the atrocities you've committed against Reveria and its people, grave enough to be in our history books," she stated, and I was a statue.

"You have the opportunity to speak on your own behalf. What do you say in your defense?" Alden called out, thus bringing me back to my senses. I steadied my feet, trying to maintain a proper posture despite my cuffed hands.

"…What I did was despicable, but you must understand that it was never in my intention to harm one of your own citizens. I know simple words won't change a thing, but I hold myself accountable."

"While many witnesses accounted for the fact that Eddy 'Shank' Delgado instigated the fight and nearly committed murder in our own streets, what you've done is nothing short of dangerous," Alden added to my declaration. "Nobody deserves to be in his position."

"Even then, Charissa's actions hold some extent of reason. Set aside the fact she left town grounds unpermitted, her altercation with the Nocturne threatened her well-being. Surely. We can't condemn her on the fact that she tried to keep her life intact." Constance tried to defend me.

Despite her disappointment, she still held a sliver of belief.

"So, you think it was justified to have his life put in stitches and tubes?" Mikhail spoke up. "Being put on life support is enough punishment for him, and Charissa deserves a similar consequence. Her crimes cannot be pardoned with sympathy. Action needs to be put forth."

Aliya stepped up to them. "Your Reverence, Charissa said it herself. She had no other way around what happened. Even after attempting to de-escalate the situation, Eddy threatened her life, and she was simply protecting herself. Wouldn't you do the same?"

Her abruption rattled the order in the court, and the crowd chattered among themselves from her display of defiance. Alden unfortunately had to interject before things would get any worse.

Not only for my sake, but for hers as well.

"Chief Morales, you're aware that based on witness testimonials, she was the first to physically initiate the fight against Delgado." The equine had to emphasize. "Whether he instigated her or not, her stance isn't completely faultless. Regrettably, she's still considered a danger."

"On the contrary, I've spent close time with her myself. She's never shown any malicious intent as you all claim, and I guarantee you, that I would have reported her behavior if I thought otherwise. Whether you believe it or not: Charissa is *no high-level threat.*"

Mikhail heard enough. "Your sole opinion isn't going to shift the hundreds here. You might uphold the highest, honorary title we could give to a Virtue, but it's irrelevant where you stand."

"Enough." Constance lifted her hand to him, easing the courtroom's tension. "Chief Morales, regardless of your personal experience with her, it's become evident that she's not as safe as we all initially made her out to be. Despite her community service and contributions, most of the people here feel differently after what happened. Many are afraid of her."

"I can attest to that." Mikhail motioned to the stand. "Asher White, please present yourself to the court." He uttered, and from the sidelines came a muttman. The name might've been unclear, but I'd seen his face.

I remembered nearly every face I met in Reveria.

"White, you were there as the events transpired. You claimed that you were too afraid to intervene, lest she 'got you next'?" Mikhail began, and to that, the grungy canine gave me jittery pupils.

"She…I know she always treated everybody well, but if I knew she was capable of—God, I don't know if I could see her the same again."

Mikhail prompted to press on. "For the sake of clarity, can you describe what exactly she did? What kind of trauma did she instill in both you and members of the community?" He asked, and breaking away from his shivers, the dog mustered up what little courage he had to speak up against me.

"She…She wasn't herself. I saw the look in her eyes, and she was far beyond insane…Not even berserk-insane." He muttered, facing the floor. "No…It was like she was haunted, out of her own mind! She beat his face until he couldn't move! His snout was dangling off and gargling blood…Even when he gave up, she didn't stop. She wanted to *kill* him…" He sniffled; the tears welled in his ducts of sincere dread. "If that old Virtue didn't hold her back, I don't know if she would've tried to do the same to anybody else…I'm sorry, Charissa. I really am."

He couldn't hold back his running rivers.

"I know that was difficult, White, but we'll see to it that she will no longer bring harm to any other citizen here." Mikhail leered at me. "That'll be all. You may return to your seat as you were."

The cowering mutt found himself back where he belonged, and if he could, wiping his face of the regret he just committed.

How could I have done this much damage?

"Never in Reveria's standing had we had a berserker case so severe. You might not be physically mutated nor inherit the permanent, mental disfigurement, but you're a ticking time bomb waiting to go off." Mikhail stated. "For the well-being of our community, she must be reprimanded for displaying such violent misdeeds within our limits."

"This is unjust!" Aliya yelled. "Haven't you considered the many other witness testimonials, or Eddy's own offenses? He instigated the entire situation, and endangered her life multiple times! It wasn't until right before she left Reveria that she confessed that he always meant physical harm to her. None of you can stand here and tell us that there isn't some sort of favor here!"

Whether or not Constance and Alden sought to find a fragment of defense for my sake, it seemed Mikhail took any opportunity to dominate.

He'd do anything to take control of the room.

"Tell us then, Chief Virtue, which would you rather have amidst our grounds?" He retorted. "A petty Nocturne that means no real threat to Reveria and its Virtues, or a potential berserker that could slaughter dozens of our citizens if given the slightest chance? One of these two evils has already been subdued. Now it is up to us to put an end to the other."

"That's ridiculous, and you know that. If somebody else was in her position, you'd understand that she did what she had to. Why do you still oppose her, even before everything unfolded?" she stated.

In that regard, he answered with a blank expression. "There's no prejudice here, Morales. Charissa showed no mercy in what she'd done. Everyone at the plaza can confirm that. It ultimately, and unfortunately, comes down to this…Whether she's truly berserk or not, we cannot take *any* risk whatsoever. Not here, not ever. For that, we must deliver the most necessary punishment we can deliver."

"High Reverence Constance, Reverence Alden? You cannot stand there and find worth in what he's saying. You both know she's not even close to a berserker, and that he's always been out for her from the start!"

Aliya made the air exceptionally frigid, and the stress in my muscles only constricted, nearly suffocating my blood flow. Constance and Alden remained silent, eyeing one another with nervous tension. The horror on my face glared on the twin screens behind the Reverences, and all the moisture dissipated from my throat. My heart raced, and all I could do was ask for my fate. "What's going to happen to me?"

Alden and Constance briefly sulked their heads, to which she struggled to fess up my verdict. Instead, she did her last-ditch effort.

"Is this really necessary?" She turned between her colleagues.

"I agree, her case isn't as simple as a case-closed berserker crime." Alden supported. "Mikhail, even if she showed any further signs, can't we help somehow? *Your* solution to these matters has always been extreme."

The reindeer gave no ounce of pity, looking me in the eye as he delivered his next words. "Someone who's willing to snuff the life of another deserves no less to be treated the same. If she's able to go as far as to kill another, who's to say she wouldn't do it again? What we'd be doing is best not only for us, but perhaps for many in Misera."

"What are you saying? What are you going to do?" Aliya questioned.

With the other two Reverences unable to voice the outcome, Mikhail experienced nothing but contentment doing so himself.

Nobody was prepared to hear it.

"You will be euthanized." He concluded.

The crowd resonated with gasps, as time stood still. There had been many times where I defied death, though to be treated like an ill dog that had no other chance of salvation…Her only choice was to perish at another's willing hand. My destiny sealed itself to a horrible plight, and I could do nothing but have my bones rattle.

Aliya refused to accept the twisted consequence.

"Your Reverence, I must insist! She doesn't deserve death! Think of how detrimental she is to us. Charissa has seen the sunlight herself, and I know she can help bring us there!" She shouted to save my skin.

"Chief Morales, that's enough! You have no power in this trial! *I do!* Unless you want to lose your badge and go back to the Commons, you withdraw your defiance this instant!" Mikhail continued to throw out threats, though, to Aliya, they were an invitation to continue fighting.

"If you kill her, it will change nothing. Misera will remain the same, and it'll only be worse without her here." She profoundly insisted, and at that rate, she was speaking to a brick wall.

"We'll be ridding of one less abomination." He seethed.

"Please, you can't do this to her—" Aliya continued to plead, but Constance interrupted her with remorse in her voice.

"We apologize, Chief Morales, but I'm afraid we must…" She regretted it, despite her higher power. "If there's a remote possibility she could turn berserk, purely human and all, we don't have the means to repair the damage. Berserkerism has never been a reversible process."

"If we had the treatment, we would give it to her…But that's just not feasible. There's nothing else that can be done and letting her walk a free woman would be another jeopardy in the making." Alden said.

"Killing her would make any possibility of treatment for anybody impossible! You've seen the work Dr. Rhodes has done with her! She's made progress! If you do this, then we have *no* future." Aliya protested.

Mikhail drew a deep breath. "You're right about one thing, Morales. One little life isn't going to change the state of Misera." He raised his hand as he was about to conduct a vote amongst her associates. "I, Reverence Mikhail, say that Charissa be put on death row and euthanized under the crimes of unpermitted departure and berserker behavior."

This couldn't be happening.

He turned between her fellow members. "Constance? Alden?"

They were about to expel me from my mortal coil, and despite all the monsters I faced, their conscience will made me most afraid. Mikhail anticipated his answer while everyone dreaded it, so much so, that two Virtues drifted from the sidelines and came to the center of the courtroom. Before Aliya could stop any of them, the representative held her back, only forcing her to watch everything that unfolded.

"Your Reverences! You have to spare her!"

Could I really not be *saved?*

"I…I, Reverence Alden, favor this notion…"

Would my death be of uncontrolled malice?

"…I," Constance struggled to give her word.

I struggled to keep my stability, and my consciousness.

"…I, High Reverence Constance, favor—"

The monumental bronze doors slammed open. Unceremoniously, two individuals stood there while everyone gawked in surprise.

Kyran and Bea came to my aid, like beacons to my darkness.

Once they caught me in their view, they ran through the aisle. During the distraction, Aliya wormed her way out of her amphibious restraint, returning to my side. Their presence altogether brought immense consolation to my worries, though it was all short-lived.

Not when I had a death warrant to my name.

"Get your hands off her now!" Kyran demanded the two Virtues, and despite his lack of status, they followed his command, letting go of my arms. The heavy weight lifted off my trembling shoulders.

"Ex-Virtue Kyran? Dr. Rhodes? What is the meaning of this disturbance?" Mikhail uttered, to which Kyran and Bea brought themselves forth to the Reverences.

"Your Reverences, you cannot execute her." Bea insisted.

He slammed his fist to the podium, gritting his teeth at the jaguars. "Why shouldn't we? She's proven to be quite the menace in our walls. You two have taken her under your care, therefore, you're only incriminating yourselves with this intrusion!"

Regardless of if Mikhail was his higher-up, Kyran had the audacity to stand his ground. From there, he only fulfilled the promise he made: to be better for me. "You can take away my badge, kick me out, and send me straight back where I came from, I don't care…This is bigger than me and Bea. If you kill Char, then you'll have plenty of more problems on your plate. We've got some info that all of you are going to want to hear."

After he confronted the stubborn antlers of his superior head-on, Mikhail stuttered. Alden scoffed at such bravado, causing him to lean over the podium to indulge the siblings. "Then please, do enlighten us. Do you have anything that can shift in Charissa's favor? Your intrusion weighs on her outcome."

When she was given the opportunity, Bea brought out the sheet from her lab coat. Upon unfolding it, the tattered edges and gruesome stains showed. It was the same map, desecrated in crude markings.

"This is an invasion ploy set up by the Vultures at Fruor Falls, and it wouldn't have stopped with us. They planned to attack every settlement they could…" She called out to the ears of everyone. "Had we never known, our town would have been in jeopardy."

Bea delivered her revelation with dignity, to which the frogman desperately got his mitts on the map. When he got to see the evidence for himself, he urgently brought it up to the Reverences, who took it in their possession with dismay, though it didn't stop there.

"You know what else? Your *Righteous Virtue of Temperance*, Yuto, has been on their trail the whole time." To everyone's shock, Kyran brought up the signature throwing knife, stained in traces of corrupted crimson. "See this? One of his special daggers that he crafted himself, covered in the same blood as those bastards. Take a long look at everything and tell me that none of this doesn't mean a damn thing to any of you." He tossed it to the Reverences himself.

Once they got their hands on it, their worries tripled.

"Where did you exactly get these?" Constance questioned.

"We didn't find them…" Bea brought up, and instead, she faced me. The dim light reflected on her lenses, though it only made that content grin of hers illuminate the most. "*Charissa* did. She returned to Reveria to warn us of this unforeseeable danger. Realistically, if she had never brought this map to our attention, everything that has been built here would very well be smithereens to Vulture hands," she claimed, and the visible devastation of the Reverences came to the display screens.

To only make matters escalate, Kyran followed up. "Hell, if anything, Shank would have doomed us all if Char didn't fight back against him. That's the truth!" He shouted, wholehearted in his belief.

"Kyran Rhodes! You've got some nerve!" Mikhail retaliated, though his frustration subsided once Alden voiced his concern.

"But he's right. This news is damned, and if they intended to invade our community…Oh, mercy on us," He fell short on his breath.

Constance shook her head at the undeniable evidence. "We've always known they might've tried to make some form of attack, but even with our numbers, the casualties would be insufferable…"

Despite the two Reverences showing their acceptance of the new details they've been given, Mikhail had to make it known that he would have none of it, as expected. "There's no possible way Charissa managed to acquire such evidence on her lonesome. This is obviously just a scheme to revoke her of any penalty!" He insisted.

All three of my closest companions did well to speak on my behalf, but it would have taken more than their voices to be heard to move forward. The final challenge fell in front of me, and I had to shake off all my nerves in order to conquer it.

Mikhail needed the *whole* truth.

"You're right, Your Reverence. I wasn't alone when I discovered everything. During my travels, I came across a group that cared for me…One you'd probably be familiar with."

Before he could surmise anything, he only allowed his temper to do the talking. "Don't provoke me! I don't trust these claims for a second! Tell us the truth or all of you will be held accountable!" Mikhail's fury showed in an act of defense, to prevent him from being in the *wrong*.

Not again. I would not gloss over my integrity.

"Nobody has been lying about anything. Want to know who I was with? I was with The Claws…*Kogti*. Heard of them?"

The moment I mentioned the clan…Mikhail's eyes sparked, and he flustered. Skeptical of my claim, he slammed his hands down, deluding himself into a warped sense of self. "Falsity will get you nowhere—" He was about to strike me down, but it would have taken more than telling their title. No, I had to recite every name.

Every Claw.

"Anastasia. Oksana. Nikolai. Lada. Your son? Your grandson? Oleg. Igor. I've met them, and I know of what happened to you." I stepped up, convicted. "You and your family were taken by Vultures. Olga, Natalya, and Mila. They were victims of their heinous atrocities."

To Mikhail's astonishment, he too couldn't deny it. He fell silent, and the anger melted away from his now-grieving face. "You…You know?"

I had him right where I wanted him.

"I don't know what they did to all of you, but I'm sorry, your Reverence, I truly am," I sympathized, but I had to seize this slim chance of appeal. "When I was with the Claws, I managed to uncover this horrid plan at Little Hopes Elementary. There, I met Yuto, and he was heading for their most active offsite hideout as far as I could tell."

Informing them further of the specifics, the Reverences could have never surmised the trial to turn out like this. Neither did I.

"These findings are unparalleled. Genuine. This indeed does change the factors on your part." Constance said, folding her hands to her waist. "While your crimes may still be evident, it doesn't compare to the carnivores that infest Misera's city carnival…We can't take any chances with them being an immediate threat to our sanctuary."

"Indeed. No matter how much we'd be prepared, none of us could foresee how horrific an onslaught from those *things* can be. As Chief Morales put it, punishing you would not change a thing." Alden shared.

Both the equine and harpy Reverences turned toward the caribou, who still had a difficult time processing my unfeigned display.

For once, he bent.

"…If you coincided with my boy and gained his trust, then I cannot refute your words. I propose a new 'punishment.'" Mikhail suggested, which brought concerning attention to the entire core of the courthouse, and intrigue to its audience.

"What do you mean?" I asked.

"I have for you, a solution." He proposed. "Seek out our most proficient *Righteous Virtue of Temperance*, hopefully before he steps foot near Fruor Falls. Bring him back here dead or alive, and his return will drop all charges against you. You have my word."

A bold task had been given to me, and it was a challenge that anyone would have struggled to accomplish alone. I only came across one live Vulture, and I barely evaded her. A live one would have torn me apart.

Even with experience, it was only so much.

"And if I don't?"

"Then you will either be on death row upon return or face a far worse demise out there in Misera's ruins," he established. "You'll have a week to complete this task, or your days are truly reduced."

Mikhail gave me the ultimatum, and I only had two real choices.

Do, or die.

Before I could accept or deny his request, Kyran brought a hand to my shoulder. His touch was so powerful, that it nearly inspired my own strength. Though his words were what truly brought me up. "There's no way she'll go out there alone." He called. "Charissa's capable, yes, but I'm in this together with her. She has my back, and I got hers."

He took my side so forthrightly, as if I had truly been a Reverian in his eyes. To say that his willingness to assist me was admirable, but considering that this was *my* duty…There was no way they'd allow it.

"Wasn't it your foolish endeavors that got you in your current position? Your willingness means nothing to us. If you insist, go on this suicide run, Mister Rhodes, but I'm afraid—"

"Permission granted, *Virtue of Courage*." Constance said.

"I— Excuse me?" The reindeer expressed his stupor.

As did Kyran himself. "Wait. What did you say?"

The High Reverence withdrew a piece of gold from her robes, a familiar gladiolus. She tossed it his way, which he caught with wide eyes. "When you first came here, you were given that title for a reason. If you're willing to stand by this human, then I expect you to bring her back with her life intact." Constance embellished.

Kyran held the badge to his chest. "I won't let you down."

Mikhail groaned. "You're going to really stand by her?"

To only flabbergast him further, Aliya stuck out for me. "He's not the only one, Your Reverence. The well-being of my Virtues is my duty, and that includes the citizens we're sworn to protect. We all have our parts to play, and I won't idly stand by. I'll be joining them."

"There's no chance we're going to let our chief throw her life away! All this commitment for this *human?*" The antler-headed Reverence squawked and to everyone's astoundment…

Bea pitched in the benevolent piece of her mind.

"This isn't just for her well-being, but for Yuto's as well." She took her stance. "Charissa has done much for me, and I owe it to her to be by her side, and the same for our fellow Virtues. My duties at the laboratories can wait if it means bringing back our colleague."

Once she offered to contribute, the caribou crumbled. "Now hold on, we can't afford to part with this many! This is not what I had in mind!"

"They're professionals, Reverence Mikhail. Had we no faith in our beloved Virtues nor scientists, our town wouldn't still be standing." Constance praised, finding faith in the forces they've built.

"And if they're all willing to go together, this brings up another possibility. If you four could do us a high favor." Alden presented, and since everything was being put out on the table…

"What's that?" I asked.

"If you're somehow able, putting any wrench into their plans would be a great service to us. It'd give us time to further prepare for whatever onslaught they'd have in store for us. Their methods might be crude, but their ruthless nature knows no bounds."

Everyone in the courtroom started to shift in their seats. The idea of their community going down in flames brought dismay, a peril that brought more fear than my wrongdoings.

"Reverence Mikhail? What say you?" the harpy asked, and the many gazes of the courtroom fell upon him.

It was either my demise or Reveria's collapse.

"…For the sake of this community's livelihood and infrastructure, I'll agree to these conditions. Though if we lose any of our good peacekeepers, let alone one of our best scientists, there will be more than hell to pay for the losses,"

The avian and equine figureheads nodded.

"Very well. I, High Reverence Constance, agree to favor this proposition," she uttered, and soon, Alden and Mikhail raised their hands as well. In unison, they agreed with one another.

"We, Reverences, agree to favor this notion."

With that, they put their arms down.

"This hearing is adjourned. Charissa, should you return to Reveria with success or failure, we will follow up on your case. We hope that fortune favors your upbringing." Constance granted me her parting words, before she lifted her dark stare towards the crowd that fumbled in their seats, bringing a gleam of hope to their woes. "To every citizen, do not let the darkness consume you. No matter the hardships, we will continue to endure until we can escape Misera's clutches. Value your days here in Reveria's embrace, as we the Reverences value you as the threads that tether our sanctuary together. Let enlightenment be with you!" Her voice echoed through the rotunda; her guiding light resonated with every Reverian who took part in my hearing. Each of the townsfolk stood from their seats, clasping their hands, bringing their eyes to the luminescence of the dome above.

"May diligence guide us toward the sun."

With that, the rows of seats emptied as everyone inside the courthouse single-filed themselves out. The screens shut off as they chattered amongst one another, and the light of the rotunda slowly dimmed to the faintest glow. I stood there, enamored with the godsends that destiny bestowed. Kyran, Bea, and Aliya gathered behind me. It had been a long time since I'd experienced such a shock. Not since Commoneo, where Narissa revealed my entire life to be a lie.

"Thank God it turned out like this," Aliya said under her breath.

Frankly, I didn't know who to properly thank. The angels? Destiny's mercy? No, all my graciousness was owed to the ones that saved me from a grim end.

"Char, that was a lot. Are you okay?" Kyran asked.

"...A thousand thank-yous wouldn't be enough to show my gratitude to you guys. I'm still shaking a bit,"

"That's alright, Charissa. We wouldn't have been here if we didn't care about you." Bea reached out to me, and I saw only humanity in her eyes. "Whether human or hybridian, you have the right to continue living your life to the fullest."

"That means a lot, coming from you all, but...I'm not out of this yet. Not until we find Yuto. He'll be the only way I can escape death row and be accepted back into this community."

"Your luck's quite impressive, Charissa," A voice called.

The four of us caught Mikhail approaching us from behind, and out of obligation, Aliya and Kyran stood front and center in his presence. I braced for whatever more brunt he had to burden.

"Reverence Mikhail?" Bea confronted.

"Your tenacity is admirable, but it's not enough. You might be aware of my bloodline, but it doesn't provide leverage to your shallow front. You care not for my people, but for your own skin."

I grew tired of his stubborn-minded doubts.

"This isn't any front, your Reverence. Whether you like it or not, Char's alive, and with her help, we can find Yuto. You and I know that he's one of our best, and you need him." Kyran did well to put Mikhail in his place, and he met the admonition with surprising grace.

But not without questioning my competence.

"Respect, Virtue of Courage. Let's just hope you'll manage to locate him before he goes fully missing in action. And while I'm still apprehensive about this wolf in sheep's clothing, let's see if she can prove me wrong." He approached me, and bringing a hand to my shoulder, he pressed down with a whisper. "Don't let everybody down now, Charissa."

With that, the high-ranked noble turned heel and marched down towards his chamber. Only our quartet remained in the quietude of the once-bustling courtroom.

"His suppositions still haven't changed, even after all that," Aliya commented with disappointment to her frown, though I certainly wasn't going to count myself out from defying him.

"He shares the same feelings as many here do, and I can't be mad at him. I have to—*We*—have to do what we can to surpass his expectations. He won't see it coming,"

"You said it. Let's bring our fellow man home." Aliya said.

"I'm with you on that, but before we make any hasty decisions, let's plot out our next steps accordingly. Perhaps we should take today to prepare, then we can set out once morning comes around. This won't be a simple task, after all." Bea reasoned.

"That's what I was thinking. We'll get our gear ready, tune up our weapons, and be prepared for anything that'll come our way. Besides, I think we've all had enough for today." Kyran assented.

To say that it was a grueling day would be an understatement. After a horrid nightmare, having Virtues break into my home to put me in cuffs, only to be thrown into a cell and put on trial that nearly ended with the death penalty...*nearly* the worst day of my life.

"Sounds good to me. I'm going to go back to the station and figure out what I'll be bringing, among other things. If any of you need something, come and find me," Aliya stated, then caught my eye. "As for you, just take it easy today. I think you've earned a rest."

Aliya waved us off before she wandered away, and as she left my sight, I couldn't help but be thankful to have her. She truly deserved her title. "There she goes. So, what should we do now?" I asked the jaguar siblings, and they hummed in unison.

They really were brother and sister.

"I want to be certain all my research equipment is still fully functional, as I'm sure I'll find plenty at Fruor Falls." Bea informed me.

Kyran scratched his chin in contemplation. "Yeah, and I'll probably go out shopping for supplies. I'd offer for you to come along, Char, but...I imagine you probably want to keep your head low after the hell that went down earlier."

He was right in that regard. When I faced the podium again, lacking its three Reverences, there was still a sinking hollowness in my belly. In a way, I'd defied death for the fourth time over, but again, I had to rely on others to pull me out of the quicksand. Perhaps my sister had always known that I couldn't fend for myself. Not in the wild, nor in the sliver of society that thrived in a dreary municipality.

Was I *truly* capable? Or did I undermine myself again?

"Maybe for a little bit. I have a lot to think about," I told him, blankly keeping to the empty screens next.

"Would you prefer us to keep you some company?" Bea consoled, though I shook my head.

"No, that's alright. I need a moment to myself," I reiterated.

"It's all good. We should be back home in a little while. Just don't stick around this place for too long, okay?" Kyran told us, and before they could take any step, another compulsion took over.

"There's one more thing I want to say."

"Of course, Charissa, what is it?" Bea's ears swiveled towards me.

I could not hold myself back. "I was sincerely wrong about both of you, and I could never have survived in this city without your guys' help. I'm so glad you guys took me off those streets and brought me here instead. Really, you rescued me."

They grinned at one another, only to reassure me that they had no regret in being my saviors. "We might've had our slumps. Though out here, we learned to be better people." Kyran assured.

"Absolutely. You're one of *us* now," Bea told me.

They left me with heartfelt smiles as they headed off. I found contentment knowing that the two of them would do what they could for me, and I would do the same for them. From there, I would never be alone again, even when the underworld was completely against me.

My future had been given a purpose, even if that ambition came with the stake of losing everything if all else failed. Nobody had truly won in this case. Those who wished for my loss were displeased to see me live, and those who wanted to witness my success had to hold patience for my outcome, and it was up to me not to disappoint them.

With the faint dimness closing in, the colors of the courtroom became transparent. For all my days, I'd been convinced that my only motive was to live for my sister's sake. It only took me twenty-two years to value my own worth. While I strived to find her again one day, I discovered more than her incentive to stay alive.

No, I had to live for *me*.

EPILOGUE

The next morning came around, and there was still no sun to insinuate a new day. Instead, it was that harrowing void. But I had learned to rise anyway. Through the artificial dusk, the only glimmers of light were the ones that came from this jubilant town, igniting a sense of meaning in a hollow abyss.

I always speculated about the future, when I could see the sun once again, and that maybe someday, these people could too. There was not a single night where I did not dream about Narissa. In a way, she was my sun, and without her, I only continued to long for her beaming gaze. I still foolishly held onto the belief that she was still alive and that perhaps she escaped the clutches of fate. Without her, I had to find the sunlight in my own way. If that meant being able to wake up every morning and face this charade, then I did what I must. Today was simply another page in the book of my new life.

After Kyran brought me back home from my jail cell, I had gotten myself dressed in travel clothes with the same worn boots that had grown on me since the first night I was here. Hair on my shoulders, I wound it with the same marigold bandana that had clung to me since the beginning. It was a reminder to find even the littlest sliver of aspiration in these bleak days. Still, I had to carry the grim reminder on my arms, covered in bandages until the wounds healed. With these same hands, I'd mend the damage I did.

Today was the day we set off to find Yuto.

Bag slung over my shoulder, my sides equipped with a gun at each hip, it was time to embark. Stepping out of my room, Bea was at the dining table, preparing all her research equipment.

"Are we all set to go?" I asked.

"Catalyst functioning as intended, sample-retrieving mechanisms in check…suit still fits. Seems like I'm ready over here."

Bea boasted an aluminized, tight-fitted jumpsuit, accompanied by heat-resistant shoes and gloves. Her thick hair was woven back into a braided bun, and her eyes were covered up with protective goggles. Catalyst-O fastened to her arm and a heavy-duty bag at the back of her waist, this was an unusual get-up for her since I was so used to her in a usual lab coat, but the new travel attire suited her well.

"I like it. You look prepared for anything."

"Well, I figured it would be a good outfit for doing some field testing. It doesn't hurt being safe," she said back, and I raised a brow.

"Oh yeah, what's this about field testing?" I asked.

Bea reached for the holster wrapped around her thigh, and she pulled out a bulky sort of contraption that appeared like a pistol of sorts, but it had a high voltage when activated. Wires tethered around the rectangular barrel, attaching to what appeared to be a battery fixated onto the gun's frame. The thing seemed hefty, but it was packed with surging firepower.

CENTAUR-LP

"An energy-powered weapon. Found it long ago out there and managed to get it fixed. Hold the trigger, charge the light within, and it fires one deadly shot. Far more powerful than the Catalyst-E, even going as far as to disintegrate organic matter."

Bea was playing with a sinister side of science.

She stowed the energy pistol away and prepared for the journey. Kyran got out of his room, wearing his leather armor once more, TAIPAN attached to his back and racks of ammo to his own thigh. "Bea, you're looking fit to blaze a trail." He chuckled and turned to me, his face softening. "I have something to give back to you."

…What could he have been talking about? "Oh?"

He leaned back into his room for a brief second. When he came back, he held something very sentimental. The same crafted bow that Narissa made for me, with the familiar quiver and arrows to match. Seeing it all now, back in my hands, I was overjoyed that he still had it with him. At the same time, having it in my grasp made me dismal, and the marigold flower that wrapped around the recurve now wilted completely. A sad remembrance of what I had lost, but I could find it again one day. I took my longbow graciously, mourning.

"I—thanks, Kyran. It's good to see it again." With a discontent sigh, I set it aside. "As much as I'd love to use it for old times' sake, I'd rather keep it here, if that's alright," I told him, and he nodded to that.

"I can tell it holds a story, I just figured you'd want it again. I knew one day it'd be good to give it back," Kyran said to me, pondering for a moment. "Well, how about this? Never know when you'll find yourself toe-to-toe with danger." He unlatched his other thigh strap, which included a serrated knife made of black carbon steel.

I wasn't certain I could accept a second gesture.

"Are you sure? That seems like it's special to you too," I told him, but he pressed it into my hands.

"Consider it a token of trust. You already have my other glove anyway, so I thought it'd match pretty well." He snickered, and it would've been foolish to refuse his kindness. Strapping the leather to my own leg and getting a feel for the knife, I stashed it.

"Anything else before we go?" I asked.

"Aliya is expecting us at the front gates. Let's not keep her waiting," Bea mentioned, and with that, we gathered ourselves and headed out to the great outdoors. It wasn't easy, treading the roads that no longer welcomed my face, but I kept my head up high, regardless of the fearful looks. After showing my testament to these people, they'd see that redemption wasn't too late for me.

And that this Beast inside me could be contained.

After departing from the plaza brimming full of wary citizens, we approached the metal gates of the town. There, the shepherd guard awaited with Aliya, fitted in tactical armor that came with a bulletproof vest. Idly tossing a bullet in the air and catching it between her fingers, she loaded her marksman rifle, making the fine gunmetal click together.

BARRUCUDA-DMR

"Right on time," Aliya called out to us, and looking at one another, we braced for what lay beyond.

"Before you go." The shepherd lifted his chin to me. "Use those pistols well. Give those kidnapping-bastards what they deserve."

To think, another Virtue would have belief in me. I needed whatever I could get. "You can count on me," I told him, and once he saluted his chief, he took his stance at the gate. I turned to Aliya. "Those slavers have made a reputation for themselves as of late, haven't they?"

"They've been every child's night terror for the past couple of decades, but their misdeeds as of late have been putting everyone on edge. If nobody else out there will put a stop to it, then it's up to us. We do what we can to shut down their activity at the park, and hopefully, our vulpine friend can handle himself if he happens to be in their territory," she said.

It was exactly like the foxhunt Narissa and I did, not long ago, it seemed. I still held a tinge of little guilt for killing that fox, but this hunt would be far more different. This time, we would find our prey alive. I made a promise to the Reverences, and I needed to fulfill it. "No time to waste, then. Let's go and find that wild card," I uttered.

"I'm with you," Bea assured me, fixing her goggles.

Kyran cocked his assault rifle. "And so am I."

"Roger that. Get these gates open, we're going out!" Aliya hollered to the watchmen, and at her command, the metal masses groaned apart, and we stepped foot beyond Reveria's limits.

I was not sure what to expect heading to the city theme park, and this would be the second time I would see our special friend, the rogue veiled in shadow. His intentions for me remained unclear, but if my new friends had good faith in him, then he was worth the trouble of searching for. With companions by my side, I could conquer anything. Narissa taught me what was necessary for my survival, and I wouldn't be selfish with my lessons. Without her, though, I had no purpose...

Or so I thought.

Narissa spent her life as my guardian angel, as I spent mine being her imperfect half. Without her in the current picture, I finally had jurisdiction over my own legacy. But until I could find her again someday, I found solace in the new people who paved their names into my prospects. I had only known one person all my life, and it was challenging to be vulnerable to those I had only been with for so long.

Aliya, Kyran, and Bea filled the void that had been left inside me, ever since I separated from the stem of my bloodline. No matter how her fate was sealed, I owed it to Narissa not to squander her sacrifices, and to my new allies to never give up on them, as they did for me.

Even with my numbered days, I had to make the most of every one that was left, because this was only the beginning. It was in my nature to persevere until my last breath.

END OF BOOK ONE

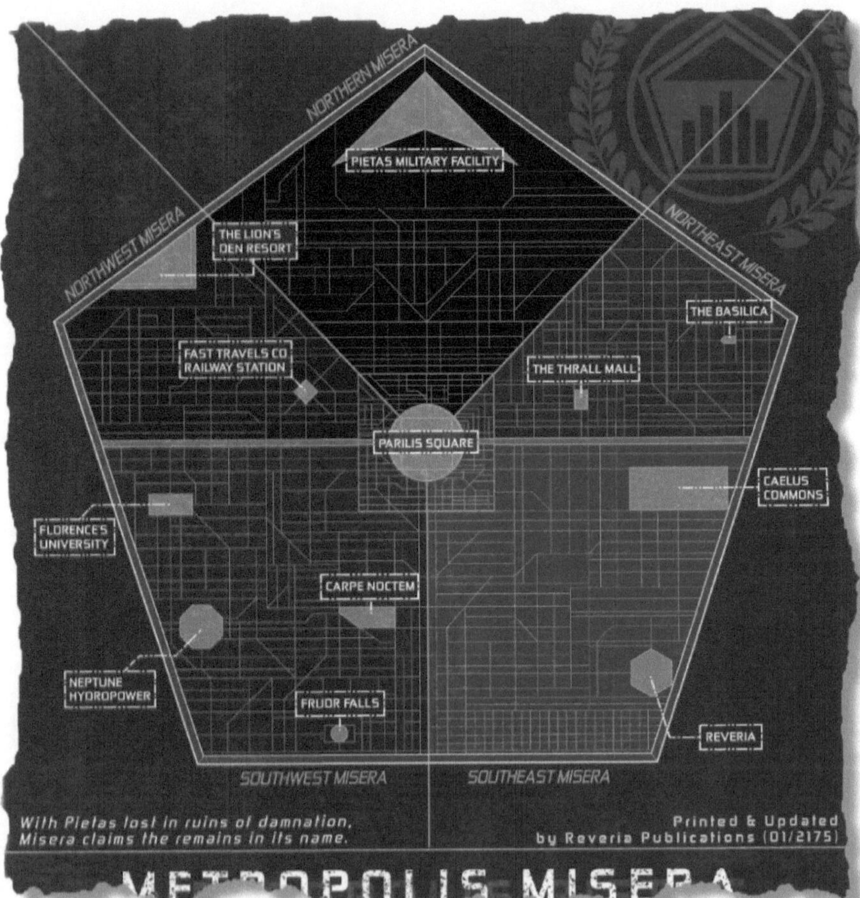

NORTHERN MISERA
NORTHWEST MISERA
NORTHEAST MISERA
PIETAS MILITARY FACILITY
THE LION'S DEN RESORT
THE BASILICA
FAST TRAVELS CO RAILWAY STATION
THE THRALL MALL
PARILIS SQUARE
CAELUS COMMONS
FLORENCE'S UNIVERSITY
CARPE NOCTEM
NEPTUNE HYDROPOWER
FRUOR FALLS
REVERIA
SOUTHWEST MISERA
SOUTHEAST MISERA
With Pietas lost in ruins of damnation,
Misera claims the remains in its name.
Printed & Updated
by Reveria Publications (01/2175)
METROPOLIS MISERA

About the Author

Z.J. Blight is an aspiring writer and fictional worldbuilder. After graduating with a bachelor's degree in fine arts, he wanted to fulfill a lifelong dream of writing his first novel. He has been striving to create a unique narrative since the age of twelve and to make a universe of his own. After all these years, he found the drive to accomplish that lifelong wish. Even as a fresh author, he aims to continue that wish by making the art of literature part of his craft. With more passion to come, he wants to share his story, *Cries of Misera*, and to hopefully inspire others to go beyond the limits of creative imagination as well; To make your own story.

Thank you for reading!

I hope you enjoyed the story,
because there will be plenty more to come!

I appreciate you, the reader,
for taking the time and part in my work.

Please be sure to leave a review on any platforms
where my book is showcased, as any feedback
or critiques are well-appreciated.

See you in the sequel!

-Z.J. Blight